The Clay Machine-Gun

Victor Pelevin has described *The Clay Machine-Gun* as the first novel in world literature to take place in an absolute void. Controversially denied the Russian Booker Prize – the Jury President branded it as a kind of computer virus designed to 'destroy the cultural memory' – the book has become a cult success in Russia, selling well over 200,000 copies.

'Pelevin is the hottest writer around. He has become an icon to the young, with fan clubs and internet sites galore, and has the added cachet of being a supreme irritant to the older, stodgier generation . . . He is a sensitive, philosophical writer of great lyrical beauty whose fiction has the power to change the reader's view of himself, and the world.' *Moscow Times*

'Even in a society where pulp fiction has never been more popular and where literary fiction is now seldom read by more than a tiny elite, Pelevin has emerged as that unusual thing: a genuinely popular serious writer. His most committed readers – who post his novels on the internet, and swap his books at nightclubs as if they were *samizdat* – are the disaffected young, who must see something of the surrealism of their own post-Soviet lives reflected in the mirror of his cool, glazed, ironic prose.' *New York Times Magazine*

D1350510

Born in 1962 in Moscow, Victor Pelevin has swiftly been recognised as the leading Russian novelist of the new generation. Before studying at Moscow's Gorky Institute of Literature, he worked in a number of jobs, including as an engineer on a project to protect MiG fighter planes from insect interference in tropical conditions. His work has been translated into fifteen languages and his novels *Omon Ra*, *The Life of Insects* and *The Clay Machine-Gun* have been published in English to great acclaim. His most recent novel *Babylon* went straight to the top of Russian bestseller lists when it was published in 1999.

The translator Andrew Bromfield was born in Hull and graduated from the University of Sussex. His career has included lecturing in Russian for 12 years in Ireland, teaching English in Yerevan, Soviet Armenia, and a brief period as an editor in Cyprus. From 1998 to 1993 he lived and worked in Moscow, where he was involved in setting up *Glas*, the English-language journal of contemporary Russian writing, of which he was co-editor. He has translated widely from Russian, including Victor Pelevin's *Omon Ra*, *The Blue Lantern*, *The Life of Insects* and *The Clay Machine-Gun*. He now lives and works in London.

by the same author

The Clay Machine-Gun

VICTOR PELEVIN

translated by Andrew Bromfield

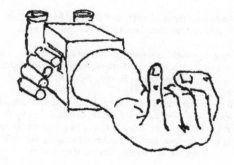

ff

faber and faber   Harbord Publishing

First published in 1999
by Faber and Faber Limited
The Bindery, 51 Hatton Garden
London EC1N 8HN
and Harbord Publishing Limited
58 Harbord Street, London SW6 6PJ
This paperback edition first published in 2000
First published in Russia in 1996 as *Chapaev I Pustota*

Typeset by Faber and Faber Ltd
Printed and bound by CPI Group (UK) Ltd, Croydon, CR0 4YY

An extract from Chapter 6 of *The Clay Machine-Gun*
first appeared in *Granta: The Wild East* in 1998

Andrew Bromfield is hereby identified as translator of this
work in accordance with Section 77 of the Copyright,
Designs and Patents Act 1988

A CIP record for this book
is available from the British Library

ISBN 978-0-571-20126-6

8 10 9 7

Gazing at the faces of the horses and the people, at this bound-less stream of life raised up by the power of my will and now hurtling into nowhere across the sunset-crimson steppe, I often think: where am I in this flux?

GHENGIS KHAN

PREFACE

For numerous reasons the name of the true author of this manuscript, written during the early 1920s in one of the monasteries of Inner Mongolia, cannot be mentioned, and it is published here under the name of the editor who prepared it for publication. This version does not include the descriptions of a number of magical procedures which figured in the original, nor does it retain the narrator's rather lengthy reminiscences of his life in pre-revolutionary St Petersburg (the so-called Petersburg Period). The author's definition of the genre of the work as 'a peculiar flight of free thought' has also been omitted: it would seem quite clear that it can only be regarded as a joke.

The story narrated by the author is of interest as a psychological journal which, while it undoubtedly possesses a number of artistic virtues, makes absolutely no claim to anything beyond that, although at times the author does undertake to discuss topics which, in our view, are in no need of discussion. The somewhat spasmodic nature of the narrative reflects the fact that the intention underlying the writing of this text was not to create a 'work of literature', but to record the mechanical cycles of consciousness in such a way as to achieve a complete and final cure for what is known as 'the inner life'. Furthermore, in two or three places, the author actually attempts to point directly to the mind of the reader, rather than force him to view yet another phantom constructed out of words; unfortunately this is far too simple a task for his attempts to prove successful. Literary specialists will most likely perceive nothing more in our narrative than yet another product of the critical solipsism which has been so fashionable in recent years, but the true value of this document lies in the fact that it represents the first attempt in the history of culture to embody in the forms of art the Mongolian Myth of the Eternal Non-Return.

Let us briefly introduce the main hero of the book. The editor of this text once read me a tanka written by the poet Pushkin:

> And yet this year of gloom, which carried off
> So many victims brave and good and beautiful,
> Is scarce remembered even
> In some simple shepherd's song
> Of sweet and soft lament.

In translation into Mongolian the phrase 'brave victim' has a strange ring to it; however, this is not the proper place to explore that theme, and we merely wished to point out that the final three lines of this verse could well be a reference to the story of Vasily Chapaev.

What is now known about this man? As far as we are able to judge, in the memory of the common people his image has assumed the features of pure myth, and Chapaev is now Russian folklore's closest equivalent of the famous Khadji Nasruddin: he is the hero of an infinite number of jokes derived from a famous film of the 1930s, in which Chapaev is represented as a Red cavalry commander fighting against the White army, who engages in long, heart-to-heart conversations with his adjutant Petka and his machine-gunner Anka and finally drowns while attempting to swim across the Ural river during a White attack. All this, however, bears absolutely no relation whatsoever to the life of the real Chapaev – or if there is some relation, then the true facts have been distorted beyond all recognition by conjecture and innuendo.

This tangled web of confusion originated with the book *Chapaev*, which was first printed in French by a Paris publishing house in 1923 and then reprinted with unaccountable haste in Russia: we shall not waste any time on demonstrating the book's lack of authenticity. Anyone who wishes to make the effort will discover in it a mass of discrepancies and contradictions, while the very spirit of the book is the best possible proof that the author (or authors) had absolutely no involvement with the events which they endeavour in vain to describe. In addition, it should be noted that although Mr Furmanov did meet the historical Chapaev on at least two occasions, he could not possibly have been the author of this book, for reasons which will emerge in the course of our narrative. It is therefore hard to credit that even now many people regard the text ascribed to him as virtually a documentary account.

In fact, it is not difficult to detect behind this forgery, now more than seventy years old, the activity of well-financed and highly active forces which were interested in concealing the truth about Chapaev from the peoples of Eurasia for as long as possible. However, the very discovery of the present manuscript seems to us a clear indication that the balance of power on the continent has shifted.

To conclude, we have altered the title of the original text (which was 'Vasily Chapaev') precisely in order to avoid any confusion with the aforementioned fake. The title 'The Clay Machine-Gun' has been chosen as being adequately indicative of the major theme, while not overly suggestive, although the editor did suggest another alternative, 'The Garden of the Divergent Petkas'.

We dedicate the merit created by this text to the good of all living creatures.

Gate Gate Paragate Parasamgate Bodhi Svaha

Urgan Jambon Tulku VII
Chairman of the Buddhist Front for Full and Final Liberation
(FFL (b))

1

Tverskoi Boulevard was exactly as it had been when I last saw it, two years before. Once again it was February, with snowdrifts everywhere and that peculiar gloom which somehow manages to infiltrate the very daylight. The same old women were perched motionless on the benches; above them, beyond the black latticework of the branches, there was the same grey sky, like an old, worn mattress drooping down towards the earth under the weight of a sleeping God.

Some things, however, were different. This winter the avenues were scoured by a blizzard straight off the steppes, and I should not have been in the least surprised to have come face to face with a pair of wolves during the course of my walk. The bronze Pushkin seemed a little sadder than usual – no doubt because his breast was covered with a red apron bearing the inscription: 'Long Live the First Anniversary of the Revolution'. I felt not the slightest inclination for ironical comment on the fact that the cheers were intended for an event which could not by definition last longer than a single day – just recently I had been afforded more than ample opportunity to glimpse the demonic face concealed behind such lapidary absurdities inscribed on red.

It was beginning to get dark, but I could still make out Strastnoi Monastery through the snowy haze. On the square in front of it were two open trucks, their tall side walls tightly strung with bright scarlet material; there was a crowd jostling around them and the orator's voice carried to where I stood. I could scarcely make out anything of what he said, but the general meaning was clear enough from his intonation and the machine-gun rattle of the 'r' in the words 'proletariat' and 'terror'. Two drunken soldiers walked past me, the bayonets on their rifles swaying behind their shoulders. They were hurrying towards the square, but one of them fixed his brazen gaze on me, slowed his pace and opened his mouth as though about to say something; fortunately – for him and for me – his companion tugged him by the sleeve and they walked on.

I turned and set off down the incline of the boulevard, guessing at what it was in my appearance that constantly aroused the suspicions of all these scum. Of course, I was dressed in outrageously bad taste; I was wearing a dirty coat cut in the English style with a broad half-belt, a military cap (naturally, without the cockade) like the one that Alexander II used to wear, and officer's boots. But it did not seem to be just a matter of my clothes. There were, after all, plenty of other people around who looked far more absurd. On Tverskaya Street, for instance, I had seen a completely insane gentleman wearing gold-rimmed spectacles holding an icon ahead of him as he walked towards the black, deserted Kremlin, but no one had paid him the slightest attention. Meanwhile, I was all the time aware of people casting sidelong glances at me, and on each occasion I was reminded that I had neither money nor documents about my person. The previous day, in the water-closet at the railway station, I had tried sticking a red bow on my chest, but I removed it as soon as I caught sight of my reflection in the cracked mirror; with the ribbon I looked not merely stupid, I looked doubly suspicious.

It is possible, of course, that no one was actually directing their gaze at me any more than at anyone else, and that my tight-strung nerves and the anticipation of arrest were to blame for everything. I did not feel any fear of death. Perhaps, I thought, it had already happened, and this icy boulevard along which I was walking was merely the threshold of the world of shadows. I had realized long before that Russian souls must be fated to cross the Styx when it is frozen, with their fare collected not by a ferryman, but by a figure garbed in grey who hires out a pair of skates – the same spiritual essence, naturally.

Suddenly I could picture the scene in the finest of detail: Count Tolstoy in black tights, waving his arms about, skates over the ice towards the distant horizon – his movements are slow and solemn, but he makes rapid progress, and the three-headed dog barking soundlessly in pursuit has no chance of overtaking him. I laughed quietly, and at that very moment a hand slapped me on the shoulder.

I stepped to one side and swung round sharply, feeling for the handle of the revolver in my pocket, when to my amazement I saw before me the face of Grigory Vorblei, an acquaintance from childhood. But, my God, his appearance! He was dressed from head to toe in black leather, a holster with a Mauser dangled at his hip, and in his hand he was clutching a ridiculous kind of obstetrician's travelling bag.

'I'm glad you're still capable of laughter,' he said.

'Hello, Grisha,' I said, 'how strange to see you.'

'Why strange?'

'It just is strange.'

'Where have you come from?' he asked in a cheerful voice. 'And where are you going?'

'From Petersburg,' I replied. 'As for where I'm going, I'd be glad if I knew that myself.'

'Then come to my place,' said Vorblei, 'I'm living just near by, with an entire flat all to myself.'

As we walked on down the boulevard we exchanged glances, smiles and meaningless snatches of conversation. Since the time of our last meeting, Vorblei had grown a beard which made his face look like a sprouting onion, and his cheeks had grown weathered and ruddy, as though his health had benefited greatly from several consecutive winters of ice-skating.

We had studied in the same grammar school, but since then we had seen each other only rarely. I had encountered him a couple of times in the literary salons of St Petersburg – he had taken to writing verse in a contrary style which was only heightened by its obvious self-satisfaction. I was rather irritated by his manner of sniffing cocaine in public and his constant hints at his connections in social-democratic circles; however, to judge from his present appearance, the hints must have been true. It was instructive to see someone who at one time was quite adept at expounding the mystical significance of the Holy Trinity now sporting the unmistakable signs of belonging to the hosts of evil. But then, of course, there was really nothing surprising in this transformation: many decadents, such as Mayakovsky, sensing the clearly infernal character of the new authority, had hastened to offer their services to it. As a matter of fact, it is my belief that they were not motivated by conscious satanism – they were too infantile for that – but by aesthetic instinct: after all, a red pentagram does complement a yellow blouse so marvellously well.

'How are things in Petersburg?' asked Vorblei.

'As if you didn't know.'

'That's right,' agreed Vorblei, suddenly seeming to lose interest. 'I do know.'

We turned off the boulevard, crossed the roadway and found ourselves in front of a seven-storey apartment house. It was directly opposite the Palace Hotel, in front of which two machine-gun installations were visible; they were manned by sailors smoking cigarettes, and a red flag flapped in the wind at the end of a long stick.

Vorblei tugged at my sleeve. 'Look over there,' he said.

I turned my head. On the street outside the entrance to the house stood a black limousine with a tiny cabin for passengers and open front seats, on which the snow had piled up.

'What?' I asked.

'It's mine,' said Vorblei. 'It goes with the job.'

'Ah,' I said, 'congratulations.'

We entered the apartment building. The lift was not working and we had to make our way up a dark staircase, from which the carpet runner had not yet been ripped away.

'What is it that you do?' I asked.

'Oh,' said Vorblei, 'it's not something I can explain in a few words. There's really a lot of work – too much, in fact. First one thing, then another, and then something else, and all the time you have to try to keep up. First one place, then another. Someone has to do it all.'

'In the cultural line, is it?'

He inclined his head to one side in a rather indefinite fashion. I did not try to ask any more questions.

When we reached the fifth floor we approached a tall door

4

on which there was a clearly defined lighter coloured rectangular area which showed where a name plaque had once been. He opened the door, and we went into a dark hallway when a telephone on the wall immediately began to jangle.

Vorblei picked up the receiver. 'Yes, comrade Babayasin,' he roared into the ebony cup of the mouthpiece. 'Yes, I remember . . . No, don't send them . . . Comrade Babayasin, I can't do that, it will look ridiculous . . . Just imagine – with the sailors, it will be a disgrace . . . What? I will follow orders, but I must register a vigorous protest . . . What?'

He glanced sideways at me and, not wishing to embarrass him, I went through into the lounge.

The floor there was covered with newspapers – most of them banned long ago. I supposed there must have been files of them left behind in the flat. Other traces of the place's former life were also visible: there was a delightful Turkish carpet hanging on the wall and below it stood a secretaire decorated with enamel rhomboids of various colours. As soon as I saw it I realized that a well-to-do bourgeois family must have lived there. A large mirror stood against the opposite wall. Beside it hung a crucifix in the art-nouveau style, and for a moment I pondered the nature of the religious feeling which might correspond to such a work of art. A considerable part of the space was occupied by an immense bed under a yellow canopy. The items that stood on the round table in the centre of the room seemed to me – possibly because of their proximity to the crucifix – to be a still-life composed of esoteric Christian motifs: a large bottle of vodka, a halvah tin shaped like a heart, a staircase leading into emptiness constructed out of pieces of black bread laid one on top of another, three tooth glasses and a cross-shaped can-opener.

Lying on the floor beside the mirror was a pile of packages whose shapes put me in mind of contraband; a sour smell of leg-wrappings and stale drink hung in the air, and there were also a great many empty bottles in the room. I sat on the table.

Shortly afterwards the door squeaked open and Vorblei came in. He took off his leather jacket, exposing an emphatically military tunic.

'The things they give you to do,' he said as he sat down. 'That was the Cheka on the phone.'

'You work for them as well?'

'I avoid them as much as I can.'

'How did you get involved with such company anyway?'

Vorblei smiled broadly. 'It couldn't have been more simple. I had a five-minute telephone conversation with Gorky.'

'And straight away they gave you a Mauser and that limousine?'

'Listen,' he said, 'life is a theatre. That's a well-known fact. But what you don't hear said so often is that every day the theatre shows a new play. And right now, Petya, I m putting on a show the like of which you can't imagine . . .'

He raised his hands above his head and shook them in the air, as though he were jingling coins in an invisible sack.

'And it's not even the play that's the thing,' he said. 'To continue the analogy, in the old days anyone who felt like it could fling a rotten egg at the stage. Today, however, it's the actors who are more likely to rake the hall with machine-gun fire – they might even toss out a bomb. Think about it, who would you rather be right now? An actor or a member of the audience?'

This was a serious question.

'What can I say? The action at this theatre of yours starts much further back than you suggest,' I said thoughtfully. 'Besides, I think that the future really belongs to the cinematograph.'

Vorblei chuckled and nodded. 'All the same, you think about what I said.'

'I promise I will,' I answered.

He poured himself some vodka and drank it.

'Ah,' he said, 'about the theatre. Do you know who the Commissar for Theatres is now? Madame Malinovskaya. Of course, you never knew her, did you?'

'I don't remember,' I replied, a little irritated. 'Who the hell was she?'

'Vorblei sighed. He stood up and walked across the room without speaking.

'Petya,' he said, sitting down facing me and gazing up into

my eyes, 'we keep on joking away, but I can see that something's wrong. What's happened to you? You and I are old friends, of course, but even setting that aside I could probably help you.'

I decided to risk it.

'I will be honest with you. Three days ago in Petersburg I had visitors.'

'Where from?'

'From that theatre of yours.'

'How do you mean?' he asked, raising his eyebrows.

'Just as I said. Three of them came from the Cheka, one introduced himself as some kind of literary functionary, and the others had no need to introduce themselves. They spoke with me for about forty minutes, mostly the literary one; then they said our conversation had been most interesting, but it would have to be continued in a different place. I did not want to go to that other place because, as you know, it's not one from which one very often returns . . .'

'But you did come back,' Vorblei interrupted.

'I did not come back,' I said, 'I never went there. I ran away from them, Grisha. You know, the way we used to run away from the doorman when we were children.'

'But why did they come for you?' asked Vorblei. 'You've got absolutely nothing to do with politics. Was it something you did?'

'I did absolutely nothing at all. It sounds stupid even to talk about it. I published a poem in a newspaper, but it was a newspaper which didn't meet their approval. And there was one rhyme in it they did not like either: "Red" and "mad". Can you imagine that?'

'And what was the poem about?'

'Oh, it was completely abstract. It was about the stream of time washing away the wall of the present so that new patterns keep appearing on it, and we call some of them the past. Our memory tells us that yesterday really existed, but how can we be sure that all of these memories did not simply appear with the first light of dawn?'

'I don't quite understand,' said Vorblei.

'Neither do I,' I said. 'But that is not the point. The main

7

thing I am trying to say is that there was no politics in it at all. At least, that was what I thought. But they thought differently, they explained that to me. The most frightening thing was that after the conversation with their consultant I actually understood his logic, I understood it so well that . . . It was so frightening that when they led me out on to the street, I ran away not so much from them as from this new understanding of mine . . .'

Vorblei frowned.

'The entire story is a load of arrant nonsense,' he said. 'They're nothing but idiots. But you're a fine fool yourself. Was that the reason you came to Moscow?'

'Well, what could I do? As I was running away, I fired. You may understand that I was firing at a spectre created by my own fear, but that is hardly something I can explain to them at the Cheka.'

Vorblei looked at me seemingly engrossed in his thoughts. I looked at his hands – he was running them across the table-cloth with a barely perceptible motion, as though he were wiping away sweat, and then suddenly he hid them under the table. There was an expression of despair on his face, and I sensed that our meeting and my account had placed him in an extremely awkward situation.

'Of course, that makes it worse,' he muttered. 'But still, it's a good thing you've confided in me. I think we'll be able to sort it out . . . Yes, yes, I'm sure we can sort it out . . . I'll give Gorky a call straight away . . . Put your hands on your head.'

I did not take in the meaning of the final words until I saw the muzzle of the Mauser lying on the tablecloth. Incredibly enough, the very next thing that he did was to take a pince-nez out of his breast pocket and set it on his nose.

'Put your hands on your head,' he repeated.

'What are you doing?' I asked, raising my hands. 'Grisha?'

'No,' he said.

'"No" what?'

'Weapon and papers on the table, that's what.'

'How can I put them on the table,' I said, 'if my hands are on my head?'

He cocked his pistol.

'My God,' he said, 'if you only knew just how often I've heard that phrase.'

'Well, then,' I said, 'the revolver is in my coat. What an incredible bastard you are. But then I've known that since we were children. What do you get out of all of this? Do you think they'll give you a medal?'

Vorblei smiled. 'Into the corridor,' he said.

When we were in the corridor he kept the gun trained on me while he rummaged through the pockets of my coat, took out the revolver and put it in his pocket. There was a furtive haste about his movements, like a schoolboy on his first visit to a brothel, and the thought occurred to me that he had probably never had to commit an act of treachery in such an obvious and commonplace fashion before.

'Unlock the door,' he ordered, 'and go out on to the landing.'

'Let me put my coat on,' I said, feverishly wondering whether there was anything I could say to this man, so excited by his own baseness, that might be capable of changing the unfolding course of events.

'We're not going far,' said Vorblei, 'just across the boulevard. But put it on anyway.'

I took the coat down from the hanger with both hands, turned slightly to thrust my arm into one of the sleeves, and the next moment, to my own amazement, I had flung the coat over Vorblei – not simply tossed it in his direction, but actually thrown it right on top of him.

To this day I do not understand how he failed to shoot me, but a fact is a fact. He pressed the trigger only as he was falling to the floor under the weight of my body and the bullet missed my side by a few inches and struck the door of the apartment. The coat covered Vorblei's head where he had fallen and I grabbed hold of his throat through the thick fabric. I managed to pin the wrist of the hand clutching the pistol to the floor with my knee, though before his fingers opened he had fired several more bullets into the wall. I was almost deafened by the thunderous noise. I think that in the course of the struggle I must have butted his covered face; in any case, I can clearly recall the quiet crunching of his pince-nez in the interlude between two shots.

Even after he had stopped moving, it was a long time before I could bring myself to release my grip on his throat. My hands scarcely obeyed me; in order to restore my breathing I performed an exercise, but it had a strange effect, inducing a mild fit of hysterics. I suddenly saw the scene from the perspective of an outside observer: a figure sitting on the corpse of a newly strangled friend and assiduously breathing according to Yogi Ramacharaki's method as described in the journal *Isida*. As I stood up, I was overwhelmed by the realization that I had committed murder.

Of course, like anyone else who did not entirely trust the authorities, I carried a revolver, and two days before I had had no qualms about using it. But this was something different, this was some dark scene out of Dostoevsky: an empty flat, a corpse covered with an English-style coat, and a door leading to a hostile world – a door perhaps already being approached by people attracted by idle curiosity. By an effort of will I banished these thoughts from my mind. The Dostoevskian atmosphere, of course, was not created by the corpse or the door with its bullet hole, but by myself, by my own consciousness, which had assimilated the forms of another's repentance.

Opening the door on to the stairs slightly, I listened for a few seconds. I could hear nothing, and I thought that perhaps the sound of a few pistol shots might not have attracted attention after all.

My revolver was still in Vorblei's trouser pocket, but I really did not feel inclined to retrieve it. I picked up his Mauser and looked it over. It had an excellent mechanism, and was quite new. I forced myself to search his jacket and discovered a packet of 'Ira' *papyrosas*, a spare cartridge clip for the Mauser and a pass for a member of the Cheka in the name of Grigory Fourply. Yes, I thought to myself – that was a typical touch; but his true character had already been clear even when we were children.

I squatted down on my haunches and opened the lock of his obstetrician's bag. Inside there was an official-looking file full of blank arrest warrants, another two cartridge clips, a tin box full of cocaine, some extremely unpleasant-looking medical forceps (I immediately flung them into the corner) and a thick wad of money, with rainbow-coloured one-hundred-rouble Duma notes on one side and dollars on the other. It was all just what I needed. In order to restore myself a little after the shock I had suffered, I stuffed a generous amount of cocaine into my nostrils. It slashed across my brain like a razor and I instantly became calm. I did not like cocaine, it made me too sentimental, but just now I needed to recover control rapidly.

Taking Vorblei under the arms, I dragged him along the corridor, kicked open the door into one of the rooms and was about to push him inside when I froze in the doorway. Despite the devastation and neglect, signs of the room's former life were still visible, illuminated by a light still there from before the war; it had been the nursery, two small beds with light bamboo railings stood in one corner and on the wall there was a charcoal drawing of a horse and a face with a moustache. There was a red rubber ball lying on the floor. When I saw it, I immediately closed the door and dragged Vorblei further along the corridor. I was startled by the funereal simplicity of the next room: standing in the centre was a black grand piano with its lid open, and beside it a revolving stool. There was nothing else.

At this moment a strange sensation came over me. Leaving Vorblei half-sitting in the corner (all the time I had been moving him I had been very careful to make sure that his face did not peep out from under the grey fabric of the coat), I sat down at the piano. How strange, I thought, comrade Fourply is here – and he is not here. Who knows what transformations his soul is now undergoing? I remembered a poem by him, published three years earlier in the *New Satiricon* – it took the form of a retelling of a newspaper article about the disbanding of some parliament or other and its acrostic read as 'Mane Tekel Fares', the words on King Belshazzar's wall. He was alive; he thought; he pondered over things. How very strange.

I turned towards the piano and began quietly playing a piece by Mozart, my favourite fugue in F, which always made me regret that I did not have the four hands the great musical madcap himself had dreamed of. The melody that engrossed

me had nothing to do with the shocking incident with Vorblei: the image that appeared before my eyes was of the small
bamboo beds in the next room, and for a second I imagined
someone else's childhood, someone else's pure glance directed at the sunset, someone else's world, deeply moving beyond all words, which had now been borne off into oblivion.
I did not play for very long, though, the piano was out of
tune, and I knew I should be leaving as quickly as possible.
But where should I go?

It was time to think about how I would spend the evening.
I went back into the corridor and glanced doubtfully at Vorblei's leather jacket, but there was nothing else. Despite the
daring nature of several of my literary experiments, I was still
not enough of a decadent to put on a coat which had now become a shroud and, moreover, had a bullet hole in its back. I
took the jacket off the hook, picked up the obstetrician's bag
and went through into the room with the mirror.

The leather jacket was just my size – the dead man and I
were almost exactly the same height. When I tightened the
belt with the holster dangling from it and looked at my reflection, what I saw was the very image of a Bolshevik. I expect that an inspection of the packages lying by the wall
would have made me a rich man in the space of a few minutes, but my squeamishness won the upper hand. Painstakingly reloading the pistol, I checked that it sprang easily from
its holster and was just about to leave the room when I heard
voices in the corridor. I realized that all this time the front
door of the apartment had been open.

I dashed over to the balcony. It looked out on to Tverskoi
Boulevard and the twenty or so yards of cold dark emptiness
beneath it held nothing but swirling snowflakes. In the circle of
light from a street lamp I could see Vorblei's automobile, and a
man wearing a Bolshevik helmet who had somehow appeared
in the front seat. I decided that Vorblei must have summoned
the Cheka when he was on the telephone. It was impossible to
clamber down on to the balcony below, so I dashed back into
the room. They were already pounding on the door. So be it, I
thought, all of this had to come to an end sooner or later. I
aimed the Mauser at the door and shouted: 'Enter!'

The door opened and two sailors in pea-jackets and rakishly flared trousers came tumbling into the room; they were hung all over with bottle-shaped hand grenades. One of them, with a moustache, was already elderly but the other was young, although his face was flaccid and anaemic. They paid not the slightest attention to the pistol in my hand.

'Are you Fourply?' asked the older one with the moustache.

'I am.'

'Here,' said the sailor, and he held out a piece of paper folded into two.

I put the Mauser back in its holster and unfolded the paper.

Com. Fourply! Go immediately to the 'Musical Snuffbox' to propound our line. To assist you I am sending Zherbunov and Barbolin, experienced comrades. Babayasin'

Below the text there was an illegible seal. While I was thinking what to say, they sat down at the table.

'Is that driver downstairs yours?' I asked.

'Yes,' said the one with the moustache. 'But we'll take your car. What's your name?'

'Pyotr,' I said, and then almost bit my tongue.

'I'm Zherbunov,' said the older one.

'Barbolin,' the younger one introduced himself. His voice was soft and almost womanish.

I sat facing them at the table. Zherbunov poured out three glasses of vodka, pushed one across to me and raised his eyes to my face. I realized that he was waiting for something.

'Well then,' I said, taking a grip on my glass, 'let us drink to the victory of world revolution!'

My toast was not greeted with any great enthusiasm.

'Of course, victory's all very well,' said Barbolin, 'but what about the works?'

'What works?' I asked.

'Don't you try playing the fool with us,' Zherbunov reproached me, 'Babayasin told us you were issued a tin today.'

'Ah, you're talking about the cocaine,' I said, reaching into the obstetrician's bag. 'Works is a word with many different meanings. Perhaps you'd like some ether, like William James?'

'Who's he?' asked Barbolin, grasping the tin in his coarse, broad palm.

'An English comrade.'

Zherbunov cleared his throat dubiously, but for a moment Barbolin's face reflected one of those feelings that nineteenth-century Russian artists loved to depict when they were creating national types – the feeling that somewhere out there is a wide and wonderful world, filled with amazing and attractive things, and though you can never seriously hope to reach it yourself, you cannot help sometimes dreaming impossible dreams.

The tension disappeared as though by magic. Zherbunov opened the tin, picked up a knife from the table, scooped up a monstrous amount of the white powder and rapidly stirred it into his vodka. Barbolin did the same, first with his own glass, and then with mine.

'Now we can do the world revolution justice,' he said.

My face must have betrayed an element of doubt, because Zherbunov chuckled and said: 'This goes right back to the *Aurora*, brother, back to the very beginning. It's called "Baltic tea".'

They raised their glasses and drained them at a gulp, and there was nothing left for me but to follow their example. Almost immediately my throat became numb. I lit a *papyrosa* and inhaled deeply, but I could not taste the smoke. We sat there without speaking for about a minute.

'We should get going,' Zherbunov said suddenly and rose from the table. 'Ivan'll freeze to death down there.'

In a state of numb torpor, I put the tin back into the bag. I hung back in the corridor, trying to find my fur hat, then put on Vorblei's peaked cap instead. We left the apartment and set off in silence down the dimly lit staircase.

I was suddenly aware that my spirits were calm and easy, and the further I went, the calmer and easier they became. I was not thinking about the future, it was enough for me that I was not threatened by any immediate danger, and as we crossed the dark landings I gazed entranced at the incredibly beautiful snowflakes swirling in the air outside the window-panes. It occurred to me that I myself was like one of those snowflakes, and the wind of fate was bearing me onwards in the wake of the two other snowflakes in black pea-jackets who were stomping down the stairs in front of me. However, despite the euphoria that had enveloped me, I remained capable of a sober assessment of reality and was able to make one interesting observation. While I was still in Petrograd I had been curious about how the sailors managed to keep up those heavy bullet harnesses they wore. On the third-floor landing, where a solitary electric bulb was shining, I spotted several hooks on Zherbunov's back which held his machine-gun belts together, rather in the manner of a brassiere. I immediately had a vision of Zherbunov and Barbolin preparing themselves for their next killing and helping one another with this difficult element of their toilet like two girls in a bathing hut. It seemed to me yet another proof of the feminine nature of all revolutions. I suddenly understood several of Alexander Blok's new moods; some involuntary exclamation must have escaped my throat, because Barbolin turned around.

'And you didn't want to try it, you nelly,' he said, exposing a gleaming gold tooth.

We went out into the street. Barbolin said something to the soldier sitting in the front seat of the car, opened the door and we climbed in. The car immediately moved off. Through the rounded windscreen of the passenger cabin I could see a snow-covered back and a sharp-pointed felt helmet. It was as though our carriage were being driven by one of Ibsen's trolls. I thought that the construction of the automobile was most uncomfortable and, moreover, humiliating for the driver, who was always exposed to the elements – but perhaps this was a deliberate arrangement, so that the passengers could enjoy not only the view through the window, but also savour the inequality of the classes.

I turned towards the side window. The street was empty and the snow falling on to the roadway was exceptionally beautiful. It was illuminated by widely spaced street lamps; by the light of one of them I caught a glimpse of a phrase of graffiti boldly daubed on the wall of a house: 'LENINE EST MERDE'.

When the automobile braked to a halt, I was already feeling

a little more normal. We alighted on an unfamiliar street beside an entirely undistinguished-looking gateway in a wall, in front of which stood a couple of automobiles and several smart cabs. A little further off I noticed a frightening-looking armoured car with its machine-gun turret buried under a cap of snow, but I had no time for a closer look, for the sailors had already plunged into the gateway. We walked across an inexpressibly bleak courtyard and found ourselves facing a door surmounted by a protruding canopy with volutes and cherubs in the old merchant style. A small signboard had been hung on the canopy: 'THE MUSICAL SNUFFBOX: LITERARY CABARET'.

There was light showing through the pink curtains drawn tightly across several windows beside the door: from behind them I could hear the plaintively beautiful note of some obscure musical instrument.

Zherbunov tugged the door open sharply, revealing behind it a short corridor hung with fur coats and greatcoats, which ended in a heavy velvet curtain. A man wearing a simple Russian shirt and looking like a convict rose from a stool to meet us.

'Citizen sailors,' he began, 'we don't . . .'

With the agility of a circus acrobat Barbolin swung his rifle around his shoulder and struck him with the butt in the base of his belly; the attendant slid down the wall and on to the floor, his hostile face suddenly expressive of weariness and revulsion. Zherbunov pulled aside the curtain, and we entered a dimly lit hall.

Feeling myself fired by an unusual burst of energy, I looked around. The place looked like an ordinary run-of-the-mill restaurant with some pretensions to chic, and the public seated among the dense clouds of smoke at small round tables was quite varied. There was a smell of opium. Nobody took any notice of us, and we sat at a small table not far from the entrance.

The hall was bounded on one side by a brightly lit stage, on which a clean-shaven gentleman in evening dress, with one bare foot, was sitting on a black velvet stool. He was sliding the bow he held in his right hand across the smooth edge of a long saw, one handle of which was pressed against the floor by his foot while the other was gripped tightly in his left hand, so that the saw bent into a trembling curve. When he needed to dampen the vibration of the gleaming strip of metal, he would press his bare foot against it for a second. Beside him on the floor stood a patent-leather shoe with a blindingly white sock protruding from it. The sound which the gentleman extracted from his instrument was absolutely unearthly, at once doleful and enchanting. I think he was playing a simple melody, but that was not important; what mattered was the timbre, the modulations of a single note that faded away over an eternity and pierced straight to the very centre of my heart.

The door-curtain at the entrance quivered and the man in the Russian shirt stuck his head and shoulders out from behind it. He clicked his fingers somewhere off into the darkness and nodded towards our table. Then he turned towards us, gave a short, formal bow and disappeared back behind the curtain. Immediately a waiter emerged out of somewhere with a tray in one hand and a copper teapot in the other (there were identical teapots standing on the other tables). The tray held a dish of small pies, three teacups and a tiny whistle. The waiter set the cups out in front of us, filled them from the teapot and then froze in motionless anticipation. I held out a bill drawn at random from my travelling bag – I think it was a ten-dollar note. I could not understand at first what the whistle was doing on the tray, but then I heard a melodic whistling from one of the neighbouring tables, and saw a waiter come dashing over at the sound.

Zherbunov swallowed a mouthful of liquid from his cup and grimaced in distaste. Then I tried a sip from mine. It was *khanja*, a bad Chinese vodka made from *kaoliang*. I started chewing on a pie, but I could not taste it at all; the freezing effect on my throat of the cocaine had still not worn off.

'What's in the pies?' Barbolin asked gingerly. 'People keep disappearing these days, after all. I don't feel like breaking my fast that way.'

'I tried it once,' Zherbunov said simply. 'It's like beef.'

Unable to bear any more of this, I took out the tin box and Barbolin set about stirring the powder into our cups.

Meanwhile the gentleman in evening dress finished playing, donned his sock and shoe with elegant rapidity, stood up, bowed, picked up the stool and quit the stage to the sound of scattered applause. A handsome-looking man with a small grey beard got up from a table beside the stage. His throat was wrapped in a grey scarf as though to conceal a love bite. I was astonished to recognize him as the poet Valery Briusov, now old and emaciated. He mounted the stage and turned to face the hall.

'Comrades! Although we live in a visual age, in which lines of printed words are being supplanted by sequences of images or . . . hmm . . . ,' he declaimed, 'still tradition does not abandon the struggle, but seeks to discover new forms. To this day the immortal Dostoevsky and his novel *Crime and Punishment* continue to inspire young seekers of truth, both with axes to grind and without. And so now a little tragedy – that is the precise definition of this play's genre, according to the author himself, the chamber poet Ioann Pavlukhin. Ladies and gentlemen, your attention please for the little tragedy *Raskolnikov and Marmeladov*.'

'Your attention please,' echoed Zherbunov, and we drank.

Briusov left the stage and returned to his table. Two men in military uniform carried a massive gilded lyre on a stand and a stool out on to the stage from the wings. Then they brought out a table, stood a pot-bellied liqueur bottle and two glasses on it, and pinned up two pieces of cardboard at either side of the stage, bearing the words 'Raskolnikov' and 'Harmeladov' (I immediately decided that the misspelling of the second name was not a mistake but a symbol of some kind), and finally they hung a board bearing the incomprehensible word 'yhvy' in the centre of the stage. Having duly situated all of these objects in their places, they disappeared. A woman in a long tunic emerged from the wings and began running leisurely fingers over the strings of the lyre. Several minutes passed in this fashion before a quartet of individuals in long black cloaks appeared on stage. Each of them went down on one knee and raised a black hem to conceal his face from the audience. Someone applauded. At the opposite end of the stage two figures appeared wearing tall buskins, long white robes and Greek masks. They began slowly moving towards each other, but stopped before they came close. One of them had an axe hanging under his arm in a noose entwined with roses – I realized that he was Raskolnikov. This, in fact, was obvious enough without the axe, because the board bearing his name was hanging by the wings on his side of the stage.

The other figure halted, slowly raised his arm in the air and began intoning in ponderous hexameters. In almost exactly the same words as his drunken prototype in the novel, he confessed that he had nowhere left to turn, then declared that Raskolnikov's blazing eyes betrayed a keen sensibility of the woes of the downtrodden and oppressed, and immediately suggested that they should drink to that (this was indeed a revolutionary innovation).

The actor with the axe declined curtly. Marmeladov quickly drained his glass and continued his oration, paying Raskolnikov a long and confused compliment, in which I found several of the images quite effective – for instance that of the arrogant strength of emptiness blossoming behind the hero's eyes and lending his face a semblance of the visage of God.

On hearing the word 'God', Zherbunov nudged me with his elbow.

'What d'you reckon?' he asked in a low voice.

'It is still too soon,' I whispered in reply. 'Carry on watching.'

Marmeladov's meaning grew more and more ambiguous. Dark hints began to surface in the flow of his words: a comparison of the grey St Petersburg morning with a blow from an axe to the back of the head, of his own world-weary soul with a dark closet in which the bodies of dead women lay. At this, Raskolnikov began showing clear signs of nervousness, and he enquired what Marmeladov wanted of him. In some confusion, Marmeladov asked him to sell the axe.

In the meantime I surveyed the hall. There were three or four people at each round table; the customers were a very mixed bunch, but as has always been the case throughout the history of humanity, it was pig-faced speculators and expensively dressed whores who predominated. Sitting at the same table as Briusov, and grown noticeably fatter since the last time I had seen him, was Alexei Tolstoy, wearing a big bow instead of a normal tie. The fat that had accumulated on him seemed to have been pumped from the skeletal frame of Briusov: together they looked quite horrific.

Looking further, at one of the tables I noticed a strange man sporting a military blouse criss-crossed with belts and an up-turned handlebar moustache. He was alone at his table, and instead of a teapot there was a bottle of champagne standing in front of him. I decided that he must be a big Bolshevik boss. I do not know what it was in his calm, powerful face that struck me as unusual, but for several seconds I was unable to take my gaze off him. His eyes met mine, but he immediately turned away to face the stage, where the meaningless dialogue was continuing.

Raskolnikov attempted to discover for what purpose Marmeladov required the axe and received replies couched in vague, flowery phrases about youth, the Grail, eternity, power, hope and – for some strange reason – the phases of the moon. Eventually Raskolnikov capitulated and handed over the axe. He was counting the wad of bills that Marmeladov had given him in payment, when he suddenly swayed back and froze in astonishment. He had noticed that Marmeladov was standing there in front of him wearing a mask. Still speaking in the same laboured hexameters, he began asking Marmeladov to remove the mask. I was particularly struck by one image which he used, 'Your eyes are like two yellow stars' – Briusov broke into applause at the words, but overall it was far too long and drawn out. After Raskolnikov had repeated his request for the third time, Marmeladov paused in silence for a long, terrible moment before tearing the mask from his face. Simultaneously the tunic attached to the mask was torn from his body, revealing a woman dressed in lacy knickers and a brassiere, sporting a silvery wig with a rat's-tail plait.

'Oh God! . . . The old woman! And I am empty-handed . . .' Having pronounced these final words in an almost inaudible voice, Raskolnikov slumped to the floor from the full height of his buskins.

What followed made me blench. Two violinists leapt out on to the stage and began frenziedly playing some gypsy melody, while the Marmeladov woman threw her tunic over

Raskolnikov, leapt on to his chest and began strangling him, wiggling her lace-clad bottom to and fro in excitement.

For a moment I thought that what was happening was the result of some monstrous conspiracy, and that everybody was looking in my direction. I glanced around like a beast at bay, my eyes once again met those of the man in the black military blouse, and I somehow suddenly realized that he knew all about the death of Vorblei – that he knew, in fact, far more serious things about me than just that.

At that moment I came close to leaping up from my chair and taking to my heels, and it took a monstrous effort of will to remain sitting at the table. The audience was applauding feebly; several of them were laughing and pointing at the stage, but most were absorbed in their own conversations and their vodka.

Having strangled Raskolnikov, the woman in the wig bounded over to the front of the stage and began dancing wildly to the insane accompaniment of the two violins, kicking her naked legs up towards the ceiling and waving the axe. The four figures in black, who had remained motionless throughout the play, now took hold of Raskolnikov, still covered by the tunic, and carried him into the wings. I had a faint inkling that this was a reference to the very end of *Hamlet*, where there is a mention of four captains who are supposed to carry away the dead prince. Strangely enough, this thought brought me to my senses straight away. I realized that what was happening was not a conspiracy against me – nobody could possibly have arranged it all in the time which had passed – but a perfectly ordinary mystical challenge. Immediately deciding to accept it, I turned to the two sailors, who had by this time retreated into themselves.

'Time to call a halt, lads. This is treason.'

Barbolin looked up at me uncomprehendingly.

'The agents of the Entente are at it again,' I threw in at random.

These words seemed to have some meaning for him, because he immediately tugged his rifle from his shoulder. I restrained him.

'Not that way, comrade. Wait.'

Meanwhile the gentleman with the saw had reappeared on the stage, seated himself on the stool and begun ceremoniously removing his shoe. Opening up my travelling bag, I took out a pencil and a blank Cheka arrest order; the plaintive sounds of the saw swept me upwards and onwards, and a suitable text was ready within a few minutes.

'What's that you're writing?' asked Zherbunov. 'You want to arrest someone?'

'No,' I replied, 'if we take anyone here, we have to take them all. We will handle this a different way. Zherbunov, remember the orders? We're not just supposed to suppress the enemy, we have to propound our line, right?'

'Right,' said Zherbunov.

'Well, then,' I said, 'you and Barbolin go backstage. I will propound our line from the stage. Once I have finished, I'll give the signal, and you come out. Then we'll play them the music of the revolution.'

Zherbunov tapped a finger against his cup.

'No, Zherbunov,' I said sternly, 'you won't be fit for work.'

An expression somewhat akin to hurt flitted across Zherbunov's face.

'What d'you mean?' he whispered. 'Don't you trust me, then? Why I, I'd . . . I'd give my life for the revolution!'

'I know that, comrade,' I said, 'but cocaine comes later. Into action!'

The sailors stood up and walked towards the stage with firm, lumbering strides, as if they were not crossing a parquet floor but the heaving deck of a battleship caught in a storm; at that moment I felt something almost like sympathy for them. They climbed up the side steps and disappeared into the wings. I tossed back the contents of my cup, rose and went over to the table where Tolstoy and Briusov were sitting. People were watching me. Gentlemen and comrades, I thought, as I strode slowly across the strangely expanded hall, today I too was granted the honour of stepping over my own old woman, but you will not choke me with her imaginary fingers. Oh, damnation take these eternal Dostoevskian obsessions that pursue us Russians! And damnation take us Russians who can see nothing else around us!

'Good evening, Valery Yakovlevich. Relaxing?'

Briusov started and looked at me for several seconds, obviously unable to place me. Then a doubtful smile appeared on his emaciated face.

'Petya?' he queried. 'Is it you? I am truly glad to see you. Join us for a minute.'

I sat at the table and greeted Tolstoy with reserve. We had met frequently enough at the *Apollo* editorial office, but hardly knew one another at all. Tolstoy was extremely drunk.

'How are you?' asked Briusov. 'Have you written anything lately?'

'No time for that now, Valery Yakovlevich,' I said.

'Yes,' said Briusov thoughtfully, his eyes skipping rapidly over my leather jacket and Mauser, 'that's true. Very true. I'm the same . . . But I didn't know you were one of us, Petya. I always thought highly of your verse, especially your first collection, *The Poems of Captain Lebyadkin*. And of course, *Songs of the Kingdom of I*. But I simply couldn't have imagined . . . You always had all those horses and emperors, and China . . .'

'Conspiracy, Valery Yakovlevich,' I said, 'conspiracy . . .'

'I understand,' said Briusov, 'now I understand. But then, I assure you, I always did sense something of the sort. But you've changed, Petya. Become so dashing . . . your eyes are positively gleaming . . . By the way, have you found time to read Blok's "Twelve"?'

'I have seen it,' I said.

'And what do you think?'

'I do not entirely understand the symbolism of the ending,' I said. 'What is Christ doing walking in front of the patrol? Does Blok perhaps wish to crucify the revolution?'

'Yes, yes,' Briusov replied quickly, 'Alyosha and I were just talking about that.'

Hearing his name mentioned, Tolstoy opened his eyes and lifted his cup, but it was empty. He fumbled about on the table until he found the whistle and then raised it to his lips, but before he could blow it, his head slumped back on to his chest.

'I have heard,' I said, 'that he has changed the ending, and now he has a revolutionary sailor walking ahead of the patrol.'

Briusov pondered this for a moment, and then his eyes lit up.

'Yes,' he said, 'that's more correct. That's more accurate. And Christ walks behind them! He is invisible and he walks behind them, dragging his crooked cross through the swirling blizzard!'

'Yes,' I said, 'and in the opposite direction.'

'You think so?'

'I am certain of it,' I said, thinking that Zherbunov and Barbolin must have fallen asleep behind the curtain at this stage. 'Valery Yakovlevich, I have something I would like to ask you. Would you announce that the poet Fourply will now present a reading of revolutionary verse?'

'Fourply?' Briusov asked.

'My party pseudonym,' I explained.

'Yes, yes,' Briusov nodded, 'and so very profound! I shall be delighted to listen to you myself.'

'I would not advise that. You had better leave straight away. The shooting will start in a minute or two.'

Briusov turned pale and nodded. Neither of us said another word; when the saw fell silent and the dandified musician had put his shoe back on, Briusov rose from the table and went up on the stage.

'Today,' he said, 'we have already spoken of the very latest forms in art. This theme will now be continued by the poet Fourply,' – he could not restrain himself, and he rolled his eyes up to the ceiling, making it clear that he was about to indulge in his typically idiotic wordplay – 'hmm . . . I have no wish to spoil the surprise, but let this poem serve as a kind of . . . hmm . . . foreplay. Your attention please for the poet Fourply, who will read his revolutionary verse!'

He walked quickly back down into the hall, smiled guiltily at me, shrugged, grabbed the weakly protesting Tolstoy under the arm and dragged him towards the exit; at that moment he looked like a retired teacher tugging along a disobedient and stupid wolfhound on a leash.

I went up on to the stage. The abandoned velvet stool stood conveniently ready at its edge. I set my boot on it and gazed out into the hall, which had fallen silent. All the faces I saw seemed to merge into a single face, at once fawning

24

and impudent, frozen in a grimace of smug servility – beyond the slightest doubt, this was the face of the old moneylender, the old woman, disincarnate, but still as alive as ever. Sitting close to the stage was Ioann Pavlukhin, a long-haired freak with a monocle; beside him a fat, pimply woman with immense red bows in her mousy hair was chewing on a pie – I thought that she must be the Theatre Commissar Madam Malinovskaya. How I hated them all for that long second!

I took the Mauser from its holster, raised it above my head, cleared my throat, and in my former manner, gazing straight ahead without expression and using no intonation whatsoever, but simply pausing briefly between quatrains, I read the poem that I had written on the Cheka arrest form:

> Comrades in the struggle! Our grief can know no bound.
> Comrade Fourply has been treacherously struck down.
> The Cheka reels now, pale and sick
> At the loss of a senior Bolshevik.
> It happened that on leaving a dangerous suspect
> He paused along the way to light a cigarette,
> When a counter-revolutionary White
> Caught him clearly in his pistol sight.
> Comrades! The muzzle thundered fierce and loud,
> The bullet smote brave comrade Fourply in the brow.
> He tried to reach a hand inside his jacket
> But his eyes closed and he fell down flat ker-smackit.
> Comrades in the struggle! Close ranks and sing in unison,
> And show the great White swine the terror of the revolution!

With these words I fired at the chandelier, but missed; immediately there was another shot from my right, the chandelier shattered and I saw Zherbunov there at my side, resetting the breech on his gun. Going down on one knee, he fired a few more shots into the hall, where people were already screaming and falling to the floor or attempting to hide behind the columns, and then Barbolin emerged from the wings. Swaying as he walked, he went up to the edge of the stage, then screeched as he tossed a bomb into the hall. There was a searing flash of white fire and a terrible bang, a table was overturned, and in the silence that followed someone gasped in astonishment. There was an awkward pause; in an attempt to fill it at least partly, I fired several times more into the ceiling, and then I suddenly caught sight again of the strange man in the military tunic. He sat unperturbed at his table, sipping from his cup, and I think he was smiling. I suddenly felt stupid.

Zherbunov fired off another shot into the hall.

'Cease fire!' I roared.

Zherbunov muttered something that sounded like 'too young to be giving me orders', but he slung his rifle back behind his shoulder.

'Withdraw,' I said, then turned and walked into the wings.

At our appearance the people who had been hiding in the wings scattered in all directions. Zherbunov and I walked along a dark corridor, turning several corners before we reached the rear door and found ourselves in the street, where once again people fled from us. We walked over to the automobile. After the stuffy, smoke-polluted atmosphere of the hall, the clean frosty air affected me like ether fumes, my head began to spin and I felt a desperate need to sleep. The driver was still sitting there motionless on the open front seat, but now he was covered with a thick layer of snow. I opened the door of the cabin and turned round.

'Where's Barbolin?' I asked.

'He'll be along,' chuckled Zherbunov, 'just something he had to see to.'

I climbed into the automobile, leaned back against the seat and instantly fell asleep.

I was woken by the sound of a woman's squeals, and I saw Barbolin emerging from a side street, carrying in his arms the girl in lace panties. She was offering token resistance and the wig with the plait had slipped to one side of her face.

'Move over, comrade,' Zherbunov said to me, clambering into the cabin. 'Reinforcements.'

I moved closer to the side wall. Zherbunov leaned towards me and spoke in an unexpectedly warm voice: 'I didn't really understand you at first, Petka. Didn't see right into your heart. But you're a good 'un. That was a fine speech you gave.'

I mumbled something and fell asleep again.

Through my slumber I could hear a woman giggling and brakes squealing, Zherbunov's voice swearing darkly and Barbolin hissing like a snake; they must have quarrelled over the unfortunate girl. Then the automobile stopped. Raising my head I saw the blurred and improbable-looking face of Zherbunov.

'Sleep, Petka,' the face rumbled, 'we'll get out here, there are things still to be done. Ivan'll get you home.'

I glanced out of the window. We were on Tverskoi Boulevard, beside the city governor's building. Snow was falling slowly in large flakes. Barbolin and the trembling semi-naked woman were already out on the street. Zherbunov shook my hand and got out. The car moved off.

I was suddenly keenly aware of how alone and vulnerable I was in this frozen world populated by people keen either to dispatch me to the Cheka or to perturb my inner soul with the dark sorcery of their obscure words. Tomorrow morning, I thought, I will have to put a bullet through my brain. The last thing I saw before I finally collapsed into the dark pit of oblivion was the snow-covered railing along the street, which came up very close to the window as the automobile finally turned.

2

To be more precise, the railings were not simply close to the window, but were part of it; in fact, it appeared that they were bars across a small window through which a narrow beam of sunshine was falling directly on to my face. I tried to turn away from it, but that proved impossible. When I attempted to press one hand against the floor in order to turn from my stomach on to my back, I found that my hands had been secured behind me: I was dressed in a garment resembling a shroud, the long sleeves of which were tied behind my back.

I felt no particular doubt as to what had happened to me. The sailors must have noticed something suspicious in my behaviour, and while I was asleep in the car they had taken me to the Cheka. By wriggling and squirming, I managed to get up on to my knees and then sit down by the wall. My cell had a rather strange appearance; up under the ceiling there was a small barred window – the point of entry for the ray of sunlight that had woken me – while the walls, the door, the floor and ceiling itself were all concealed beneath a thick layer of padding, which meant that romantic suicide in the spirit of Dumas ('one more step, milord, and I dash my brains out against the wall') was quite out of the question. The Chekists had obviously built cells like this for their specially honoured guests, and I must confess that for a second I was flattered at the thought.

A few minutes went by as I gazed at the wall, recalling the frightening details of the previous day, and then the door swung open.

Standing in the doorway were Zherbunov and Barbolin – but, my God, how changed they were! They were dressed in white doctors' coats, and Barbolin had a genuine stethoscope protruding from his pocket. This was simply too much for me, and my chest heaved abruptly with nervous laughter that erupted from my cocaine-scorched throat in an explosion of hoarse coughing. Barbolin, who was standing in front, turned to Zherbunov and said something. I suddenly stopped laughing, struck by the thought that they were going to beat me.

I should say that I was not in the least bit afraid of death. In my situation to die was every bit as natural and reasonable as to leave a theatre that has caught fire in the middle of a lack-lustre performance. But I most definitely did not want my final departure to be accompanied by kicks and punches from people I hardly knew – in the depths of my soul I was clearly not sufficiently a Christian for that.

'Gentlemen,' I said, 'I am sure you must understand that soon they will kill you too. Out of respect for death, therefore – if not for mine, then at least for your own – I ask you to get it over with quickly, without any unnecessary humiliation. I shall not be able to tell you anything, in any case. I am no more than an ordinary private citizen and . . .'

'That's a bit feeble,' Zherbunov interrupted me with a chuckle. 'But that stuff you were giving us yesterday, that was something else. And that poetry you read! D'you re-member any of that?'

There was something strangely incongruous about the way he spoke, something rather odd, and I decided that he must have been tippling his Baltic tea already that morning.

'My memory is excellent,' I replied, looking him straight in the face.

The emptiness in his eyes was impenetrable.

'I don't know why you bother talking to that asshole,' Bar-bolin hissed in his thin voice. 'Let Timurich handle it, that's what he's paid for.'

'Let's go,' said Zherbunov, putting an end to the conversa-tion. He came over to me and took hold of my arm.

'Can you not at least untie my hands?' I asked. 'There are two of you, after all.'

'Oh, yeah? And what if you try strangling one of us?'

I cringed as though I had been struck. They knew everything. I had an almost physical sensation of the crushing weight of Zherbunov's words tumbling down on top of me.

Barbolin gripped me by my other arm. They easily stood me on my feet and dragged me out into the dimly lit, deserted corridor, which did actually have a vague hospital smell about it, not unlike the smell of blood. I made no attempt to resist, and a few minutes later they pushed me into a large room, sat me down on a stool at its centre and withdrew.

Directly in front of me stood a large desk piled high with bureaucratic-looking files. Sitting behind the desk was a gentleman of intellectual appearance wearing a white doctor's coat just like those of Zherbunov and Barbolin. He was listening attentively to a black ebonite telephone receiver squeezed between his ear and his shoulder, while his hands mechanically sorted through some papers on the desk; from time to time he nodded, saying nothing, and he paid not the slightest attention to me. Another man wearing a white doctor's coat and green trousers with red stripes down their sides was sitting by the wall, on a chair placed between two tall windows over which dusty blinds had been lowered.

Something indefinite in the arrangement of the room reminded me of General HQ, which I had visited frequently in 1916, when I was trying my hopeful but inexperienced hand at patriotic journalism. But instead of a portrait of the Emperor (or at the very least that infamous Karl who had left a trail of indelible marks across half the kingdoms of Europe), hanging on the wall above the head of the gentleman in the white coat was something so terrible that I bit my lip, drawing blood.

It was a poster, printed in the colours of the Russian flag and mounted on a large piece of cardboard, depicting a blue man with a typically Russian face. His chest had been cleaved open and the top of his skull sawn off to expose his red brain. Despite the fact that his viscera had been extracted from his abdomen and labelled with Latin numerals, the expression in his eyes seemed one of indifference, and his face appeared frozen in a calm half-smile; on the other hand, perhaps that was simply the effect created by a wide gash in his cheek, through which I could see part of his jaw and teeth as flawless as in an advertisement for German tooth powder.

'Get on with it, then,' the man in the white coat barked, dropping the receiver back into its cradle.

'I beg your pardon,' I said, lowering my eyes to look at him.

'Granted, granted,' he said, 'bearing in mind that I already have some experience in dealing with you. Allow me to remind you that my name is Timur Timurovich.'

'Pyotr. For obvious reasons I am not able to shake your hand.'

'No need for that. Well, well, Pyotr, my lad. How did you manage to get yourself into such a mess?'

The eyes that watched me were friendly, even sympathetic, and the goatee beard made him look like an idealistic supporter of the liberal reform movement, but I knew a great deal about the Cheka's cunning tricks, and my heart remained unstirred by even the slightest flickering of trust.

'I do not believe that I have got myself into any particular mess,' I said. 'But if that is how you choose to put things, then I did not get into it on my own.'

'Then with whom exactly?'

This is it, I thought, it has begun.

'If I understand you correctly, you expect me to provide you with details of addresses and hiding places, but I am afraid I shall be obliged to disappoint you. My entire life since childhood is the story of how I have shunned all company, and in such a context one can only speak of other people in terms of a general category, if you take my meaning?'

'Naturally,' he said, and wrote something down on a piece of paper. 'No doubt about that. But there is a contradiction in what you say. First you tell me you didn't get into your present condition on your own, and then you tell me you shun other people.'

'Oh, come now,' I replied, crossing my legs at some risk to my immediate equilibrium, 'that is merely the appearance of a contradiction. The harder I try to avoid other people's company, the less successful I am. Incidentally, it was only quite recently that I realized why this is the case. I was walking past St Isaac's and I looked up at the dome – you know how it is, a

31

frosty night, the stars shining . . . and I understood.'

'And what is the reason?'

'If one tries to run away from other people, one involuntarily ends up actually following in their path throughout the course of one's life. Running away does not require knowing where one is running to, only what one is running from. Which means that one constantly has to carry before one's eyes a vision of one's own prison.'

'Yes,' said Timur Timurovich. 'Yes indeed, when I think of the trouble I'm going to have with you, it terrifies me.'

I shrugged and raised my eyes to the poster above his head. Apparently it was not a brilliant metaphor after all, merely a medical teaching aid, perhaps something taken from an anatomical atlas.

'You know,' Timur Timurovich continued, 'I have a lot of experience. Plenty of people pass through my hands here.'

'Indeed, I do not doubt it,' I said.

'So let me tell you something. I'm less interested in the formal diagnosis than the internal event which has prised someone loose from his normal socio-psychological niche. And as far as I can see, yours is a very straightforward case. You simply will not accept the new. Can you remember how old you are?'

'Of course. Twenty-six.'

'There you are, you see. You belong to the very generation that was programmed for life in one socio-cultural paradigm, but has found itself living in a quite different one. Do you follow what I'm saying?'

'Most definitely,' I replied.

'So what we have is a *prima facie* internal conflict. But let me reassure you straight away that you're not the only one struggling with this difficulty. I have a similar problem myself.

'Oh, really?' I exclaimed in a rather mocking tone. 'And just how do you deal with it?'

'We can talk about me later,' he said, 'let's try sorting you out first. As I've already said, nowadays almost everyone suffers from the same subconscious conflict. What I want you to do is to recognize its nature. You know, the world around us is reflected in our consciousness and then it becomes the object of our mental activity. When established connections in the real world collapse, the same thing happens in the human psyche. And this is accompanied by the release of a colossal amount of psychic energy within the enclosed space of your ego. It's like a small atomic explosion. But what really matters is how the energy is channelled after the explosion.'

The conversation was taking a curious turn.

'And what channels, if I may ask, are available?'

'If we keep it simple, there are two. Psychic energy can move outwards, so to speak, into the external world, striving towards objects like . . . well, shall we say, a leather jacket or a luxury automobile. Many of your contemporaries . . .'

I remembered Vorblei and shuddered. 'I understand. Please do not continue.'

'Excellent. In the other case, for one reason or another, this energy remains within. This is the less favourable course of events. Imagine a bull locked inside a museum . . .'

'An excellent image.'

'Thank you. Well then, this museum, with its fragile and possibly beautiful exhibits, is your personality, your inner world. And the bull rushing about inside it is the release of psychic energy that you are unable to cope with. The reason why you are here.'

He really is very clever, I thought – but what an utter scoundrel!

'I can tell you more,' continued Timur Timurovich. 'I've given a great deal of thought as to why some people have the strength to start a new life – for want of a better term, we can call them the "New Russians", although I detest that expression . . .'

'Indeed, it is quite repulsive. And also inaccurate; if you are quoting the revolutionary democrats of the last century, then I believe that they called them the new people.'

'Possibly. But the question remains the same: why do some people actively strive, as it were, towards the new, while others persist in their attempts to clarify their non-existent relations with the shadows of a vanished world?'

'Now that really is magnificent. You're a genuine poet.'

'Thank you once again. The answer, in my view, is very

33

simple – I'm afraid you might even find it rather primitive. Let me build up to it. The life of a man, a country, a culture and so on, is a series of constant metamorphoses. Sometimes they extend over a period of time and so are imperceptible, sometimes they assume acute forms, as in the present case. And it is precisely the attitude to these metamorphoses that determines the fundamental difference between cultures. For instance, China, the culture you are so crazy about . . .'

'What makes you think that?' I asked, feeling my tightly bound hands clench into fists behind my back.

'Your case history,' said Timur Timurovich, picking up the very fattest of the files on his desk. 'I was just leafing through it.'

He threw the file back down again. 'Yes, China. As you may recall, their entire world view is constructed on the principle that the world is constantly degenerating as it moves from a golden age towards darkness and stagnation. For them, absolute standards have been left far behind in the past, and all that is new is evil insofar as it leads the world still further away from those standards.'

'I beg your pardon,' I said, 'but this is a typical aspect of human culture in general. It is even present in language itself. In English, for instance, we are the *descendants* of the past. The word signifies movement downwards, not upwards. We are not *ascendants*.'

'Possibly,' Timur Timurovich answered. 'I don't know any foreign languages except Latin. But that's not the point here. When this type of consciousness is embodied in an individual personality, then the person concerned begins to regard his childhood as a lost paradise. Take Nabokov. His endless musings on the early years of his life are a classic example of what I'm talking about. And the classic example of recovery, of the reorientation of consciousness to the real world is the contra-sublimation, as I would call it, that he achieved in such a masterly fashion by transforming his longing for an unattainable paradise which may never have existed at all into a simple, earthly and somewhat illegitimate passion for a little girl, a child. Although at first . . .'

'Excuse me,' I interrupted, 'but which Nabokov are you

talking about? The leader of the Constitutional Democrats?'

Timur Timurovich smiled with emphatic politeness. 'No,' he said, 'his son.'

'Little Vovka from the Tenishevsky school? You mean you have picked him up as well? But he's in the Crimea! And what kind of nonsense is all this about little girls?'

'Very well, very well. He's in the Crimea,' Timur Timurovich replied briskly. 'In the Crimea. But we were talking about China. And the fact that for the classic Chinese mentality, any advance is bound to mean degeneration. But there is another path, the one followed by Europe throughout its history, no matter what you might tell me about language. The path that Russia has been struggling to follow for so many years, as it enters again and again into its ill-fated alchemical wedlock with the West.'

'Remarkable.'

'Thank you. In this case the ideal is conceived not as something left behind in the past, but as something potentially existing in the future. Do you understand me? This is the idea of development, progress, movement from the less perfect to the more perfect. The same thing occurs at the level of the individual personality, even if individual progress takes such petty forms as redecorating an apartment or changing an old car for a new one. It makes it possible to carry on living – but you don't want to pay for any of this. The metaphorical bull we were talking about rushes about in your soul, trampling everything in its path, precisely because you are not prepared to submit to reality. You don't want to let the bull out. You despise the positions that the times require us to adopt. And precisely this is the cause of your tragedy.'

'What you say is interesting, of course, but far too complicated,' I said, casting a sideways glance at the man in military trousers over by the wall. 'And now my hands have gone numb. As for progress, I can easily provide you with a brief explanation of what that is.'

'Please do so.'

'It is very simple. If we put everything that you were saying in a nutshell, then we are left with the simple fact that some people adapt themselves to change more quickly than others. But have you ever asked yourself why these changes take place at all?'

Timur Timurovich shrugged.

'Then let me tell you. You would not, I trust, deny that the more cunning and dishonourable a man is, the easier his life is?'

'No, I wouldn't.'

'And his life is easier precisely because he adapts more rapidly to change?'

'Perhaps.'

'Well then, there exists a level of dishonourable cunning, my dear sir, at which a man anticipates the outcome of change even before it is completed, and as a result he is able to adapt far more rapidly than everyone else. But far worse than that, the most sensitive of scoundrels actually adapt to change before it has even begun.'

'What of it?'

'In actual fact, all the changes that happen in the world only take place because of such highly sensitive scoundrels. Because, in reality, they do not anticipate the future at all, but shape it, by creeping across to occupy the quarter from which they think the wind will blow. Following which, the wind has no option but to blow from that very quarter.'

'Why is that?'

'It is obvious, surely. As I told you, I am speaking of the most villainous, sly and shameless of scoundrels. Surely you can believe them capable of persuading everyone else that the wind is blowing from the precise quarter in which they have established themselves? Especially since this wind we are talking about blows only within this idiom of ours . . . But now I am talking too much. In all honesty, I had intended to keep silent right up to the final shot.'

The officer sitting by the wall grunted suddenly and gave Timur Timurovich a meaningful glance.

'I haven't introduced you,' said Timur Timurovich. 'This is Major Smirnov, a military psychiatrist. He is here for other reasons, but your case has attracted his interest.'

'I am flattered, Major,' I said, inclining my head in his direction.

Timur Timurovich leaned over his telephone and pressed a button. 'Sonya, four cc's as usual, please,' he spoke into the receiver. 'Here in my office, while he's in the jacket. Yes, and then straight into the ward.'

Turning to me, Timur Timurovich sighed sadly and scratched his beard.

'We'll have to continue the course of medication for the time being,' he said. 'I tell you honestly, I regard it as a defeat. A small one, but nonetheless a defeat. I believe that a good psychiatrist should avoid using medication, it's – how can I explain it to you? – it's cosmetic. It doesn't solve any of the problems, it merely conceals them from view. But in your case I can't think of anything better. You'll have to help me. If you want to save a drowning man, it's not enough just to reach out to him, he has to offer his hand too.'

The door opened behind me and I heard quiet footsteps, then gentle woman's hands grasped me by the shoulder and I felt the small cold sting of a needle piercing my skin through the cloth of the strait-jacket.

'By the way,' said Timur Timurovich, rubbing his hands as though to warm them, 'one small comment; in madhouse slang the term "final shot" isn't used for what we're injecting you with, that is, an ordinary mixture of aminazine and perevitine. It's reserved for the so-called sulphazine cross, that is, four injections in . . . But then, I hope we're never going to reach that stage.'

I did not turn my head to look at the woman who had given me the injection. I looked at the dismembered red-white-and-blue man on the poster, and when he began looking back at me, smiling and winking, I heard Timur Timurovich's voice coming from somewhere very far away:

'Yes, straight to the ward. No, he won't cause any problems. There may be at least some effect . . . He'll be going through the same procedure himself soon enough.'

Somebody's hands (I think they belonged to Zherbunov and Barbolin again) pulled the shirt off my body, picked me up by the arms and dumped me like a sack of sand on to some kind of stretcher. Then the door-frame flashed past my eyes and we were in the corridor.

My unfeeling body floated past tall white doors with numbers on them, and behind me I could hear the distorted voices and laughter of the sailors in doctors' coats, who appeared to be conducting a scurrilous conversation about women. Then I saw Timur Timurovich's face peering down at me – apparently he had been walking along beside me.

'We've decided to put you back in the Third Section,' he said. 'At present there are four others in there, so you'll make five. Do you know anything about Kanashnikov group therapy? My group therapy, that is?'

'No,' I mumbled with difficulty.

The flickering of the doors as they passed me had become quite unbearable, and I closed my eyes.

'To put it simply, it means patients pooling their efforts in the struggle for recovery. Imagine that for a time your problems become the collective problems, that for a certain time everyone taking part in a session shares your condition. They all identify with you, so to speak. What do you think the result of that would be?'

I did not answer.

'It's very simple,' Timur Timurovich went on. 'When the session comes to an end, a reaction sets in as the participants withdraw from the state that they have been experiencing as reality; you could call it exploiting man's innate herd instinct in the service of medicine. Your ideas and your mood might infect the others taking part in the session for a certain time, but as soon as the session comes to an end, they return to their own manic obsessions, leaving you isolated. And at that moment – provided the pathological psychic material has been driven up to the surface by the process of catharsis – the patient can become aware of the arbitrary subjectivity of his own morbid notions and can cease to identify with them. And from that point recovery is only a short step away.'

I did not follow the meaning of his words very clearly, assuming, that is, that there was any. But nonetheless, something stuck in my mind. The effect of the injection was growing stronger and stronger. I could no longer see anything around me, my body had become almost totally insensitive, and my spirit was immersed in a dull, heavy indifference. The most unpleasant thing about this mood was that it did not seem to have taken possession of me, but of some other person – the person into whom the injected substance had transformed me. I was horrified to sense that this other person actually could be cured.

'Of course you can recover,' Timur Timurovich confirmed. 'And we will cure you, have no doubt about it. Just forget the very notion of a madhouse. Treat it all as an interesting adventure. Especially since you're a literary man. I sometimes encounter things here that are just begging to be written down. What's coming up now, for instance – we're due for an absolutely fascinating event in your ward, a group session with Maria. You do remember who I'm talking about?'

I shook my head.

'No, of course not, of course not. But it's an extremely interesting case. I'd call it a psychodrama of genuinely Shakespearean proportions, the clash of such apparently diverse objects of consciousness as a Mexican soap opera, a Hollywood blockbuster and our own young, rootless Russian democracy. Do you know the Mexican television serial *Just Maria*? So you don't remember that either. I see. Well, in a word, the patient has taken on the role of the heroine, Maria herself. It would be a quite banal case, if not for the subconscious identification with Russia, plus the Agamemnon complex with the anal dynamics. In short, it's exactly my field, a split false identity.'

Oh, God, I thought, how long the corridors here are.

'Of course, you won't be in any fit state to take a proper part in the proceedings,' Timur Timurovich's voice continued, 'so you can sleep. But don't forget that soon it will be your turn to tell your own story.'

I think we must have entered a room – a door squeaked and I caught a fragment of interrupted conversation. Timur Timurovich spoke a word of greeting to the surrounding darkness and several voices answered him. Meanwhile I was transferred to an invisible bed, a pillow was tucked under my head and a blanket thrown over me. For a while I paid attention to the disembodied phrases that reached my ears – Timur Timurovich was explaining to somebody why I had been absent for so long; then I lost contact with what was happening, being visited instead by a quite momentous hallucination of an intimately personal character.

I do not know quite how long I spent alone with my conscience, but at some point my attention was caught again by the monotonous voice of Timur Timurovich.

'Watch the ball closely, Maria. You are quite calm. If your mouth feels dry, it's only because of the injection you were given – it will soon pass. Can you hear me?'

'Yes,' came the reply, in what seemed to me more like a high male voice than a low female one.

'Who are you?'

'Maria,' answered the voice.

'What's your surname?'

'Just Maria.'

'How old are you?'

'They say I look eighteen,' replied the voice.

'Do you know where you are?'

'Yes. In a hospital.'

'And what brought you here?'

'It was the crash, what else? I don't understand how I survived at all. I couldn't possibly have guessed he was that kind of man.'

'What did you crash into?'

'The Ostankino television tower.'

'I see. And how did it happen?'

'It's a long story.'

'That's all right,' Timur Timurovich said kindly, 'we're not in any hurry, we have time to listen. How did it all begin?'

'It began when I went for a walk along the embankment.'

'And where were you before that?'

'I wasn't anywhere before that.'

'All right, carry on.'

'Well then, I'm walking, you know, just walking along, and all around me there's some kind of smoke. And the further I go, the more there is . . .'

I suddenly realized that the longer I tried to listen to the words, the harder it was to make out their meaning. It felt as though the meaning were attached to them by pieces of string, which kept getting longer and longer. I found myself unable to keep up with the conversation, but that was not important, because at the same time I began to see the wavering outline of a picture – a river embankment enveloped in clouds of smoke and a woman with broad muscular shoulders walking along it, looking more like a man dressed in women's clothes. I knew that she was called Maria and I could see her, and see the world through her eyes at the same time. A moment later I realized that in some way I was perceiving everything that she was thinking and feeling: she was thinking that however hard she tried, this walk was never going to lead to anything; the sunny morning at the beginning of which she had arrived in this world of suffering had given way to this unholy mess, and it had happened so smoothly that she had not even noticed.

At first there was a smell of burning in the air, and Maria thought that someone somewhere must be burning fallen leaves. Then the first smell became mingled with that of scorched rubber, and soon she was swamped by a fog-like smoke that grew thicker and thicker until it hid everything from sight apart from the iron railings along the embankment and the few yards of space immediately around her.

Soon Maria felt as though she were walking through a long hall in an art gallery: in their trite ordinariness the segments of the surrounding world which appeared from time to time out of the all-enveloping gloom looked very much like bizarrely fashioned works of modern art. Drifting out of the gloom towards her came signboards bearing the words 'Bureau de Change', benches scored all over by penknives and a vast quantity of empty cans, bearing witness to the fact that the generation next still chooses beer.

Groups of agitated men carrying automatic rifles emerged from the mist and then disappeared back into it. They pretended not to notice Maria and she reacted in the same way. She already had more than enough people to remember her and think of her. How many was it – millions? Tens of millions? Maria didn't know the exact number of them, but she was sure that if all the hearts in which fate had inscribed her name were to beat in unison, then their combined beating would be much louder than the deafening explosions she could hear from the other side of the river.

Maria looked round and screwed up her radiant eyes as she tried to understand what was going on.

Every now and then from somewhere close by – because of the smoke she couldn't see exactly where – there was a thunderous crash; the booming sound was followed immediately by the barking of dogs and the roaring of a multitude of voices, like the noise from the crowd when a goal is scored at the stadium. Maria didn't know what to make of it. Perhaps they were shooting a film near the White House on the other bank of the river, or perhaps some new Russians were squabbling about which of them was the newest. I wish they'd get on with it and finish dividing everything up, she thought. How many more of our handsome young men must we see fall on the roadway and spill out their heart's blood on the asphalt?

Maria began thinking about how she could lighten the unbearable burden of this life for everyone who was writhing, God knows for what reason, in the grip of these black coils of smoke that obscured the sky and the sun. Her head was filled with clear, bright, uncomplicated images – there she was in a simple dress, entering a modest flat tidied specially for the occasion by its occupants. And there they were, sitting at the table with the samovar and gazing at her lovingly, and she knew that she didn't have to say anything, all she had to do was sit opposite them and gaze tenderly back, paying as little attention as she could to the whirring of the camera. And there was a hospital ward full of people all bandaged up and lying on uncomfortable beds, and there was her image hanging on the wall in a place where everyone could see it. They gazed at her from their beds and for a while they forgot all about their woes, their aches and pains . . .

This was all wonderful, but she vaguely realized that it was not enough. No, what the world needed was a strong hand, stern and unrelenting, capable of resisting evil whenever the need arose. But where was this strength to be found? And what would it look like? These were questions Maria couldn't answer, but she sensed that they were the very reason why she was walking along this embankment in this city that was expiring in its suffering.

42

For a second a puff of wind dispersed the smoke surrounding Maria and a ray of sunshine fell on her. Shielding her face with her hand, she suddenly understood where she should seek the answer. Of course, it lay in those innumerable hearts and minds that had summoned her and incarnated her here, on this smoky embankment. Through the millions of pairs of eyes staring at their television screens, they were fused into a single oceanic consciousness, and this entire ocean lay open to her gaze. She looked across it, at first seeing nothing that might help her. But no, of course there was an image of all-conquering power reflected in this consciousness, and in most cases its form was much the same: the figure of a young man with a small head and wide shoulders, wearing a double-breasted crimson sports jacket and standing beside a long, low-slung automobile with his feet planted wide apart. The image of the automobile was a little bit vague and somehow blurred, because all the people whose souls Maria could see imagined it in different ways. The young man's face was much the same, it was a very generalized face, and only the hairstyle, a slightly curly chestnut-brown crew cut, was rather more clearly defined. The jacket, however, was drawn with quite remarkable precision, and with a little effort Maria could even have managed to read the words on its gold buttons. But she didn't try. It didn't matter what was written on the buttons, what mattered was how this all-conquering power could be united with her own meek and gentle love.

Maria stopped and leaned on one of the low granite posts that punctuated the iron railings of the fence. Once again she had to seek an answer in the minds and hearts that had placed their trust in her, but this time – Maria was quite certain of this – the lowest common denominators of thought would not do. What was needed . . .

There must be at least one intelligent woman out there, she thought.

And the intelligent woman appeared almost immediately. Maria didn't know who she was, or even what she looked like, she just caught a glimpse of tall bookshelves, a desk with heaps of papers and a typewriter, and a photograph hanging over the desk showing a man with an enormous curling moustache and intense, moody eyes. It was all in flickering, hazy black and white, as though Maria were viewing it from inside an ancient television with a screen the size of a cigarette packet that was standing somewhere off in the corner of the room. But the images disappeared too quickly for Maria to reflect on what she had seen, and then they were replaced by thoughts.

Maria understood almost nothing at all in the swirling vortex of ideas that appeared before her; apart from anything else, it was somehow musty and oppressive, like the cloud that appears when you disturb the dust of a long-forgotten lumber room. Maria decided she must be dealing with a consciousness that was extremely cluttered and not entirely normal, and she felt very relieved when it was all over. The catch netted by the pink void of her soul consisted of words whose meanings were not entirely clear – there was a brief glimpse of the word 'Bridegroom' (for some reason, with a capital letter), and then the word 'Visitor' (another capital letter), followed by the incomprehensible words 'Alchemical Wedlock' and after that the totally obscure phrase, sounding like a snatch of Silver Age poetry: 'all repose is vain, I knock at the gates'. With this the thoughts ended, and then there was another brief glimpse of the man with the ecstatic eyes and the long, droopy moustache which looked like a beard growing from right under his nose.

She looked around her in bewilderment. Still more or less surrounded by smoke, she thought that perhaps somewhere close by there might be a gate she was supposed to knock at, and she took several timid steps through the murk. Immediately she was enveloped by total darkness on every side, and felt so afraid that she scurried back on to the embankment, where at least a little light remained.

And if I do knock, she thought, will anybody actually open the gate? Hardly.

Behind her Maria heard the quiet growling of a car engine. She pressed herself against the railings of the embankment and waited apprehensively to see what would emerge from the smoke. Several seconds went by, and then a long black automobile slowly swam past her, a 'Chaika' decorated with ribbons of various colours – she realized it was a wedding car. It was full of silent, serious-looking people; the barrels of several automatic rifles protruded from the windows and on the roof there were two gleaming yellow rings, one larger and one smaller.

Maria watched the 'Chaika' as it drove away, then suddenly slapped herself on the forehead. But of course, now she understood. Yes – that was it. Two interlinked rings – Bridegroom, Visitor, Sponsor. She still couldn't understand what alchemical wedlock was supposed to be, but if anything untoward happened, she had a good lawyer. Maria shook her head and smiled. It was so simple, how could she have failed to see the most important thing of all for so long? What could she have been thinking of?

She looked around, orientating herself approximately by the sun, and held out her arms towards the West – somehow it seemed clear that the Bridegroom would appear from that direction.

'Come!' she prayed in a whisper, and immediately she could sense that a new presence had appeared in the world.

Now all she had to do was wait for the meeting to take place. She ran on joyfully, sensing the distance between herself and the Bridegroom diminishing. Like her, he already knew, he was walking towards her along this very embankment – but unlike her he wasn't hurrying, because it wasn't in his nature to hurry.

Miraculously managing to leap across an open manhole that appeared suddenly out of the smoke, Maria slowed down and began feverishly rummaging in her pockets. She had suddenly realized that she had no mirror and no make-up with her. For a moment she was plunged into despair, and she even tried to recall whether she had passed a puddle in which she could view her own reflection. But then, when she remembered that she could appear to her beloved in whatever form she wished, Maria's despair vanished as quickly as it had appeared.

She thought about this for a while. Let him see a very young girl, she decided, with two ginger plaits, a freckled face and . . . and . . . She needed some final touch, some naive and endearing detail – perhaps earrings? A baseball cap? Maria had almost no time left, and at the very final moment she adorned herself with padded pink earphones which looked like a continuation of the flame-bright flush of her cheeks. Then she raised her eyes and looked ahead.

In front of her, among the tattered wisps of smoke, something metallic gleamed for a moment and then immediately vanished. Then it appeared a little closer, only to be concealed again in the murk. A sudden gust of wind drove the smoke aside and Maria saw a tall glittering figure advancing slowly towards her. At the same moment she noticed, or so she thought, that with every step the figure took the ground shook. The metal man was much taller than her and his impassively handsome face expressed not the slightest trace of emotion. Maria was frightened and stumbled backwards – she remembered that somewhere behind her there was an open manhole, but she couldn't tear her eyes away from the metal torso bearing down on her like the bow of some immense destroyer approaching an ice floe.

At the very moment when she was about to scream, the metal man underwent an astonishing transformation. First of all his gleaming thighs were suddenly clad in very domestic-looking striped underpants, then he acquired a white vest and his body took on the normal colour of tanned human skin and was promptly clad in canary-yellow trousers, a shirt and tie and a wonderful crimson sports jacket with gold buttons. That was enough to lay Maria's fears to rest. But the delightful sight of the crimson jacket was soon concealed beneath a long grey raincoat. Black shoes appeared on the Visitor's feet and sun-glasses with glittering lenses on his face, his hair set itself into a gingerish crew cut and Maria's heart skipped a beat for joy when she recognized that her bridegroom was Arnold Schwarzenegger – but then she realized it could never have been anyone else.

He stood there saying nothing and staring at her with those black rectangles of glass; the ghost of a smile played about his lips. Maria caught a glimpse of her reflection in his glasses and adjusted her earphones.

'Ave Maria,' said Schwarzenegger quietly.

He spoke without expression, in a voice that was hollow but pleasant.

'No, my sweet,' said Maria, smiling mysteriously and clasping her hands together over her breast, 'just Maria.'

'Just Maria,' Schwarzenegger repeated.

'Yes,' said Maria. 'And you're Arnold?'

'Sure,' said Schwarzenegger.

46

Maria opened her mouth to say something, but suddenly she realized she had absolutely nothing to say. Schwarzenegger carried on looking at her and smiling. Maria lowered her gaze and blushed, and then, with a gentle but irresistibly powerful movement, Schwarzenegger turned her round and led her away beside him. Maria looked up at him and smiled her famous stupid-mysterious smile. Schwarzenegger put his hand on her shoulder. Maria sank slightly under the weight, and suddenly her memory threw up something unexpected, a picture of Lenin carrying a beam at one of those communist working Saturdays. In the picture only the edge of the beam could be seen above Lenin's shoulder and Maria thought that perhaps it wasn't a beam after all, but the hand of some mighty creature at which Lenin could only glance up with a defenceless smile, as she was now glancing up at Schwarzenegger. But a moment later Maria realized that such thoughts were entirely out of place, and she promptly banished them from her mind.

Schwarzenegger turned his face towards her.

'Your eyes,' he intoned monotonously, 'are like a landscape of the dreamy south.'

Maria trembled in surprise. She hadn't been expecting words like these, and Schwarzenegger seemed to understand this immediately. Then something strange happened – or perhaps it didn't really happen, and Maria simply imagined the faint red letters flickering across the inside surface of Schwarzenegger's glasses, like running titles on a TV screen, and the soft whirring sound inside his head, as though a computer hard disk drive had been switched on. Maria started in fright, but then she remembered that Schwarzenegger, like herself, was a purely conventional being woven by the thousands of individual Russian consciousnesses which were thinking about him at that very second – and that different people could have very different thoughts about him.

Schwarzenegger raised his empty hand in front of him and flicked his fingers in the air as he looked for the right words.

'No,' he said at last, 'your eyes aren't eyes – they're orbs!'

Maria clung tightly to him and looked up trustingly. Schwarzenegger tucked his chin into his neck, as though to prevent Maria from seeing under his glasses.

'There's a lot of smoke here,' he said, 'why are we walking along this embankment?'

'I don't know,' answered Maria.

Schwarzenegger turned round and led her away from the railings, straight into the smoke. After they'd gone a few steps Maria felt frightened: the smoke was so thick now that she couldn't see anything, not even Schwarzenegger – all she could make out was his hand where it clutched her shoulder.

'Where's all this smoke from?' asked Maria. 'Nothing seems to be burning.'

'C-N-N,' Schwarzenegger replied.

'You mean they're burning something?'

'No,' said Schwarzenegger, 'they're shooting something.'

Aha, thought Maria, probably everybody who was thinking about her and Schwarzenegger was watching CNN, and CNN was showing some kind of smokescreen. But what a long time they were showing it for.

'It's okay,' said the invisible Schwarzenegger, 'it'll soon be over.'

But there seemed to be no end to the smoke, and they were getting further and further away from the embankment. Maria suddenly had the terrible thought that for several minutes someone else could have been walking along beside her instead of Schwarzenegger, perhaps even the being that had put its arm round Lenin's shoulder in that same picture, and this thought frightened her so badly that she automatically adjusted her earphones and switched on the music. The music was strange, chopped into small incoherent fragments. No sooner had the guitars and trumpets launched into a sweet song of love than they were swamped by a sudden electronic wailing, like the howling of wolves. But anything was better than listening to the sound of distant explosions from the area of the parliament building and the indistinct hubbub of human voices.

Suddenly a figure came hurtling straight at Maria out of the smoke so that she shrieked in fright. In front of her she saw a man in blotchy camouflage fatigues, carrying an automatic rifle. He looked up at Maria and opened his mouth to speak, but then Schwarzenegger took his hand from Maria's shoulder, grabbed hold of the man's head, twisted it gently to one side and tossed the limp body away beyond the bounds of their vision. His hand returned to Maria's shoulder, and Maria pressed herself against his monumental torso.

'Ah, men, men,' she cooed softly.

Gradually the smoke began to disperse until once again Maria could see Schwarzenegger's face, and then the entire massive body, concealed beneath the light grey shroud of the raincoat like a monument waiting to be unveiled.

'Arnold,' she asked, 'where are we going?'

'Don't you know?' said Schwarzenegger.

Maria blushed and lowered her eyes.

What is an alchemical wedlock, though? she thought. And will it hurt me, I wonder? Afterwards, I mean? I've been hurt so many times before.

Looking up at him she saw the famous dimples in his cheeks – Schwarzenegger was smiling. Maria closed her eyes and walked on, hardly daring to believe in her own happiness, guided by the hand that lay on her shoulder.

When Schwarzenegger stopped, she opened her eyes and saw that the smoke had almost completely disappeared. They were standing on a street she didn't recognize, between rows of old houses faced with granite. The street was deserted except for a few stooped figures with automatic rifles darting about aimlessly in the distance, nearer the embankment which was still hidden behind a pall of smoke. Schwarzenegger seemed to loiter in an odd, indecisive fashion, giving Maria the impression that he was tormented by some strange kind of doubt, and she was frightened at the thought that the doubt might concern her.

I have to say something romantic quickly, she thought. But what exactly? I suppose it doesn't really matter.

'You know, Arnold,' she said, squeezing herself against his side, 'I suddenly . . . I don't know, perhaps you'll think it's silly . . . I can be honest with you, can't I?'

'Of course,' said Schwarzenegger, turning his black lenses towards her.

'When I'm with you, I want so much to soar up into the sky! I feel as though the sky is so very close!'

Schwarzenegger raised his head and looked upwards.

There actually were glimpses of bright blue sky between the

streams of smoke. It didn't seem particularly close, but then neither was it that far away.

Ah, thought Maria, what nonsense I do talk.

But it was too late to stop now.

'What about you, Arnold, wouldn't you like to soar up into the sky?'

Schwarzenegger thought for a second.

'Yes,' he said.

'And will you take me with you? You know, I . . .' – Maria smiled shyly – 'I'm so very earthbound.'

Schwarzenegger thought for another second.

'Okay,' he said. 'I'll take you up into the sky.'

He looked around, as though he were trying to locate landmarks that only he knew, and then he seemed to have found them, because he grabbed Maria decisively by the arm and dragged her onwards. Maria was startled by this sudden transition from poetic abstraction to concrete action, but then she realized that this was the way real men were supposed to behave.

Schwarzenegger dragged her along the façade of a long Stalin-era apartment block. After a few steps she managed to adjust to his rapid stride and began trotting along beside him, holding on to the sleeve of his raincoat. She sensed that if she slowed her pace at all, Schwarzenegger's arm would change from a gallantly proffered fulcrum into a steel lever that would drag her implacably along the pavement, and for some reason the thought filled her with a feeling of boundless happiness that sprang from the very depths of her belly and spread in warm waves throughout her body.

On reaching the end of the building, Schwarzenegger turned through an arch. Once in the courtyard of the building, Maria felt as though they had been transported to a different city. Here the peace of the morning was still unbroken; there was no smoke to be seen, and it was hard to believe that somewhere close at hand there were crazy people dashing about shooting off their automatic rifles.

Schwarzenegger definitely knew where he was taking Maria. They made their way round a small children's playground with swings and dived into a labyrinth of narrow alleys between rusting garages. Maria was thinking with sweet terror in her heart that somewhere here, quickly and rather awkwardly, their al-chemical wedlock would probably be consummated, when sud-denly the passageway led out into an empty space surrounded on all sides by sheet-iron walls of various colours and heights.

The space wasn't entirely empty, though. Beneath their feet lay the usual collection of bottles, and there were a couple of old car tyres, a crumpled door from a Lada and other assorted quasi-mechanical garbage of the kind that always accumulates beside garages.

And, next to them, there was a jet fighter.

Although it took up almost all of the space, it was the very last thing that Maria noticed, probably because for several seconds her brain filtered out the signals it was receiving from her eyes as a hallucination. Maria felt afraid.

How could a plane get in here? she thought. On the other hand, how could Schwarzenegger have got here? But even so, this is really strange.

'What is it?' she asked.

'A model A-4 "Harrier" jump-jet vertical take-off and landing pursuit craft,' said Schwarzenegger.

Maria saw the famous dimples in his cheeks again – Schwarzenegger was smiling. She frowned slightly, drawing her frizzy eyebrows together, and the fear in her heart was replaced by a feeling of jealousy for this immense insect of glass and metal, which clearly occupied quite as important a place in Schwarzenegger's heart as she did herself.

He approached the plane. Sunk in thought, Maria remained standing on the spot until she was jerked forward in turn – rather as if Schwarzenegger were a tractor and she were some piece of agricultural machinery casually hooked on to it.

'But there's only room for one,' she said when she caught sight of the back of the seat through the glass canopy.

'Don't worry,' said Schwarzenegger, and in a single light movement he lifted her up and sat her on the wing.

Maria drew in her legs and stood up on the angled aluminium surface. A gust of wind fluttered through her clothes, and she thought how well romantic roles had always suited her.

'What about you?' she asked.

But Schwarzenegger was already in the cockpit. He had

clambered in with amazing speed and agility, and Maria realized it must have been a montage sequence or a piece of slick editing. He stuck his head out of the cabin and smiled, gesturing to her with his thumb and forefinger joined to form a ring; Maria decided she could think of it as her wedding ring.

'Sit on the fuselage,' said Schwarzenegger, 'at the base of the wings. Don't be afraid. Imagine it's a carousel. Imagine you're sitting on one of the horses.'

'You mean, you're going to . . .'

Schwarzenegger nodded.

His dark glasses gazed straight into the depths of Maria's soul and she realized her fate was being decided right here and now. She was being tested, there was no doubt about it: the woman worthy of standing beside Schwarzenegger could not be some feeble coward good for nothing more than multi-episode domestic and sexual intrigue. She had to be able to meet mortal danger face to face without betraying her feelings with anything more than a smile. Maria tried adjusting her expression accordingly, but felt that the smile turned out a little contrived.

'Great idea,' she said. 'But won't I get cold?'

'It won't take long,' said Schwarzenegger. 'Get up.'

Maria shrugged and took a cautious step towards the point where the fuselage protruded above the flat surface of the wings like the curved spine of a fish, and then sat down on it neatly.

'No,' said Schwarzenegger, 'you can ride side-saddle when we go to my ranch in California. Right now you had better sit the ordinary way, or the wind'll blow you off.'

Maria hesitated for a moment. 'Look the other way,' she said.

Schwarzenegger smiled with the left corner of his mouth and turned away. Maria threw her leg over the aluminium crest and straddled the fuselage. Underneath her the metal was cold and slightly damp with dew; she hoisted herself up slightly in order to tuck the hem of her jacket underneath her, and suddenly had the strange sensation that the very tenderest parts of her body had been flattened across the angular hips of a metal man lying on his back – some mutant cross between the iron Dzerzhinsky toppled by the wind of change and a robot from hell. She shuddered, but the brief hallucination disappeared abruptly, to be replaced by the feeling that she was sitting on a frying-pan which had just been taken out of the fridge. She was feeling worse and worse about what was happening.

'Arnold,' she called, 'are you sure we ought to do this?'

She usually reserved these words for entirely different circumstances, but this time they just seemed to come out on their own.

'It was you who wanted to soar up into the sky,' he said, 'but if you're afraid . . .'

'No,' said Maria, pushing aside her fear, 'I'm not afraid in the slightest. It's just that I'm being such a bother to you.'

'No bother,' said Schwarzenegger. 'It's going to be very noisy, better put your earphones on. What is it you're listening to, anyway?'

'Jihad Crimson,' said Maria, settling the small pink pads on her ears.

Schwarzenegger's face froze absolutely still. A strange flickering red light ran across the lenses of his dark glasses – Maria thought it must be the reflection of the leaves falling from the maple trees that stood just behind the garages.

'Arnie,' she called.

The corner of Schwarzenegger's mouth twitched a few times, and then he seemed to recover the power of movement. He turned his head with difficulty, as though it were rotating on a bearing clogged with sand.

'Crimson Jihad?' he asked.

'Jihad Crimson,' answered Maria. 'Nushrat Fatekh Ali Khan and Robert Fripp. Why?'

'Nothing,' said Schwarzenegger, 'it's not important.'

His head disappeared into the cockpit. Underneath her, somewhere deep in the plane's metal belly, she heard an electrical hum that expanded in the space of just a few seconds into a monstrous loud roaring until it seemed to Maria that she could feel the foam-plastic pads being forced into her ears. Then she was tilted smoothly over to one side and the garages drifted down and away behind her.

Swaying from side to side like a boat, the Harrier rose up vertically into the air – Maria had not even been aware that aeroplanes could fly like that. She thought that if she closed her eyes it might be less frightening, but her curiosity proved stronger than her fear, and in less than a minute she had opened them again.

The first thing she saw was a window moving straight towards her. It was so close already that Maria had a perfectly clear view of a tank turning the muzzle of its gun in her direction from the screen of the television in the room. The tank on the screen fired, and at that precise moment the plane banked steeply and soared away from the wall. Maria almost slid across on to the wing, and she squealed in fear, but the plane soon righted itself.

'Hold on to the antenna!' shouted Schwarzenegger, poking his head out of the cabin and waving to her.

Maria looked down. Protruding out of the fuselage directly in front of her was a long metal form with a rounded, slightly swollen tip – it was strange that she hadn't noticed it before. It looked like a narrow vertical wing, and it immediately roused immodest associations in Maria's mind, although its dimensions were significantly larger than any encountered in real life. One glance at this powerful protuberance was enough to quell her fear and replace it with a joyful inspiration that had always been so lacking with all those languid Miguels and drunken Ivans from the television.

Everything was quite different this time. The rounded swelling at the tip of the antenna was covered with small holes which reminded her slightly of a shower head and at the same time set her thinking of strange, non-terrestrial forms of life and love. Maria pointed to it and glanced inquiringly at Schwarzenegger. He nodded and gave a broad smile, and the sun glinted on his teeth.

Maria decided that what was happening to her now must be a childhood dream coming true. In some film or other she had spent a lot of time poring over fairy-tales in books, looking at the pictures and imagining herself flying through the sky on the back of a dragon or a huge bird, and now it was actually happening. Maybe not exactly the way she'd dreamed it, but then, she thought as she laid her palm on the steel projection of the antenna, dreams don't always come true in the way we expect.

The plane banked slightly and Maria noticed it was obviously responding to her touching the antenna. More than that, the movement seemed to her to be incredibly animated, as though the plane were alive and the antenna were its most sensitive part. Maria ran her hand along the steel rod and squeezed its upper part tight in her fist. The Harrier twitched its wings nervously and rose a few yards higher. Maria thought to herself that the plane was behaving exactly like a man tied to a bed, unable to take her in his arms, incapable of anything but twitching and jerking his entire body. The similarity was enhanced by the fact that she was sitting just behind the wings, which looked like a pair of wide-spread legs, incredibly muscly, but quite incapable of movement.

This was certainly amusing, but it was all a bit too complicated. Instead of this huge steel bird, Maria would have preferred to have come across an ordinary camp-bed in the empty space between the garages. But then, she thought, with Schwarzenegger it couldn't really have been any other way. She glanced at the cockpit. She couldn't see much, because the sun was reflected in the glass, but he seemed to be sitting there, moving his head gently from side to side in time with the movement of her hand.

Meanwhile, the plane was rising higher and higher. The roofs of the houses were now far below them, and Maria had a magnificent panoramic view of the city of Moscow.

There were church domes gleaming on all sides, making the city look like an immense biker's jacket embellished at random with a remarkable quantity of studs and rivets. There was far less smoke hanging over Moscow than Maria had imagined from down below on the embankment; though some was still visible here and there above the houses, it wasn't always clear whether it was a fire, pollution from factory chimneys or simply low cloud.

Despite the revolting ugliness of each of its component parts, viewed as a whole the city looked extremely beautiful, but the source of this beauty was beyond all understanding. That's always the way with Russia, thought Maria, as she ran her hands up and down the cold steel – when you see it from afar, it's so beautiful it's enough to make you cry, but when you take a closer look, you just want to puke.

The plane suddenly jerked beneath her, and she felt the upper part of the steel rod dangling loosely in her hand. She jerked her hand away, and immediately the metal knob with the small holes fell away from the antenna, struck the fuselage and flew off into space; the powerful protuberance was reduced to a short hollow tube with a screw thread around its top, with the torn blue and red strands of two wires twisted together protruding from its end.

Maria glanced in the direction of the cockpit. Through the glass she could make out the blond back of Schwarzenegger's motionless head. At first she thought that he hadn't noticed anything. Then she thought he must have fainted. She looked around in confusion, saw that the nose of the plane was wavering uncertainly, and immediately her suspicion hardened into certainty. Hardly even aware of what she was doing, she slumped down from the fuselage on to the small flat area between the wings (the stump of the antenna ripped her jacket as she fell) and crawled towards the cockpit.

The cockpit was open. Lying there on the wing, Maria propped herself up and shouted:

'Arnie! Arnie!'

There was no answer. She fearfully manoeuvred herself on to all fours and saw the back of his head with a single lock of hair fluttering in the wind.

'Arnie!' she called again.

Schwarzenegger turned to face her.

'Thank God!' Maria exclaimed.

Schwarzenegger took off his glasses.

His left eye was half-closed in a way that expressed an absolutely clear and at the same time immeasurably complex range of feelings, including a strictly proportioned mixture of passion for life, strength, a healthy love for children, moral support for the American automobile industry in its difficult struggle with the Japanese, acknowledgement of the rights of sexual minorities, a slightly ironical attitude towards feminism and the calm assurance that democracy and Judaeo-Christian values would eventually conquer all evil in this world.

But his right eye was quite different. It could hardly even be called an eye. A round glass lens looking like a huge wall-eye, set in a complicated metal holder connected to wires that ran out from under the skin, peered out at Maria from a tattered socket surrounded by streaks of dried blood. A beam of blinding red light shone directly out from the centre of the lens – Maria only noticed it when the beam shone into her own eyes.

Schwarzenegger smiled, and the left side of his face expressed exactly what the face of Arnold Schwarzenegger is supposed to express when it smiles – an indefinable boyish quality between mischief and cunning, immediately making it clear that this is a man who will never do anything bad, and if he should happen to kill a few assholes now and then, it's not until the camera has repeatedly revealed from several different angles what despicable trash they are. But the smile only affected the left side of his face, the right side remained absolutely unchanged – cold, focused and terrifying.

'Arnold,' Maria said in confusion, rising to her feet. 'What are you doing that for? Stop it!'

But Schwarzenegger didn't answer, and a moment later the plane banked steeply and Maria was sent tumbling along the wing. On the way she banged her face several times against various protruding objects, and then suddenly there was nothing holding her up any longer. She decided she must be falling and squeezed her eyes shut in order not to see the trees and roofs hurtling up towards her, but several seconds went by and nothing happened. Maria realized that the roaring of the engine was still as close to her as ever and she opened her eyes again.

She was hanging under the wing. The hood of her jacket had snagged on the empennage of some protrusion, which she recognized with some effort as a rocket. The sight of the rocket's swollen head rather reminded her of the antenna she had been handling just a few minutes earlier, and she decided Schwarzenegger must be continuing with his loveplay. But this was too much – her face was probably covered in bruises, and she could taste the blood from a cut on her lip.

'Arnold,' she yelled, waving her arms furiously in an attempt to turn towards the cockpit, 'stop it! I don't want to do this! Do you hear me? I don't want to!'

She finally managed to catch a glimpse of the cockpit and Schwarzenegger's smiling face.

'I don't want to do this, d'you hear me? It's hurting me that way!'

'You won't?' he asked.

'No! No!'

'Okay,' said Schwarzenegger. 'You're fired.'

A moment later his face zoomed back and away from Maria as she was thrust ahead of the plane by a force of unimaginable power; in just a few seconds the plane was transformed into a tiny silver bird which was connected to her only by a long streak of smoke. Maria turned her head to see where she was going and saw the spire of the Ostankino television tower veering towards her. The swollen lump at its centre grew rapidly as she watched and a split second before the impact came Maria had a clear view of some men in white shirts and ties sitting at a table and gazing at her in amazement through a thick pane of glass.

There was the ringing sound of a glass shattering and then something heavy fell to the floor. Someone started crying loudly.

'Careful, careful,' said Timur Timurovich. 'There now, that's better.'

Realizing that it was all over, I opened my eyes. By this time I could more or less see. Everything close to me was quite distinct, but objects further away shifted and blurred, and the overall perspective was as though I were sitting inside a large Christmas-tree decoration with the outside world daubed on its inner surface. Timur Timurovich and Colonel Smirnov towered up over me like twin cliffs.

'Well,' said someone in the corner. 'So much for Arnold Schwarzenegger and Just Maria.'

'I would like to point out,' said Colonel Smirnov, clearing his throat and turning to Timur Timurovich, 'the distinctly phallic relevance of the fact that the patient sees dicks everywhere. Did you notice that? The antenna, the rocket, the Ostankino tower?'

'You military men always take things too literally,' replied Timur Timurovich. 'Not everything's that simple. Russia cannot be grasped by logic, as the saying goes – but neither can it be entirely reduced to sexual neurosis. Let's not be too hasty. What's important here is that the cathartic effect is quite evident, even if it is attenuated.'

'Yes,' agreed the colonel, 'the chair's even broken.'

'Precisely,' agreed Timur Timurovich. 'When blocked pathological material rises to the surface of consciousness it has to overcome powerful resistance, and so it often produces visions of catastrophes or conflicts of various kinds, as we've just seen. It's the clearest possible sign that we're working along the right lines.'

'Maybe it's just the shell-shock?' said the colonel.

'What shell-shock?'

'What, didn't I tell you about that? Well, when they were shelling the White House, a few of the shells went straight through, in the windows on one side and out of the windows on the other. And one of them landed in a flat just at the very moment when . . .'

The colonel leaned over to Timur Timurovich and whispered something in his ear. 'Well, of course . . .' – I could just make out odd words here and there – '. . . to smithereens . . . under security with the corpses at first, and then we saw something moving . . . Massive concussion, obviously.'

'But why on earth have you kept this to yourself for so long, my good fellow? It changes the entire picture,' said Timur Timurovich reproachfully. 'I've been struggling so hard . . .'

He leaned down over me, parted one of my eyelids with two fat fingers and looked into my eye. 'How about you?'

'I'm not quite sure,' I replied. 'Of course, it was not the most interesting vision I have ever had, but I . . . How can I put it? I found the dreamlike facility with which these delirious ravings acquired for several minutes the status of reality quite amusing.'

'How do you like that?' asked Timur Timurovich, turning to Colonel Smirnov.

The colonel nodded without speaking.

'My dear fellow, I was not inquiring as to your opinion, but your condition,' said Timur Timurovich.

'I feel quite well, thank you,' I replied. 'But I am sleepy.'

This was no more than the simple truth.

'Then sleep.'

He turned away from me.

'Tomorrow morning,' he said to an invisible nurse, 'please give Pyotr four cc's of taurepam immediately before the hydraulic procedures.'

'Can we have the radio on?' asked a quiet voice in the corner.

Timur Timurovich clicked a switch on the wall, took the colonel by the arm and led him in the direction of the door. I closed my eyes and realized that I did not have enough strength to open them again.

'Sometimes I think that all our soldiers brave,' a man began singing in a mournful voice, 'Who fell on battle's bloody hills and plains, Were never buried in their native graves, But turned into a soaring flight of cranes . . .'

At these final words turmoil broke out in the ward.

'Keep tight hold of Serdyuk!' yelled a voice right beside my ear. 'Who put those blasted cranes on? Have you forgotten, or what?'

'It was you asked for it to be turned on,' answered another voice. 'Let's change channels.'

There was another click.

'Is the time now past,' an ingratiating voice asked from the ceiling, 'when Russian pop music was synonymous with provincialism? Here's the chance to judge for yourself. The "Inflamed Ovaries" are a rare kind of Russian pop group, consisting entirely of women whose stage gear weighs as much as a "T-90" tank. Despite such ultra-modern features, the "Inflamed Ovaries" play mostly classical music, but in their own interpretation. Listen to what the girls make of a simple fugue in F by the Austrian composer Mozart, who is well known to many of our listeners from the cream liqueur that bears the same name, which can be bought wholesale from our sponsor, the trading firm "Third Eye".'

I heard the beginning of wild music, like the wind howling in a prison chimney, but I was already, thank God, only half-conscious. At first I was overwhelmed by tormenting thoughts about what was happening, and then I had a brief nightmare about an American wearing dark glasses which seemed to continue the story told by the unfortunate Maria.

The American landed his plane in a yard, soaked it with

kerosene and set fire to it. Into the flames he threw the crimson jacket, the dark glasses and the canary-yellow trousers, until he was left wearing nothing but the skimpy trunks. Rippling his magnificently developed muscles he searched for something in the bushes for a long time, but failed to find it. Then there was a gap in my dream, and the next time I saw him – horror of horrors! – he was pregnant: the encounter with Maria had obviously not been without its consequences. At that precise moment he was transformed into a terrifying metal figure with a sketchy mask in place of a face, and the sun glinted furiously on his swollen belly.

3

The melody seemed at first to be floating up the staircase towards me, briefly marking time before it dashed in desperation on to the landing – that was when I could hear the short moments of quietness between its sounds. Then the pianist's fingers picked up the tune, set it back on the steps, and the whole thing was repeated one flight of stairs lower. The place where all this was taking place seemed very much like the staircase in house number eight on Tverskoi Boulevard, except that in my dream the staircase extended upwards and downwards as far as the eye could see and was clearly infinite. I suddenly understood that every melody has its own precise meaning, and that this was one of the proofs of the metaphysical impossibility of suicide – not of its sinfulness, but precisely of its impossibility. And I felt that all of us are nothing more than sounds drifting through the air from the fingers of some unknown pianist, nothing more than short thirds, smooth sixths and dissonant sevenths in a mighty symphony which none of us can ever hear in its entirety. This thought induced a profound sadness in me, which remained in my heart as I came plummeting out of the leaden clouds of sleep.

For several seconds I struggled to understand where I actually was and what was taking place in this strange world into which some unknown force had been thrusting me every morning for the past twenty-six years. I was dressed in a heavy jacket of black leather, riding breeches and boots, and there was a pain in my hip where something was sticking into me. I turned over on to my side, reached under my leg and felt the holster with the Mauser, and then I looked around me. Above my head hung a silk canopy with astoundingly beautiful yellow tassels. The sky outside the window was a cloudless blue, and the roofs in the distance glowed a dull red in the rays of the winter sun. Directly opposite my window on the other side of the boulevard I could see a dome clad in tin-plate, which for some reason reminded me of the belly of a huge metal woman in childbirth.

Suddenly I realized that I had not been dreaming the music – I could hear it playing clearly just beyond the wall. I began trying to grasp how I had come to be here and suddenly, like an electric shock, yesterday's memories came flooding back in a single second, and I realized that I was in Vorblei's apartment. I leapt up from the bed, dashed across to the door and froze.

On the other side of that wall, in the room where I had left Vorblei, not only was someone playing the grand piano – they were playing the very Mozart F Minor fugue which cocaine and melancholia had drawn to the surface of my own mind only the evening before. The world quite literally went dark before my eyes as I imagined the cadaver pounding woodenly on the keys, fingers protruding from beneath the coat which I had thrown over him, and I realized that the previous day's nightmare was not yet over. Glancing round the room I spotted a large wooden crucifix hanging on the wall, with a small, elegant silver figure of Christ, the sight of which briefly induced in me the strangest sense of *déjà vu*, as though I had seen this metal body in some recent dream. I took down the crucifix, drew my Mauser and tiptoed out into the corridor. My approximate reasoning was that, if I could accept that a dead man could play the piano, then there was some likelihood that he might be afraid of the cross.

The door into the room where the piano was playing stood ajar. Trying to tread as quietly as possible, I went up to it and glanced inside, but I could see no more than the edge of the grand piano. I took several deep breaths and then kicked open the door and stepped into the room, grasping the heavy cross in one hand and holding my gun ready to shoot in the other. The first things I saw were Vorblei's boots protruding from the corner; he was still lying at peace under his grey English shroud.

I turned towards the piano.

Sitting at the keyboard was the man in the black military

tunic whom I had seen the day before in the 'Musical Snuff-box'. He appeared to be about fifty years old, with a thick black handlebar moustache and a sprinkling of grey at his temples. He gave no sign of having noticed my appearance; his eyes were closed as though he were entirely absorbed in the music, and his playing was truly excellent. Lying on the lid of the piano I saw a tall hat of the finest astrakhan fur with a red ribbon of watered silk and a sabre of an unusual form in a magnificent scabbard.

'Good morning,' I said, lowering the Mauser.

The man at the piano raised his eyelids and looked me up and down. His eyes were black and piercing, and it cost me a certain effort to withstand their almost physical pressure. Noticing the cross in my hand he gave a barely perceptible smile.

'Good morning,' he said, continuing to play. 'It is gratifying to see that you give thought to your soul at such an early hour.'

'What are you doing here?' I asked, carefully placing the crucifix on the lid of the piano beside his sabre.

'I am attempting,' he replied, 'to play a rather difficult piece of music. But unfortunately it was written for four hands and I am now approaching a passage which I shall not be able to manage on my own. Perhaps you would be kind enough to assist me? I believe you are acquainted with the piece in question?'

As though in a trance, I thrust the Mauser back into its holster, stood beside him and waited for the right moment before lowering my fingers on to the keys. My counterpoint scarcely managed to limp along after the theme, and I made several mistakes; then my gaze fell once again on Vorblei's splayed legs, and the absurdity of the entire situation came home to me. I shrank sharply away from my companion and stared at him wide-eyed. He stopped playing and sat motionless for a while, as though he were deeply absorbed in his own thoughts. Then he smiled, reached out his hands and lifted the crucifix from the piano.

'Splendid,' he said. 'I could never understand why God should manifest himself to people in the ugly form of a

64

human body. It has always seemed to me that the perfection of a melody would have been far more appropriate – a melody that one could listen to on and on for ever.'

'Who are you?' I asked.

'My name is Chapaev,' the stranger replied.

'I am afraid it means nothing to me,' I said.

'Which is precisely why I use it,' he said. 'My full name is Vasily Ivanovich Chapaev. I trust that means even less to you?'

He rose from the stool and stretched himself. As he did so his joints gave out a loud cracking sound. I caught a slight whiff of expensive English eau-de-Cologne.

'Yesterday,' he said, looking intently at me, 'you left your travelling bag behind at the "Musical Snuffbox". There it is.'

I glanced down at the floor and saw Vorblei's black bag standing by the leg of the grand piano.

'Thank you,' I said, 'but how did you manage to get into the apartment?'

'I tried ringing,' he said, 'but the doorbell appeared not to be working. And the keys were in the lock. I saw that you were sleeping and I decided to wait.'

'I see,' I replied, although in actual fact it all remained a complete mystery to me. How had he discovered where I was? Who had he actually come to see – me or Vorblei? Who was he and what did he want? And why – this was the question that tormented me beyond all endurance – why had he been playing that cursed fugue? Did he suspect something? (Apropos of suspicion, I was discomfited least of all by the corpse beneath the coat in the corner – that, after all, was a perfectly ordinary element in the decor of many a Chekist apartment.)

Chapaev seemed to have read my thoughts.

'You must obviously have guessed,' he said, 'that I came to see you about more than just your travelling bag. I am leaving today for the eastern front, where I command a division. I need a commissar. The last one . . . Well, let us simply say that he did not justify the hopes placed in him. I saw your agit-performance yesterday and you made quite an impression on me. Babayasin was very pleased as well, by the way. I would like the political work in the units entrusted to me to be conducted by yourself.'

With these words he unbuttoned the pocket of his tunic and held out to me a sheet of paper folded into four. I unfolded it and read the following:

> To Com. Fourply. By order of Com. Dzerzhinsky you are immediately transferred to the staff of commander of the Asiatic Division Com. Chapaev in order to intensify political work. Babayasin.

Below the message stood the now familiar blurred and fuzzy purple stamp. Who is this Babayasin, I thought in confusion as I raised my eyes from the sheet of paper.

'So what exactly is your name?' Chapaev asked, screwing up his eyes as he looked at me, 'Grigory or Pyotr?'

'Pyotr,' I said, licking my dry lips. 'Grigory is my old literary *nom de plume*. It constantly causes confusion. Out of habit some people still call me Grigory, others call me Pyotr . . .'

He nodded and picked up his sabre and astrakhan hat from the grand piano.

'Very well then, Pyotr,' he said, 'It may not seem very convenient for you, but our train leaves today. There is nothing to be done about that. Do you have any unfinished business here in Moscow?'

'No,' I said.

'In that case I suggest that you leave with me without delay. I have to attend the embarkation of the Ivanovo weavers' regiment immediately, and I would like you to be present. You might even be required to speak. Do you have many things?'

'Only this,' I said, nodding towards the travelling bag.

'Splendid. I shall give orders today for you to be issued your allowances at the staff carriage.'

He walked towards the door.

I picked up the travelling bag and followed him out into the corridor. My thoughts were in a state of confused chaos. The man walking ahead of me frightened me. I could not understand who he was – the very last thing he reminded me of was a Red commander and yet, he very clearly was one of them. The signature and stamp on today's order were exactly the same as those which I had seen yesterday, which indi-

cated that he possessed enough influence to extract the decision he required from the bloody Dzerzhinsky and the shady
Babayasin in the space of a single morning.

In the hallway Chapaev halted and took down from the
coat-stand a long dove-grey greatcoat with three stripes of
shimmering scarlet watered silk running across the chest.
Greatcoats ornamented in this manner were the latest Red
Guard fashion, but normally the strip fastenings on the chest
were made out of ordinary cloth. Chapaev put on his greatcoat and hat and fastened on a belt from which hung a holster
with a Mauser, clipped on his sabre and turned to face me. On
his chest I noticed a rather strange-looking medal, a silver star
with small spheres on its points.

'Have you been decorated for the New Year?' I asked.

Chapaev laughed good-naturedly.

'No,' he said, 'that is the Order of the October Star.'

'I have never heard of it.'

'If you are lucky, you might even earn one yourself,' he
said. 'Are you ready?'

'Comrade Chapaev,' I said, deciding to take advantage of
the informal tone of our conversation. 'I would like to ask you
a question which you might find rather strange.'

'I am all attention,' he said and smiled politely, tapping the
long yellow cuff of a glove against his scabbard.

'Tell me,' I said, looking him straight in the eye, 'why were
you playing the piano? And why precisely that piece?'

'Well you see,' he said, 'when I glanced into your room you
were still sleeping, and you were whistling that fugue in your
sleep – not entirely accurately, I am afraid. For my own part,
I am simply very fond of Mozart. At one time I studied at the
Conservatory and intended to become a musician. But why
does this concern you?'

'It is nothing of importance,' I said. 'Merely a strange coincidence.'

We went out on to the landing. The keys really were hanging in the door. Moving like an automaton, I locked the apartment, dropped the keys into my pocket and followed
Chapaev down the stairs, thinking that I had never in my life
been in the habit of whistling, especially in my sleep.

The first thing that I saw when I emerged on to the frosty, sunny street was a long grey-green armoured car, the same one that I had noticed the previous day outside the 'Musical Snuffbox'. I had never seen a vehicle like it before – it was clearly the very latest word in the science of destruction. Its body was thickly studded with large round-headed rivets, the blunt snout of the motor protruded forwards and was crowned with two powerful headlights; on its high steel forehead, sloping slightly backwards, two slanting observation slits peered menacingly towards Nikitsky Square, like the half-closed eyes of a Buddha. On the roof was a cylindrical machine-gun turret, pointing in the direction of Tverskoi Boulevard. The barrel of the machine-gun was protected on both sides by two long plates of steel. There was a small door in the side.

A crowd of boys was swarming around the vehicle, some of them with sledges, others on skates; the thought automatically came to mind that while the idiot adults were busy trying to rearrange a world which they had invented for themselves, the children were still living in reality – among mountains of snow and sunlight, on the black mirrors of frozen ponds and in the mystic night silence of icy yards. And although these children were also infected with the bacillus of insanity that had invaded Russia – this was obvious enough from the way in which they looked at Chapaev's sabre and my Mauser – their clear eyes still shone with the memory of something which I had long ago forgotten; perhaps it was some unconscious reminiscence of the great source of all existence from which they had not yet been too far distanced in their descent into this life of shame and desolation.

Chapaev walked over to the armoured car and rapped sharply on its side. The motor started up and the rear end of the car was enveloped in a cloud of bluish smoke. Chapaev opened the door and at that precise moment I heard a screeching of brakes behind me. An enclosed automobile drew up right beside us and four men in black leather jackets leapt out of it and disappeared into the doorway from which we had emerged only a moment before. My heart sank – I thought they must have come for me. Probably this idea was prompted by the fact that the foursome reminded me of the actors in black cloaks who had borne Raskolnikov's body from the stage the previous day. One of them actually paused in the doorway and glanced in our direction.

'Quickly,' shouted Chapaev from inside the armoured car. 'You will let the cold in.'

I tossed in my travelling bag, clambered in hastily after it and slammed the door behind me.

The interior decor of this engine of doom enchanted me from the very first glance. The small space separated from the driver's cabin reminded me of a compartment in the Nord-Express; the two narrow leather divans, the table set between them and the rug on the floor created a cosy, if rather cramped, atmosphere. There was a round hole in the ceiling, through which I could see the massive butt-stock of the machine-gun in its cover; a spiral staircase ending at something shaped like a revolving chair with footrests led up into the turret. The whole was illuminated by a small electric bulb, by the light of which I could make out a picture fastened to the wall by bolts at the corners of its frame. It was a small landscape in the style of Constable – a bridge over a river, a distant thundercloud and romantic ruins.

Chapaev reached for the bell-shaped mouthpiece of the speaking tube and spoke into it: 'To the station.'

The armoured car moved away gently, with scarcely any sensation of motion inside. Chapaev sat on a divan and gestured to me to sit opposite him.

'A magnificent machine,' I said in all sincerity.

'Yes,' said Chapaev, 'this is not at all a bad armoured car. But I am not very fond of machinery in general. Wait until you see my horse . . .

'How about a game of backgammon?' he asked, putting his hand under the table and taking out a board.

I shrugged. He opened up the board and began setting out the black and white pieces.

'Comrade Chapaev,' I began, 'what will my work consist of? What questions are involved?'

Chapaev adjusted his moustache with a careful gesture.

'Well, you see, Pyotr, our division is a complex organism. I expect that you will gradually be drawn into its life and find your own niche, as it were. As yet it is still too early to say exactly what that will be, but I realized from the way you conducted yourself yesterday that you are a man of decisive character and at the same time you have a subtle appreciation of the essential nature of events. People like you are in great demand. Your move.'

I threw the dice on to the board, pondering on how I should behave. I still found it hard to believe that he really was a Red commander; somehow I felt that he was playing the same insane game as myself, only he had been playing longer, with greater skill and perhaps of his own volition. On the other hand, all my doubts were founded exclusively on the intelligent manner of his conversation and the hypnotic power of his eyes, and in themselves these factors meant nothing at all: the deceased Vorblei, for instance, had also been a man of reasonable culture, and the head of the Cheka, Dzerzhinsky, was quite a well-known hypnotist in occult circles. And then, I thought, the very question itself was stupid – there was not a single Red commander who was really a Red commander; every one of them simply tried as hard as he could to emulate some infernal model, pretending in just the same way as I had done the previous day. As for Chapaev, I might not perceive him as playing the role suggested by his military garb, but others evidently did, as was demonstrated by Babayasin's order and the armoured car in which we were riding. I did not know what he wanted from me, but I decided for the time being to play according to his rules; furthermore, I felt instinctively that I could trust him. For some reason I had the impression that this man stood several flights above me on the eternal staircase of being which I had seen in my dream that morning.

'Is there something on your mind?' Chapaev asked as he tossed the dice. 'Perhaps there is some thought bothering you?'

'Not any more,' I replied. 'Tell me, was Babayasin keen to transfer me to your command?'

'Babayasin was against it,' said Chapaev. 'He values you very highly. I settled the question with Dzerzhinsky.'

'You mean,' I asked, 'that you are acquainted?'

'Yes.'

'Perhaps, comrade Chapaev, you are acquainted with Lenin as well?' I asked with a gentle irony.

'Only slightly,' he replied.

'Can you demonstrate that to me somehow?' I asked.

'Why not? This very moment, if you wish.'

This was too much for me to take in. I gazed at him in bewilderment, but he was not embarrassed in the slightest. Moving aside the board, he drew his sabre smoothly from its scabbard and laid it on the table.

The sabre, it should be said, was rather strange. It had a long silver handle covered in carvings showing two birds on either side of a circle containing a hare, with the rest of the surface covered in the finest possible ornament. The handle ended in a jade knob to which was tied a short thick cord of twisted silk with a purple tassel at the end. At its base was a round guard of black iron; the gleaming blade was long and slightly curved. Strictly speaking, it was not even a sabre, but some kind of Eastern sword, probably Chinese. However, I did not have time to study it in detail, because Chapaev switched off the light.

We were left in total darkness. I could not see a single thing, I could only hear the low, level roaring of the engine (the soundproofing on this armour-plated vehicle, I noticed, was quite excellent – not a single sound could be heard from the street), and I could feel a slight swaying motion.

Chapaev struck a match and held it up above the table. 'Watch the blade,' he said.

I looked at the blurred reddish reflection that had appeared on the strip of steel. There was a strange profundity to it, as though I were gazing through a slightly misted pane of glass into a long illuminated corridor. A gentle ripple ran across the surface of the image, and I saw a man in an unbuttoned military jacket strolling along the corridor. He was bald and unshaven; the reddish stubble on his cheeks merged into an unkempt beard and moustache. He leaned down towards the floor and reached out with trembling hands, and I noticed a kitten with big sad eyes cowering in the corner. The image was very clear, and yet distorted, as though I were seeing a reflection in the surface of a Christmas-tree ball. Suddenly a cough rose unexpectedly in my throat and Lenin – for undoubtedly it was he – started at the sound, turned around and stared in my direction. I realized that he could see me. For a second his eyes betrayed his fright, and then they took on a cunning, even guilty look. He gave a crooked smile and wagged his finger at me threateningly.

Chapaev blew on the match and the picture disappeared. I caught a final glimpse of the kitten fleeing along the corridor and suddenly realized that I had not been seeing things on the sabre at all, I had simply, in some incomprehensible fashion, actually been there and I could probably have reached out and touched the kitten.

The light came on. I looked in amazement at Chapaev, who had already returned the sabre to its scabbard.

'Vladimir Ilyich is not quite well,' he said.

'What was that?' I asked.

Chapaev shrugged. 'Lenin,' he said.

'Did he see me?'

'Not you, I think,' said Chapaev. 'More probably he sensed a certain presence. But that would hardly have shocked him too much. He has become used to such things. There are many who watch him.'

'But how can you . . . In what manner . . . Was it hypnosis?'

'No more than everything else,' he said, and nodded at the wall, evidently referring to what lay beyond it.

'Who are you really?' I asked.

'That is the second time you have asked me that question today,' he said. 'I have already told you that my name is Chapaev. For the time being that is all that I can tell you. Do not try to force events. By the way, when we converse in private you may call me Vasily Ivanovich. "Comrade Chapaev" sounds rather too solemn.'

I opened my mouth, intending to demand further explanations, when a sudden thought halted me in my tracks. I realized that further insistence from my side would not achieve anything; in fact, it might even do harm. The most astonish-

72

ing thing, however, was that this thought was not mine – I sensed that in some obscure fashion it had been transferred to me by Chapaev.

The armoured car began to slow down, and the voice of the driver sounded in the speaking tube:

'The station, Vasily Ivanovich!'

'Splendid,' responded Chapaev.

The armoured car manoeuvred slowly for several minutes until it finally came to a halt. Chapaev donned his astrakhan hat, rose from the divan and opened the door. Cold air rushed into the cabin, together with the reddish light of winter sunshine and the dull roar of thousands of mingled voices.

'Bring your bag,' said Chapaev, springing lightly down to the ground. Screwing up my eyes slightly after the cosy obscurity of the armoured car, I climbed out after him.

We were in the very centre of the square in front of the Yaroslavl Station. On every side we were surrounded by an agitated, motley crowd of armed men drawn up in the ragged semblance of a parade. Several petty Red commanders were striding along the ranks, their sabres drawn. At Chapaev's appearance there were shouts, the general hubbub grew louder and after a few seconds it expanded into a rumbling 'Hoorah!' that resounded around the square several times.

The armoured car was standing beside a wooden platform decorated with crossed flags, which resembled, more than anything else, a scaffold. There were several military men standing on it, engaged in conversation: when we appeared they began applauding. Chapaev quickly ascended the squeaky steps; I followed him up, trying not to lag behind. Exchanging hurried greetings with a pair of officers (one of them was wearing a beaver coat criss-crossed with belts and straps), Chapaev walked over to the railing of the scaffold and raised his hand with the yellow cuff in a gesture calling for silence.

'Now, lads!' he shouted, straining his voice to make it sound hoarse. 'Y'all know what you're here for. No bloody shilly-shallying about the bush . . . You're all stuck in there and you've got to get your fingers out . . . Ain't that just the way of things, though? Once you get down the front you'll be

73

up to your neck in it and get a bellyful soon enough. Didn't reckon you was in for any spot of mollycoddling, did you . . .'

I paid close attention to the way Chapaev moved – as he spoke, he turned smoothly from side to side, incisively slicing the air in front of his chest with his extended yellow palm. The meaning of his ever more rapid speech escaped me, but to judge from the way in which the workers strained their necks to hear and nodded their heads, sometimes even grinning happily, what he was saying made good sense to them.

Someone tugged at my sleeve. With an inward shiver, I turned round to see a short young man with a thin moustache, a face pink from the frost and voracious eyes the colour of watered-down tea.

'Fu fu,' he said.

'What?' I asked him.

'Fu-Furmanov,' he said, thrusting out a broad hand with short fingers.

'A fine day,' I replied, shaking the hand.

'I'm the co-commissar with the weavers' regiment,' he said. 'We'll b-be working together. If you're go-going to speak, k-keep it short if you can. We're boarding soon.'

'Very well,' I said.

He glanced doubtfully at my hands and wrists. 'Are you in the p-p-party?'

I nodded.

'For long?'

'About two years now,' I replied.

Furmanov looked over at Chapaev. 'An eagle,' he said, 'but he has to be watched. They s-s-say he often gets c-c-carried away. But the s-s-soldiers love him. They understand him.'

He nodded at the silent crowd above which Chapaev's words were drifting. 'You've got to go, no two ways round it, and here's my hand-deed to you as a commander on the nail . . . and now the commissar's going to have a word.'

Chapaev moved back from the railing.

'Your turn, Petka,' he ordered in a loud voice.

I walked over to the railing.

It was painful to look at those men and imagine the dark maze woven by the pathways of their fates. They had been deceived since childhood, and in essence nothing had changed for them because now they were simply being deceived in a different fashion, but the crude and insulting primitiveness of these deceptions – the old and the new – was genuinely inhuman. The feelings and thoughts of the men standing in the square were as squalid as the rags they wore, and they were even being seen off to their deaths with a stupid charade played out by people who were entirely unconnected to them. But then, I thought, was my situation really any different? If I, just like them, am unable to understand, or even worse, merely imagine I understand the nature of the forces which control my life when I do not, then how am I any better than a drunken proletarian sent off to die for the word 'Internationalism'? Because I have read Gogol, Hegel and even Herzen? The whole thing was merely a bad joke.

However, I had to say something.

'Comrade workers!' I shouted. 'Your commissar comrade Furmanov has asked me to be as brief as I can, because boarding is due to begin any moment. I think that we shall have time to talk later, but now let me simply tell you of the flame that is blazing here in my heart. Today, comrades, I saw Lenin! Hoorah!'

A long roar rumbled across the square. When the noise had died down, I said:

'And now, comrades, here with his parting words is comrade Furmanov!'

Furmanov nodded gratefully to me and stepped towards the railing. Chapaev was laughing and twirling his moustache as he talked about something with the officer in the beaver coat. Seeing me approach, he clapped the officer on the shoulder, nodded to the others and climbed down the steps from the tribune. Furmanov began speaking:

'Comrades! We have only a few minutes left here. The final chimes will sound, and we shall set sail for that mighty shore of marble – for those cliffs on which we shall establish our bridgehead . . .'

He spoke now without stammering, intoning smoothly.

We made our way through the ranks of workers which parted before us – my sympathy for them almost evaporated

75

when I saw them at close quarters – and set off towards the station. Chapaev walked quickly, and I found it hard to keep up with him. Sometimes, as he responded to greetings from someone, he would raise a yellow cuff briefly to his astrakhan hat. To be on the safe side, I began copying this gesture and had soon mastered it so well that I actually began to feel quite at home among all these super-neanderthals scurrying about the station.

On reaching the edge of the platform, we jumped down on to the frozen earth. Ahead of us on the shunting lines and sidings stood a labyrinth of snow-covered carriages. There were tired people watching us from every side; the grimace of despair repeated on all of their faces seemed to form them into some new race of men.

I turned to Chapaev and asked: 'Can you explain to me the meaning of "hand-deed"?'

'What?' Chapaev asked with a frown.

'"Hand-deed,"' I repeated.

'Where did you hear that?'

'If I am not mistaken, only a moment ago you were speaking from the platform on the subject of your commander's hand-deed.'

'Ah,' said Chapaev with a smile, 'so that's what you are talking about. You know, Pyotr, when one has to address the masses, it is quite unimportant whether one understands the words that one speaks. What is important is that other people understand them. One has simply to reflect the expectations of the crowd. Some achieve this by studying the language in which the masses speak, but I prefer to act in a more direct fashion. In other words, if you wish to learn what "hand-deed" means, then it is not me you should be asking, but the men standing back there on the square.'

I thought I understood what he was saying. Indeed, I had long before come to very similar conclusions myself, only in regard to conversations about art, which had always depressed me with their monotony and pointlessness. Since I was obliged by virtue of my activities to meet large numbers of chronic imbeciles from literary circles, I had deliberately cultivated the ability to participate in their discussions without paying any particular attention to what was being spoken about, simply by juggling with such absurd words as 'realism' and 'theurgy', or even 'theosophical value'. In Chapaev's terminology this was learning the language in which the masses speak. However, I realized that he himself did not even burden himself with the knowledge of the words which he pronounced; of course, it was not clear to me how he was able to do this. Perhaps, having fallen into some kind of trance, he could sense the vibrations of anticipation projected by the crowd and somehow weave them into a pattern which it understood.

We walked the rest of the way in silence. Chapaev led me on, further and further; two or three times we stooped to dive under empty, lifeless trains. It was quiet, with no sound except the occasional frenzied whistling of steam locomotives in the distance. Eventually we halted beside a train which included an armoured carriage in its complement. The chimney above the roof of the carriage was smoking cosily, and an impressive Bolshevik with an oak-stained Asiatic face was standing on guard at the door – for some reason I immediately dubbed him a Bashkir.

We walked past the saluting Bashkir, climbed into the carriage and found ourselves in a short corridor. Chapaev nodded towards one of the doors.

'That is your compartment,' he said, taking his watch out of his pocket. 'With your permission, I shall leave you for a short while, I must issue a few instructions. They have to couple us to the locomotive and the carriages with the weavers.'

'I did not like the look of their commissar,' I said, 'that Furmanov. He and I may not be able to work well together in the future.'

'Don't go worrying your head about things that have no connection with the present,' said Chapaev. 'You have yet to reach this future of which you speak. Perhaps you will reach a future in which there will be no Furmanov – or, perhaps you might even reach a future in which there will be no you.'

I said nothing, not knowing what reply to make to his strange words.

'Make yourself comfortable and rest,' he said. 'We shall meet again at supper.'

I was astounded by the absolutely peaceful atmosphere of the compartment; the window in the armoured wall was tightly curtained, and there was a vase of carnations standing on the small table. I felt absolutely exhausted; once I had sat down on the divan, it was some time before I felt able to move again. Then I remembered that I had not washed for several days, and I went out into the corridor. Amazingly enough, the very first door that I opened led into the shower room and toilet.

I took a hot shower with immense pleasure (the water must have been heated by a coal stove) and returned to my compartment to discover that the bed had been made and a glass of strong tea was waiting for me on the table. Having drunk my fill, I slumped on to the divan and almost immediately fell asleep, intoxicated by the long-forgotten scent of stiffly starched sheets.

When I awoke the carriage was shuddering to a regular rhythm as its wheels hammered over the joints of the rails. On the table where I had left my empty tea glass, in some mysterious fashion a bundle had now appeared. Inside it I found an immaculate two-piece black suit, a gleaming pair of patent-leather shoes, a shirt, a change of underwear and several ties, clearly intended to offer me a choice. I was no longer capable of surprise at anything that happened. The suit and the shoes fitted me perfectly; after some hesitation, I selected a tie with fine black polka dots and when I inspected myself in the mirror on the door of the wall cupboard I was entirely satisfied with my appearance, although it was spoilt just a little by several days' unshaven stubble. Pulling out a pale-purple carnation from the vase, I broke off its stem and threaded the flower into my buttonhole. How beautiful and unattainable the old life of St Petersburg seemed at that moment!

Going out into the corridor, I saw that it was almost dark already. I walked up to the end door and knocked. Nobody answered. Opening the door, I saw the interior of a large saloon car. At its centre stood a table set with a light supper for three and two bottles of champagne; above the table candle flames flickered to and fro in time with the swaying of the train. The walls were covered with light-coloured wallpaper with a pattern of gold flowers; opposite the table there was a large window, beyond which the lights of the night slowly cut their way through the darkness.

There was a movement at my back. I started and looked round. Standing behind me was the same Bashkir whom I had seen outside the carriage. After glancing at me without the slightest expression of any kind, he wound up the gramophone with the glinting silverish horn that was standing in the corner and lowered the needle on to the record that had begun to revolve. Chaliapin's solid cast-bronze bass began singing – it was something from Wagner, I think. Wondering for whom the third place was intended, I reached into my pocket for a *papyrosa*.

I was not left to wonder for very long before the door opened and I saw Chapaev. He was wearing a black velvet jacket, a white shirt and a scarlet bow-tie made of the same shimmering watered silk as the red stripes on his greatcoat. He was followed into the saloon car by a girl.

Her hair was cut very short – it could hardly even be called a style. Down across her scarcely formed breasts, clad tightly in dark velvet, there hung a string of large pearls; her shoulders were broad and strong, while her hips were a little on the narrow side. Her eyes were slightly slanted, but that only added to her charm.

Beyond the slightest doubt, she was fit to serve as a model of beauty – but a beauty which could hardly have been called womanly. Not even my uninhibited fantasy was capable of transporting that face, those eyes and shoulders to the passionate, furtive gloom of a lovers' alcove. But it was easy to imagine her, for example, on an ice-rink. There was something sobering about her beauty, something simple and a little sad; I am not speaking of that decoratively lascivious chastity with which everyone in St Petersburg was already so thoroughly fed up even before the war. No, this was a genuine, natural, self-aware perfection, beside which mere lust becomes as boring and vulgar as the raucous patriotism of a policeman.

She glanced at me, then turned to Chapaev, and the pearls gleamed against the skin of her neck.

'And is this our new commissar?' she asked. The tone of her voice was slightly flat, but pleasant nonetheless.

Chapaev nodded. 'Let me introduce you,' he said, 'Pyotr, Anna.'

I got up from the table, took her cold palm in my hand and would have raised it to my lips, but she prevented me, replying with a formal handshake in the manner of a St Petersburg *emancipée*. I retained her hand in mine for a moment.

'She is a magnificent machine-gunner,' said Chapaev, 'so beware of irritating her.'

'Could these delicate fingers really be capable of dealing death to anyone?' I asked, releasing her hand.

'It all depends,' said Chapaev, 'on what exactly you call death.'

'Can there really be any difference of views on that account?'

'Oh, yes, indeed,' said Chapaev.

We sat down at the table. With suspicious facility the Bashkir opened the champagne and filled our glasses.

'I wish to propose a toast,' said Chapaev, resting his hypnotic gaze on me, 'for the terrible times in which it has been our lot to be born, and for all those who even in such days as these do not cease to strive for freedom.'

His logic seemed strange to me, because our times had been made terrible precisely because of the striving, as he had put it, of 'all those' for their so-called 'freedom' – but whose freedom, and from what? Instead of objecting, however, I took a sip of champagne – this was the simple precept which I always followed when there was champagne on the table and the conversation turned to politics. I suddenly realized how hungry I was, and I set about the food with vigour.

It is hard to express what I was feeling. What was happening was so very improbable that I no longer felt its improbability; this is what happens in a dream, when the mind, cast into a whirlpool of fantastic visions, draws to itself like a magnet some detail familiar from the everyday world and focuses on it completely, transforming the most muddled of nightmares into a simulacrum of daily routine. I once dreamed that through some exasperating contingency I had become the angel on the spire of the Peter and Paul Cathedral and in order to protect myself against the bitterly cold wind I was struggling to fasten my jacket, but the buttons simply would not slip into the buttonholes – and what surprised me was not that I had suddenly found myself suspended high in the night sky above St Petersburg, but the fact that I was incapable of completing this familiar operation.

I was experiencing something similar now. The unreality of what was happening was somehow bracketed out of my consciousness; in itself the evening was entirely normal, and if it had not been for the gentle swaying of the carriage, I might easily have assumed that we were sitting in one of St Petersburg's small cafés with the lamps of cabs drifting past the windows.

I ate in silence and only rarely glanced at Anna. She replied briefly to Chapaev when he spoke to her of gun-carts and machine-guns, but I was so engrossed by her that I failed to follow the thread of their conversation. I felt saddened by the absolute unattainability of her beauty; I knew that it would be as pointless to reach out to her with lustful hands as it would be to attempt to scoop up the sunset in a kitchen bucket.

When supper was finished, the Bashkir cleared the plates from the table and served coffee. Chapaev leaned back on his chair and lit a cigar. His face had acquired a benevolent and slightly sleepy expression; he looked at me and smiled.

'Pyotr,' he said, 'you seem thoughtful, perhaps even – pardon me for saying so – a little absent-minded. But a commissar . . . He has to carry people along with him, you understand . . . He has to be absolutely sure of himself. All the time.'

'I am entirely sure of myself,' I said. 'But I am not entirely sure of you.'

'How do you mean? What can be bothering you?'

'May I be candid with you?'

'Certainly. Both Anna and I are absolutely counting on it.'

'I find it hard to believe that you really are a Red commander.'

Chapaev raised his left eyebrow.

'Indeed?' he asked, with what seemed to me to be genuine astonishment. 'But why?'

'I do not know,' I said. 'This all reminds me very much of a masquerade.'

'You do not believe that I sympathize with the proletariat?'

'Certainly I believe it. On that platform today I even experienced a similar feeling myself. And yet . . .'

Suddenly I no longer understood what exactly I wanted to say. Silence hung over the table, broken only by the tinkling of the spoon with which Anna was stirring her coffee.

'Well, in that case, just what does a Red commander look like?' asked Chapaev, brushing the cigar ash from the flap of his jacket.

'Furmanov,' I replied.

'Forgive me, Pyotr, but that is the second time today that you have mentioned that name. Who is this Furmanov?'

'The gentleman with the voracious eyes,' I said, 'who addressed the weavers after me.'

Anna suddenly clapped her hands.

'That reminds me,' she said, 'we have entirely forgotten about the weavers, Vasily Ivanovich. We should have paid them a visit long ago.'

Chapaev nodded.

'Yes, yes,' he said, 'you are quite right, Anna. I was just about to suggest it myself, but Pyotr set me such a puzzle that everything else entirely slipped my mind.'

He turned towards me. 'We must certainly return to this topic. But for the present, would you not like to keep us company?'

'Yes, I would.'

'Then, forward,' said Chapaev, rising from the table.

We left the staff carriage and went towards the rear of the train. Events now began to seem even stranger to me: several of the carriages through which we walked were dark and seemed entirely empty. There was not a single light burning anywhere and not a sound could be heard behind their closed doors. I could not really believe that there were Red Army soldiers sleeping behind those walnut panels which reflected the glow of Chapaev's cigar in their polished surface, but I tried not to ponder too much on the matter.

One of the carriages did not end in the usual little lobby, but in a door in the end wall, beyond the window of which the dark winter night rushed away from us. After fumbling briefly with the lock the Bashkir opened it and the corridor was suddenly filled with the sharp clattering of wheels and a swarm of tiny, prickly snowflakes. Outside the door there was a small fenced-in area beneath a canopy, like the rear platform of a tram, and beyond it loomed the heavy carcass of the next carriage. There was no way of crossing over to it, so it remained unclear just how Chapaev had intended to pay a visit to his new men. I followed the others out on to the platform. Leaning on the railing, Chapaev drew deeply on his cigar, from which the wind snatched several bright crimson sparks.

'They are singing,' said Anna, 'can you hear?'

She raised an open hand, as though to protect her hair from the wind, but lowered it immediately – her hairstyle made the gesture entirely meaningless. The thought struck me that she must have worn a different style only a very short time before.

'Can you hear?' she repeated, turning to face me.

And indeed, through the rumbling of the carriage wheels I could make out a rather lovely and harmonious singing. Listening more closely, I could even catch the words:

Blacksmiths are we, our spirit is an anthill,
We forge the keys of happiness.
Oh, hammer mighty, rise up higher still,
Smite harder, harder yet upon this iron breast!

'Strange,' I said, 'why do they sing that they are smiths, if they are weavers? And why is their spirit an anthill?'

'Not an anthill, but an anvil,' said Anna.

'An anvil?' I echoed. 'Ah, but of course. It is an anvil because they are smiths – or rather, because they sing that they are smiths, although in actual fact they are weavers. One devil of a confused mess.'

Despite the absurdity of the text there was something ancient and bewitching about this song ringing out in the winter night. Perhaps it was not the song itself, but the strange combination of innumerable male voices, the piercingly bitter wind, the snow-covered fields and the small stars scattered sparsely across the night sky. When the train curved as it went round a bend we could make out the string of dark carriages – the men travelling in them must have been singing in total darkness – and this filled out the picture, making it even more mysterious and strange. For some time we listened without speaking.

'Perhaps it is something Scandinavian,' I said. 'You know, they had a god there, and he had a magic hammer that he used as a weapon. In the Old Edda saga I think it was. Yes, yes, see how well everything else fits! This dark frost-covered carriage before us, why should it not be Thor's hammer hurled at some unknown enemy! It hurtles relentlessly after us, and there is no force capable of halting its flight!'

'You have a very lively imagination,' Anna replied. 'Can the sight of a dirty railway carriage really arouse such a train of thoughts in you?'

'Of course not,' I said. 'I am simply endeavouring to make conversation. In actual fact I am thinking about something else.'

'About what?' asked Chapaev.

'About the fact that man is rather like this train. In exactly the same way he is doomed for all eternity to drag after him out of the past a string of dark and terrible carriages inherited from goodness knows whom. And he calls the meaningless rumbling of this accidental coupling of hopes, opinions and fears his life. And there is no way to avoid this fate.'

'Why not?' asked Chapaev. 'There is a way.'

'Do you know it?' I asked.

'Of course,' said Chapaev.

'Perhaps you would share it with us?'

'Gladly,' said Chapaev, and he clicked his fingers.

The Bashkir seemed to have been waiting for precisely this signal. Setting his lamp on the floor, he ducked nimbly under the railings, leaned out in the darkness over the invisible elements of the carriage coupling and began making rapid movements with his hands. There was a dull clanging sound and the Bashkir returned to the platform with the same alacrity with which he had left it.

The dark carriage wall facing us began slowly receding.

I looked up at Chapaev. He met my gaze calmly.

'It is getting cold,' he said, as though nothing had happened. 'Let us return to the table.'

'I will follow on after you,' I replied.

Left alone on the platform, I went on gazing into the distance for some time. I could still make out the singing of the weavers, but with every second that passed the string of carriages fell further and further behind; suddenly they seemed to me like a tail cast off by a fleeing lizard. It was a beautiful sight. Oh, if only it were really possible, as simply as Chapaev had parted from these men, to leave behind me that dark crowd of false identities which had been tearing my soul apart for so many years!

Soon I began to feel cold. Turning back into the carriage and closing the door behind me, I felt my way along by touch. When I reached the staff carriage I felt such a great weariness that without even pausing to shake the snowflakes from my jacket, I went straight into my compartment and collapsed on to the bed.

I could hear Chapaev and Anna talking and laughing in the saloon car.

'Pyotr!' Chapaev shouted. 'Don't go to sleep! Come and join us!'

After the cold wind which had chilled me through on the platform, the warm air in the compartment was remarkably pleasant. It even began to feel more like water than air, as though at long last I were taking the hot bath I had been dreaming about for so many days. When the sensation became absolutely real, I realized that I was falling asleep, which I might have guessed anyway from the fact that instead of Chaliapin, the gramophone suddenly began playing the same Mozart fugue with which my day had begun. I sensed that I should not on any account fall asleep, but there was no longer anything I could do to resist; having abandoned the struggle, I hurtled down headlong between the minor piano chords into the same stairwell of emptiness which had so astounded me that morning.

4

'Hey there! No sleeping!'

Someone shook me carefully by the shoulder. I lifted my head, opened my eyes and saw a face I did not recognize, round and plump, framed in a painstakingly tended beard. Although it wore an affable smile, it did not arouse any desire to smile in return. I understood why immediately – it was the combination of the carefully trimmed beard with a smoothly shaven skull. The gentleman leaning over me reminded me of one of those speculators trading in anything they could lay their hands on who appeared in such abundance in St Petersburg immediately after the start of the war. As a rule they came from the Ukraine and had two distinguishing features – a monstrous amount of vitality and an interest in the latest occult trends in the capital.

'Vladimir Volodin,' the man introduced himself. 'Just call me Volodin. Since you've decided to lose your memory one more time, we might as well introduce ourselves all over again.'

'Pyotr,' I said.

'Better not make any sudden movements, Pyotr,' said Volodin. 'While you were still sleeping they gave you four cc's of taurepam, so your morning's going to be a bit on the gloomy side. Don't be too surprised if you find the things or people around you depressing or repulsive.'

'Oh, my friend,' I said, 'it is a long time now since I have been surprised by that kind of thing.'

'No,' he said, 'what I mean is that the situation you find yourself in might seem quite unbearably loathsome. Inexpressibly, inhumanly monstrous and absurd. Entirely incompatible with life.'

'And what should I do?'

'Take no notice. It's just the injection.'

'I shall try.'

'Splendid.'

I suddenly noticed that this Volodin was entirely naked. Moreover, he was wet and he was squatting on a tiled floor, on to which copious amounts of water were dripping from his body. But what was most intolerable in this entire spectacle was a certain relaxed freedom in his pose, an elusive monkey-like lack of constraint in the way he rested his long sinewy arm against the tiles. This lack of constraint somehow seemed to proclaim that the world around us is such that it is only natural and normal for large hairy men to sit on the floor in such a state – and that if anyone thinks otherwise, then he will certainly find life difficult.

What he had said about the injection seemed to be true. Something strange really was happening to my perception of the world. For several seconds Volodin had existed all alone, without any background, like a photograph in a residence permit. Having inspected his face and body in their full detail, I suddenly began to think about where all this was happening, and it was only after I had done so that the place actually came into being – at least, that was how I experienced it.

The space around us was a large room covered throughout with white tiles, with five cast-iron baths standing in a row on the floor. I was lying in one of the end baths and I suddenly realized with disgust that the water in it was rather cold. Offering a final smile of encouragement, Volodin turned round on the spot and from his squatting position leapt with revolting agility into the bath next to mine, scarcely even raising a splash in the process.

In addition to Volodin, I could see two other people in the room: a long-haired, blue-eyed blond with a sparse beard who looked like an ancient Slavic knight, and a dark-haired young man with a rather feminine, pale face and an excessively developed musculature. They were looking at me expectantly.

'Seems like you really don't remember us,' the bearded blond said after several seconds of silence. 'Semyon Serdyuk.'

'Pyotr,' I replied.

'Maria,' said the young man in the far bath.

'I beg your pardon?'

'Maria, Maria,' he repeated, obviously annoyed. 'It's a name. You know, there was a writer, Erich Maria Remarque? I was named after him.'

'I have not come across him,' I replied. 'He must be one of the new wave.'

'And then there was Rainer Maria Rilke. Haven't you heard of him either?'

'Why, certainly I have heard of him. We are even acquainted.'

'Well then, he was Rainer Maria, and I'm just Maria.'

'Pardon me,' I said, 'but I seem to recognize your voice. Was it not by any chance you who related that strange story with the aeroplane, about Russia's alchemical wedlock with the West and so forth?'

'Yes,' replied Maria, 'but what do you find so strange about it?'

'Nothing in general terms,' I said, 'but for some reason I had the impression that you were a woman.'

'Well, in a certain sense, that's right,' replied Maria. 'According to the boss here, my false personality is definitely that of a woman. You wouldn't by any chance be a heterosexual chauvinist would you?'

'Certainly not,' I said, 'I am simply surprised at how easily you accept that this personality is false. Do you really believe that?'

'I don't believe anything at all,' said Maria. 'My concussion's to blame for everything. And they keep me here because the boss is writing his dissertation.'

'But who is this boss?' I asked in bewilderment, hearing the word a second time.

'Timur Timurovich,' Maria replied. 'The head of the department. False personalities are his line.'

'That's not exactly right,' Volodin countered. 'The title of the dissertation he is working on is "The Split False Personality". Maria here is a fairly simple and uncomplicated case and you really have to strain the term a bit to talk about him having a split personality, but you, Pyotr, are a prize exhibit. Your false personality is developed in such fine detail that it outweighs the real one and almost entirely displaces it. And the way it's split is simply magnificent.'

'Nothing of the sort,' objected Serdyuk, who had so far remained silent. 'Pyotr's case isn't really very complicated. At a structural level it's no different from Maria's. Both of them have identified with names, only Maria's identification is with the first name, and Pyotr's is with the surname. But Pyotr's displacement is stronger. He can't even remember his surname. Sometimes he calls himself Fourply, sometimes something else.'

'Then what is my surname?' I asked anxiously.

'Your surname is Voyd,' Volodin replied, 'and your madness is caused by your denying the existence of your own personality and replacing it with another, totally invented one.'

'Although in structural terms, I repeat, it's not a complicated case,' added Serdyuk.

I was annoyed – I found the idea of some strange psychic deviant telling me that my case was not complicated rather offensive.

'Gentlemen, you are reasoning like doctors,' I said. 'Does that not seem to you to represent a certain incongruity?'

'What kind of incongruity?'

'Everything would be perfectly fine,' I said, 'if you were standing here in white coats. But why are you lying here yourselves, if you understand everything so very clearly?'

Volodin looked at me for several seconds without speaking.

'I am the victim of an unfortunate accident,' he said.

Serdyuk and Maria burst into loud laughter.

'And as for me,' said Serdyuk, 'I haven't even got any false personalities. Just an ordinary suicide attempt due to chronic alcoholism. They're keeping me here because you can't build a dissertation around just three cases. Just to round out the statistics.'

'Never mind all that,' said Maria. 'You're next in line for the garrotte. Then we ll hear all about your alcoholic suicide.'

By this time I felt thoroughly chilled; furthermore, I was unable to decide whether the explanation lay in the injection which, according to Volodin, ought to have made everything that was happening to me seem intolerable, or whether the water really was as cold as it seemed.

Thankfully, however, the door opened at this point and two men in white coats entered the room. I remembered that one of them was called Zherbunov, the other Barbolin. Zherbunov held a large hourglass in his hand, while Barbolin was carrying an immense heap of linen.

'Out we get,' said Zherbunov merrily, waving the timer in front of him.

They wiped down each of us in turn with huge fluffy sheets and helped us to put on identical pyjamas with horizontal stripes, which immediately lent events a certain naval flavour. Then they led us out through the door and down a long corridor, which also seemed somehow familiar – not the corridor itself, however, but the vaguely medical smell that hung in its air.

'Tell me,' I said quietly to Zherbunov, who was walking along just behind me, 'why am I here?'

He opened his eyes wide in surprise.

'As if you didn't know,' he said.

'No,' I said, 'I am prepared to admit that I am not well, but what was the cause? Have I been here for a long time? And what specific acts am I actually charged with?'

'Ask Timur Timurovich all your questions,' said Zherbunov. 'We've no time for idle chatter.'

I felt extremely depressed. We stopped at a white door bearing the number '7'. Barbolin opened it with a key and they allowed us through into a rather large room with four beds standing along the wall. The beds were made, there was a table by the barred window and standing by the wall was something that looked like a combination of a couch and a low armchair, with elastic loops for the sitter's hands and feet. Despite these loops, there was nothing at all menacing about the contrivance. Its appearance was emphatically medical, and the absurd phrase 'urological chair' even came into my mind.

'I beg your pardon,' I said, turning to Volodin, 'but is this the garrotte of which you spoke?'

Volodin gave me a brief glance and nodded towards the

door. I turned to look. Timur Timurovich was standing in the doorway.

'Garrotte?' he asked, raising one eyebrow. 'The garrotte, if I am not mistaken, is a chair on which people were executed by strangulation in medieval Spain, is that not so? What a dark and depressive perception of surrounding reality! Of course you, Pyotr, had your injection this morning, so it's nothing to be surprised at. But you, Vladimir? I am astonished, astonished.'

As he rattled off this speech, Timur Timurovich gestured for Zherbunov and Barbolin to leave and walked to the centre of the room.

'It's not a garrotte at all,' he said. 'It's a perfectly ordinary couch for our group therapy sessions. You, Pyotr, have already attended one of these sessions, immediately after you returned to us from the isolation ward, but you were in rather poor condition, so it's unlikely that you can remember anything.'

'That is not the case,' I said, 'I do remember something.'

'All the better. Then let me briefly remind you what takes place here. The method which I have developed and employ could be provisionally classified as turbo-Jungian. You are, of course, acquainted with the views of Jung . . .'

'I beg your pardon, of whom?'

'Karl Gustav Jung. Very well, I perceive that your mental activity is currently subject to powerful censorship from your false personality. And since your false personality is living in 1918 or 1919, we should hardly be surprised if you seem unable to remember who he is – or perhaps you really never have heard of Jung?'

I shrugged my shoulders in a dignified manner.

'To put it simply, there was a psychologist by the name of Jung. His therapeutic methods were based on a very simple principle. He attempted to draw to the surface of his patient's consciousness the symbols which he could use to form a diagnosis. By means of deciphering them, that is.'

At this point Timur Timurovich gave a cunning little smile.

'But my method is a little different,' he said, 'although the fundamentals are the same. With Jung's method we would have to take you off somewhere to Switzerland, to some sanatorium up in the mountains, sit you down on a *chaise-longue*, enter into long-drawn-out conversations and wait for God knows how long before the symbols began to surface. We can't do that sort of thing. Instead of the *chaise-longue* we sit you down over there,' – Timur Timurovich pointed to the couch – 'we give you a little injection, and then we observe the symbols that start floating to the surface in simply va-a-ast quantities. After that it's up to us to decipher them and cure you. Is that clear?'

'More or less,' I said. 'How do you go about deciphering them?'

'You'll see that, Pyotr, for yourself. Our sessions take place on Fridays, which means that in three . . . no, in four weeks it will be your turn. I must say, I am really looking forward to it, working with you is so very interesting. But then, of course, the same applies to all of you, my friends.'

Timur Timurovich smiled, flooding the room with the warm radiance of his love, then he bowed and shook his own left hand with his right one.

'And now it's time for class to begin.'

'What class?' I asked.

'Why,' he said, looking at his watch, 'it's already half past one. Practical aesthetics therapy.'

With the possible exception of the psycho-hydraulic procedures which had roused me from sleep, I have never experienced anything quite so distressing as that session of practical aesthetics therapy – but then, perhaps the injection was really to blame. The exercises were held in a room adjacent to our ward; it was large and dimly lit, with a long table in its corner heaped with lumps of Plasticine of various colours, ugly mis-shapen toy horses of the kind moulded by artistically gifted children, paper models of ships, broken dolls and balls. At the centre of the table was a large plaster bust of Aristotle, and we sat opposite him, on four chairs covered with brown oilcloth, with drawing-boards on our knees. The aesthetics therapy consisted in our drawing the bust with pencils which were attached to the board and had also been covered in soft black rubber.

Volodin and Serdyuk remained in their striped pyjamas,

while Maria removed his jacket and put on instead an under-shirt with a long slit reaching almost down to his navel. They all seemed quite accustomed to this procedure and sat there patiently pushing their pencils across the surface of the paper. Just to be on the safe side, I made a quick, rough sketch and then set the board aside and began inspecting my sur-roundings.

The injection was certainly still working – I was still suffer-ing from the same effect that I had felt in the bathroom and was incapable of perceiving external reality in its totality. El-ements of the surrounding world appeared at the moment when my gaze fell on them, and I was developing a giddy feeling that my gaze was actually creating them.

Suddenly I noticed that the walls of the room were hung with drawings on small sheets of paper, some of which ap-peared to be very curious indeed. Some of them obviously be-longed to Maria. These were extremely clumsy, almost childish scribbles which all repeated in various forms the theme of an aeroplane adorned with a massive phallic projec-tion. Sometimes the aeroplane was standing on its tail and the images acquired Christian overtones of a somewhat sacrile-gious nature. In general though, Maria's drawings were of no particular interest.

However, another set appeared curious in the extreme, and not merely because the artist possessed indisputable talent. These were drawings united by a Japanese theme, represented in a strange, uneven fashion. Most of the drawings, seven or eight in number, attempted to reproduce an image seen some-where previously: a samurai with two swords and the lower half of his body indecently exposed, standing on the edge of an abyss with a stone hung round his neck. Another two or three drawings depicted horsemen at rest against a background of distant mountains, which were drawn with astonishing skill in the traditional Japanese style. The horses in these images were tethered to trees and their dismounted riders, clad in loose, colourful garments, were sitting near by on the grass and drinking from shallow bowls. The drawing which made the strongest impression on me had an erotic theme; it showed an other-worldly man in a tiny blue cap astride a woman with broad Slavic cheekbones who was giving herself to him. There was something horrifying about her face.

'Excuse me, gentlemen,' I said, unable to restrain myself, 'to whom do these drawings on Japanese themes belong?'

'Semyon,' said Volodin, 'who do your drawings belong to? The hospital, I suppose?'

'Are they yours, Mr Serdyuk?'

'Yes,' answered Serdyuk, glancing sideways at me with his bright blue eyes.

'Quite exquisite,' I said. 'Only, perhaps, rather sombre.'

He gave no answer.

The third series of drawings, which I guessed must be those of Volodin, was very abstract and impressionistic in manner. Here also there was a leitmotif – three dark blurred silhouettes around a burst of flame, with a broad beam of light falling on them from above. In compositional terms it was reminiscent of a well-known Russian painting of three hunters sitting round a camp-fire, except that in this work it was a high-explosive shell that had exploded in the flames just a moment before.

I looked over at the other wall and started violently in surprise.

It was probably the most acute attack of *déja vu* I have ever suffered in my life. From my very first glance at the six-foot-long sheet of cardboard, covered with its tiny figures in various colours, I sensed a profound connection with the strange object. I rose from my chair and went across to it.

My gaze fell on the upper part of the sheet, which showed something like the plan of a battle, in the way they are usually drawn in history textbooks. At its centre was a solid blue oval, where the word 'SCHIZOPHRENIA' was written in large letters. Approaching it from above were three broad red arrows; one ran directly into the oval and the two others curved round to bite into its sides. Written on them were the words 'insulin', 'aminazine' and 'sulphazine', and running down from the oval in a broken line was a blue arrow, beneath which were the words 'illness retreats'. I studied this plan and then turned my attention to the drawing below it.

With its numerous characters, abundant detail and

94

crowded composition it reminded me of an illustration to Tolstoy's *War and Peace* – one including all of the novel's characters and the entire scope of its action. At the same time the drawing was very childish in nature, because it broke all of the rules of perspective and common sense, exactly like a child's drawing. The right-hand section of the drawing was occupied by a representation of a big city. When I spotted the bright yellow dome of St Isaac's, I realized that it must be St Petersburg. Its streets, in some places drawn in detail and in others merely represented by simple lines, as though on a map, were filled with arrows and dotted lines which clearly represented the trajectory of someone's life. From St Petersburg a dotted line led to a similar image of Moscow which was close beside it. In Moscow only two places were represented in real detail – Tverskoi Boulevard and the Yaroslavl Station. Leading away from the station was the fine double cobweb-line of a railway track, which widened as it approached the centre of the sheet and acquired a third dimension, turning into a drawing rendered more or less according to the laws of perspective. The track ran off to a horizon overgrown with bright yellow wheat, where a train stood on its rails, wreathed in clouds of smoke and steam.

The train was drawn in detail. The locomotive had been badly damaged by several direct hits from shells; thick clouds of steam were pouring from the holes in the sides of the barrel-shaped boiler, and the driver's dead body was hanging out of the cabin. Behind the locomotive there was an open goods truck with an armoured car standing on it – my heart began to race at this – with its machine-gun turret turned towards the yellow waves of wheat. The trapdoor of the turret was open and I saw Anna's close-cropped head protruding from it. The ribbed barrel of the machine-gun was spitting fire in the direction of the wheatfield; Chapaev, wearing a tall astrakhan hat and a shaggy black cloak buttoned from his neck to his feet, stood on the platform beside the armoured car and waved his raised sabre in the direction of its fire. His pose seemed a little too theatrical.

The train in the picture had halted only a few yards short of a station, the greater part of which was invisible beyond the edge of the sheet of cardboard; all I could see was the platform barrier and a sign bearing the words 'Lozovaya Junction'.

I tried to spot the enemies at whom Anna was firing from her turret, but all I could discover in the drawing were numerous vaguely sketched silhouettes largely hidden by the wheat. I was left with the impression that the artist responsible for the work did not have a very clear idea of why and against whom the military action shown was being conducted. But I had little doubt as to the identity of the author.

Written in large letters under the drawing were the words: 'The Battle at Lozovaya Junction'. Close by, other words had been added in a different hand: 'Chapaev's waving, Petka's raving'.

I whirled round to face the others.

'Come now, gentlemen, does it not seem to you that this rather exceeds the bounds of what is acceptable among decent people, eh? What if I should start acting in the same way, eh? Then what would happen?'

Volodin and Serdyuk averted their gaze. Maria pretended that he had not heard. I carried on looking at them for some time, attempting to guess which of them was responsible for this vile act, but no one responded. Besides, I was not in all honesty particularly concerned and my annoyance was to a large extent feigned. I was far more interested in the drawing, which from my very first glance had given me the impression that it was somehow incomplete. Turning back to the cardboard, I struggled for some time to understand exactly what it was that was bothering me. It seemed to be the section between the plan of the battle and the train, where in principle the sky should have been – a large area of the cardboard was blank, which somehow produced the impression of a gaping void. I went over to the table and rummaged in its clutter until I found a stub of sanguine and an almost complete stick of charcoal.

I spent the next half-hour adding black blotches of shrapnel shell-bursts to the sky over the wheatfield. I drew them all identically – a small dense black cloud of solid charcoal, and fragments scattering like arrows in all directions, leaving long trails of dark red behind them.

The result was very similar to that well-known painting by Van Gogh, the name of which I cannot recall, where a black cloud of crows looking like thick, crudely drawn 'V's circles above a field of wheat. I thought of how hopelessly despairing the condition of the artist is in this world: at first the thought gave me a certain bitter satisfaction, but then I suddenly felt it to be unbearably false. It was not merely a question of its banality, but of its institutional meanness: everybody involved in art repeated it in one way or another, classifying themselves as members of some special existential caste, but why? Did the life of a machine-gunner or a medical orderly, for instance, lead to any other outcome? Or were they any less filled with the torment of the absurd? And was the unfathomable tragedy of existence really linked in any way with the pursuits in which a person was engaged in their lifetime?

I turned to look at my companions. Serdyuk and Maria were absorbed in the bust of Aristotle (Maria was concentrating so hard that he had even stuck the tip of his tongue out of his mouth), but Volodin was attentively following the changes in the drawing on my sheet of cardboard. Catching my gaze on him, he smiled inquiringly at me.

'Volodin,' I began, 'may I ask you a question?'

'By all means.'

'What is your profession?'

'I am an entrepreneur,' said Volodin, 'or a new Russian, as they say nowadays. At least, I was. But why do you ask?'

'You know, I was just thinking . . . People go on and on about the tragedy of the artist, the tragedy of the artist. But why the artist in particular? It is really rather unfair. The fact is, you see, that artists are very visible individuals and therefore the troubles that they encounter in life are bandied about and exposed to the public eye . . . but does anyone ever think about . . . Well, no, they might well remember an entrepreneur . . . Let us say, an engine-driver? No matter how tragic his life might be?'

'You're coming at the question from the wrong side entirely, Pyotr,' said Volodin.

'What do you mean?'

'You're getting your concepts confused. The tragedy

doesn't happen to the artist or the engine-driver, it takes place in the mind of the artist or the engine-driver.'

'I beg your pardon?'

'Granted, granted,' Volodin purred and turned back to his drawing-board.

It was several seconds before Volodin's words sank in and I realized what he meant. But the mental listlessness induced by the injection completely blocked out any response.

Turning back to my sheet of cardboard, I drew in several columns of thick black smoke above the field, using up all my charcoal. Together with the dark spots of the shrapnel-bursts, they lent the picture a certain air of menace and hopelessness. I suddenly felt unwell, and I dedicated myself to covering the horizon with small figures of horsemen galloping through the wheat to cut off the attackers.

'You missed your vocation – you should have been a battle artist,' observed Volodin. From time to time he would look up to glance at my sheet of cardboard.

'A fine comment, coming from you,' I replied. 'After all, you are the one who keeps drawing an explosion in a camp-fire.'

'An explosion in a camp-fire?'

I pointed to the wall where the drawings hung.

'If you think that's an explosion in a camp-fire, then I have nothing more to say to you,' replied Volodin, 'nothing what-soever.'

He seemed to have taken offence.

'What is it, then?'

'It's the descent of the light of heaven,' he answered. 'Can't you see that it comes down from on high? It's drawn like that deliberately.'

My mind raced through several consecutive conclusions.

'Can I assume, then, that they're keeping you here because of this heavenly light?'

'You can,' said Volodin.

'That's hardly surprising,' I said politely. 'I sensed immedi-ately that you were no ordinary man. But what exactly have they charged you with? With having seen that light? Or with attempting to tell others about it?'

'With being the light,' said Volodin. 'As is usual in such cases.'

'I must assume that you are joking,' I said. 'But seriously?'

Volodin shrugged.

'I had two assistants,' he said, 'about your age. You know, garbage men – they were very useful for cleaning up reality, you can't do business without them these days. They're in the drawing here, by the way – see, those two shadows. Well, to cut it short, I made it a rule to discuss such exalted subjects with them. And then one day we happened to go into the forest and I showed them – I don't even know how to explain it – the way everything is. I didn't even show them – they saw it all for themselves. That's the moment shown in the drawings. And it had such an effect on them that a week later they ran off and turned me in. Stupid idiots, each of them had a dozen stiffs to answer for, but they still reckoned that was nothing compared with what they had to report. Modern man has the very basest of instincts, let me assure you.'

'Indeed you are right,' I replied, thinking of something else entirely.

For lunch Barbolin led us to a small dining-room rather like the room with the baths, except that the place of the baths was taken by plastic tables situated next to a serving-hatch. Only one of the tables was laid. We hardly spoke at all during the meal. When I had finished my soup and begun eating my gruel I suddenly noticed that Volodin had pushed away his plate and was staring hard at me. At first I tried not to pay any attention, but then I could stand it no longer, and I looked up and stared boldly into his eyes. He smiled peaceably – in the sense that there was nothing menacing in his expression, and said:

'You know, Pyotr, I have the feeling that you and I have met in circumstances that were extremely important – for me, at least.'

I shrugged.

'Do you by any chance have an acquaintance with a red face, three eyes and a necklace of skulls,' he asked, 'who

99

dances between fires? Mm? Very tall, he was. And he waves these crooked swords around.'

'Maybe I do,' I said politely, 'but I cannot quite tell just who it is you have in mind. The features you mention are very common, after all. It could be almost anybody.'

'I see,' said Volodin, and he went back to his plate.

I reached out for the teapot in order to pour some tea into my glass, but Maria shook his head.

'Better not,' he said. 'Bromide. Takes away your natural sexuality.'

Volodin and Serdyuk, however, drank the tea without appearing in the slightest manner concerned.

After lunch we went back to the ward and Barbolin immediately disappeared off somewhere. My three companions were obviously accustomed to such a routine and fell asleep almost as soon as they had laid down on their beds. I stretched out on my back and stared at the ceiling for a long time, savouring the state, rare for me, of an entirely empty mind, which was possibly a consequence of the morning's injection.

In fact, it would not be entirely correct to say that my mind was empty of all thoughts, for the simple reason that my consciousness, having entirely liberated itself of thought, continued nonetheless to react to external stimuli, but without reflecting upon them. And when I noticed the total absence of thoughts in my head, that in itself became already a thought about the absence of thoughts. Thus, I reasoned, a genuine absence of thoughts appeared impossible, because it cannot be recorded in any way – or one might say that it was equivalent to non-existence.

But this was still a marvellous state, as dissimilar as possible from the routine internal ticking of the everyday mind. Incidentally, I have always been astounded by one particular feature typical of people who are unaware of their own psychological processes. A person of that kind may be isolated for a long period from external stimuli, without experiencing any real needs, and then, for no apparent reason, a spontaneous psychological process suddenly arises within him which compels him to launch into a series of unpredictable actions in the external world. It must appear very strange to anyone who happens to observe it: there is the person lying on his back, he lies there for an hour, for two, for three, and then suddenly leaps up, thrusts his feet into his slippers and sets out for goodness knows where, simply because for some obscure reason – or perhaps without any reason at all – his train of thought has gone dashing off in some entirely arbitrary direction. The majority of people are actually like that, and it is these lunatics who determine the fate of our world.

The universe that extended in all directions around my bed was full of the most varied sounds. Some of them I recognized – the blows of a hammer on the floor below, the sound of a shutter banging in the wind somewhere in the distance, the cawing of the crows – but the origin of most of the sounds remained unclear. It is astonishing how many new things are immediately revealed to a man who can empty out the fossilized clutter of his conscious mind for a moment! It is not even clear where most of the sounds that we hear actually come from. What then can be said about everything else, what point is there in attempting to discover an explanation for our lives and our actions on the basis of the little that we believe we know! One might just as well attempt to explain the inner life-processes of another individual's personality through the kinds of phantasmagorical social constructs employed by Timur Timurovich, I thought, and suddenly remembered the thick file on my case that I had seen on his desk. Then I remembered that when he left, Barbolin had forgotten to lock the door. And instantly, in a mere split second, an insane plan had taken shape in my mind.

I examined my surroundings. No more than twenty minutes had passed since the beginning of the rest hour, and my three companions were asleep. It seemed as though the entire building had fallen asleep together with them – in all that time not a single person had passed the door of our ward. Carefully pulling off my blanket, I thrust my feet into my slippers, stood up and stealthily made my way over to the door.

'Where are you going?' came a whisper from behind my back.

I turned round. Maria's eyes were focused keenly on me

from the corner of the room. I could just see him through the narrow gap in the blanket in which he had wrapped himself from head to toe.

'To the toilet,' I said in a similar whisper.

'Don't play the brave soldier,' whispered Maria, 'the pot's over there. If they catch you it's a day in the isolation ward.'

'They won't catch me,' I whispered in reply and slipped out into the corridor.

It was empty.

I vaguely remembered that Timur Timurovich's office was located beside a tall semi-circular window, which looked straight out on to the crown of a huge tree. Far ahead of me, at the point where the corridor in which I was standing turned to the right, I could see bright patches of daylight on the linoleum. Crouching down, I crept as far as the corner and saw the window. I immediately recognized the door of the office by its magnificent gilt handle.

For several seconds I stood there with my ear pressed to the keyhole. I could not hear a sound from inside the office, and finally I ventured to open the door slightly – the room was empty. Several files were lying on the desk, but mine, which was the thickest (I remembered its appearance very clearly) was no longer in its former place.

I glanced around in despair. The dismembered gentleman on the poster returned my gaze with inhuman optimism; I felt sick and terrified. For some reason I felt that the orderlies were sure to enter the office at any moment. I was on the point of turning and running out into the corridor when I suddenly noticed a file lying open beneath other papers which were set out on the table.

'A course of taurepam injections prescribed to precede the hydraulic procedures. Purpose – to block speech and motor functions with simultaneous activation of the psycho-motor complex . . .'

There were a few more words in Latin. Pushing these papers to one side, I turned over the cardboard sheet of the file beneath and read the words on it:

'Case: Pyotr Voyd.'

I sat in Timur Timurovich's chair.

The very first entry, on a few bound sheets of paper placed in the file, was so very old that the purple ink in which it had been written had faded, acquiring the kind of historical colour that one finds in documents which speak of people long since dead and buried. I was soon absorbed in what I read.

'In early childhood no signs of psychological deviance were detected. He was a cheerful, affectionate, sociable child. Studied well at school, enjoyed writing verse which did not demonstrate any particular aesthetic merit. First pathological deviations recorded at about fourteen years of age. Tendency to withdrawal and irritability observed, unrelated to any external causes. According to parents he 'abandoned the family'; moved into a state of emotional alienation. Stopped associating with his friends – which he explains by the fact that they teased him about his Estonian surname "Voyd". Says that his teacher of geography used to do the same, repeatedly calling him an "empty shell". Began to make much slower progress at school. At the same time began intensively reading philosophical literature – the works of Hume, Berkeley, Heidegger – everything which in one way or another deals with the philosophical aspects of emptiness and non-existence. As a result began to analyse the simplest events from a "metaphysical" point of view and declared that he is superior to his peers in "the heroic valour of life". Began frequently skipping classes, following which his family were obliged to contact a doctor.

'Willingly enters into contact with the psychologist. Trusting. Concerning his inner world declares as follows: he has "a special conception of the world". The patient reflects "long and vividly" on all objects around him. In describing his psychological activity he declares that his thought "gnaws its way deeper and deeper into the essence of a particular phenomenon". Due to this feature of his thinking he is able to "analyse any question asked, each word and each letter, laying them out like an anatomical specimen", while in his mind he has a "ceremonial choir of numerous selves arguing with each other". Has become extremely indecisive, which he explains, in the first instance, by the experience of "the ancient Chinese" and secondly by the fact that "it is difficult to make sense of the whirlwind of scales and colours of the contradictory inner life". On the other hand, according to his own words, he is gifted with a "peculiar flight of free thought" which "elevates

103

*him above all other laymen". In this connection complains of lone-
liness and lack of understanding from those around him. The patient says there is no one capable of thinking "on his wavelength".*

*'Believes he can see and feel things unattainable to "laymen".
For instance, in the folds of a curtain or tablecloth, the patterns of
wallpaper etc. he distinguishes lines, shapes and forms which express "the beauty of life". According to his words, this is his
"golden joy", that is, the reason for which he daily repeats the
"involuntary heroism of existence".*

*'Regards himself as the only successor to the great philosophers
of the past. Spends much time rehearsing "speeches to the people".
Does not find placement in a psychiatric hospital oppressive, since
he is confident that his "self-development" will proceed by "the
right path" no matter where he lives.'*

Someone had crossed out several purple phrases with a thick
blue pencil. I turned the page. The next text was titled
'organoleptic indications', and was obviously burdened with
a superfluity of Latin terms. I began rapidly leafing through
the pages. Those written in purple were not even bound into
the file – they had most probably slipped in there by accident
from some other file. A page had been inserted in front of the
following set of papers, which was the thickest, and on it I
read the words:

THE PETERSBURG PERIOD
*(Provisional title taken from the most persistent feature of
delusions. Repeated hospitalization.)*

But I had no chance to read a single word from the second
part. I heard Timur Timurovich's voice in the corridor, exas-
peratedly explaining something to someone else. Rapidly returning the papers on the desk to approximately the same
position in which they had been lying before my arrival, I
dashed over to the window – the idea occurred to me of hiding behind the curtains, but they hung almost flush against
the glass.

Timur Timurovich's rumbling voice sounded very close
to the door by this time. He seemed to be giving one of the
orderlies a dressing-down. Stealing over to the door, I
glanced through the keyhole. I could see no one – the owner

of the office and his companion were apparently standing several yards away round the corner.

The action I took then was in large measure instinctive. I quickly left the office, tip-toed across to the door opposite and dived into the dark and dusty broom-cupboard behind it. I was only just in time. The conversation round the corner stopped abruptly and a second later Timur Timurovich appeared in the narrow space which I could observe through the crack of the door. Cursing quietly to himself, he disappeared into his office. I counted to thirty-five (I do not know why it was thirty-five – nothing in my life has ever been associated with that number), then darted out into the corridor and ran noiselessly back to my ward.

Nobody noticed my return – the corridor was empty, and my companions were asleep. A few minutes after I lay down on my bed the melodic chimes of reveille came drifting along the corridor; almost simultaneously Barbolin came in and said they were going to defumigate the ward, and so today we would be having a second session of practical aesthetics therapy.

The atmosphere of a madhouse obviously must instil submissiveness into a person. Nobody even thought of expressing indignation or saying that it was impossible to spend so many hours on end drawing Aristotle. Maria was the only one to mutter something dark and incomprehensible under his breath. I noticed that he had woken in a bad mood. Possibly he had had a dream, for immediately on waking he began to study his reflection in the mirror. He did not seem to like what he saw very much, and he spent several minutes massaging the skin under his eyes and running his fingers round them.

Arriving very late in the practical aesthetics room, he made not the slightest pretence of drawing Aristotle as everyone else, including myself, was doing. Taking a seat in the corner he wound a yellow ribbon round his head, evidently intended to protect his hair against the winds raging in his psychological space, and began looking us up and down as if he had never seen us before.

There may not have been any wind in the room, but dark

clouds certainly seemed to have gathered there. Volodin and Serdyuk did not pay the slightest attention to Maria, and I decided that I had been mistaken to attach so much weight to minor details. But the silence oppressed me nonetheless, and I decided to break it.

'I beg your pardon, Mr Serdyuk, but will you not be offended if I attempt to engage you in conversation?' I inquired.

'Certainly not, indeed,' Serdyuk replied politely, 'by all means, do so.'

'I hope very much that you will not find my question tactless, but can you tell me what it was that brought you here?'

'Otherworldliness,' said Serdyuk.

'Indeed? But can one really be hospitalized for otherworldliness?'

Serdyuk measured me up with a long glance.

'They registered it as suicidal vagrancy syndrome arising from *delirium tremens*. Although no one has any idea what that is.'

'Tell me more about it,' I asked.

'What is there to tell? I was just lying there in a basement out on the Nagornoe road – for entirely personal and highly important reasons. I was fully and agonizingly conscious. Then this copper with a torch and an automatic appeared. Wanted to see my documents, so I showed him. Then, of course, he asked for money. I gave him all I had – about twenty roubles. He took the money, but kept on hanging about, wouldn't go away. I should have just turned to face the wall and forgotten about him, but I had to go and start up a conversation; what d'you mean poking your porkies out at me like that, are you short of bandits upstairs or something? This pig turns out to be fond of talking – I found out later he'd graduated from the philosophy faculty. No, he says, there's more than enough of them up there, only they're not disturbing the social order. What d'you mean by that, I asked him. Well, he says, your ordinary bandit, what is he? Sure, take a look at him and you can see that all he's got on his mind is how he can find someone to kill and rob, but so what? And the guy who's just been robbed, he's not breaking any laws either. He just lies there with his fractured skull and thinks –

so now I've gone and got robbed. And you're lying down there – he's talking to me now – and I can see you're thinking about something . . . Like you don't believe in anything around you. Or at least you have your doubts.'

'So what did you say?'

'What did I say?' echoed Serdyuk. 'I only went and told him that maybe I did have my doubts. The sages of the East all told us that this world is an illusion – I just mentioned the sages of the East in a way he'd be able to handle, on his own primitive level. Then he suddenly goes all red and says to me: "What the hell's going on here? I wrote my diploma on Hegel, and here you've read something in *Science and Religion* and you think you can crawl into some basement and lie around doubting the reality of the world?" In short, first they dragged me round to the station, and then round here. I had a scratch on my belly – I cut myself on a broken bottle – so they registered that as attempted suicide.'

'What I'd do with anyone who doubts the reality of the world,' Maria unexpectedly interrupted, 'is put them away for ever. They don't belong in the madhouse, they should be in prison. Or worse.'

'And why's that?' asked Serdyuk.

'You want an explanation?' Maria asked in an unfriendly voice. 'Come over here and I'll give you one.'

Getting up from his place beside the door, he went over to the window, waited for Serdyuk and then pointed outside with his muscular arm.

'See that Mercedes-600 standing over there?'

'Yes,' said Serdyuk.

'Are you telling me that's an illusion too?'

'Very probably.'

'You know who drives around in that illusion? The commercial director of our madhouse. He's called Vovchik Maloi, and his nickname's "the Nietzschean". Have you seen him around?'

'Yes.'

'What do you think of him?'

'It's obvious. He's a bandit.'

'So think about it – that bandit could have killed a dozen people to buy himself a car like that. Are you telling me they all gave their lives for nothing, if it's only an illusion? Why don't you say something? Can't you see where that leads?'

'Yes, I can see,' Serdyuk said gloomily and went back to his chair.

Maria apparently felt a sudden desire to draw. Picking up his drawing-board from the corner, he sat down beside the rest of us.

'No,' he said, peering through half-closed eyes at the bust of Aristotle, 'if you want to get out of here some time, you have to read the newspapers and experience real feelings while you're doing it. And not start doubting the reality of the world. Under Soviet power we were surrounded by illusions. But now the world has become real and knowable. Understand?'

Serdyuk went on drawing without speaking.

'Well, don't you agree?'

'It's hard to say,' Serdyuk replied gloomily. 'I don't agree that it's real. But as for it being knowable, I guessed that for myself a long time ago. From the smell.'

'Gentlemen,' I intervened, sensing that a quarrel was ripening and attempting to lead the conversation into neutral territory, 'do you have any idea why it's Aristotle we are drawing in particular?'

'So it's Aristotle, is it?' said Maria. 'I thought he looked pretty serious. God knows why. Probably the first thing they came across in the junk-room.'

'Don't be stupid, Maria,' said Volodin. 'Nothing happens by accident in here. Just a moment ago you were calling things by their real names. What are we all doing here in the madhouse? They want to bring us back to reality. And the reason we're sitting here drawing this Aristotle is because he *is* that reality with the Mercedes-600s that you, Maria, wanted to be discharged into.'

'So before him it didn't exist?' asked Maria.

'No, it didn't,' snapped Volodin.

'How so?'

'You won't understand,' said Volodin.

'You just try explaining,' said Maria. 'Maybe I will understand.'

'Okay, you tell me why the Mercedes is real,' said Volodin.

Maria struggled painfully with his thoughts for a few seconds.

'Because it's made of iron,' he said, 'that's why. And you can go up to the iron and touch it.'

'So you're telling me that it's rendered real by a certain substance of which it consists?'

Maria thought.

'Yeah, more or less,' he said.

'Well, that's why we're drawing Aristotle. Because before him there was no substance,' said Volodin.

'What was there then?'

'There was the number one heavenly automobile,' said Volodin, 'compared with which your Mercedes-600 is nothing but a heap of shit. This heavenly automobile was absolutely perfect. And every single concept and image relating to automobiles was contained in it and it alone. And the so-called real automobiles that drove around the roads in ancient Greece were no more than its imperfect shadows. Projections, so to speak. Understand?'

'Yeah. So what came next?'

'Next came Aristotle and he said that of course the number one heavenly automobile existed, and of course all the earthly automobiles were simply its distorted reflections in the dim and crooked mirror of existence. At that time there was no way you could argue with all that. But, said Aristotle, in addition to the prototype and the reflection, there is one other thing. The material that takes the form of the automobile. Substance, possessing an existence of its own. Iron, as you called it. And it was this substance that made the world real. This entire fucking market economy started up from it. Because before then all the things on earth were merely reflections, and what reality can a reflection have, I ask you? The only reality is what makes the reflections.'

'You know,' I said quietly, 'that really is quite a big question.'

Volodin ignored what I had said.

'Understand?' he asked Maria.

'Yeah,' Maria answered.

'What do you understand?'

'I understand that you're a psycho all right. How could they have automobiles in ancient Greece?'

'Ugh,' said Volodin, 'how petty and precisely correct. They really will discharge you soon.'

'God willing,' said Maria.

Serdyuk raised his head and looked attentively at Maria.

'You know, Maria,' he said, 'just recently you've turned real bitchy. In the spiritual sense.'

'I've got to get out of here, don't you understand? I don't want to spend all my life stuck in here. Who's going to want me ten years from now?'

'You're a fool, Maria,' Serdyuk said scornfully. 'Can't you understand that the love you and Arnold have can only exist in here?'

'You watch your mouth, stork-face! Or I'll smash this bust over your stupid head.'

'Go on, just you try it, you berk,' said Serdyuk, rising from his chair with a face that had turned pale. 'Just you try it!'

'I won't have to try,' answered Maria, also rising to his feet. 'I'll just do it, that's all. People get killed for saying things like that.'

He stepped towards the table and took hold of the bust.

What followed lasted no more than a few seconds. Volodin and I leapt up from our seats. Volodin wrapped his arms around Serdyuk, who was advancing on Maria. Maria's face twisted in a grimace of fury; he raised the bust above his head, swung it back and stepped towards Serdyuk. I pushed Maria away and saw that Volodin had seized Serdyuk in such a way that his arms were pinned to his body, and if Maria were to strike him with the bust, he would not even be able to protect himself with his hands. I tried to pull Volodin's hands apart where they were clasped on Serdyuk's chest. Meanwhile Serdyuk had closed his eyes and was smiling blissfully. Suddenly I noticed that Volodin was staring aghast over my shoulder. I turned my head and saw a lifeless plaster face with dusty wall-eyes slowly descending out of a fly-spotted sky.

5

The bust of Aristotle was the only thing I retained in my memory when I came round, although I am far from certain that the expression 'to come round' is entirely appropriate. Ever since my childhood I have sensed in it a certain shame-faced ambiguity. Round what exactly? To where? And, most intriguing of all, from where? Nothing, in short, but a cheating sleight of hand, like the card-sharps on the Volga steamers. As I grew older, I came to understand that the words 'to come round' actually mean 'to come round *to other people's point of view*', because no sooner is one born than these other people begin explaining just how hard one must try to force oneself to assume a form which they find acceptable.

However, that is not the point. I regard the expression as not entirely appropriate to describe my condition because when I awoke I did not do so completely – instead, I became aware of myself, so to speak, in that non-material world familiar to everyone on the borderline between sleep and wakefulness, where one's surroundings consist of visions and thoughts which momentarily arise and dissolve in consciousness, while the person around whom they arise is entirely absent. One usually flits through this state instantaneously, but for some reason I remained stuck in it for several long seconds; my thoughts were mostly of Aristotle. They were incoherent and almost entirely meaningless; the ideological great-grandfather of Bolshevism was not the object of any particular sympathy on my part, but neither did I feel any personal hatred for him as a consequence of the previous day's events – the concept of substance which he had invented was evidently insufficiently substantial to have inflicted upon me any truly serious damage. Curiously enough, in my half-dreaming state I was furnished with the most convincing of proofs for this – when the bust shattered into shards under the force of the blow, it proved to have been hollow all the time.

If I had been struck on the head with a bust of Plato, I thought, then the result would have been far more serious. At this point I remembered that I had a head, the final fragments of sleep scattered and evaporated, and events began to follow the normal sequence of human awakening, as it became apparent that all of these thoughts had their existence inside the head, and that the head in question was aching intolerably.

I opened my eyes cautiously.

The first thing that I saw was Anna, sitting close to my bed. She had not noticed that I had woken, probably because she was absorbed in reading – there was a volume of Knut Hamsun lying open in her hands. I watched her for some time through my eyelashes. I was unable to add anything substantial to my first impression of her, but no additions were necessary: perhaps her beauty appeared even more tormenting in its indifferent perfection. I thought with sadness that when a woman like her does fall in love with a man it is always either a commercial traveller with a moustache or some red-faced artillery major – the mechanism is the same as that by which the most beautiful schoolgirls are bound to choose ugly friends. It is not, of course, a matter of wishing to emphasize their own beauty by means of the contrast (an explanation on the level of Ivan Bunin), but of compassion.

There were some changes in her, however. Her hair seemed to be shorter and a little lighter, but that was probably a trick of the light. Instead of the previous day's dark dress she was wearing a strange semi-military uniform – a black skirt and a loose sandy-coloured tunic, dappled now with trembling rainbow spots of colour from a ray of sunlight that was split as it passed through the carafe that stood on a table, which stood in turn in a room I had never seen before. But the most astonishing thing was that outside the window it was summer – through the pane I could see what appeared to be the silvery-green crowns of poplars soaring upwards through the noonday heat.

This room in which I was lying reminded me of a suite in

an inexpensive provincial hotel; a small table, two firmly up-holstered armchairs, a washbasin on the wall and a lamp with a shade. One thing it did not resemble in the slightest, how-ever, was the compartment of the train hurtling through the winter night in which I had fallen asleep the previous evening.

I propped myself up on my elbow. My movement evidently took Anna entirely by surprise – she dropped her book on the floor and stared at me in confusion.

'Where am I?' I asked, sitting up in bed.

'For God's sake, lie down,' she said, leaning towards me. 'Everything is all right. You are safe.'

The gentle pressure of her hands forced me back down on to the bed.

'But may I not at least know where I am? And why it is suddenly summer?'

'Yes,' she said, going back to her chair, 'it is summer. Do you not remember anything at all?'

'I remember everything perfectly well,' I said. 'I simply cannot understand how it happens that one moment I was riding in a train and now suddenly I find myself in this room.'

'You began talking quite often while you were delirious,' she said, 'but you never once came round fully. Most of the time you were in a coma.'

'What coma? I remember that we were drinking champagne, and Chaliapin was singing . . . Or was it the weavers . . . And then that strange gentleman . . . Comrade . . . In short, Chapaev. Chapaev uncoupled the carriages.'

Anna must have stared doubtfully into my eyes for an entire minute.

'How strange,' she said at last.

'What is strange?'

'That you should remember precisely that. And afterwards?'

'Afterwards?'

'Yes, afterwards. For instance, do you remember the Battle of Lozovaya Junction?'

'No,' I said.

'Or what came before that?'

'Before that?'

'Yes, before that. At Lozovaya you were already commanding a squadron.'

'What squadron?'

'Petya, at Lozovaya you distinguished yourself. If you had not moved in from the left flank with your cavalry squadron, they would have wiped us all out.'

'What is the date today?'

'The third of June,' she said. 'I know that such instances do occur in cases of head wounds, but . . . I could understand it if you had lost your memory completely, but this strange selectivity is quite astonishing. But then, I am not a doctor. Perhaps this is also part of the normal order of things.'

I raised my hands to my head and shuddered – it was as though my palms had touched a billiard ball that had sprouted short stubble. I had been completely shorn, like a typhus case. And there was also something strange, some kind of hairless projection running through the skin. I ran my fingers along it and realized that it was a long scar lying diagonally right across my skull. It felt as though a section of a leather belt had been glued to my scalp with gum arabic.

'Shrapnel,' said Anna. 'The scar is impressive, but it is nothing to worry about. The bullet only grazed you. But the concussion is apparently rather more serious.'

'When did it happen?' I asked.

'On the second of April.'

'And since then I have not recovered consciousness?'

'Several times. But for just a few moments, no more.'

I closed my eyes and tried to conjure up a memory of at least some of what Anna had spoken about. But the darkness into which I gazed held nothing except the streaks and spots of light that appeared behind my eyelids.

'I do not remember a thing,' I said, and felt my head again. 'Absolutely nothing. I can only remember a dream I had – that in some dark hall in St Petersburg I am being beaten on the head with a bust of Aristotle, and every time it shatters into fragments. But then it happens all over again – pure Gothic . . . But now I understand what was going on.'

'Your ravings were really quite intriguing,' said Anna. 'You spent half of yesterday remembering some Maria who had been hit by a shell. It was a rather incoherent tale, though, and I never did understand just what relationship you had with the girl. I suppose you must have been thrown together by the whims of war?'

'I have never known anyone called Maria. Excluding, that is, a recent nightmare . . .'

'Please do not be concerned,' said Anna, 'I have no intention of being jealous.'

'That is a shame,' I replied, then I sat up and lowered my legs to the floor. 'Please, do not think that I am trying to shock you by talking to you in nothing but my underwear.'

'You must not get up.'

'But I feel perfectly well,' I replied. 'I would like to take a shower and get dressed.'

'Quite out of the question.'

'Anna,' I said, 'if I command a squadron, I must have an orderly.'

'Certainly you have one.'

'While you and I are talking here, he is most probably swinishly drunk yet again. Do you think you could send him to me? And another thing – where is Chapaev?'

The strange thing was that my orderly (he was a taciturn, yellow-haired, stocky individual with a long body and the short, crooked legs of a cavalryman – a ridiculous combination which made him look like an inverted pair of pincers) really was drunk. He brought me my clothes: a greyish-green military jacket with no shoulder-stripes (but with one sewn on to the arm for my wound), blue breeches with a double red stripe down the side and a pair of excellent short boots made of soft leather. Also thrown on to the bed were a fuzzy black astrakhan hat, a sabre with the inscription 'To Pyotr Voyd for valour', a holster containing a Browning and Vorblei's travelling bag, the very sight of which suddenly made me feel unwell.

All of its contents were still in place, except that there was a little less cocaine in the tin. In addition, I discovered in the bag a small pair of binoculars and a notebook about one-third full of writing which was undoubtedly my own. I found most of the notes quite incomprehensible – they dealt with horses, hay and people whose names meant nothing to me. But apart from that, my eyes did encounter a few phrases which resembled those which I had been in the habit of noting down:

'Christianity and other religs. can be regarded as a totality of variously remote objects radiating a certain energy. How blindingly the figure of the crucified God shines! And how stupid it is to call Chr. a primitive system! If one thinks about it, it was not Rasputin who plunged Russia into revolution, but his murder.'

And then, two pages further on:

'In life all "successes" have to be measured against the period of time over which they are achieved; if this interval is excessively long, then most achievements are rendered meaningless to a greater or lesser degree; the value of any achievement (at least, any practical achievement) is reduced to zero if the effort extends throughout the length of one's life, because after death nothing any longer has any meaning. Do not forget the inscription on the ceiling.'

Despite this last exhortation, I seemed to have forgotten the inscription on the ceiling quite irretrievably. There had been times when I would use up an entire notebook every month on jottings of this kind, and every one of them had seemed genuinely significant and filled with a meaning which would be required in the future. But when this future arrived, the notebooks had been misplaced, life outside had completely changed, and I had found myself on the dank and miserable Tverskoi Boulevard with a revolver in my coat pocket. It was a good thing, I thought, that I had happened to meet an old friend.

Once I was dressed (the orderly had not brought any footbindings, and I was obliged to tear up the sheet to make some) I hesitated for some time before eventually donning the astrakhan hat -- it smelt of something rotten - but my shaven head seemed to me to present an extremely vulnerable target. I left the sabre on the bed, but extracted the pistol from its holster and hid it in my pocket. I cannot bear to upset people's nerves with the sight of a weapon, and in any case it made it easier to reach the weapon quickly if necessary. When I took a look at myself in the mirror above the washbasin I was quite satisfied – the astrakhan hat even lent my unshaven face a certain crazed haughtiness.

Anna was standing downstairs at the foot of the broad curved staircase which I descended after leaving my room.

'What kind of place is this?' I asked. 'It looks like an abandoned manor-house.'

'So it is,' she said. 'This is our HQ. And not only our HQ – we live here as well. Since you became a squadron commander, Pyotr, a great deal has changed.'

'But where is Chapaev?'

'He is out of town just at the moment,' Anna replied, 'but he should be back soon.'

'And what town is this, by the way?'

'It is called Altai-Vidnyansk, and it is surrounded on every side by mountains. I cannot understand how towns appear in such places. Society here consists of no more than a few officers, a couple of strange individuals from St Petersburg and the local intelligentsia. The locals have, at best, heard something about the war and the revolution, while the Bolsheviks are stirring things up on the outskirts. In short, a real hole.'

'Then what are we doing here?'

'Wait for Chapaev,' said Anna. 'He'll explain everything.'

'In that case, with your permission, I shall take a stroll around the town.'

'You must not do that under any circumstances,' Anna insisted. 'Think for yourself. You have only just come round – you might suffer some kind of fit. What if you were to faint out on the street?'

'I am deeply touched by your concern,' I replied, 'but if it is sincere, you will have to keep me company.'

'You leave me no choice,' she said with a sigh. 'Exactly where would you like to go?'

'If perhaps there is some kind of hostelry,' I said, 'you know, the usual kind for the provinces – with a wilting palm tree in a tub and warm sherry in carafes – that would do very nicely. And they must serve coffee.'

'There is one such place here,' said Anna, 'but it has no palm tree, and no sherry either, I expect.'

*

117

The town of Altai-Vidnyansk consisted for the most part of small wooden houses of one or two storeys set rather widely apart from one another. They were surrounded by tall fences of wooden planks, most of which were painted brown, and were almost totally concealed behind the dense greenery of neglected gardens. Closer to the centre, which Anna and I approached by descending the steep slope of a cobbled street, buildings of brick and stone appeared, also as a rule no more than two storeys high; I noted a couple of picturesque cast-iron fences and a fire-observation tower with something elusively Germanic about its appearance. It was a typical small provincial town, not without a certain unspoilt charm, calm and bright and drowned in blossoming lilac. The mountains towered up around it on all sides; it seemed to lie at the bottom of the chalice which was formed by them – with the central square with its repulsively ugly statue of Alexander II at its very lowest point: the windows of the 'Heart of Asia' restaurant to which Anna took me happened to look out on that particular monument. The thought came to me that it was all just begging to be put into some poem or other.

It was cool and quiet in the restaurant; there was no palm-tree in a tub, but there was a stuffed bear standing in the corner clutching a halberd in its paws, and the room was almost empty. At one of the tables two rather seedy-looking officers were sitting and drinking – when Anna and I walked past they looked up at me and then turned their eyes away with indifference. I must confess that I was not really sure whether my present status obliged me to open fire on them with my Browning or not, but to judge from Anna's calm demeanour, nothing of the kind seemed to be required; in any case, the shoulder-straps had been torn off their uniform jackets. Anna and I sat at the next table and I ordered champagne.

'You wanted to drink coffee,' said Anna.

'True,' I said. 'Normally I never drink in the daytime.'

'Then why the exception?'

'It is made entirely in your honour.'

Anna laughed. 'That's very kind, Pyotr. But I want to ask you a favour – for God's sake, please don't start courting me again. I do not find the prospect of an affair with a wounded cavalry officer in a town where there are shortages of water and kerosene very attractive.'

I had expected nothing else.

'Well, then,' I said, when the waiter had set the bottle on the table, 'if you choose to see me as a wounded cavalry officer, who am I to object? But in that case, how shall I regard you?'

'As a machine-gunner,' said Anna. 'Or if you prefer to be more accurate, as a Lewis gunner. I prefer the disc-loading Lewis.'

'As a cavalry officer, of course, I detest your profession. Nothing could be more depressing than the prospect of attacking a machine-gun emplacement in mounted formation. But since we are talking about you, I raise my glass to the profession of gunner.'

We clinked glasses.

'Tell me, Anna,' I asked, 'whose officers are those at the next table? Who actually holds this town?'

'Broadly speaking,' said Anna, 'the town is held by the Reds, but there are some Whites here as well. Or you might say it is held by the Whites, but there are some Reds here as well. So it is best to dress in a neutral style – much as we are dressed now.'

'And where is our regiment?'

'Our division, you mean. Our division has been dissipated in battle. We now have very few men left, a third of a squadron at the most. But since there are no enemy forces of any substance here we can regard ourselves as safe. This is the backwoods, everything is perfectly quiet here. You walk along the streets, you see yesterday's enemies and you think to yourself – is the reason for which we were trying to kill one another only a few days ago real?'

'I understand you,' I said. 'War coarsens the sinews of the heart, but one only has to glance at the lilac blossom and it seems that the whistling of shells, the wild whooping of cavalrymen, the scent of gunpowder mingled with the sweet smell of blood are all unreal, no more than a mirage or a dream.'

'Exactly,' said Anna. 'The question is, how real is the lilac blossom? Perhaps it is just another dream.'

Well, well, I thought to myself, but I refrained from expanding any further on the theme.

'Tell me, Anna, what is the present situation at the fronts? In general, I mean.'

'To be quite honest, I do not know. Or as they say nowadays, I'm not posted on that. There are no newspapers here and the rumours are all different. And then, you know, I have had enough of all that. They take and lose towns one has never heard of with wild-sounding names like Buguruslan, Bugulma and . . . what is it now . . . Belebei. And where it all goes on, who takes the town and who loses it, is not really clear and, more importantly, it is not particularly interesting either. The war goes on, of course, but talking about it has become rather *mauvais genre*. I would say the general atmosphere is one of weariness. Enthusiasm has slumped badly.'

I sat in silence, thinking about what she had said. Somewhere far away a horse neighed in the street, followed by the long-drawn-out yell of the coachman. One of the officers at the next table finally managed to get the needle into his vein: he had been trying unsuccessfully for the past five minutes, leaning far back in his chair to get a good view of his arms concealed under the table – all this time his chair had been balanced on its two back legs and there were moments when I thought he was certain to fall. Putting the syringe back into its nickel-plated box, he hid it in his holster. Judging from the oily gleam that immediately appeared in his eyes, the syringe must have contained morphine. For a minute or two he sat swaying on his chair, then he slumped forward on to the table with his elbows, took his comrade by the hand and in a voice filled with a sincerity beyond my power to convey, he said:

'I just thought, Nikolai . . . D'you know why the Bolsheviks are winning?'

'Why?'

'Because their teaching contains a vital, passionate . . .' he closed his eyes and shuffled the fingers of one hand as he searched agonizingly for the right word, 'a love of humanity, a love full of ecstasy and bliss. Once you accept it fully and completely, Bolshevism is capable of kindling a certain higher hope that lies dormant in the heart of man, don't you agree?'

The second officer spat on the floor.

'You know what, Georges,' he said sullenly, 'if it was your auntie they'd hanged in Samara, I'd like to hear what you had to say about higher hopes.'

The first officer closed his eyes and said nothing for several seconds. Then suddenly he went on: 'They say Baron Jungern was seen in the town recently. He was riding on a horse, wearing a red robe with a gold cross on the chest, and acting as though he wasn't afraid of anyone . . .'

At that moment Anna was lighting a cigarette – when she heard these words she started and the match almost slipped out of her fingers. I thought it would be best to distract her by making conversation.

'Tell me, Anna, what has actually been going on all this time? I mean, since the day when we left Moscow?'

'We have been fighting,' said Anna. 'You gave a good account of yourself in battle and became very close to Chapaev – you would spend several nights in a row in conversation with him. And then you were wounded.'

'I wonder what it was we talked about.'

Anna released a fine stream of smoke in the direction of the ceiling.

'Why not wait for him to get back? I can guess at the approximate content of your discussions, but I would not like to go into any detail. It really concerns nobody but the two of you.'

'But give me at least a general indication, Anna,' I said.

'Chapaev,' she said, 'is one of the most profound mystics that I have ever known. I believe that he has found in you a grateful audience and, perhaps, a disciple. I suspect, furthermore, that the misfortune which you have suffered is in some way connected with your conversations with him.'

'I do not understand a thing.'

'That is hardly surprising,' said Anna. 'He has attempted on several occasions to talk with me, and I have also failed to understand a thing. The one thing of which I am sure is that he is capable of reducing a credulous listener to total insanity within the space of a few hours. My uncle is a very unusual man.'

'He is your uncle then,' I said. 'So that's it! I was beginning to think that you and he must be bound by ties of a different nature.'

'How dare you . . . But then, you can think what you like.'

'Please, I beg you, forgive me,' I said, 'but after what you just said about a wounded cavalry officer I thought that perhaps you might be more interested in healthy cavalry officers.'

'One more boorish outburst of that kind and I shall entirely lose interest in you, Pyotr.'

'So you do at least feel some interest. That is comforting.'

'Do not go clutching at words.'

'Why may I not clutch at words if I like the sound of them?'

'Out of simple considerations of safety,' said Anna. 'While you were lying unconscious you put on a lot of weight, and you might find the words are not able to support you.'

She was obviously quite capable of standing up for herself. But this was going just a little too far.

'My dearest Anna,' I said, 'I cannot understand why you are trying so hard to insult me. I know for certain that it is a pretence. You are not, in actual fact, indifferent to me, I realized that immediately I came round and saw you sitting there beside my bed. And you have no idea of how deeply I was touched.'

'I am afraid that you will be disappointed if I tell you why I was sitting there.'

'What do you mean? What other motive can there be for sitting beside the bed of a wounded man, apart from sincere . . . I don't know – concern?'

'Now I really do feel embarrassed. But you asked for it yourself. Life here is boring, and your ravings were most picturesque. I must confess that I sometimes came to listen – but I came out of nothing but boredom. I find the things you are saying now far less interesting.'

I had not expected this. I counted slowly to ten as I attempted to recover from the blow. Then I counted again. It was no good – I still felt the same bright flame of hatred, a hatred pure and unadulterated.

'Would you mind giving me one of your cigarettes?'

Anna proffered her open cigarette case.

'Thank you,' I said. 'You make very interesting conversation.'

'You think so?'

'Yes,' I said, feeling the cigarette trembling in my fingers, and becoming even more irritated. 'What you say is very thought-provoking.'

'In what way?'

'Well, for instance, several minutes ago you cast doubt on the reality of the lilac in which this town is enveloped. It was unexpected – and yet at the same time very Russian.'

'What do you see in the remark that is specifically Russian?'

'The Russian people realized very long ago that life is no more than a dream. You know what a succubus is?'

'Yes,' said Anna, with a smile. 'A demon that takes female form to seduce a sleeping man. But what's the connection?'

I counted to ten again. My feelings had not changed.

'The most direct one possible. When they say in Russian vernacular that all women suck, the word "suck" as used in the phrase is actually derived from the word "succubus". An association which came to Russia via Catholicism. No doubt you remember – the seventeenth century, the Polish invasion, in other words, the Time of Troubles. That's what it goes back to. But I am wandering. All I wished to say was that the very phrase "all women suck",' – I reiterated the words with genuine relish – 'means in essence that life is no more than a dream. And so are all the bitches. That is, I meant to say, the women.'

Anna drew deeply on her cigarette. There was a very slight flush on the line of her cheekbones, and I could not help noticing that it suited her pale face remarkably well.

'I am wondering,' she said, 'whether or not I should throw this glass of champagne in your face.'

'I really cannot say,' I said. 'In your place I believe I would not do that. We are not as yet sufficiently intimate.'

A moment later a shower of transparent drops struck me in the face – her glass had been almost full, and she flung the champagne out of it with such force that for a second I was blinded.

'I'm sorry,' Anna said in confusion, 'but you yourself . . .'

'Think nothing of it,' I replied.

Champagne possesses one very convenient quality. If one picks up a bottle, closes off the mouth with one's thumb and shakes it really well several times, the foam will force its way out in a stream which exhausts virtually the entire contents of the bottle. It seems to me that this method must have been known to the poet Lermontov – he has a line which quite clearly reflects direct experience of a similar kind: *'thus does the ancient moss-covered bottle yet store its stream of frothing wine'*. Of course, it is hard to hypothesize about the inner world of a man who, intending to turn his face towards the Prince of Darkness, wrote as a result a poem about a flying colonel of the hussars. I would not therefore claim that Lermontov did actually spray women with champagne, but I do believe that the probability of his having done so was very high, in view of his continuous obsession with matters of sex and the immodest but entirely inescapable associations which this operation always arouses when its object is a beautiful young woman. I must confess that I fell victim to them in full measure.

Most of the champagne caught Anna on her tunic and skirt. I had been aiming for her face, but at the final moment some strange impulse of chastity must have forced me to divert the flow downwards.

She looked at the dark blotch on the chest of her tunic and shrugged.

'You are an idiot,' she said calmly. 'You should be in a home for the mentally disturbed.'

'You are not alone in thinking that,' I said, setting the empty bottle on the table.

An oppressive silence fell. It seemed to me entirely pointless to engage in any further attempts to clarify our relations, and sitting opposite each other in silence was even more stupid. I think that Anna was feeling the same; probably in the entire restaurant only the fat black fly methodically beating itself against the window-pane knew what to do next. The situation was saved by one of the officers sitting at the next table – by this time I had completely forgotten that they even existed, but I am sure that in the wider sense they also had no idea of what to do next. The one who had been injecting himself rose to his feet and approached us.

'My dear sir,' I heard him say in a voice filled with feeling, 'my dear sir, would you mind if I were to ask you a question?'

'Not at all, please do,' I said, turning to face him.

He was holding an open wallet in his hands, which he glanced into as he spoke as though it contained the crib for his speech.

'Allow me to introduce myself,' he said. 'Staff Captain Lambovsky. By pure chance I happened to overhear part of your conversation. I was not eavesdropping, naturally. You were simply talking loudly.'

'And what of it?'

'Do you genuinely believe that all women are a dream?'

'You know,' I replied, trying to speak as politely as possible, 'that is really a very complex question. In short, if one regards the entire Universe as no more than a dream, then there is no reason at all for placing women in any kind of special category.'

'So they are a dream, then,' he said sadly. 'I feared as much. But I have a photo here. Take a look.'

He held out a photograph. It showed a girl with an ordinary face sitting beside a potted geranium. I noticed that Anna also stole a glance at the photograph out of the corner of her eye.

'This is my fiancée, Nyura,' said the staff captain. 'That is, she was my fiancée. Where she is now I have not the slightest idea. When I recall those bygone days, it all seems so very real . . . The skating rink at the Patriarch's Ponds, or summer out at the estate . . . But in reality it has all disappeared, disappeared irretrievably – and if it had all never been, what would have been changed in the world? Do you understand how terrible that is? It makes no difference.'

'Yes,' I said, 'I understand, believe me.'

'So it would seem that she is a dream too?'

'So it would seem,' I echoed.

'Aha!' he said with satisfaction, and glanced round at his companion who was smiling as he smoked. 'Then must I understand you to be saying, my dear sir, that my fiancée Nyura sucks?'

'What?'

'Well, now,' said Staff Captain Lambovsky, glancing round once more at his companion, 'if life is but a dream, then all women are also no more than visions in dreams. My fiancée Nyura is a woman, and therefore she is also a vision in a dream.'

'Let us assume so. What of it?'

'Was it not you who only a moment ago said that the word "suck" in the idiom "all women suck" is derived from the word "succubus". Let us assume that Nyura excites me as a woman, and is at the same time a vision in a dream – does it not inevitably follow that she also sucks? It does. And are you aware, my dear sir, of the consequences of speaking words of this kind in public?'

I looked closely at him. He was about thirty years old, he had a mousy moustache, a high forehead with a receding hairline and blue eyes; the impression of concentrated provincial demonism produced by the combination of these features was so powerful that I experienced a distinct sense of irritation.

'Now listen,' I said, imperceptibly slipping my hand into my pocket and taking hold of the handle of my Browning, 'you really are taking things too far. I have not had the honour of being acquainted with your fiancée, so I cannot possibly possess any opinions regarding her.'

'Nobody dares to make assumptions,' said the staff captain, 'from which it follows that my Nyura is a bitch. It is very sad, but I can see only one way out of the situation which has arisen.'

Fixing me with a piercing gaze, he placed his hand on his holster and slowly unbuttoned it. I was about to fire, but I remembered that the holster contained his syringe-box. It was all actually becoming rather funny.

'Did you wish to give me an injection?' I asked. 'Thank you, but I cannot tolerate morphine. In my opinion it dulls the brain.'

The staff captain jerked his hand away from the holster and glanced at his companion, a plump young man with a face that was red from the heat, who had been following our conversation closely.

'Stand back Georges,' he said, rising ponderously from the

table and drawing his sabre from its scabbard. 'I will give this gentleman his injection myself.'

God only knows what would have happened next. In another second I should probably have shot him, with all the less regret since the colour of his face clearly indicated a tendency towards apoplexy, and he could hardly have been fated to live long. But at this point something unexpected occurred.

I heard a loud shout from the direction of the door.

'Everybody stay right where they are! One movement and I shoot!'

I looked round. Standing in the doorway was a broad-shouldered man in a grey two-piece suit and a crimson Russian shirt. Strength of will was stamped on his powerful face – if it had not been spoiled by his short, receding chin, it would have looked magnificent in an antique bas-relief. His head was completely shaven, and he was holding a revolver in each hand. The two officers froze where they stood; the shaven-headed gentleman approached our table and stopped, setting his revolvers to their heads. The staff captain began blinking rapidly.

'Stand still,' said the stranger. 'Stand still . . . Easy now . . .'

Suddenly his face was distorted by a grimace of fury and he pressed the triggers twice. They clicked and misfired.

'Have you heard of Russian roulette, gentlemen?' he asked. 'Hey?'

'Yes,' answered the officer with the red complexion.

'You may regard yourselves at the present moment as playing that game, and that I am your croupier. I can inform you confidentially that the third chamber in each drum holds a live round. Please indicate whether you understand what I have said as quickly as possible.'

'How?' asked the staff captain.

'Raise your hands,' said the shaven-headed gentleman.

The officers raised their hands; the clatter of the sabre falling to the floor made me wince.

'Get out of here,' said the stranger, 'and please do not look behind you on your way. I cannot tolerate that.'

The officers gave him no reason to repeat himself – they quit the dining-hall in dignified haste, leaving behind their half-drunk glasses of champagne and a *papyrosa* smoking in the ashtray. When they had left, the stranger placed his revolvers on our table and leaned towards Anna; it seemed to me that there was something very favourable in the way she returned his gaze.

'Anna,' he said, raising her hand to his lips, 'what a great joy it is to see you here.'

'Hello, Grigory,' said Anna. 'Have you been in town long?'

'I have just this moment arrived,' he answered.

'Are those your trotters outside the window?'

'They are,' said the shaven-headed gentleman.

'And do you promise to take me for a ride?'

The gentleman smiled.

'Grigory,' said Anna, 'I love you.'

The gentleman turned to me and held out his hand. 'Grigory Kotovsky.'

'Pyotr Voyd,' I replied, shaking his hand.

'So you are Chapaev's commissar? The one who was wounded at Lozovaya? I have heard a great deal about you. I am truly glad to see you in good health.'

'He is not entirely well yet,' said Anna, casting a brief glance in my direction.

Kotovsky sat at the table.

'And what exactly happened between you and those gentlemen?'

'We had a quarrel concerning the metaphysics of dreams,' I replied.

Kotovsky chortled. 'That is what you deserve for discussing such matters in provincial restaurants. Which reminds me, did I not hear that at Lozovaya everything started from a conversation in the station buffet too?'

I shrugged.

'He remembers nothing about it,' said Anna. 'He has partial amnesia. It happens sometimes with serious concussion.'

'I hope that you will soon be fully recovered from your wound,' said Kotovsky, picking up one of the revolvers from the table. He slipped the drum out to one side, then raised and lowered the hammer several times, swore under his breath and shook his head in disbelief. I was astonished to see that there were rounds set in all the chambers of the drum.

'God damn these Tula revolvers,' he said, looking up at me. 'You can never trust them. On one occasion they got me into such a pickle . . .'

He tossed the revolver back on to the table and shook his head, as though he were driving away dark thoughts. 'How is Chapaev?'

Anna gestured with her hand.

'He drinks,' she said. 'God knows what is going on, it really is quite frightening. Yesterday he ran out into the street with his Mauser, wearing nothing but his shirt, fired three times at the sky, then thought for a moment, fired three times into the ground and went to bed.'

'Stunning, absolutely stunning,' muttered Kotovsky. 'Are you not afraid that in this state he might bring the clay machine-gun into action?'

Anna gave me a sideways glance, and I instantly felt that my presence at the table was superfluous. My companions evidently shared this feeling – the pause lasted so long that it became unbearable.

'Tell me, Pyotr, what did those gentlemen think about the metaphysics of dreams?' Kotovsky asked eventually.

'Oh, nothing significant,' I said. 'They weren't very intelligent. Excuse me, but I feel a need for some fresh air. My head has begun to ache.'

'Yes, Grigory,' said Anna, 'let us see Pyotr home, and then we can decide what to do with the evening.'

'Thank you,' I said, 'but I can manage on my own. It is not very far, and I remember the way.'

'Until later then,' said Kotovsky.

Anna did not even look at me. I had scarcely left the table before they launched into an animated conversation. On reaching the door I glanced round: Anna was laughing loudly and tapping Kotovsky's hand with her open palm, as though she was begging him to stop saying something unbearably funny.

Stepping outside I saw a light-sprung carriage with two grey trotters harnessed to it. It was obviously Kotovsky's *équipage*. I turned the corner and set off up the slope of the street along which Anna and I had so recently been walking.

It was about three o'clock in the afternoon and the heat was unbearable. I thought of how everything had changed since the moment of my awakening – there was not a trace left of my pacific mood; most unpleasant of all was the fact that I simply could not get Kotovsky's trotters out of my head. It seemed absurd that such a petty detail could have depressed me so much – or rather, I wished to regain my normal state, in which such things appeared absurd to me, but I could not. I was in fact deeply wounded.

The reason, of course, did not lie in Kotovsky and his trotters. The reason lay in Anna, in the elusive and inexpressible quality of her beauty, which from the very first moment had made me invent and ascribe to her a soul of profound and subtle feeling. I could not possibly have dreamed that an ordinary pair of trotters might be capable of rendering their owner attractive in her eyes. And yet it was so. The strangest thing of all, I thought, was that I had assumed that a woman needs something else. But what might that be – the riches of the spirit?

I laughed out loud and two chickens walking along the edge of the road fluttered away from me in fright.

Now that was interesting, I reasoned, for if I were truthful with myself, that was precisely what I had thought – that there existed in me something capable of attracting this woman and raising me in her eyes immeasurably higher than any owner of a pair of trotters. But the very comparison already involved a quite intolerable vulgarity – in accepting it I was myself reducing to the level of a pair of trotters what should in my view seem of immeasurably greater value to her. If for me these were objects of one and the same order, then why on earth should she make any distinction between them? And just what was this object which was supposed to be of immeasurably greater value to her? My inner world? The things that I think and feel? I groaned out loud in disgust at myself. It was time I stopped deceiving myself, I thought. For years now my main problem had been how to rid myself of all these thoughts and feelings and leave my so-called inner world behind me on some rubbish tip. But even if I assumed for a moment that it did have some kind of value, at least of an aesthetic kind, that did not change a thing – everything beautiful that can exist in a human being is inaccessible to others, because it is in reality inaccessible even to the person in whom it exists. How could it really be possible to fix it with the eye of introspection and say: 'There it was, it is and it will be?' Was it really possible in any sense to possess it, to say, in fact, that it belonged to anyone? How could I compare with Kotovsky's trotters something that bore no relation to myself, something which I have merely glimpsed in the finest seconds of my life? And how could I blame Anna if she refused to see in me what I have long ago ceased to see in myself? No, this was genuinely absurd – even in those rare moments of life when I have perhaps discovered this most important of things, I have felt quite clearly that it was absolutely impossible to express it. It might be that someone utters a succinct phrase as he gazes out of the window at the sunset, and no more. But what I myself say when I gaze out at sunsets and sunrises has long irritated me beyond all tolerance. My soul is not endowed with any special beauty, I thought, quite the opposite – I was seeking in Anna what had never existed in myself. All that remained of me when I saw her was an aching void which could only be filled by her presence, her voice, her face. So what could I offer her instead of a ride with Kotovsky on his trotters – myself? In other words, my hope that in intimacy with her I might discover the answer to some vague and confused question tormenting my soul? Absurd. Had I been in her position myself, I would have chosen to ride the trotters with Kotovsky.

I stopped and sat down on a worn milestone at the edge of the road. It was quite impossibly hot. I felt shattered and depressed; I could not recall when I had ever felt so disgusted with myself. The sour stench of champagne that had permeated my astrakhan hat seemed at that moment truly to symbolize the state of my spirit. I was surrounded on all sides by the indifferent torpidity of summer, somewhere there were dogs barking lazily, while the overheated machine-gun barrel of the sun was strafing the earth in a continuous, never-ending burst of fire. No sooner had this comparison come to mind than I remembered that Anna had called herself a machine-gunner. I felt tears well up in my eyes and I buried my face in my hands.

A few minutes later I got to my feet and set off up the hill again. I was feeling better; more than that, the thoughts that had just passed rapidly through my mind and seemingly crushed me had suddenly become a source of subtle pleasure. The sadness that had enveloped me was inexpressibly sweet, and I knew that in an hour's time or so I would attempt to summon it again, but it would not come.

I soon reached the manor-house. I noticed that there were several horses tethered in the courtyard that had not been there before, and that smoke was rising from the chimney of one of the outhouses. I halted at the gates. The road continued on up the hill and disappeared around a bend into dense greenery; not a single building was visible above me, and it was quite incomprehensible where it might lead to. I did not wish to encounter anyone, so I entered the courtyard and made my way furtively round the house.

'You've lost again, you idiot!' shouted a bass male voice on the first floor.

They must have been playing cards. I reached the edge of the building, turned round the corner and found myself in a back yard, which proved to be unexpectedly picturesque – several steps away from the wall the ground fell away steeply, forming a natural depression concealed beneath the shade of the trees that overhung it. A babbling brook ran through the dip and I could see the roofs of two or three outbuildings, while further off, in a small open area, there was a tall stack of hay, exactly like those depicted in the idyllic rural scenes to be found in the journal *Niva*. I felt a sudden, crazy desire to tumble in the hay, and I set off towards the stack. Then suddenly, when I was only ten paces away from it, a man with a rifle leapt out from beneath the trees and barred my way.

Standing before me was the very same Bashkir who had served us dinner in the staff car and then uncoupled the weavers' carriages from our train, but now his face was covered by a sparse black beard.

'Listen,' I said, 'we know each other, don't we? All I want to do is take a roll in the hay. I promise you not to smoke.'

The Bashkir did not react to my words in any way; his eyes gazed at me without the slightest trace of expression. I attempted to walk round him, and then he stepped backwards, raised his rifle and set the bayonet against my throat.

I turned and walked away. I must confess that there was something in the Bashkir's manner which I found genuinely frightening. When he pointed his bayonet at me he had gripped his rifle as though it were a spear, as if he had no notion that one could shoot from it, and the movement had hinted at such wild strength born of the steppe that the Browning in my pocket had seemed no more than a simple child's firecracker. But it was all surely no more than nerves. When I reached the brook I looked back, but the Bashkir was no longer anywhere to be seen. I squatted down by the water and carefully washed my astrakhan hat in it.

Suddenly I noticed that the murmuring of the brook was overlaid, like the strains of some obscure instrument, by the tones of a low, rather pleasant-sounding voice. In the building nearest to me which, judging from the chimney in its roof, had once been a bathhouse, someone was intoning:

'Calmly I walk the open field in my white shirt . . . And the storks are like the crosses on the bell towers . . .'

Something in these words moved me, and I decided to see who was singing. Wringing the water from my hat, I thrust it into my belt, walked across to the door and swung it open without knocking.

Inside there was a wide table made of freshly planed boards and two benches. On the table stood an immense bottle containing a turbid liquid, a glass and several onions. Sitting on the nearer of the benches with his back to me was a man wearing a white Russian shirt hanging loose outside his trousers.

'I beg your pardon,' I asked, 'but is that not perhaps vodka in your bottle?'

'No,' said the man, turning round as he spoke, 'this is moonshine.'

It was Chapaev.

I started in surprise. 'Vasily Ivanovich!'

'Hi there, Petka,' he answered with a broad smile. 'Back on your feet already, I see.'

I had absolutely no memory of when we had moved on to such familiar terms. Chapaev glanced at me with gentle cunning; a damp lock of hair had fallen across his forehead and his shirt was unbuttoned down to the middle of his belly. His appearance was so absolutely ordinary and so far removed from the image that I carried in my memory that I hesitated for several seconds, thinking it was a mistake.

'Siddown, Petka, siddown,' he said, nodding towards the other bench.

'I thought you were out of town, Vasily Ivanovich,' I said as I took a seat.

'I got back an hour ago,' he said, 'and came straight to the bathhouse. Just the job in this heat. But why are you asking about me, tell me about yourself. How're you feeling?'

'Fine,' I said.

'Gets up just like that, puts on his hat and goes off into town. You should stop playing the bleeding hero. What's this talk I hear about your losing your memory somewhere?'

'I have,' I said, trying not to pay any attention to his buffoonery and perverse use of uncultured language. 'But who could have told you already?'

'Why Semyon, who else? Your orderly. You really can't remember anything then, eh?'

'All I remember is getting into the train in Moscow,' I said. 'Everything after that is a blank. I cannot even recall under what circumstances you began calling me Petka.'

Chapaev stared me in the face for a minute or so with his eyes screwed up, as though he were looking straight through me.

'Yes,' he said finally, 'I see. A bad business. I reckon that you, Petka, are simply muddying the water.'

'What water?'

'Carry on muddying it if you like,' Chapaev said mysteriously, 'you're still young yet. And I began calling you Petka at Lozovaya Junction, not long before the battle.'

'I know nothing of this battle,' I said, frowning. 'I keep hearing about it all the time, but I cannot remember a single thing. It just makes my head start aching.'

'Well, if it makes your head ache, don't think about it. You wanted a drink, didn't you? So have one!'

Tipping the bottle Chapaev filled the glass to the brim and pushed it across to me.

'Many thanks,' I said ironically and drank. Despite its frightening murky sheen, the moonshine proved to be quite excellent – it must have been distilled with some kind of herbs.

'Like some onion?'

'Not at the moment. But I do not rule out the possibility that in a while I might indeed reach a state in which I am able and even eager to chew onions with my moonshine.'

'Why so down in the dumps?' asked Chapaev.

'Oh, just thoughts.'

'And what thoughts might they be?'

'Surely, Vasily Ivanovich, you cannot really be interested in what I am thinking?'

'Why not?' said Chapaev. 'Of course I am.'

'I am thinking, Vasily Ivanovich, that the love of a beautiful woman is always in reality a kind of condescension. Because it is simply impossible to be worthy of such a love.'

'You what?' said Chapaev, wrinkling up his forehead.

'Enough of this swaggering foolery,' I said, 'I am being serious.'

'Serious are you?' asked Chapaev. 'All right then, try this for size – condescension is always movement down from something to something else. Like down into this little gully here. So where does this condescension of yours go to – and from where?'

I started thinking about it. I could see what he was getting at: if I had said that I was talking about the condescension of the beautiful to the ugly and the suffering, he would immediately have asked me whether beauty is aware of itself, and whether it can remain beauty having once become conscious of itself in that capacity. To that question, which had driven me almost insane through long sleepless nights in St Petersburg, I had no answer. And if the beauty I was speaking of was a beauty unconscious of itself, then there could surely be no talk of condescension? Chapaev was very definitely far from simple.

'Let us say, Vasily Ivanovich, not the condescension of something to something else, but the act of condescension in itself. I would even call it ontological condescension.'

'And where exactly does this an-ta-logical condescension happen, then?' asked Chapaev, obviously relishing his mimicry. He took another glass from under the table.

'I am not prepared to converse in that tone.'

'Let's have another drink, then,' said Chapaev.

We drank. I stared dubiously at an onion for several seconds.

'But really,' said Chapaev, wiping his moustache, 'you tell me where it all happens.'

'If you are in a fit state to talk seriously, Vasily Ivanovich, then I will tell you.'

'Go on then, tell me.'

'It would be more correct to say that there is no condescension involved. It is simply that such love is felt as condescension.'

'And which parts is it felt in?'

'In the mind, Vasily Ivanovich, in the perception of the conscious mind,' I said sarcastically.

'Ah, in simple terms you mean here in the head, right?'

'Roughly speaking, yes.'

'And where does the love happen?'

'In the same place, Vasily Ivanovich. Roughly speaking.'

'Right,' said Chapaev in a satisfied voice. 'So you were asking about, what was it now . . . Whether love is always condescension, right?'

'Correct.'

'And it seems that love takes place inside your head, right?'

'Yes.'

'And is that condescension too?'

'So it appears, Vasily Ivanovich. What of it?'

'Tell me, Petka, how on earth you have managed to get yourself into a state where you ask me, your commanding officer, whether what happens in your head is always what happens in your head, or not always?'

'Sophistry,' I said and drank. 'Unadulterated sophistry. And anyway, I cannot understand why I continue to torment myself. I have endured all this before in St Petersburg, and the beautiful young woman in the maroon velvet dress set her empty goblet on the tablecloth in exactly the same fashion and I took my handkerchief out of my pocket in exactly the same way . . .'

Chapaev cleared his throat loudly, drowning out what I was saying. I finished in a quiet voice, not quite sure to whom I was actually speaking:

'What do I want from this girl? Am I not aware that one can never return to the past? One might skilfully reproduce all of its external circumstances, but one can never recover one's former self, never . . .'

'Oi-oi, you spin a very fine line in garbage, Petka,' Chapaev said with a laugh. 'Goblet, tablecloth.'

'What is wrong with you, Vasily Ivanovich,' I asked, restraining myself with some difficulty. 'Have you been rereading Tolstoy? Have you decided to become more simple?'

'We've no need to reread any of your Tol-stoys,' said Chapaev, chuckling again. 'But if you're pining because of our Anka, then I can tell you that every woman has to be approached in the right way. Pining away for our Anka, are you? Have I guessed right?'

His eyes had become two narrow slits of cunning. Then he suddenly struck the table with his fist.

'You answer when your divisional commander asks you a question!'

There was definitely no way I was going to be able to break through his strange mood today.

'It is of no importance,' I said. 'Vasily Ivanovich, let us have another drink.'

Chapaev laughed quietly and filled both glasses.

My memories of the hours which followed are rather vague. I got very drunk. I think we talked about soldiering – Chapaev was reminiscing about the Great War. He made it sound quite convincing: he spoke about the German cavalry, about some positions above some river, about gas attacks and mills with machine-gunners sitting in them. At one point he even became very excited and began shouting, glaring at me with gleaming eyes:

'Ah, Petka! D'you know the way I fight? You can't know anything about that! Chapaev uses only three blows, you understand me?'

I nodded mechanically, but I was listening carefully.

'The first blow is where!'

He struck the table so hard with his fist that the bottle almost toppled over.

'The second is when!'

Again he smote the boards of the table.

'And the third is who!'

In a different situation I would have appreciated this performance, but despite all his shouting and striking the table, I soon fell asleep right there on the bench; when I awoke it was already dark outside and somewhere in the distance I could hear sheep bleating.

I lifted my head from the table and surveyed the room – I felt as though I were in a cab drivers' tavern somewhere in St Petersburg. A paraffin lamp had appeared on the table. Chapaev was still sitting opposite me holding his glass, humming something to himself and staring at the wall. His eyes were almost as clouded as the moonshine in the bottle, which was already half-empty. Perhaps I should talk with him in his own manner, I thought, and thumped the table with my fist in a gesture of exaggerated familiarity.

'Tell me now, Vasily Ivanovich, straight from the heart. Are you a Red or a White?'

'Me?' asked Chapaev, shifting his gaze to me. 'You want to know?'

He picked up two onions from the table and began cleaning them. One of them he cleaned until its flesh was white, but from the other he removed only the dry outer skin, exposing the reddish-purple layer underneath.

'Look here, Petka,' he said, placing them on the table in front of him. 'There are two onions in front of you, one white, the other red.'

'Well,' I said.

'Look at the white one.'

'I am looking at it.'

'And now at the red one.'

'Yes, what of it?'

'Now look at both of them.'

'I am looking,' I said.

'So which are you, red or white?'

'Me? How do you mean?'

'When you look at the red onion, do you turn red?'

'No.'

'And when you look at the white onion, do you turn white?'

'No,' I said, 'I do not.'

'Let's proceed then,' said Chapaev. 'There are such things as topographical maps. And this table is a simplified map of consciousness. There are the Reds. And there are the Whites. But just because we're aware of Reds and Whites, do we take on any colours? And what is there in you that can take them on?'

'You are deliberately confusing things, Vasily Ivanovich. If we are not Reds and not Whites, then just who are we?'

'Petka, before you try talking about complicated questions, you should settle the simple ones. "We" is more complicated than "I", isn't it?'

'It is,' I said.

'What do you call "I"?'

'Clearly, myself.'

'Can you tell me who you are?'

'Pyotr Voyd.'

'That's your name. But who is it bears that name?'

'Well,' I said, 'one could say that I am a psychological individual. A totality of habits, experience . . . And knowledge and preferences.'

'And just whose are these habits, Petka?' Chapaev asked forcefully.

'Mine,' I shrugged.

'But you just said yourself, Petka, that you are a totality of habits. If they are your habits, does that mean that these habits belong to a totality of habits?'

'It sounds funny,' I said, 'but in essence, that is the case.'

'And what kind of habits do habits have?'

I began to feel irritated.

'This entire conversation is rather primitive. We began, after all, from the question of who I am, of what my nature is. If you have no objection, then I regard myself as . . . Well, let us say, a monad. In Leibniz's sense of the word.'

'Then just who is it who goes around regarding himself as this gonad?'

'The monad itself,' I replied, determined to maintain a grip on myself.

'Good,' said Chapaev, screwing up his eyes in a cunning fashion, 'we'll talk about "who" later. But first, my dear friend, let us deal with "where". Tell me, where's it live, this gonad of yours?'

'In my consciousness.'

'And where is your consciousness?'

'Right here,' I said, tapping myself on the head.

'And where is your head?'

'On my shoulders.'

'And where are your shoulders?'

'In a room.'

'And where is the room?'

'In a building.'

'And where is the building?'

'In Russia.'

'And where is Russia?'

'In the deepest trouble, Vasily Ivanovich.'

'Stop that,' he shouted seriously. 'You can joke when your commander orders you to. Answer.'

'Well, of course, on the Earth.'

We clinked glasses and drank.

'And where is the Earth?'

'In the Universe.'

'And where is the Universe?'

I thought for a second.

'In itself.'

'And where is this in itself?'

'In my consciousness.'

'Well then, Petka, that means your consciousness is in your consciousness, doesn't it?'

'It seems so.'

'Right,' said Chapaev, straightening his moustache. 'Now listen to me carefully. Tell me, what place is it in?'

'I do not understand, Vasily Ivanovich. The concept of place is one of the categories of consciousness, and so ... .'

140

'Where is this place? In what place is this concept of place located?'

'Well now, let us say that it is not really a place. We could call it a real . . .'

I stopped dead. Yes, I thought, that is where he is leading me. If I use the word 'reality', he will reduce everything to my own thoughts once again. And then he will ask where they are located. I will tell him they are in my head, and then . . . A good gambit. Of course, I could resort to quotations, but then, I thought in astonishment, any of the systems which I can cite either sidesteps this breach in the logic of thought or plugs it with a couple of dubious Latinisms. Yes, Chapaev was very far indeed from being simple. Of course, there is always the foolproof method of concluding any argument by pigeon-holing your opponent – nothing could be easier than to de-clare that everything he is trying to demonstrate is already well known under such-and-such a name, and human thought has advanced a long way since then. But I felt ashamed to behave like some self-satisfied evening-class stu-dent who has leafed ahead through a few pages of the philos-ophy textbook during breaks. And had not I myself only recently told some St Petersburg philosopher, who had launched into a drunken discussion of the Greek roots of Russian communism, that philosophy would be better called sophisilly?

Chapaev laughed.

'And just where can human thought advance to?' he asked.

'Eh?' I asked in confusion.

'Advance from what? Where to?'

I decided that in my absent-mindedness I must have spo-ken out loud.

'Vasily Ivanovich, let us talk about all that when we are sober. I am no philosopher. Let us have a drink instead.'

'If you were a philosopher,' said Chapaev, 'I wouldn't trust you with anything more important than mucking out the sta-bles. But you command one of my squadrons. At Lozovaya you understood everything just fine. What's happening to you? Too afraid, are you? Or maybe too happy?'

'I do not remember anything,' I said, once again experiencing that strange tension in all my nerves. 'I do not remember.'

'Ah, Petka,' Chapaev sighed, filling the glasses with moonshine. 'I just don't know what to make of you. Understand yourself first of all.'

We drank. Mechanically I reached for an onion and bit out a large chunk.

'Perhaps we should go for a breath of air before bed?' asked Chapaev, lighting up a *papyrosa*.

'We could,' I replied, replacing the onion on the table.

There had obviously been a brief shower of rain while I was sleeping and the slope of the gully that rose towards the manor-house was damp and slippery. I discovered that I was absolutely drunk – having almost reached the top, I slipped and tumbled back down into the wet grass. My head was flung back on my neck and I saw above me the sky full of stars. It was so beautiful that for several seconds I simply lay there in silence, staring upwards. Chapaev gave me his hand and helped me to my feet. Once we had scrambled out on to level ground, I looked up again and was suddenly struck by the thought that it must have been ages since I had last seen the starry sky, although it had been there all the time right above my head, and all I had to do was look up. I laughed.

'What's up?' asked Chapaev.

'Nothing special,' I said and pointed up at the sky. 'The sky is beautiful.'

Chapaev looked upwards, swaying on his feet.

'Beautiful?' he queried thoughtfully. 'What is beauty?'

'Come now,' I said. 'What do you mean? Beauty is the most perfect objectivization of the will at the highest possible level of its cognizability.'

Chapaev looked at the sky for another few seconds and then transferred his gaze to a large puddle which lay at our feet and spat the stub of his *papyrosa* into it. The Universe reflected in the smooth surface of the water suffered a momentary cataclysm as all its constellations shuddered and were transformed into a twinkling blur.

'What I've always found astounding,' he said, 'is the starry sky beneath our feet and the Immanuel Kant within us.'

'I find it quite incomprehensible, Vasily Ivanovich, how a man who confuses Kant with Schopenhauer could have been given the command of a division.'

Chapaev looked at me with dull eyes and opened his mouth to say something, but at this point we heard a clatter of wheels and the whinnying of horses. Someone was driving up to the house.

'It is probably Kotovsky and Anna,' I said. 'It would seem, Vasily Ivanovich, that your machine-gunner has a penchant for strong personalities in Russian shirts.'

'So Kotovsky's in town, is he? Why didn't you say so?'

He turned and walked quickly away, completely forgetting about me. I plodded slowly after him as far as the corner of the house and then stopped. The carriage stood by the porch, while Kotovsky himself was in the act of assisting Anna out of it. When he saw Chapaev approaching, Kotovsky saluted and went to meet him and they embraced. This was followed by a series of exclamations and slaps of the kind that occur at every meeting between two men who both wish to demonstrate how well they are able to keep their spirits up as they wander through the shifting sands of life. They wandered in the direction of the house, while Anna remained beside the carriage. Acting on a sudden impulse I set off towards her – on the way I almost fell again when I stumbled over an empty shell crate, and I had a brief presentiment that I would regret my impetuousness.

'Anna, please! Do not go!'

She stopped and turned her head towards me. My God, how beautiful she was at that moment!

'Anna,' I blurted out, for some reason pressing my hands to my breast as I spoke, 'please believe me when I say . . . How badly I feel just thinking about my behaviour in the restaurant. But you must admit that you did give me cause. I understand that this unremittingly self-assertive suffragism is not the real you at all, it is nothing more than conformity to a certain aesthetic formula, and that is merely the result . . .'

She suddenly pushed me away.

'Get away from me, Pyotr, for God's sake,' she said with a

frown. 'You smell of onions. I'm willing to forgive you everything, but not that.'

I turned and rushed into the house. My face was burning so hotly that one could probably have lit a cigarette on it, and all the way to my room – I have no idea how I managed to find it in the darkness – I roundly cursed Chapaev with his moonshine and his onions. I flung myself on to the bed and fell into a state close to coma, no doubt similar to the state from which I had emerged that morning.

After a while somebody knocked.

'Petka!' called Chapaev's voice. 'Where are you?'

'Nowhere!' I mumbled in reply.

'Now then!' Chapaev roared unexpectedly. 'That's my lad! Tomorrow I'll thank you formally in front of the ranks. You understand everything so well! So what were you up to, acting the fool all evening?'

'How am I to understand you?'

'You work it out for yourself. What can you see in front of you right now?'

'A pillow,' I answered, 'but not very clearly. And please do not explain to me yet again that it is located in my consciousness.'

'Everything that we see is located in our consciousness, Petka. Which means we can't say that our consciousness is located anywhere. We're nowhere for the simple reason that there is no place in which we can be said to be located. That's why we're nowhere. D'you remember now?'

'Chapaev,' I said, 'I would like to be alone for a while.'

'Whatever you say. Report to me in the morning, fresh as a cucumber. We advance at noon.'

He retreated along the corridor over the squeaking floorboards. For a while I pondered over what he had said – at first over this 'nowhere', and then over the inexplicable advance that he had set for noon the next day. Of course, I could have left my room and explained to him that it was impossible for me to advance because I was 'nowhere', but I did not want to do that – I was overwhelmed by a terrible desire to sleep, and everything had begun to seem boring and unimportant. I fell asleep and dreamed of Anna's fingers caressing the ribbed barrel of a machine-gun. I was awakened by another knock at the door.

'Chapaev! I asked you to leave me alone! Let me get some rest before battle!'

'It's not Chapaev,' said a voice outside the door. 'It's Kotovsky.'

I half sat up in my bed. 'What do you want?'

'I must talk to you.'

I took my pistol out of my pocket and laid it on the bed, covering it with the blanket. God alone knew what he could want. I had a presentiment that it was somehow connected with Anna.

'Come in then.'

The door opened and Kotovsky entered. He looked quite different from when I had seen him during the day – now he was wearing a dressing-gown with tassels, from beneath which protruded the striped legs of a pair of pyjama trousers. In one hand he held a candlestick with three lighted candles, and in the other he had a bottle of champagne and two glasses – when I spotted the champagne my guess that Anna had complained to him about me became a near certainty.

'Have a seat.' I pointed to the armchair.

Setting the champagne and the candlestick on the table, he sat down.

'May I smoke here?'

'By all means.'

When he had lit his cigarette, Kotovsky made a strange gesture – he ran his open hand across his bald head, as though he were pushing back an invisible lock of hair that had fallen across his forehead. I realized that I had seen the movement somewhere before, and immediately remembered where – on our first meeting, in the armoured train, Anna had smoothed down her non-existent locks in almost exactly the same way. The idea flitted through my mind that they must be members of some strange sect headed by Chapaev, and these shaven heads were connected with their rituals, but a moment later I realized that we were all members of this sect – all of us, that is, who had been obliged to suffer the consequences of Russia's latest attack of freedom and the lice that inevitably accompanied it. I laughed.

'What are you laughing at?' Kotovsky asked, raising an eyebrow.

'I was thinking about how we live nowadays. We shave our heads in order not to catch lice. Who could have imagined it five years ago? It really is incredible.'

'Remarkable,' said Kotovsky, 'I was thinking about just the same thing – about what is happening to Russia. That's why I came to see you. On a kind of impulse. I wanted to talk.'

'About Russia?'

'Precisely,' he said.

'What is there to say?' I said. 'Everything is abundantly clear.'

'No, what I meant was – who is to blame?'

'I do not know,' I said, 'what do you think?'

'The intelligentsia. Who else?'

He held out a full glass towards me.

'Every member of the intelligentsia,' he continued, his face showing a dark grimace, 'especially in Russia, where he can only survive if someone else supports him, possesses one revoltingly infantile character trait. He is never afraid to attack that which subconsciously he feels to be right and lawful. Like a child who is not afraid to do his parents harm, because he knows that they may put him in the corner, but they won't throw him out. He is more afraid of strangers. And it's the same with this vile class.'

'I do not quite follow you.'

'No matter how much the intelligentsia may like to deride the basic principles of the empire from which it has sprung, it knows perfectly well that within that empire the moral law retained its vital strength.'

'How? How does it know?'

'From the fact that if the moral law were dead, the intelligentsia would never have dared to trample the cornerstones of the empire under foot. Just recently I was rereading Dostoevsky – do you know what I thought?'

I felt one side of my face twitch.

'What?' I asked.

'Good is by its very nature all-forgiving. Just think, all of these butchers who are so busy killing people nowadays used to be exiled to villages in Siberia, where they spent days at a time hunting hares and hazel-hens. No, the intelligentsia is not afraid of sacrilege. There's only one thing it is afraid of – dealing with the question of evil and its roots, because it understands, and quite rightly, that here it could get shafted with a telegraph pole.'

'A powerful image.'

'Toying with evil is enjoyable,' Kotovsky continued passionately. 'There's no risk whatsoever and the advantages are obvious. That's why there's such a vast army of villainous volunteers who deliberately confuse top with bottom and right with left, don't you see? All of these calculating pimps of the spirit, these emaciated Bolsheviks, these needle-punctured liberals, these cocaine-soaked social-revolutionaries, all these . . .'

'I understand.'

Kotovsky took a sip of champagne.

'By the way, Pyotr,' he said casually, 'while we're on the subject, I heard you have some cocaine.'

'Yes,' I said, 'I do. Now that the subject has come up anyway.'

I reached into my travelling bag, took out the tin and put it on the table.

'Please help yourself.'

Kotovsky needed no further persuasion. The white tracks he sprinkled on the surface of the table looked like two major highways under construction. He went through all the requisite manipulations and leaned back in his armchair. After waiting a minute or so, I asked out of politeness:

'And do you often think about Russia in that manner?'

'When I lived in Odessa, I thought about her at least three times a day,' he said in a dull voice. 'It was giving me nosebleeds. Then I gave it up. I didn't want to become dependent on anything.'

'And what happened now? Was it Dostoevsky who tempted you?'

'Oh no,' he said. 'A certain inner drama.'

I suddenly had an unexpected idea.

'Tell me, Grigory, are you very fond of your trotters?'

'Why?' he asked.

'We could swap. Half of this tin for your carriage.'

Kotovsky gave a me a sharp glance, then he picked up the tin from the table, looked into it and said:

'You really know how to tempt a man. Why would you want my trotters?'

'To go driving. Why else?'

'Very well,' said Kotovsky, 'I agree. As it happens, I have a set of chemical scales in my luggage . . .'

'Measure it by eye,' I said, 'I came by it very easily.'

Extracting a silver cigarette case from the pocket of his dressing-gown, he emptied out the *papyrosas* from it and then took out a penknife and used its blade to transfer part of the powder to the case.

'Won't it spill?' I asked.

'Don't worry, I got this cigarette case in Odessa. It's special. The trotters are yours.'

'Thank you.'

'Shall we drink to our deal?'

'Gladly,' I said, raising my glass.

Kotovsky drained his champagne, put the cigarette case in his pocket and picked up the candlestick.

'Well, thank you for the conversation. Please forgive me, I beg you, for intruding during the night.'

'Good night to you. Would you permit me to ask you one question? Since you have already mentioned it yourself – what is the inner drama which is eased so well by cocaine?'

'In the face of the drama of Russia it dwindles to nothing,' said Kotovsky. He nodded curtly in military fashion and left the room.

I tried for some time to get to sleep, but was unsuccessful. At first I thought about Kotovsky – I must admit that he had made a rather pleasant impression on me, there was a sense of style to him. Then my thoughts turned back to Chapaev. I began thinking about his 'nowhere' and our conversation. At first glance it seemed far from complicated: he had asked me to answer the question, whether I exist because of the world, or the world exists because of me. Of course, it all amounted to nothing more than banal dialectics, but there was a rather frightening aspect to it, which he had pointed out in a masterly fashion with his questions, at first sight so idiotic, about the place where it all happens. If the entire world exists within me, then where do I exist? And if I exist within this world, then where, in what place in the world, is my consciousness located? One might say, I thought, that on the one hand the world exists in me and on the other I exist in the world, and these are simply the poles of a single semantic magnet, but the tricky thing was that there was no peg on which to hang this magnet, this dialectical dyad.

There was nowhere for it to exist!

Because its existence required an individual in whose consciousness it could come into being. And that individual had nowhere to exist, because any 'where' could only arise in a consciousness for which there was simply no place other than one created by itself . . . But then where was it before it created this place for itself? If within itself, then where?

I suddenly felt afraid of being alone. Throwing my military jacket over my shoulders, I went out into the corridor, saw the blue radiance of the moon shining through the window on to the staircase and descended to the hallway.

The horseless carriage was standing near the door. I walked round it a couple of times, admiring its clean lines – the moonlight seemed to lend it additional charm. A horse snorted somewhere close to me. I turned round and saw Chapaev standing with a curry-comb in his hand, brushing the animal's mane. I walked over and stood beside him; he looked at me. I wonder, I thought, what he will say if I ask him where this 'nowhere' of his is located. He will have to define the word in terms of itself, and will find his position in the conversation no better than my own.

'Can't sleep?' asked Chapaev.

'Yes,' I said. 'Something is bothering me.'

'What is it, never seen the void before?'

I realized that by the word 'void' he meant precisely the 'nowhere' which I had become aware of only a few minutes earlier.

'No,' I answered. 'Never.'

'Then just what have you been seeing, Petka?' Chapaev asked gently.

'Let's change the subject,' I said. 'Where are my trotters?'

'In the stable,' said Chapaev. 'And just how long have they been yours and not Kotovsky's?'

'About a quarter of an hour now.'

Chapaev laughed.

'You be careful with Grigory,' he said. 'He's not as straight-forward as he seems.'

'I have already realized that,' I replied. 'You know, Vasily Ivanovich, I just cannot get your words out of my head. You certainly know how to drive a person into a corner.'

'That's right,' said Chapaev, forcing the curry-comb through the tangles of horsehair, 'I do. And then I give them a good burst from the machine-gun . . .'

'But I think,' I said, 'that I can do it too.'

'Try it.'

'Very well,' I said. 'I shall also ask a sequence of questions about place.'

'Ask away, ask away,' muttered Chapaev.

'Let us start at the beginning. There you stand combing a horse. But where is this horse?'

Chapaev looked at me in amazement. 'Petka, have you gone completely off your chump?'

'I beg your pardon?'

'It's right here in front of your face.'

I said nothing for several seconds. I had not been prepared for such a turn of events. Chapaev shook his head doubtfully.

'You know, Petka,' he said, 'I reckon you'd better get off to bed.'

I smiled stupidly and wandered back towards the house. Somehow managing to reach my bed, I collapsed on to it and began tumbling down into the next nightmare; I had sensed its inevitable onset as I was still climbing the stairs.

I did not have to wait for long. I began dreaming of a blue-eyed, blond-haired man tethered with loops to a strange-look-ing seat like a dentist's chair. In the dream I knew for certain that his name was Serdyuk, and that what was happening to him now was soon going to happen to me. Coloured wires connected Serdyuk's arms to a menacing-looking dynamo-like machine standing on the floor; I was sufficiently conscious to guess that this mechanism had been added to the picture by my own mind. The handle of the machine was being turned by two men in white coats who were leaning over it. At first they turned the handle slowly, and the man in the armchair merely trembled and bit his lip, but gradually their movements grew faster, and one after another huge shuddering movements began sweeping in waves through the bound man's body. At last he could no longer restrain himself from crying out.

'Stop it!' he said.

But his tormentors only worked even faster.

'Stop the dynamo,' he roared as loudly as he could, 'turn off the dynamo! The dynamo! The dynamo! The DY-NA-MO!!!'

6

'Next station – "Dynamo".'

The voice from the loudspeaker brought Serdyuk to attention.

The passenger sitting opposite, a weird-looking type with a round, pockmarked face, dressed in a dirty padded kaftan and a turban streaked with splashes of green paint, caught Serdyuk's senseless glance, touched two fingers to his turban and said loudly:

'Heil Hitler!'

'Hitler heil,' Serdyuk replied politely and turned his gaze away.

He couldn't figure out who the man was or what he was doing riding in the metro, when an ugly mug like that should have been driving around in at least a BMW.

Serdyuk sighed, squinted down to his right and began reading the book which lay open on the knees of his neighbour. It was a thin, tattered brochure wrapped in newsprint, on which the words 'Japanese Militarism' had been scrawled in ballpoint pen. The brochure was obviously some kind of semi-secret Soviet textbook: the paper was yellow with age and the typeface was peculiar, with a text made up of large numbers of Japanese words set in italics.

'The concept of social duty,' read Serdyuk, 'is interwoven for the Japanese with a sense of natural human duty in a way that generates the emotional energy of high drama. This duty is expressed in the concepts *on* and *giri* (derived from the hieroglyphs meaning "to prick" and "to weigh down" respectively) which are still very far from being historical curiosities. *On* is the "debt of gratitude" owed by a child to its parents, a vassal to his suzerain, a citizen to the state. *Giri* is "obligation and responsibility", and requires that each individual act in accordance with his station and position in society. It is also obligation in relation to one's own self, the preservation of the honour and dignity of one's own person, of one's name. Duty consists in being prepared to sacrifice oneself in the name of *on* and *giri*, which define a specific code of social, professional and human behaviour.'

His neighbour apparently noticed that Serdyuk was reading his book, and he lifted it closer to his face, half-closing it for good measure, so that the text was completely hidden. Serdyuk closed his eyes.

That's why they're able to live like normal human beings, he thought, because they never forget about their duty. Don't spend all their time getting pissed like folks here.

It's not really possible to say what exactly went on in his head over the next few minutes, but when the train stopped at Pushkinskaya station and Serdyuk emerged from the carriage his own soul had become filled with the fixed desire to have a drink – in fact, to take an entire skinful of something. Initially this desire remained formless and unrecognized, acknowledged merely as a vague melancholy relating to something unattainable and seemingly lost for ever, and it only assumed its true form when Serdyuk found himself face to face with a long rank of armour-plated kiosks, from inside which identical pairs of Caucasian eyes surveyed enemy territory through narrow observation slits.

Deciding on what exactly he wanted proved more difficult. There was a very wide, but fairly second-rate selection – more like an election than a piss-up, he thought. Serdyuk hesitated for a long time, until he finally spotted a bottle of port wine bearing the name 'Livadia' in one of the glass windows.

Serdyuk's very first glance at the bottle brought back clear memories of a certain forgotten morning in his youth; a secluded corner in the yard of the institute where he studied, stacked high with crates, the sun on the yellow leaves and a group of laughing students all from the same year, handing round a bottle of that same port wine (with a slightly different label, it was true – in those days they hadn't started putting dots on the Russian 'i's yet). Serdyuk also recalled that to reach that secluded spot, secure against observation from all sides, you had to slip through between some rusty railings, usually messing up your jacket in the process. But the most important thing in all of this wasn't the port wine or the railings, it was the fleeting reminiscence that triggered a pang of sadness in his heart – the memory of all the limitless opportunities and endless highways there used to be in the world that stretched away from that corner of the yard.

This memory was followed rapidly by the absolutely unbearable thought that the world itself had not changed at all since those old days, it was just that he couldn't see it any more with the same eyes as he had then: he could no longer squeeze through those railings, and there was nowhere left to squeeze into either – that little patch of emptiness behind the railings had long since been completely paved over with zinc-plated coffins of experience.

But if he couldn't view the world through those same eyes any more, he could at least try for a glimpse of it through the same glass, darkly. Thrusting his money in through the embrasure of the kiosk, Serdyuk scooped up the green grenade that popped out through the same opening. He crossed the street, picked his way carefully between the puddles that reflected the sky of a late spring afternoon, sat down on a bench opposite the green figure of Pushkin and pulled the plastic stopper out of the bottle with his teeth. The port wine still tasted exactly the same as it had always done – one more proof that reform had not really touched the basic foundations of Russian life, but merely swept like a hurricane across its surface.

Serdyuk polished off the bottle in a few long gulps, then carefully tossed it into the bushes behind the low granite kerb; an intelligent-looking old woman who had been pretending to read a newspaper went after it straight away. Serdyuk slumped back against the bench.

Intoxication is by its nature faceless and cosmopolitan. The high that hit him a few minutes later had nothing in common with the promise implied by the bottle's label with its cypresses, antique arches and brilliant stars in a dark-blue sky. There was nothing in it to indicate that the port wine actually came from the left bank of the Crimea, and the suspicion even flashed through his mind that if it had come from the right bank, or even from Moldavia, the world around him would still have changed in the same fashion.

The world was changed all right, and quite noticeably – it stopped feeling hostile, and the people walking past him were gradually transformed from devoted disciples of global evil into its victims, although they themselves had no inkling that was what they were. After another minute or two something happened to global evil itself – it either disappeared or simply stopped being important. The intoxication mounted to its blissful zenith, lingered for a few brief seconds at the highest point, and then the usual ballast of drunken thoughts dragged him back down into reality.

Three schoolboys walked past Serdyuk and he heard their breaking voices repeating the words 'you gotta problem?' with forceful enthusiasm. Their backs receded in the direction of an amphibious Japanese Jeep parked at the edge of the pavement with a big hoist on the front of its snout. Jutting up directly above the Jeep on the other side of Tverskaya Street he could see the McDonald's sign, looking like the yellow merlon of some invisible fortress wall. Somehow it all left Serdyuk in no doubt as to what the future held for them.

His thoughts moved back to the book he had read in the metro. 'The Japanese,' Serdyuk thought, 'now there's a great nation! Just think – they've had two atom bombs dropped on them, they've had their islands taken away, but they've survived . . . Why is it nobody here can see anything but America? What the hell good is America to us? It's Japan we should be following – we're neighbours, aren't we? It's the will of God. And they need to be friends with us too – between the two of us we'd polish off your America soon enough . . . with its atom bombs and asset managers . . .'

In some imperceptible fashion, these thoughts developed into a decision to go for another bottle. Serdyuk thought for a while about what to buy. He didn't fancy any more port wine. The right thing to follow the playful left-bank adagio seemed like a long calm andante – he wanted something simple and straightforward with no boundaries to it, like the sea in the TV programme *Travellers' Club*, or the field of wheat on the share certificate he'd received in exchange for his privatization voucher. After a few minutes' thought, Serdyuk decided to get some Dutch spirit.

Going back to the same bench, he opened the bottle, poured out half a plastic cupful, drank it, then gulped at the air with his scorched mouth as he tore open the newspaper wrapped around the hamburger he'd bought to go with his drink. His eyes encountered a strange symbol, a red flower with asymmetrical petals set inside an oval. There was a notice below the emblem:

'The Moscow branch of the Japanese firm Taira Incorporated is interviewing potential employees. Knowledge of English and computer skills essential.'

Serdyuk cocked his head sideways. For a second he thought he'd seen a second notice printed beside the first one, decorated with a similar emblem, but when he took a closer look at the sheet of newspaper, he realized that there really were two ovals – right beside the flower inside its oval border there was a ring of onion, a wedge of dead grey flesh protruding from under the crust of bread and a bloody streak of ketchup. Serdyuk noted with satisfaction that the various levels of reality were beginning to merge into each other, carefully tore the notice out of the newspaper, licked a drop of ketchup off it, folded it in two and stuck it in his pocket.

Everything after that went as usual.

He was woken by a sick feeling and the grey light of morning. The major irritant, of course, was the light – as always, it seemed to have been mixed with chlorine in order to disinfect it. Looking around, Serdyuk realized he was at home, and apparently he'd had visitors the evening before – just who, he couldn't remember. He struggled up from the floor, took off his mud-streaked jacket and cap, went out into the corridor and hung them on a hook. Then he was visited by the comforting thought that there might be some beer in the fridge – that had happened several times before in his life. But when he was only a few feet from the fridge the phone on the wall began to ring. Serdyuk took the receiver off the hook and tried to say 'hello', but the very effort of speaking was so painful that instead he gave out a croak that sounded something like 'Oh-aye-aye'.

'*Okhae dzeimas*,' the receiver echoed cheerfully. 'Mr Serdyuk?'

'Yes,' said Serdyuk.

'Hello. My name is Oda Nobunaga and I had a conversation with you yesterday evening. More precisely, last night. You were kind enough to give me a call.'

'Yes,' said Serdyuk, clutching at his head with his free hand.

'I have discussed your proposal with Mr Esitsune Kawabata, and he is prepared to receive you today at three o'clock for purposes of an interview.'

Serdyuk didn't recognize the voice in the receiver. He could tell straight away it was that of a foreigner – although he couldn't hear any accent, the person talking to him made pauses, as though he were running through his vocabulary in search of the right word.

'Much obliged,' said Serdyuk. 'But what proposal's that?'

'The one you made yesterday. Or today, to be precise.'

'Aha!' said Serdyuk. 'A-a-ha!'

'Write down the address,' said Oda Nobunaga.

'Hang on,' said Serdyuk, 'just a moment. I'll get a pen.'

'But why do you not have a notepad and a pen by the telephone?' Nobunaga asked with obvious irritation in his voice. 'A man of business should do so.'

'I'm writing now.'

'Nagornaya metro station, the exit on the right. There will be an iron fence facing you and a house, with an entrance to the yard. The precise address is Pyatikhlebny Lane, house number five. There will be a . . . What is it now . . . A plaque.'

'Thank you.'

'That is all from me. *Sayonara*, as they say,' said Nobunaga and hung up.

There was no beer in the fridge.

Emerging on to the surface of the earth from Nagornaya metro station long before the appointed time, Serdyuk immediately saw a fence covered with battered and peeling tin-plate, but he didn't believe it could be the same one mentioned by Mr Nobunaga – this fence was somehow too plain and too dirty. He walked around the area for a while, stopping the rare passers-by and asking where Pyatikhlebny Lane was. This was something nobody seemed to know, however, or perhaps they simply didn't want to tell him – most of the people Serdyuk found to ask were old women in dark clothes plodding slowly on their way to some mysterious destination.

It was a wild place, like the remnants of some industrial region bombed to smithereens in the distant past and now overgrown with wild grass, through which, here and there, pieces of rusty iron protruded. There was plenty of open space and sky, and he could see dark strips of forest on the horizon. But despite these banal commonplaces, this region was very unusual: if he looked to the west, where the green fence was, he saw a normal panoramic cityscape, but if he turned his gaze to the east, his field of view was entirely filled with a vast stretch of emptiness, with a few street lamps towering above it like gallows trees. It was as though Serdyuk had found his way precisely to the secret border between post-industrial Russia and primordial Rus.

It was not one of the areas where serious foreign companies opened their offices, and Serdyuk decided this must be some two-bit firm staffed by Japanese who had failed to adjust fully to the demands of the changing world (for some reason he thought of the peasants from the film *The Seven Samurai*). It was clear now why they'd taken such an interest in his drunken phone call, and Serdyuk even felt a surge of sympathy and warm fellow-feeling for these slightly dull-witted foreigners who, just like himself, had not been able to find themselves a comfortable niche in life – and now, of course, the doubt that had been nagging at him all the way there, the idea that he really should have had a shave, quite simply disappeared.

Mr Nobunaga's direction that 'there will be a house' could have applied to several dozen buildings in his field of view. Serdyuk decided for no particular reason that the one he was looking for was a grey eight-storey building with a glass-fronted delicatessen on the ground floor. Remarkably enough, after he had spent about three minutes walking around the yard behind the building, he spotted a brass oblong on the wall with the inscription 'TAIRA TRADING HOUSE' and a tiny bell-push, at first glance invisible against the uneven surface of the wall. About a yard away from the plaque there was a crude iron door hanging on immense hinges, painted with green paint. Serdyuk looked around in consternation – apart from the door, the only other thing the plaque could possibly relate to was a cast-iron manhole cover in the asphalt. Serdyuk waited until his watch showed two minutes to three and rang the bell.

The door opened immediately. Standing behind it was the inevitable hulk in camouflage gear, holding a rubber truncheon. Serdyuk nodded to him and opened his mouth in order to explain the reason for his visit – but then his jaw dropped.

Beyond the door there was a small hallway with a desk, a telephone and a chair, and on the wall of this hallway there was a large mural, showing a corridor extending into infinity. But on looking more closely at the mural, Serdyuk realized it wasn't a mural at all, it was a genuine corridor, which began on the other side of a glass door. This corridor was very strange: there were lanterns hanging on its walls – he could actually see flickering flames through their thin rice-paper shades – and scattered over the floor was a thick layer of yellow sand, across the surface of which narrow mats made of slivers of split bamboo lay side by side to form a kind of carpet-runner. The same emblem that he had seen in the newspaper was drawn in bright red paint on the lanterns – a flower with four diamond-shaped petals (the side petals were longer than the others), enclosed in an oval. The corridor did not actually run off into infinity, as he'd thought at first, it simply curved smoothly to the right (it was the first time Serdyuk had seen that kind of layout in a building in Moscow), and its far end was hidden from sight.

'What'yer want?' said the security guard, breaking the silence.

'I've a meeting with Mr Kawabata,' said Serdyuk, pulling himself together, 'at three o'clock.'

'Ah. Come inside then, quick. They don't like it when the door's left open for long.'

Serdyuk stepped inside and the guard closed the door and locked it with something that looked like a massive valve-wheel.

'Take your shoes off, please,' he said. 'The *geta* are over there.'

'The what?' asked Serdyuk.

'The *geta*. What they use for slippers. They don't wear any other shoes inside. That's a strict rule.'

Serdyuk saw several pairs of wooden shoes lying on the floor.

They looked very clumsy and uncomfortable, something like tall shoe-stretchers with a strap made out of a split string, and you could only put the shoe-stretchers on your bare feet, because the strap had to be inserted between the big toe and the second toe. Just for a second he thought the security guard was joking, but then he noticed several pairs of shiny black shoes with socks protruding from them standing in the corner. He sat down on a low bench and began removing his own shoes. When the procedure was complete, he stood up and noticed that the *geta* had made him three or four inches taller.

'Can I go in now?' he asked.

'Go ahead. Take a lantern and go straight down the corridor. Room number three.'

'Why the lantern?' Serdyuk asked in amazement.

'That's the rule here,' said the security guard, taking one of the lanterns down from the wall and holding it out to Serdyuk, 'you don't wear a tie to keep you warm, do you?'

Serdyuk, who had knotted a tie round his neck that morning for the first time in many years, found this argument quite convincing. At the same time he felt a desire to take a look inside the lantern to see whether there was a real flame in there or not.

'Room number three,' repeated the security guard, 'but the numbers are in Japanese. It's the one with three strokes one above the other. You know, like the trigram for "sky".'

'Aha,' said Serdyuk, 'I'm with you.'

'And whatever you do, don't knock. Just let them know you're outside – try clearing your throat, or say a few words. Then wait for them to tell you what to do.'

Serdyuk set off, lifting his feet high in the air like a stork and clutching the lantern at arm's length. Walking was very awkward, the shoe-stretchers squeaked indignantly under his feet and Serdyuk blushed at the thought of the security guard laughing to himself as he watched. Around the smooth bend he found a small dimly lit hall with black beams running across the ceiling. At first Serdyuk couldn't see any doors there, but then he realized the tall wall panels were doors that moved sideways. There was a sheet of paper hanging on one of the panels. Serdyuk held his lantern close to it and when he saw the three lines drawn in black ink, he knew this must be room number three.

There was music playing quietly behind the door. It was some obscure string instrument: the timbre of the sound was unusual, and the slow melody, built upon strange and – as it seemed to Serdyuk – ancient harmonies, was sad and plaintive. Serdyuk cleared his throat. There was no response from beyond the wall. He cleared his throat again, louder this time and thought that if he had to do it again he would probably puke.

'Come in,' said a voice behind the door.

Serdyuk slid the partition to the left and saw a room with its floor carpeted with simple dark bamboo mats. Sitting on a number of coloured cushions scattered in the corner with his legs folded under him was a barefooted man in a dark suit. He was playing a strange instrument that looked like a long lute with a small sound-box, and he took absolutely no notice of Serdyuk's appearance. His face could hardly have been called mongoloid, though you could say there was something southern about it – Serdyuk's thoughts on this point followed a highly specific route as he recalled a trip he'd made to Rostov-on-Don the year before. Standing on the floor of the room was a small electric cooker with a single ring, supporting a voluminous saucepan, and a black, streamlined fax machine, with a lead that disappeared into a hole in the wall. Serdyuk went in, put down his lantern on the floor and closed the door behind him.

The man in the suit gave a final touch to a string and raised his puffy, red eyes in a gesture of farewell to the note as it departed this world for ever, before carefully laying his instrument on the floor. His movements were very slow and economical, as though he were afraid a clumsy or abrupt gesture might offend someone who was present in the room but invisible to Serdyuk. Taking a handkerchief from the breast pocket of his jacket he wiped away the tears from his eyes and turned towards his visitor. They looked at each other for a while.

'Hello. My name is Serdyuk.'

'Kawabata,' said the man.

He sprang to his feet, walked briskly over to Serdyuk and took him by the hand. His palm was cold and dry.

'Please,' he said, literally dragging Serdyuk over to the scattered cushions, 'sit down. Please, sit down.'

Serdyuk sat down.

'I . . .' he began, but Kawabata interrupted him:

'I don't want to hear a word. In Japan we have a tradition, a very ancient tradition which is still alive to this day, which says that if a person enters your house with a lantern in his hand and *geta* on his feet, it means that it is dark outside and the weather is bad, and the very first thing you must do is pour him some warm sake.'

With these words Kawabata fished a fat bottle with a short neck out of the saucepan. It was sealed with a watertight stopper and there was a long thread tied to its neck, which Kawabata used to extract it. Two small porcelain glasses with indecent drawings on them appeared – they depicted beautiful women with unnaturally high arched eyebrows giving themselves in intricately contrived poses to serious-looking men wearing small blue caps. Kawabata filled the glasses to the brim.

'Please,' he said, and held out one of the glasses to Serdyuk.

Serdyuk tipped the contents into his mouth. The liquid reminded him most of all of vodka diluted with rice water. Worse still, it was hot – perhaps that was the reason why he puked straight on to the floor mats as soon as he swallowed it. The feeling of shame and self-loathing that overwhelmed him was so powerful that he just covered his face with his hands.

'Oh,' said Kawabata politely, 'there must be a real storm outside.'

He clapped his hands.

Serdyuk half-opened his eyes. Two girls had appeared in the room, dressed in a manner very similar to the women shown on the glasses. They even had the same high eyebrows – Serdyuk took a closer look and realized they were drawn on their foreheads with ink. In short, the resemblance was so complete that Serdyuk's thoughts were only restrained from running riot by the shame he had felt a few seconds earlier. The girls quickly rolled up the soiled mats, laid out fresh ones in their place and left the room – not by the door that Serdyuk had used to enter, but by another; apparently there was another wall panel that moved sideways.

'Please,' said Kawabata.

Serdyuk raised his eyes. The Japanese was holding out another glass of sake, Serdyuk gave a pitiful smile and shrugged.

'This time,' said Kawabata, 'everything will be fine.'

Serdyuk drank it. And this time the effect really was quite different – the sake went down very smoothly and a healing warmth spread through his body.

'You know what the trouble is,' he said, 'yesterday . . .'

'First another one,' said Kawabata.

The fax machine on the floor jangled and a sheet of paper thickly covered with hieroglyphics came slithering out of it. Kawabata waited for the paper to stop moving, then tore the sheet out of the machine and became engrossed in studying it, completely forgetting about Serdyuk.

Serdyuk examined his surroundings. The walls of the room were covered with identical wooden panels, and now that the sake had neutralized the consequences of yesterday's bout of nostalgia, each of them had assumed the appearance of a door leading into the unknown. But then one of the panels, which had a printed engraving hanging on it, was quite clearly not a door.

Like everything else in Mr Kawabata's office, the print was strange. It consisted of an immense sheet of paper in the centre of which a picture seemed gradually to emerge out of a mass of carelessly applied yet precisely positioned lines. It showed a naked man (his figure was extremely stylized, but it was clear from the realistically depicted sexual organ that he was a man) standing on the edge of a precipice. There were several weights of various sizes hung around his neck, and he had a sword in each hand; his eyes were blindfolded with a white cloth, and the edge of the precipice was under his very feet. There were a few other minor details – the sun setting into a bank of mist, birds in the sky and the roof of a pagoda in the distance – but despite these romantic digressions, the main sensation aroused in Serdyuk's soul by the engraving was one of hopelessness.

'That is our national artist Aketi Mitsuhide,' said Kawabata, 'the one who died recently from eating *fugu* fish. How would you describe the theme of this print?'

Serdyuk's eyes slithered over the figure depicted in the print, moving upwards from its exposed penis to the weights hanging on its chest.

'Yes, of course,' he said, surprising even himself. '*On* and *giri*. He's showing his prick and he's got weights round his neck.'

Kawabata clapped his hands and laughed.

'More sake?' he asked.

'You know,' replied Serdyuk, 'I'd be glad to, but perhaps we could do the interview first? I get drunk very quickly.'

'The interview is already over,' said Kawabata, filling the glasses. 'Let me tell you all about it. Our firm has existed for a very long time, so long in fact that if I told you, I'm afraid you wouldn't believe me. Our traditions are more important to us than anything else. We can only be approached, if you will allow me to use a figurative expression, through a very narrow door, and you have just stepped through it with confidence. Congratulations.'

'What door's that?' asked Serdyuk.

Kawabata pointed to the print.

'That one,' he said. 'The only one that leads into Taira Incorporated.'

'I don't really understand,' said Serdyuk. 'As far as I was aware, you're traders, and for you . . .'

Kawabata raised an open palm.

'I am frequently horrified to observe,' he said, 'that half of Russia has already been infected with the repulsive pragmatism of the West. Present company excepted, of course, but I have good reason for saying so.'

'But what's wrong with pragmatism?' asked Serdyuk.

'In ancient times,' said Kawabata, 'in our country officials were appointed to important posts after examinations in which they wrote an essay on beauty. And this was a very wise principle, for if a man has an understanding of that which is immeasurably higher than bureaucratic procedures, then he will certainly be able to cope with such lower matters. If your mind has penetrated with such lightning swiftness the mystery of the ancient allegory encoded in the drawing, then could all those price lists and overheads possibly cause you the slightest problem? Never. Moreover, after your answer I would consider it an honour to drink with you. Please do not refuse me.'

Serdyuk downed another one and unexpectedly found he had fallen into reminiscing about the previous day – it seemed he'd gone on from Pushkin Square to the Clean Ponds, but it wasn't clear to him why: all that was left in his memory was the monument to Griboedov, viewed in an odd perspective, as though he were looking at it from underneath a bench.

'Yes,' said Kawabata thoughtfully, 'but if you think about it, it's a terrible picture. The only things that differentiate us from animals are the rules and rituals which we have agreed on among ourselves. To transgress them is worse than to die, because only they separate us from the abyss of chaos which lies at our very feet – if, of course, we remove the blindfold from our eyes.'

He pointed to the print.

'But in Japan we have another tradition – sometimes, just for a second, deep within ourselves – to renounce all traditions, to abandon, as we say, Buddha and Mara, in order to experience the inexpressible taste of reality. And this second sometimes produces remarkable works of art . . .'

Kawabata glanced once again at the man with the swords standing on the edge of the abyss and sighed.

'Yes,' said Serdyuk. 'Life here nowadays is enough to make a man give up on everything too. And as for traditions . . . well, some go to different kinds of churches, but of course most just watch the television and think about money.'

He sensed that he had seriously lowered the tone of the conversation and he needed quickly to say something clever.

'Probably,' he said, holding out his empty glass to Kawabata, 'the reason it happens is that by nature the Russian is not inclined to a search for metaphysical meaning and makes do with a cocktail of atheism and alcoholism which, if the truth be told, is our major spiritual tradition.'

Kawabata poured again for himself and Serdyuk.

'On this point I must take the liberty of disagreeing with you,' he said. 'And this is the reason. Recently I acquired it for our collection of Russian art.'

'You collect art?' asked Serdyuk.

'Yes,' said Kawabata, rising to his feet and going over to one of the sets of shelves. 'That is also one of our firm's principles. We always attempt to penetrate the inner soul of any nation with whom we do business. It is not a matter of wishing to extract any additional profit in this way by understanding the . . . What is the Russian word? Mentality, isn't it?'

Serdyuk nodded.

'No,' Kawabata continued, opening a large file. 'It's more a matter of a desire to raise to the level of art even those activities that are furthest removed from it. You see, if you sell a consignment of machine-guns, as it were, into empty space, out of which money that might have been earned any way at all appears in your account, then you are not very different from a cash register. But if you sell the same consignment of machine-guns to people about whom you know that every time they kill someone they have to do penance before a tripartite manifestation of the creator of the world, then the simple act of selling is exalted to the level of art and acquires a quite different quality. Not for them, of course, but for you. You are in harmony, you are at one with the Universe in which you are acting, and your signature on the contract acquires the same existential status . . . Do I express this correctly in Russian?'

Serdyuk nodded.

'The same existential status as the sunrise, the high tide or the fluttering of a blade of grass in the wind . . . What was I talking about to begin with?'

'About your collection.'

'Ah, that's right. Well then, would you like to take a look at this?'

He held out to Serdyuk a large sheet of some material covered with a thin protective sheet of tracing-paper.

'But please, be careful.'

Serdyuk took hold of the sheet. It was a piece of dusty greyish cardboard, apparently quite old. A single word had been traced on it in black paint through a crude stencil – 'God'.

'What is it?'

'It's an early-twentieth-century Russian conceptual icon,' said Kawabata. 'By David Burliuk. Have you heard of him?'

'I've heard the name somewhere.'

'Strangely enough, he's not very well known in Russia,' said Kawabata. 'But that's not important. Just look at it!'

Serdyuk took another look at the sheet of cardboard. The letters were dissected by white lines that must have been left by the strips of paper holding the stencil together. The word was crudely printed and there were blobs of dried paint all around it

– the overall impression was strangely reminiscent of a print left by a boot.

Serdyuk looked up at Kawabata and drawled something that sounded like 'Ye-ea-es'.

'How many different meanings there are here!' Kawabata continued. 'Wait a moment, don't speak – I'll try to describe what I see, and if I miss anything, then you can add it. All right?'

Serdyuk nodded.

'Firstly,' said Kawabata, 'there is the very fact that the word "God" is printed through a stencil. That is precisely the way in which it is imprinted on a person's consciousness in childhood – as a commonplace pattern identical with the pattern imprinted on a myriad other minds. But then, a great deal depends on the quality of the surface to which it is applied – if the paper is rough and uneven, the imprint left on it will not be sharp, and if there are already other words present, it is not even clear just what mark will be left on the paper as a result. That's why they say that everyone has his own God. And then, look at the magnificent crudeness of these letters – their corners simply scratch at your eyes. It's hard to believe anyone could possibly imagine this three-letter word to be the source of the eternal love and grace, the reflection of which renders life in this world at least partially tolerable. But on the other hand, this print, which looks more like a brand used for marking cattle than anything else, is the only thing a man has to set his hopes on in this life. Do you agree?'

'Yes,' said Serdyuk.

'But if that were all there were to it, the work which you hold in your hands would not be anything particularly outstanding – the entire range of these arguments can be encountered at any atheist lecture in a village club. But there is one small detail which makes this icon a genuine work of genius, which sets it – and I am not afraid to say this – above Rublyov's "Trinity". You, of course, understand what I mean, but please allow me to say it myself.'

Kawabata paused in solemn triumph.

'What I have in mind, of course, are the empty stripes left from the stencil. It would have been no trouble to colour them in – but then the result would have been so different. Yes indeed, most certainly. A person begins by looking at this word, from the appearance of sense he moves on to the visible form and suddenly he notices the blank spaces that are not filled in with anything – and only there, in this nowhere, is it possible to encounter what all these huge, ugly letters strive in vain to convey, because the word "God" denominates that which cannot be denominated. This is a bit like Meister Eckhart, or . . . But that's not important. There are many who have attempted to speak of this in words. Take Lao-tzu. You remember – about the wheel and the spokes? Or about the vessel whose value is determined solely by its inner emptiness? And what if I were to say that every word is such a vessel, and everything depends on how much emptiness it can contain? You wouldn't disagree with that, surely?'

'No,' said Serdyuk.

Kawabata wiped away the drops of noble sweat from his forehead.

'Now take another look at the print on the wall,' he said.

'Yes,' said Serdyuk.

'Do you see how it is constructed? The segment of reality in which the *on* and the *giri* are contained is located in the very centre, and all around it is a void, from which it appears and into which it disappears. In Japan we do not torment the Universe with unnecessary thoughts about its cause and origin. We do not burden God with the concept of "God". But nonetheless, the void in this print is the same void as you see in Burliuk's icon. A truly significant coincidence, is it not?'

'Of course,' said Serdyuk, holding out his empty glass to Kawabata.

'But you will not find this void in Western religious painting,' Kawabata said as he poured. 'Everything there is filled up with material objects – all kinds of curtains and folds and bowls of blood and God only knows what else. The unique vision of reality reflected in these two works of art is common to only you and us, and therefore I believe what Russia really needs is alchemical wedlock with the East.'

'I swear to God,' said Serdyuk, 'only yesterday evening I was . . .'

'Precisely with the East,' interrupted Kawabata, 'and not the West. You understand? In the depths of the Russian soul lies the same gaping void we find deep in the soul of Japan. And from this very void the world comes into being, constantly, with every second. Cheers.'

Kawabata drank up, as Serdyuk had already done, and twirled the empty bottle in his fingers.

'Yes,' he said, 'most certainly, the value of a vessel lies in its emptiness. But in the last few minutes the value of this particular vessel has increased excessively. That disrupts the balance between value and the absence of value, and that is intolerable. That's what we must fear the most, a loss of balance.'

'Yes,' said Serdyuk. 'Definitely. So there's none left then?'

'We could go and get some,' Kawabata replied with a glance at his watch. 'Of course, we'd miss the football . . .'

'D'you follow the game?'

'I'm a "Dynamo" fan,' Kawabata answered, giving Serdyuk a very intimate kind of wink.

In an old, worn jacket with a hood and rubber boots Kawabata lost all resemblance to a Japanese, becoming instead the absolute picture of a visitor to Moscow from down south – the kind whose appearance alone was enough to prompt suspicions about the real reason for his visit.

But then Serdyuk had long known that most of the foreigners he encountered on the streets of Moscow were not really foreigners at all, but petty trader riff-raff who'd scrabbled together a bit of cash and then tarted themselves up at the Kalinka-Stockman shop. The genuine foreigners, who had multiplied to a quite incredible extent in recent years, had been trying to dress just like the average man on the street, for reasons of personal safety. Naturally enough, most of them got their idea of what the average Moscow inhabitant on the street looked like from CNN. And in ninety cases out of a hundred CNN, in its attempts to show Muscovites doggedly pursuing the phantom of democracy across the sun-baked desert of reform, showed close-ups of employees of the American embassy dressed up as Muscovites, because they looked a lot more natural than Muscovites dressed up as foreigners. And so despite Kawabata's similarity to a visitor from Rostov – or rather, precisely because of that similarity – and especially because his face didn't look particularly Japanese, it was really clear from the start that he was actually a pure-blooded Japanese who had just slipped out of his office for a minute into the Moscow twilight.

Furthermore, Kawabata led Serdyuk along one of those routes that only foreigners ever use – slipping across dark yards, in and out of buildings, through gaps in wire fences, so that after a few minutes Serdyuk was completely disoriented and had to rely entirely on his impetuous companion. Before very long they emerged on to a dark, crooked street where there were several trading kiosks and Serdyuk realized they'd reached their destination.

'What shall we get?' asked Serdyuk.

'I think a litre of sake would do the job –' said Kawabata. 'And a bit of grub to go with it.'

'Sake?' said Serdyuk in astonishment. 'Have they got sake here?'

'This is the place all right,' said Kawabata. 'There are only three kiosks in Moscow where you can get decent sake. Why do you think we set up our office here?'

He's joking, thought Serdyuk, and looked into the kiosk window. The selection was the usual one, except for a few unfamiliar litre bottles with labels crammed with hieroglyphics visible in among the others.

'Black sake,' Kawabata spoke gruffly. 'Two. Yes.'

Serdyuk was given one bottle, which he stuck in his pocket. Kawabata kept hold of the other one.

'Now just one other thing,' said Kawabata. 'It won't take a moment.'

They walked along the line of kiosks and soon found themselves in front of a large tin-plated pavilion with a door pockmarked with holes, either from bullets or from nails or – as was more usual – from both. Both of the pavilion's windows were protected with a traditional decorative grating, consisting of a metal rod bent into a semicircle in one bottom corner with rusty rays of iron radiating from it in all directions. The sign hanging above the door said 'Jack of All Trades'.

Inside, there were tins of enamel paint and drying-oil on the shelves, with samples of tiles hanging from the walls and a separate counter piled high with various types of gleaming locks for safes. But in the corner, on an upturned plastic bath, there was something that Serdyuk had never seen before.

It was a black cuirass finished in gleaming lacquer, with small gold encrustations. Beside it lay a horned helmet with a fan of dangling neck-plates, also covered in black lacquer; on the helmet's forehead there was a gleaming five-pointed silver star. On the wall beside the cuirass were several swords of various lengths and a long, asymmetrical bow.

While Serdyuk was inspecting this arsenal, Kawabata engaged the salesman in quiet conversation – they seemed to be talking about arrows. Then he asked him to take down a long sword in a scabbard decorated with white diamond shapes. He drew it half-way out of the scabbard and tried the blade with his thumbnail (Serdyuk noticed that Kawabata was very careful about the way he handled the sword and even when he was testing its cutting edge, he tried not to touch the blade with his fingers). Serdyuk felt as though Kawabata had completely forgotten that he existed, so he decided to remind him.

'Tell me,' he said, turning to Kawabata, 'what could that star on the helmet mean? I suppose it's a symbol of some sort?'

'Oh yes,' said Kawabata. 'It's a symbol, and a very ancient one. It's one of the emblems of the Order of the October Star.'

Serdyuk chortled.

'What kind of order's that?' he asked. 'One they gave to the milkmaids in the ancient world?'

Kawabata gave him a long look, and the corner of his mouth turned up in an answering smile.

'No,' he said. 'This order has never been awarded by anyone to anyone. Certain people have simply realized that they are entitled to wear it. Or rather that they had always been entitled to wear it.'

'But what is it for?'

'There is nothing that it could be for.'

'The world's full of idiots, all right,' Serdyuk said vehemently.

Kawabata slammed the sword back into its scabbard. The air was suddenly thick with embarrassment.

'You're joking,' said Serdyuk, instinctively trying to smooth things over. 'You might as well have said the Order of the Red Labour Banner.'

'I have never heard of . . . that decoration,' said Kawabata.

171

'The Order of the Yellow Flag certainly does exist, but that's from a quite different area. And why do you think I'm joking? I very rarely joke. And when I do, I give warning by laughing softly.'

'I'm sorry if I said something wrong,' said Serdyuk. 'It's just that I'm drunk.'

Kawabata shrugged and handed the sword back to the salesman.

'Are you taking it?' the salesman asked.

'Not this one,' said Kawabata. 'Wrap up that one over there, the small one.'

While Kawabata was paying, Serdyuk went out on to the street. He had a terrible feeling that he'd done something irredeemably stupid, but he soon felt calmer once he'd looked up a few times at the damp spring stars that had appeared in the sky. Then his eye was caught once again by the splayed metal rays of the window gratings and he thought sadly that when it came down to it, Russia was a land of the rising sun too – if only because the sun had never really risen over it yet. He decided this was an observation he could share with Kawabata, but by the time Kawabata emerged from the pavilion with a slim parcel tucked under his arm, this thought had already been forgotten, its place taken instead by an all-consuming desire for a drink.

Kawabata seemed to take in the situation at a glance. Moving several steps away from the doorway, he put his bundle down beside the dark, wet trunk of a tree growing out of a hole in the asphalt and said:

'You know, of course, that in Japan we warm our sake before we drink it. And naturally, nobody would ever dream of drinking it straight from the bottle – that would totally contradict the spirit of the ritual. And drinking on the street is deeply dishonourable. But there is a certain ancient form which allows us to do this without losing face. It is called the "horseman's halt". It could also be translated as the "horseman's rest".'

Keeping his eyes fixed on Serdyuk's face, Kawabata drew the bottle out of his pocket.

'According to tradition,' he continued, 'the great poet Arivara Narihira was once dispatched as hunting ambassador to the province of Ise. The road was long, and in those times they travelled on horseback, so the journey took many days. It was summer. Narihira was travelling with a group of friends, and his exalted soul was filled with feelings of sadness and love. When the horsemen grew weary, they would dismount and refresh themselves with simple food and a few mouthfuls of sake. In order not to attract bandits, they lit no fire and drank the sake cold as they recited to each other marvellous verses about what they had seen on the way and what was in their hearts. And then they would set off again . . .'

Kawabata twisted open the screw-cap.

'That is where the tradition comes from. When you drink sake in this fashion, you are supposed to think of the men of old, and then these thoughts should gradually merge into that radiant sadness that is born in your heart when you are aware of the fragility of this world and at the same time captivated by its beauty. So let us . . .'

'With pleasure,' said Serdyuk, reaching out for the bottle.

'Not so fast,' said Kawabata, jerking it away from him. 'This is the first time you have taken part in this ritual, so allow me to explain the sequence of the actions involved and their significance. Do as I do and I will explain to you the symbolic meaning of what is happening.'

Kawabata set down the bottle beside his bundle.

'First of all we must tether our horses,' he said.

He tugged at the tree's lowest branch to test its strength and then wove his hands around it as though he were winding a string on to it. Serdyuk realized he was supposed to do the same. Reaching up to a branch a little higher, he roughly repeated Kawabata's manipulations under his watchful gaze.

'No,' said Kawabata, 'he's uncomfortable like that.'

'Who?' asked Serdyuk.

'Your horse. You've tethered him too high. How will he graze? Remember, it's not just you that's resting, it's your faithful companion as well.'

An expression of puzzlement appeared on Serdyuk's face, and Kawabata sighed.

'You must understand,' he said patiently, 'that in performing this ritual we are transported back, as it were, to the Heian era. At present we are riding through the summer countryside to the province of Ise. I ask you, please, retie the bridle.'

Serdyuk decided it would be best not to argue. He waved his hands over the upper branch and then wove them around the lower one.

'That's much better,' said Kawabata. 'And now we should compose verses about what we see around us.'

He closed his eyes and waited in silence for several seconds, then pronounced a long, guttural phrase in which Serdyuk was unable to detect either rhythm or rhyme.

'That's more or less about what we've been saying,' he explained. 'About invisible horses nibbling at invisible grass and about how it's far more real than this asphalt which, in essence, does not exist. But in general it's all built on word-play. Now it's your turn.'

Serdyuk suddenly felt miserable.

'I really don't know what to say,' he said in an apologetic tone. 'I don't write poems, I don't even like them very much. And who needs words with the stars up in the sky?'

'Oh,' Kawabata exclaimed, 'magnificent! Magnificent! How right you are! Only thirty-two syllables, but worth an entire book!'

He took a step backwards and bowed twice.

'And how good that I recited my verse first!' he said. 'After you I wouldn't have dared to do it! But where did you learn to write *tanka*?'

'Oh, around,' Serdyuk said evasively.

Kawabata held out the bottle to him. Serdyuk took several large gulps and handed it back. Kawabata also applied himself eagerly, drinking in small sips, holding his free hand behind him – there was obviously some ritual meaning to the gesture, but to be on the safe side Serdyuk avoided asking any questions. While Kawabata was drinking, he lit a cigarette. Two or three drags restored his self-confidence and he even began to feel slightly ashamed of his recent state of timidity.

'And by the way, about the horse,' he said. 'I didn't actually tether him too high. It's just that recently I've been getting tired very quickly, and I take halts of up to three days at a time. That's why he has a long bridle. Otherwise he'd eat all the grass the first day . . .'

Kawabata's face changed. He bowed once more, walked off to one side and began unfastening the buttons of his jacket over his stomach.

'What are you doing?' asked Serdyuk.

'I am so ashamed,' said Kawabata. 'I can't carry on living after suffering such dishonour.'

He sat down on the asphalt surface, unwrapped the bundle, took out the sword and bared its blade – a glimmering patch of lilac slithered along it, reflected from the neon lamp above their heads. Serdyuk finally realized what Kawabata was about to do and managed to grab hold of his hands.

'Stop that will you, please,' he said in genuine fright. 'How can you give such importance to trifles like that?'

'Will you be able to forgive me?' Kawabata asked emotionally, rising to his feet.

'Please, please, let's just forget about this stupid misunderstanding. And anyway, a love of animals is a noble feeling. Why should you be ashamed of that?'

Kawabata thought for a moment and the wrinkles on his brow disappeared.

'You're right,' he said. 'I really was motivated by sympathy for a tired animal, not the desire to show that I understood something better than you. There really is nothing dishonourable about that. I may have said something stupid, but I have not lost face.'

He put the sword back into its scabbard, swayed on his feet and applied himself to the bottle once again.

'If some petty misunderstanding should arise between two noble men, surely it will crumble to dust if they both attack it with the keen edge of their minds,' he said, handing the bottle to Serdyuk.

Serdyuk finished off what was left.

'Of course it will,' he said. 'That's as clear as day, that is.'

Kawabata raised his head and looked dreamily up at the sky.

'And who needs words with stars up in the sky?' he declaimed. 'How very fine. You know, I would really like to celebrate this remarkable moment with a gesture of some kind. Why don't we release our horses? Let them graze on this beautiful plain, and retreat into the mountains during the nights. Surely they have deserved their freedom?'

'You're a very kind-hearted man,' said Serdyuk.

Kawabata walked unsteadily over to the tree, drew the sword from its scabbard and sliced off the lower branch with a movement that was almost invisible. It fell on to the asphalt of the pavement. Kawabata waved his arms in the air and shouted something loud and incomprehensible – Serdyuk realized that he was driving away the horses. Then he came back, picked up the bottle and with disappointment tipped out the last few drops on to the ground.

'It's getting cold,' Serdyuk observed, looking around and instinctively sensing that any moment now the damp Moscow air would weave itself into the solid shape of a police patrol. 'Shouldn't we be getting back to the office?'

'Of course,' said Kawabata, 'of course. And we can have a bite to eat there too.'

Serdyuk didn't remember the way back at all. He only became aware of himself again when they were back in the same room from which their journey had started. Kawabata and he were sitting on the floor and eating noodles out of soup plates. The second bottle was already half-empty, but Serdyuk realized that he was completely sober and in a distinctly exalted mood. Kawabata must have been feeling good as well, because he was humming quietly and beating time with his chopsticks, sending slim vermicelli snakes flying off in all directions around the room. Some of them landed on Serdyuk, but he didn't find it annoying.

When he'd finished eating, Kawabata set his plate aside and turned towards Serdyuk.

'Now tell me,' he said, 'what does a man want after returning home from a dangerous journey, once he has satisfied his hunger and thirst?'

'I don't know,' said Serdyuk. 'Round here they usually turn on the television.'

'Nah-ah,' said Kawabata. 'In Japan we make the finest televisions in the world, but that doesn't prevent us from realizing that a television is just a small transparent window in the pipe of a spiritual garbage chute. I wasn't thinking of those unfortunates who spend their whole lives in a trance watching an endless stream of swill and only feeling alive when they recognize a familiar tin can. I'm talking about people who are worthy of mention in our conversation.'

Serdyuk shrugged.

'Can't think of anything in particular,' he said.

Kawabata screwed up his eyes, moved closer to Serdyuk and smiled, so that just for a moment he really did look like a cunning Japanese.

'You remember, just a little while ago, when we set the horses loose, then forded the Tenzin river and walked on foot to the gates of Rasemon, you were talking of the warmth of another body lying beside you? Surely this is what your spirit was seeking at that moment?'

Serdyuk shuddered.

He's gay, he thought, I should have guessed it right from the start.

Kawabata moved even closer.

'After all, it is one of the few remaining natural feelings which a man may still experience. And we did agree that what Russia needs is alchemical wedlock with the East, didn't we?'

'We did,' said Serdyuk, squirming inwardly. 'Of course it does. I was just thinking about it only yesterday.'

'Good,' said Kawabata, 'but there is nothing that happens to nations and countries that is not repeated in symbolic form in the life of the individuals who live in those countries and make up those nations. Russia, in the final analysis, is you. So if you spoke sincerely, and of course I cannot at all believe otherwise, then let us perform this ritual immediately. Let us, as it were, reinforce our words and thoughts with a symbolic fusion of basic principles . . .'

Kawabata bowed and winked.

'In any case, we shall be working together, and there is nothing which brings men so close together as . . .'

He winked again and smiled. Serdyuk bared his teeth mechanically in response and noticed that one of Kawabata's own teeth was missing. But there were other things that struck him as far more significant: first of all, Serdyuk remembered the danger of AIDS, and then he recalled that his underwear wasn't particularly clean. Kawabata got up and went across to the cupboard, rummaged in it and tossed Serdyuk a piece of cloth. It was a blue cap, exactly like those shown on the heads of the men on the sake glasses. Kawabata put one on his head, gestured for Serdyuk to do the same and clapped his hands.

Immediately one of the panels in the wall slid to one side and Serdyuk became aware of a rather wild-sounding music. Behind the panel, in a small room that looked more like a broom cupboard, there was a group of four or five girls wearing long colourful kimonos and holding musical instruments. For a moment Serdyuk thought they weren't actually wearing kimonos, but some kind of long, badly cut dressing-gowns belted at the waist with towels and tucked up so as to look like kimonos, but then he decided that dressing-gowns like that were essentially kimonos after all. The girls waved their heads from side to side and smiled as they played. One had a balalaika, another one was banging together a pair of painted wooden Palekh spoons, and another two were holding small plastic harmonicas which made a fearful, piercing squeaking noise; this was only natural, Serdyuk thought, since harmonicas like that were never actually made to play on, merely to create a happy atmosphere at children's parties.

The girls' smiles were a little forced and the layer of rouge on their cheeks looked a bit too thick. Their features were not even slightly Japanese, either – they were just ordinary Russian girls, and not even particularly beautiful. One of them looked like a student from Serdyuk's year at college, a girl called Masha.

'Woman, Semyon,' Kawabata said thoughtfully, 'is by no means created for our downfall. In that marvellous moment when she envelops us in her body, it is as though we are transported to that happy land from which we came and to which we shall return after death. I love women and I am not ashamed to admit it. And every time I am joined with one of them, it is as though I . . .'

Without bothering to finish, he clapped his hands and the girls danced forward in close formation, gazing straight ahead into empty space as they moved directly towards Serdyuk.

'Sixth rank, fifth rank, fourth rank, and now our horses turn to the left, and the longed-for palace of Suzdaku emerges from the mist,' said Kawabata as he buttoned up his pants, gazing attentively all the while at Serdyuk.

Serdyuk raised his head from the floor-covering. He must have fallen asleep for a few minutes – Kawabata was obviously continuing with some story, but Serdyuk couldn't remember the beginning. He took a look at himself. He was wearing nothing but an old washed-out T-shirt with Olympic symbols; the rest of his clothing was scattered about the room. The girls, tousled, half-naked and passionless, were fussing around the electric kettle that was boiling in the corner. Serdyuk started getting dressed quickly.

'Further on, by the left wing of the castle,' Kawabata continued, 'we take a turn to the right, and there are the gates of Blissful Light rushing towards us . . . And now everything depends on which poetic style is in closest harmony with your soul at this moment. If you are inwardly attuned to simplicity and joy, you will gallop straight forward. If your thoughts are far removed from this frail and perishable world, then you will turn to the left and see before you the gates of Eternal Peace. And finally, if you are young and hot-headed and your soul thirsts for delights, you will turn to the right and enter in at the gates of Enduring Joy.'

Squirming under Kawabata's unwavering gaze, Serdyuk pulled on his trousers, his shirt and his jacket, and began knotting the tie round his neck, but his fingers got tangled up in the knots and he gave up, dragged the tie off over his head and shoved it back into his pocket.

'But then,' Kawabata continued, raising one finger in a solemn gesture – he seemed so absorbed in what he was saying that Serdyuk realized there was no need to feel embarrassed or hurry – 'then, whatever gateway you may have chosen to enter the imperial palace, you find yourself in the same courtyard! Think what a revelation this is for a man accustomed to reading the language of symbols! Whatever road your heart has followed, whatever route your soul may have mapped out, you always return to the same thing! Remember what is said – all things return to the one, but where does the one return to? Ah?'

Serdyuk raised his eyes from the floor.

'Well, where does the one return to?' Kawabata repeated, and his eyes narrowed into two slits.

Serdyuk coughed and opened his mouth to say something,

but before he could speak Kawabata had clapped his hands in delight.

'Oh,' he said, 'profound and accurate as always. And especially for those rare horsemen who have risen to the height of this truth, growing in the first courtyard of the imperial palace there is an orange-blossom tree and a . . . What would you plant to pair with an orange blossom?'

Serdyuk sighed. There was only one Japanese plant he knew.

'What's it called . . . Sakura,' he said. 'A blossoming sakura.'

Kawabata took a step backwards and added yet another bow to the long sequence he had already made that evening. There seemed to be tears gleaming in his eyes.

'Yes, yes,' said Kawabata. 'Precisely so. Orange blossom and cherry blossom in the first courtyard, and further on, by the Chambers of the Drifting Scents there is a wistaria, by the Chambers of the Frozen Flowers there is a plum tree, by the Chambers of the Reflected Light there is a pear tree. Oh how ashamed I am that I have subjected you to the insult of this interrogation! Please believe me, I am not to blame for this. Such are . . .'

He glanced across at the girls sitting round the electric kettle and clapped his hands twice. The girls gathered up the kettle and their scattered clothes and quickly disappeared into the broom cupboard from which they had emerged; the screen closed behind them and nothing, apart perhaps from a few spots of something white on the fax machine, was left to remind Serdyuk of the bonfire of passion that had been blazing in the room only a few minutes earlier.

'Such are the rules of our firm,' Kawabata finished his sentence. 'I've already told you that when I use the word "firm" I am not translating absolutely accurately. In actual fact it would be more correct to say "clan". But if this term is used too early, it may arouse suspicion and fear. We therefore prefer first to find out what kind of man we are dealing with and then go into the details. Even though in your case the answer was clear to me from the moment when you recited that magical poem . . .'

Kawabata stood absolutely still and closed his eyes, and for several seconds his lips moved silently. Serdyuk guessed that he was repeating the phrase about the stars in the sky, which Serdyuk couldn't remember exactly himself.

'Quite remarkable words. Yes, from that moment on everything was absolutely clear to me. But there are rules, very strict rules, and I was obliged to ask you the required questions. Now I must tell you the following,' Kawabata continued. 'Since I have already mentioned that our firm is in reality more like a clan, it follows that our employees are more like members of a clan. And the obligations which they take upon themselves are also different from the usual obligations that hired hands accept. To put it simply, we accept you as a member of our clan, which is one of the most ancient in Japan. The title of the vacant post which you will occupy is "Assistant Manager for the Northern Barbarians". I understand that the title might possibly seem offensive to you, but this is a tradition older than the city of Moscow. It is a beautiful city, by the way, especially in summer. This is a post for a samurai, and a layman may not occupy it. Therefore, if you are willing to accept the post, I will make you a samurai.'

'But what kind of work is it?'

'Oh, nothing complicated,' said Kawabata. 'Papers, clients. From the outside it all looks just the same as in any other firm, except that your inner attitude to events must match the harmony of the cosmos.'

'And what's the pay like?'

'You will receive two hundred and fifty *koku* of rice a year,' said Kawabata, and frowned as he calculated something in his head. 'That's about forty thousand of your dollars.'

'In dollars?'

'However you wish,' Kawabata said with a shrug.

'I'll take it,' said Serdyuk.

'As I expected. Now tell me, are you ready to accept that you are a samurai of the Taira clan?'

'I should say so.'

'Are you willing to link your life and your death with the destiny of our clan?'

All these crazy rituals they have, thought Serdyuk. Where do they find the time to make all those televisions?

'I am,' he said.

'Will you be prepared, as a real man, to cast the ephemeral blossom of this life over the edge of the abyss and into the void if this is required of you by your *giri*?' Kawabata asked with a nod in the direction of the print on the wall.

Serdyuk took another look at it.

'I will,' he said, 'of course. Chuck the blossom down the abyss – no problem.'

'You swear?'

'I swear.'

'Splendid,' said Kawabata, 'splendid. Now there is only one small formality left, and we'll be finished. We must receive confirmation from Japan. But that will only take a few minutes.'

He sat down facing the fax machine, rummaged through a pile of papers until he found a clean sheet, and then a brush appeared in his hand.

Serdyuk changed his position. His legs had gone numb from sitting too long on the floor and he thought it would be a good idea to ask Kawabata whether he would be allowed to bring a stool – just a small one – to work with him. Then he looked around for the remains of the sake, but the bottle had disappeared. Kawabata was busy with his sheet of paper and Serdyuk was afraid to ask – he couldn't be sure that he wouldn't disrupt the ritual. He remembered the oath he had just taken. God almighty, he thought, the number of oaths I've sworn in my life! Promised to struggle for the cause of the Communist Party, didn't I? Half a dozen times, probably, going back to when I was just a kid. Promised to marry Masha, didn't I? Sure I did. And yesterday, after the Clear Ponds, when I was drinking with those idiots, didn't I promise we'd get another bottle on me? And now look where it's got me – chucking blossoms down an abyss.

Meanwhile Kawabata finished pushing his brush around the sheet of paper, blew on it and showed it to Serdyuk. It was a large chrysanthemum drawn in black ink.

'What is it?' asked Serdyuk.

'Oh,' said Kawabata, 'it's a chrysanthemum. You understand, when a new member joins us, it is such a great joy for the entire Taira clan that it would be inappropriate to entrust it to marks on paper. In such cases, we usually inform our leaders by drawing a flower. What's more, this is the very flower of which we were just speaking. It symbolizes your life, which now belongs to the Taira clan, and at the same time it testifies to your final awareness of its fleeting ephemerality . . .'

'I get it,' said Serdyuk.

Kawabata blew on the sheet of paper once more, then set it in the crack of the fax machine and began dialling some incredibly long number.

He got through only at the third attempt. The fax hummed into life, a little green lamp on its corner lit up and the page slowly slid out of sight into the black maw.

Kawabata stared fixedly at the fax machine, without moving or changing his pose. Several long and weary minutes went by, and then the fax began to hum again and another sheet of paper slid out from underneath its black body. Serdyuk understood immediately that this was the reply.

Kawabata waited until the full length of the page had emerged and then tore it out of the fax, glanced at it and looked slowly round at Serdyuk.

'Congratulations,' he said, 'my sincere congratulations! The reply is most propitious.'

He held out the sheet of paper to Serdyuk, who took it and saw a different drawing – this time it was a long, slightly bent stick with some kind of pattern on it and something sticking out from it at one side.

'What is it?' he asked.

'It's a sword,' Kawabata said solemnly, 'the symbol of your new status in life. And since I never had any doubt that this would be the outcome, allow me to present you, so to speak, with your passport.'

With these words Kawabata held out the short sword he had bought earlier in the tin-plated pavilion.

Perhaps it was Kawabata's fixed, unblinking stare, or perhaps it was the result of some chemical reaction in his own alcohol-drenched metabolism, but for some reason Serdyuk became aware suddenly of the significance and solemnity of the moment. He almost went down on his knees, but just in time he remembered that it was the medieval European knights who did that, not the Japanese – and not even the knights, if he thought about it, but only the actors from the Odessa film studios who were playing them in some intolerably dreary old Soviet film. So he just held out his hands and took a cautious grip on the cold instrument of death. There was a design on the scabbard that he hadn't noticed before: it was a drawing of three cranes in flight – the gold wire impressed into the black lacquer of the scabbard traced a light and dashing contour of exceptional beauty.

'Your soul,' said Kawabata, gazing into Serdyuk's eyes again, 'lies in this scabbard.'

'What a beautiful drawing,' said Serdyuk. 'You know, it reminds me of a song I know, about cranes. How does it go, now? "... And in their flight I see a narrow gap, perhaps that is a place for me ..."'

'Yes, yes,' Kawabata cut in. 'And why would a man need any greater gap? The Lord Buddha can easily fit the entire world with all its problems into the gap between two cranes. Why, it would be lost in the gaps between the feathers of either of them ... How poetical this evening is! Why don't we have another drink? For the place in the flight of cranes which you have finally occupied?'

Serdyuk thought he sensed something ominous in Kawabata's words, but he paid no attention, because Kawabata could hardly have known the song was about the souls of dead soldiers.

'Gladly,' said Serdyuk, 'in just a while. I ...'

Suddenly there was a loud knock at the door. Kawabata turned and shouted something in Japanese, the panel slid to one side and a man's face, also with southern features, appeared in the gap. The face said something and Kawabata nodded.

'I shall have to leave you for a few minutes,' he said to Serdyuk. 'It seems there is some serious news coming in. If you wish, please look through any of the print albums while you are waiting,' – he nodded in the direction of the bookshelf – 'or simply amuse yourself.'

Serdyuk nodded. Kawabata quickly left the room and closed the panel behind him. Serdyuk went over to the shelves and glanced at the long row of different-coloured spines, then went over to the corner of the room and sat down on a bamboo mat, leaning his head against the wall. He had no appetite left for all those prints.

It was quiet in the building. He could hear someone hammering on a wall somewhere above him – they must be installing a metal door. Behind the sliding panel he could hear the whispers

184

of the girls swearing at each other; they were very close, but he could hardly make out any of their obscenities, and the muffled voices mingled together to produce a gentle, calming rustling sound, as though there were a garden behind the wall and the leaves of the blossoming cherries were murmuring in the wind.

Serdyuk was woken by a low moaning. He couldn't tell how long he'd been asleep, but it must have been quite a long time – Kawabata was sitting in the centre of the room, already changed and shaved. He was wearing a white shirt and his hair, so recently tousled and untidy, was combed back neatly. He was the source of the moaning that had woken Serdyuk – it was some kind of mournful melody, a long-drawn-out dirge. Kawabata was holding the long sword in his hands and wiping it with a white piece of cloth. Serdyuk noticed that Kawabata's shirt was unbuttoned, and his hairless chest and belly were exposed.

Kawabata realized that Serdyuk had woken up and turned to face him with a broad smile.

'Did you sleep well?' he asked.

'I wasn't exactly sleeping,' said Serdyuk, 'I just . . .'

'Had a doze,' said Kawabata, 'I understand. All of us are merely dozing in this life. And we only wake when it ends. Do you recall how we forded the brook when we were walking back to the office?'

'Yes,' said Serdyuk, 'that stream coming out of the pipe.'

'Pipe or no pipe, that is not important. Do you recall the bubbles on the surface of that brook?'

'Yes. They were big ones all right.'

'Truly,' said Kawabata, raising the blade to the level of his eyes and gazing at it intently, 'truly this world is like bubbles on the water. Is that not so?'

Serdyuk thought that Kawabata was right, and he wanted very much to say something so that his companion would realize how well he understood his feelings and how completely he shared them.

'Not even that,' he said, raising himself up on one elbow. 'It's like . . . let me think now . . . It's like a photograph of those bubbles that has fallen down behind a chest of drawers and been gnawed by the rats.'

Kawabata smiled once again.

'You are a genuine poet,' he said. 'I have no doubt at all about that.'

'And what's more,' Serdyuk went on, inspired, 'it could well be that the rats got to it even before it had been developed.'

'Splendid,' said Kawabata, 'quite splendid. This is the poetry of words, but there is also the poetry of deeds. I hope that your final poem without words will prove a match for the verses that have brought me so much delight today.'

'What d'you mean?'

Kawabata carefully set his sword down on a bamboo mat.

'Life is uncertain and changeable,' he said thoughtfully. 'In the early morning no one can say what awaits him in the evening.'

'Has something happened, then?'

'Oh, yes. You know, of course, that business is like war. The Taira clan has an enemy, a mighty enemy – Minamoto.'

'Minamoto?' echoed Serdyuk, feeling a shiver run down his spine. 'So what?'

'Today news came that cunning treachery on the Tokyo stock exchange has allowed the Minamoto Group to acquire a controlling interest in Taira Incorporated. A certain English bank and the Singapore mafia were involved, but that is not important. We are destroyed. And our enemy is triumphant.'

Serdyuk said nothing for a while as he tried to work out what this meant. Only one thing was clear, though – it didn't mean anything good.

'But you and I,' said Kawabata, 'we two samurai of the clan of Taira – surely we shall not allow our spirits to be overcast by the shifting shadows of these insignificant bubbles of existence?'

'Er . . . no,' Serdyuk answered.

Kawabata laughed fiercely and his eyes flashed.

'No,' he said. 'Minamoto shall not behold our degradation and dishonour. One should leave this life as the white cranes disappear into the clouds. Let not a single petty feeling remain in our hearts at a moment of such beauty.'

He swung round sharply where he sat, turning the bamboo mat with him, and bowed to Serdyuk.

'I wish to ask you a favour,' he said. 'When I rip open my belly, please cut off my head!'

'What?'

'My head, please cut off my head. We call this rendering the final service. And a samurai who is asked to do this may not refuse without covering himself in great dishonour.'

'But I never . . . That is, before . . .'

'It's very simple. One stroke and it's done. Wh-oo-oosh!' Kawabata waved his hands rapidly through the air.

'But I am afraid I won't manage it,' said Serdyuk. 'I don't have any experience of that kind of thing.'

Kawabata pondered for a moment, then suddenly his face darkened as though he had been struck by some exceptionally unpleasant thought. He slapped his hand against his *tatami*.

'It's good that I am leaving this life soon,' he said, looking up guiltily at Serdyuk. 'What a coarse and ignorant brute I am!'

He covered his face with his hands and began rocking from side to side.

Serdyuk quietly stood up, tiptoed over to the screen, silently slid it to one side and went out into the corridor. The cold concrete felt unpleasant under his bare feet, and Serdyuk suddenly realized that while he and Kawabata had been wandering around dark and dubious alleyways in search of sake, his socks and shoes had been standing in the corridor by the door, where he'd left them in the afternoon; he couldn't remember what he'd been wearing on his feet at all, just as he couldn't recall how he and Kawabata had got out on to the street or how they'd got back in.

'Split, I've got to split right now,' he thought as he turned the corner in the corridor. 'First I split, then there'll be time for a bit of thinking.'

The security guard rose from his stool as Serdyuk approached.

'And where are we off to at a time like this?' he asked with a yawn. 'It's half past three in the morning.'

'We got a bit involved,' said Serdyuk. 'You know, with the interview.'

'Okay then,' said the security guard. 'Let's have your pass.'

'What pass?'

'To get out.'

'But you let me in without any pass.'

'That's right,' said the security guard, 'but to get out, you need a pass.'

The lamp on the desk cast a dim glow on Serdyuk's shoes standing over by the wall. The door was only a yard away from them, and beyond the door lay freedom. Serdyuk took a small step towards the shoes. Then another one. The security guard cast an indifferent glance at his bare feet.

'And then,' he said, toying with his rubber truncheon, 'we've got regulations. The alarm's on. The door's locked until eight o'clock in the morning. If I open it the pigs'll be round in a flash. That means hassle, official statements. So I can't open up. Not unless there's a fire. Or a flood.'

'But this world,' Serdyuk began ingratiatingly, 'is like bubbles on the water.'

The security guard laughed and shook his head.

'Sure, sure,' he said. 'We know what kind of place it is we work in. But you've got to understand where I'm coming from. Just imagine that along with those bubbles there's a set of instructions drifting along on the water. And just as long as it's reflected in one of those bubbles, we lock up at eleven and open the door at eight. And that's it.'

Serdyuk sensed a note of uncertainty in the security guard's voice and he tried pressing his point home a little harder.

'Mr Kawabata will be very surprised at your behaviour,' he answered. 'You're supposed be responsible for security in a serious firm, and you need such simple things explained to you. It must be obvious that if the world is only a mirage . . .'

'A mirage, a mirage,' said the security guard in a thoughtful voice, and he focused his eyes on a point that was obviously a long way beyond the wall. 'We know all about that. We haven't just started here, you know. And we have training sessions every week. But I'm not trying to tell you that door's real. Shall I tell you what I think?'

'Go on then.'

'The way I reckon, there isn't any substantial door at all, there's nothing but a provisional totality of essentially empty elements of perception.'

'Precisely!' said Serdyuk, delighted, and he took another little step in the direction of his shoes.

'But there's no way I'm opening up that totality before eight o'clock,' said the security guard, slapping himself on the palm with his rubber truncheon.

'Why?' asked Serdyuk.

The security guard shrugged.

'Karma for you,' he said, 'dharma for me, but it's all really just the same old crap. The void. And even that doesn't really exist.'

'Ye-es,' said Serdyuk. 'That's some serious training they give you.'

'What'd you expect? The Japanese security forces run it.'

'So what am I supposed to do?' Serdyuk asked.

'What can you do? Wait until eight. And ask them to write you out a pass.'

Serdyuk cast a final glance at the security guard's burly shoulders and the truncheon in his hands, then slowly turned on his heel and started trudging back to Kawabata's room. He had the unbearable feeling that there were words which would have made the guard give in and open the door, but that he had failed to find them. If I'd read the Sutras, I'd know what was trumps, he thought dejectedly.

'Listen,' the security guard called out behind him, 'better not go walking about without your *geta*. The floor in here's concrete. You'll get a chill in your kidneys.'

When he reached Kawabata's office again and noiselessly slid the panel open, Serdyuk noticed there was a strong smell in the room of stale drink and female sweat. Kawabata was still sitting there on the floor, his face in his hands, rocking from side to side, as though he hadn't even noticed that Serdyuk had gone out.

'Mr Kawabata,' Serdyuk called quietly.

Kawabata lowered his hands.

'Are you feeling bad?'

'I feel terrible,' said Kawabata, 'I feel absolutely terrible. If I had a hundred bellies, I would slit them all without a moment's delay. Never in my life have I felt such shame as I am feeling now.'

'Why, what's the problem?' Serdyuk asked sympathetically, kneeling down to face the Japanese.

'I made bold to ask you to render me the final service without thinking that there would be no one to render the service to you if I commit seppuku first. Such monstrous dishonour.'

'Me?' said Serdyuk, rising to his feet. 'Me?'

'Why yes,' said Kawabata, also rising and fixing Serdyuk with his blazing eyes. 'Who will cut off your head? Not Grisha, I suppose?'

'Who's Grisha?'

'The security guard. You were just talking to him. He's no good for anything except breaking heads with his truncheon. The rules say it has to be cut off, and not just any old way, it has to be left hanging on a scrap of skin. Imagine how terrible it would look if it went rolling across the floor! But sit down, sit down.'

There was such hypnotic power in Kawabata's gaze that Serdyuk involuntarily lowered himself on to a bamboo mat. It was all he could do to tear his eyes away from Kawabata's face.

'And anyway, I suspect you don't know what the doctrine of the direct and fearless return to eternity tells us about seppuku,' said Kawabata.

'What?'

'Do you know how to slit open your belly?'

'No,' said Serdyuk, staring blankly at the wall.

'There are various ways of doing it. The simplest is a horizontal incision. But there's nothing special in that. As we say in Japan, five minutes' dishonour and Amidha's your Buddha. Like driving into the Pure Land in an old Lada. A vertical incision is a little bit better, but that's the lower-middle-class style, and it's a bit provincial too. You can use crossed incisions, but I wouldn't advise that either. If you cut vertically, they'll pick up a Christian allusion, and if you cut on the diagonal, you get the St Andrew's Cross, which is the Russian naval flag. They'll think you're from the Black Sea Fleet – but you're not a naval officer, are you?'

'No, I'm not,' Serdyuk confirmed in an expressionless voice.

'That's what I'm saying, there's no point. Two years ago a double parallel incision was all the fashion, but that's difficult. So what I would suggest is a long diagonal cut from the lower left to the upper right with a slight turn back towards the centre at the end. From the strictly aesthetic point of view it's quite beyond reproach, and when you've done it, I'll probably do it the same way.'

Serdyuk attempted to stand up, but Kawabata placed a hand on his shoulder and forced him back down.

'Unfortunately, we shall have to do everything in a rush,' he said with a sigh. 'We don't have any white blinds or anything suitable to smoke. There are no warriors with drawn swords waiting at the edge of the platform . . . We do have Grisha, I suppose, but then, what kind of a warrior is he? Anyway, they're not really necessary, they're only there in case a samurai betrays his oath and refuses to commit seppuku. Then they beat him to death like a dog. There haven't been any cases like that in my time – but then, it's really beautiful when there are men with drawn swords standing around the border of the fenced-off area, the sun glinting on their steel. Yes, perhaps . . . Do you want me to call Grisha? And maybe Shura from the first floor as well? To bring it closer to the original ritual?'

'Don't bother,' said Serdyuk.

'That's right,' said Kawabata, 'that's right. Of course, you understand that the most important thing in any ritual is not the external form, but the internal content that fills it.'

'I understand, I understand. I understand everything,' said Serdyuk, staring with hatred at Kawabata.

'I am therefore absolutely certain that everything will proceed excellently.'

Kawabata lifted the short sword he had bought from the floor, drew it out of its scabbard and sliced through the air a couple of times.

'It will do,' he said. 'Now let me tell you something. There are always two problems. Not to fall over on your back after the incision – that's really most inelegant, but I can help you there – and the other problem is not to catch the spinal column with the blade. Therefore the blade should not be inserted too far. Let's do it this way . . .'

He picked up several sheets of paper with fax messages on them – Serdyuk noticed that the sheet with the drawing of the chrysanthemum was among them – stacked them into a neat pile and then carefully wrapped them round the blade, leaving four or five inches of steel projecting.

'That's it. So, you take the handle in your right hand, and you hold it here with your left hand. You don't need to push it in very hard, or it might get stuck and then . . . All right, and then upwards to the right. And now you probably want to focus your mind. We don't have much time, but at least there's enough for that.'

Serdyuk was sitting there in a kind of a trance, staring at the wall. Feeble thoughts ran through his head about pushing Kawabata aside and running out into the corridor and . . . But the door out there was locked, and there was Grisha with his truncheon. And there was supposed to be someone called Shura on the first floor, too. In theory he could phone the police, but Kawabata was right there beside him with his sword . . . And the police wouldn't turn out at this hour of the night. But the most unpleasant thing of all was that any such course of action would bring an expression of astonishment to Kawabata's face, to be followed rapidly by a grimace of fierce contempt. There was something in what had happened that day which Serdyuk didn't want to betray, and he even knew what it was – it was that moment after they'd tethered their horses, when they recited poetry to each other. And even though, if he really thought about it, there hadn't actually been any horses or any poems, the moment had been real, and so had the wind from the south that brought the promise of summer, and the stars in the sky. There couldn't be the slightest doubt that it had all been real – that is, just the way it should have been. But as for the world waiting for him behind that door which was due to be opened at eight in the morning . . .

Serdyuk's thoughts paused briefly, and he could suddenly hear quiet noises all around him. Kawabata's stomach was gurgling as he sat there beside the fax with his eyes closed, and Serdyuk thought that his companion was sure to complete the entire procedure with brilliant ease. And the world that the Japanese was preparing to quit – if by 'world' we mean everything that a man can feel and experience in his life – was certainly far more attractive than the stinking streets of Moscow that closed in on Serdyuk every morning to the accompaniment of the songs of Filipp Kirkorov.

Serdyuk realized why he'd suddenly thought of Kirkorov – the girls sitting behind the wall were listening to one of his songs. Then he heard the sounds of a brief quarrel, stifled weeping and the click of a switch. The invisible television began transmitting a news programme, but it seemed to Serdyuk that the channel hadn't really changed and Kirkorov had simply stopped singing and begun talking in a quiet voice. Then he heard one of the girls whispering agitatedly:

'He is, look! Pissed again! Look at him embracing Chirac! I tell you, he's pissed as a newt!'

Serdyuk thought for a few more seconds.

'Ah, to hell with the lot of it,' he said decisively. 'Give me the sword.'

Kawabata walked quickly over to him, went down on one knee and held out the handle of the sword to him.

'Hang on,' said Serdyuk, and he unbuttoned his shirt under his jacket. 'Can I do it through the T-shirt?'

Kawabata thought for a moment.

'It has been done on occasion. In 1454 after he lost the Battle of Okehajama, Takeda Katsueri slit open his belly through his hunting costume. So it's okay.'

Serdyuk took hold of the sword.

'Na-ah,' said Kawabata, 'I told you, take the handle in your right hand and use your left hand to grip the blade where it's wrapped. Like that.'

'So I just cut and that's all?'

'Hang on a second. I'll be right with you.'

Kawabata ran across the room and picked up his big sword, then came back to Serdyuk and stood behind him.

'You don't have to cut very deep. I'll have to cut deep though. I won't have a second to assist. You're lucky. You must have lived a good life.'

Serdyuk smiled wanly.

'Just an ordinary life,' he said. 'Like all the others.'

'But then, you are dying like a true warrior,' said Kawabata. 'Right then, I'm all set. Let's do it on the count of three.'

'Okay,' said Serdyuk.

'Take a deep breath,' said Kawabata, 'and we're off. One . . . two . . . two and a half . . . And three!'

Serdyuk stuck the sword into his belly.

The paper jammed tight against the T-shirt. It wasn't particularly painful, but the blade felt extremely cold.

The fax machine on the floor began to ring.

'That's it,' said Kawabata. 'And now up and to the right. Harder, harder . . . That's it, that's right.'

Serdyuk's legs began to tremble.

'Now a quick turn in towards the centre and push it into yourself with both hands. That's it, that's it . . . That's right . . . Now just an inch more . . .'

'I can't,' Serdyuk said with a struggle, 'everything's on fire!'

'So what did you expect?' said Kawabata. 'Just a moment.'

He skipped over to the fax machine and picked up the receiver.

'Hello! Yes! That's right, this is the place. Yes, a 1996 model, it's done two thousand miles.'

Serdyuk dropped the sword on the floor and pressed his hands to his bleeding belly.

'Quickly!' he wheezed. 'Quickly!'

Kawabata frowned and gestured for him to wait.

'What?' he yelled into the receiver. 'What do you mean, three and a half thousand is too much? I paid five thousand for it only a year ago!'

The light in Serdyuk's eyes slowly faded and went out, like the lights in a cinema just before the film. He began slowly slumping over to one side, but before his shoulder reached the floor, all awareness of his body had disappeared; there was nothing left but an all-consuming agony. Through a red, pulsating mist he heard Kawabata's voice:

'What d'you mean damaged? Where's it damaged? You call two scratches on the bumper damage? What? What? Arsehole yourself! You shit, you fucking wanker! What? You can go fuck yourself!'

The receiver clanged back into place and the fax machine immediately began ringing again.

Serdyuk noticed that the space in which the telephone was ringing and Kawabata was swearing and everything else was happening was somewhere very far away from him; it was such an insignificant segment of reality that he had to focus with all his strength to follow what was going on there. At the same time, there was absolutely no sense in this act of concentration: Serdyuk realized that this concentration was life. It turned out that his entire, long existence as a human being, with all its longings, hopes and fears, had been nothing more than a fleeting thought that had momentarily attracted his attention. And now Serdyuk – although it was not really Serdyuk at all – was drifting through a qualityless void and he sensed he was coming close to something huge that radiated an intolerable heat. The most terrible thing was that this immense thing that breathed fire was approaching him from behind, which meant that it was impossible for him to see what it actually was. The sensation was quite unbearable, and Serdyuk began feverishly searching for the spot where he had left behind the old, familiar world. By some miracle he found it, and Kawabata's voice sounded in his head like the tolling of a bell:

'On the islands they didn't believe at first that you would manage it. But I knew you would. And now, allow me to render you the final service. Huh-u-up!'

For a long time after that there was nothing at all – although it was not really even correct to say that it was a long time, because there was no time either. And then there was a cough, and a squeaking of floorboards and Timur Timurovich's voice said:

'Yes, Senya. They found you there like that by the heater with the neck of a broken bottle in your hand. Who were you really drinking with, can you remember?'

There was no answer.

'Tatyana Pavlovna,' said Timur Timurovich, 'two cc's please. Yes, now.'

'Timur Timurovich,' Volodin said unexpectedly from the corner, 'they were spirits, you know.'

'Oh yes?' Timur Timurovich asked politely. 'Who were spirits?'

'All of them from the House of Taira. I swear they were. And he behaved with them like he wanted to die. Probably he really did want to.'

'Then why is he still alive?' asked Timur Timurovich.

'He was wearing that T-shirt with the Olympic symbols.

You remember the year they held the Olympic Games in Moscow, don't you? Lots and lots of those little symbols, right? He was cutting through the T-shirt.'

'What of it?'

'Well, we should think of them as magic hieroglyphs. I read in a book about a case in ancient times when they drew protective symbols all over this monk, but they forgot about his ears. And when the spirits of Taira came, they took his ears, because as far as they were concerned everything else was invisible.'

'But why did they come to him? I mean, to the monk?'

'He played the flute very well.'

'Ah, the flute,' said Timur Timurovich. 'Well, that's logical enough, I suppose. But don't you find it odd that these spectres are "Dynamo" fans?'

'There's nothing surprising about that,' Volodin replied. 'Some spectres support "Spartak", others support the Army Club. Why shouldn't some of them support "Dynamo"?'

7

'Dinama! Dinama! Where the fuck you goin'?'

I leapt up from my bed. A man was chasing a horse around the yard and yelling: 'Dinama! Where d'ya think you're off to? Come 'ere, yer bugger!'

There were horses snorting and whinnying under my window; looking out, I saw a huge jostling crowd of Red Army men who had not been there the day before. I could only actually tell that they were Red Army men from their ragamuffin appearance: they were clearly dressed in the first garments that had come to hand, for the most part in civilian garb, and it seemed that their preferred method for equipping themselves must have been pillage. Standing in the centre of the crowd was a man wearing a pointed Red Army helmet with a crookedly tacked-on red star, waving his arms about and issuing some kind of instruction. He bore a striking resemblance to the weavers' commissar, Furmanov, whom I had seen at the meeting in front of the Yaroslavl Station in Moscow, except that now he had a crimson scar from a sabre cut across his cheek.

I did not, however, waste long contemplating this motley crew, for my attention was drawn to the carriage standing in the very centre of the yard. Four black horses had been harnessed to a long open landau with pneumatic tyres, soft leather seats and a frame made of expensive timber which still bore lingering traces of gilt. There was something quite unbearably nostalgic in this object of luxury, this fragment of a world which had disappeared for ever into oblivion; its inhabitants had naively supposed that they would be riding into the future in vehicles just like this one. In the event, it was only the vehicles which had survived their jaunt into the future, and only then at the cost of transformation into parodies of

Hunnish war chariots – such were the associations triggered by the sight of the three Lewis machine-guns tied together by a metal beam which had been installed in the rear section of the landau.

As I moved back from the window I suddenly remembered that in Russian the soldiers called this kind of chariot a *tachanka*. The origins of this word were mysterious and obscure, and although I mentally reviewed all of the possible etymologies as I pulled on my boots, I could not find one that really suited the case. I did, however, come up with a humorous play on words in English: *tachanka* – 'touch Anka'. But since the memory of my declaration of feelings the previous day to the lady in question was enough to bring a sullen flush to my cheeks, I felt unable to share my joke with anyone.

These, more or less, were the thoughts that filled my head as I went down the stairs and out into the yard. Someone said that Kotovsky had asked me to come into the staff barn, and I set off in that direction immediately. Two soldiers in black uniforms were standing on guard at the entrance. As I walked past, they stood to attention and saluted. From the look of concentration on their faces, I realized that they knew me well, but unfortunately the concussion had completely erased their names from my memory.

Kotovsky was sitting on the table wearing a tightly buttoned brown service jacket. He was alone in the room. I noted the deathly pallor of his face, as though a thick layer of powder had been applied to it. Standing beside him on the table was a transparent cylinder inside which clouds of some molten white substance were clumped together. It was a lamp made out of a spirit-stove and a long glass retort, inside which lumps of wax floated in tinted glycerine: five years before they had been the height of fashion in St Petersburg.

Kotovsky held out his hand. I noticed that his fingers were trembling slightly.

'Since early this morning,' he said, raising his cool, limpid eyes to my face, 'for some reason I have been thinking about what awaits us beyond the grave.'

'Then you believe that something does await us?' I asked.

'Perhaps I didn't express myself very well,' said Kotovsky.

'Let us just say I have been pondering on death and immortality.'

'What could have brought on such a mood?'

'It has never really left me since a certain memorable day in Odessa,' Kotovsky answered with a cold smile. 'But that is not important.'

He folded his arms on his chest and pointed to the lamp with his chin.

'Look at that wax,' he said. 'Watch carefully what happens to it. As the spirit-stove heats up, it rises upwards in drops that assume the most fantastic forms. As it rises, it cools. The higher the pieces rise, the more slowly they move. And finally, at some point they stop and begin to fall back towards the very place from which they have just risen, often without ever reaching the surface.'

'There's a tragedy straight out of Plato in it,' I said thoughtfully.

'Possibly. But that is not what I have in mind. Imagine that the solidified drops rising upwards in the lamp are endowed with consciousness. In this case they will immediately encounter the problem of self-identification.'

'Undoubtedly.'

'Now this is where it becomes really interesting. If one of those lumps of wax believes that it is the form which it has assumed, then it is mortal, because that form will be destroyed – but if it understands that it is wax, then what can happen to it?'

'Nothing,' I replied.

'Precisely,' said Kotovsky. 'In that case it is immortal. But the tricky part is, it's very difficult for the wax to understand that it is wax – it's almost impossible to grasp one's own primordial nature. How can you notice what has been there right in front of you since the beginning of time? And so the only thing that the wax does notice is its temporary form. But the form is arbitrary every time it arises, influenced by thousands and thousands of different circumstances.'

'A quite magnificent allegory. But what conclusion can we draw from it?' I asked, recalling our conversation of the previous evening concerning the fate of Russia, and the facility with which he had directed the subject towards cocaine. It might well prove to be that he was simply trying to obtain the remainder of the powder and was gradually leading the conversation around to that topic.

'The conclusion is that the only route to immortality for a drop of wax is to stop thinking of itself as a drop and to realize that it is wax. But since our drop is capable only of noticing its own form, all its brief life it prays to the Wax God to preserve this form, although, if one thinks about it, this form possesses absolutely no inherent relation to the wax. Any drop of wax possesses exactly the same properties as its entire volume. Do you understand me? A drop of the great ocean of being is the entire ocean, contracted for a moment to the scope of that drop. But now, tell me how to explain this to these drops of wax that fear most of all for their own fleeting form? How can we instil this thought into them? For it is thoughts that drive them towards salvation or destruction, because in their essence both salvation and destruction are also thoughts. I believe it is the Upanishads that tell us that mind is a horse harnessed to the carriage of the body . . .'

At this point he clicked his fingers, as though he had been struck by an unexpected idea, and again raised his cold gaze to my face:

'By the way, while we are on the subject of carriages and horses, don't you think that, after all, half a tin of cocaine for a pair of Oryol trotters is just a bit . . .'

A sudden thunderous crash burst upon my ears, startling me so badly that I staggered backwards. The lamp standing beside Kotovsky had exploded, splattering a cascade of glycerine across the table and over the map which was spread on it. Kotovsky leapt off the table and a revolver appeared in his hand like magic.

Chapaev was standing in the doorway with his nickel-plated Mauser in his hand; he was wearing a grey jacket with a high collar, a shoulder-belt, an astrakhan hat with a slanting watered-silk ribbon and black riding breeches trimmed with leather and decorated with a triple stripe. A silver pentagram gleamed on his chest – I remembered that he had called it

'The Order of the October Star' – and a small pair of black binoculars hung beside it.

'That was smart talking there, Grisha, about the drop of wax,' he said in a thin, hoarse tenor, 'but what're you going to say now? Where's your great ocean of beans now?'

Kotovsky glanced in perplexity at the spot where the lamp had been standing only a moment before. A huge greasy spot had spread across the map. Thankfully, the wick of the lamp had been extinguished by the explosion, otherwise the room would already have been ablaze.

'The form, the wax – who created it all?' Chapaev asked menacingly. 'Answer me!'

'Mind,' replied Kotovsky.

'Where is it? Show me.'

'Mind is the lamp,' said Kotovsky. 'I mean, it was.'

'If mind is the lamp, then where do you go to now it's broken?'

'Then what is mind?' Kotovsky asked in confusion.

Chapaev fired another shot, and the bullet transformed the ink-well standing on the table into a cloud of blue spray.

I felt a strange momentary dizziness.

Two bright red blotches had appeared on Kotovsky's pallid cheeks.

'Yes,' he said, 'now I understand. You've taught me a lesson, Vasily Ivanovich. A serious lesson.'

'Ah, Grisha,' Chapaev said sadly, 'what's wrong with you? You know yourself you can't afford to make any mistakes now – you just can't. Because where you're going there won't be anyone to point out your mistakes, and whatever you say, that's how it'll be.'

Without looking up, Kotovsky turned on his heels and ran out of the barn.

'We're just about to advance,' said Chapaev, putting his smoking pistol back into its holster. 'Why don't we go in that carriage you won from Grisha yesterday? While we're at it we can have a little chat.'

'With pleasure,' I said.

'I've already ordered it to be harnessed,' said Chapaev. 'Anka and Grisha can ride the *tachanka*.'

A dark shadow must have flitted across my face, because Chapaev laughed loudly and slapped me on the back with all his might.

We went out into the yard and pushed our way through the crowd of Red Army men to the stables, where the prevailing mood was that bustling confusion of alarm and jollity so dear to the heart of every true cavalryman, the mood that always envelops a detachment as it prepares for imminent battle. The soldiers were tightening saddle girths, checking hooves and conversing loudly, but behind the merriment one could sense the sober concentration and the supreme tension in every fibre of their spirit. These human feelings seemed to infect the horses, which were shifting from one foot to the other, whinnying occasionally as they attempted to spit out their bits, and squinting sideways out of their large, magnetic eyes, which seemed to shine with an insane joy.

I too felt myself falling under the hypnotic influence of imminent danger. Chapaev began explaining something to two soldiers and I went over to the nearest horse and sank my fingers into his mane. I can recall that second perfectly – coarse hairs under my fingers, the slightly sour smell of a new leather saddle, a spot of sunlight on the wall in front of my face and a quite incredible, incomparable feeling of the completeness, the total reality of this world. I suppose it was the feeling which people attempt to express in phrases like 'living life to the full'. It lasted for no more than a single brief second, but that was long enough for me to realize yet again that this full, authentic sense of life can never, by its very nature, last any longer.

'Petka!' Chapaev shouted behind me. 'Time to be off!'

I slapped the horse on the neck and set off towards the carriage, glancing sideways at the *tachanka*, in which Kotovsky and Anna were already seated. Anna was wearing a white peaked cap with a red band and a simple soldier's blouse with a narrow belt on which hung a small suede holster; her blue riding breeches with the narrow red piping were tucked into high lace-up boots. Decked out in that fashion, she looked unbearably young, almost like a schoolgirl. When she caught my glance, she turned away.

Chapaev was already in the carriage. Sitting in front was the silent Bashkir, the same one who had poured the champagne in the train and later had almost skewered me with his bayonet as he stood on his absurd guard duty over a haystack. As soon as I had taken my seat, the Bashkir jerked the reins, clicked his tongue and we rolled out through the gates.

Travelling behind us came the *tachanka* with Kotovsky and Anna, followed by the cavalrymen. We turned to the right and set off up the road, which rose steeply, then curved to the right into a green wall of foliage.

We drove into something like a tunnel, formed by branches that wove themselves together above the road – the trees were rather strange, rather more like overgrown bushes than real trees; the tunnel proved to be very long, or perhaps I had that impression because we were moving slowly. Sunlight filtered through the branches and glinted in the final drops of the morning dew. The brilliant green of the foliage was so dazzling that at one point I completely lost all orientation and I felt as though we were falling slowly down a bottomless green well. I closed my eyes and the feeling passed.

The thickets on each side of us came to an end as abruptly as they had begun and we found ourselves on an earth road leading uphill. On the left there was a shallow rocky slope, on the right a weathered stone cliff of an incredibly beautiful pale lilac colour, with little trees sprouting here and there in cracks in the stone. We continued our ascent for about a quarter of an hour.

Chapaev sat with his eyes closed and his hands clasped together on the handle of his sabre, which was thrust against the floor. He seemed to be absorbed in profound thought on some subject, or to have fallen into a light sleep. Suddenly he opened his eyes and turned towards me.

'Are you still suffering from those nightmares you were complaining about?' he asked.

'As always, Vasily Ivanovich,' I replied.

'And still about that clinic?'

'Oh, if they were only about that. As in every dream, everything changes at a most fantastic pace. Last night, for instance, I dreamed about Japan. But the night before I did dream about the clinic, and do you know what happened? That butcher in charge of everything that goes on there asked me to write down in detail what happens to me here. He said he needed it for his work. Can you imagine it?'

'I can,' said Chapaev. 'Why don't you do as he says?'

I stared at him in amazement.

'You mean to say you would seriously advise me to do it?'

He nodded.

'But why?'

'You told me yourself that in your nightmares everything changes with fantastic speed. Any consistent activity that you repeatedly come back to makes it possible to create something like a fixed centre to the dream. Then the dream becomes more real. You couldn't possibly think up any better idea than making notes in your dream.'

I pondered the idea.

'But what good is a fixed centre to my nightmares if what I really want is to get rid of them?'

'It's precisely in order to get rid of them – you can only get rid of something that is real.'

'I suppose so. You mean, then, that I can write down absolutely everything that takes place here?'

'Of course.'

'But what should I call you in this journal of mine?'

Chapaev laughed.

'Petka, it's no accident you're dreaming about a mental hospital. What difference does it make what you call me in the notes you make in a dream?'

'That's true enough,' I said, feeling like a complete fool. 'I was simply afraid that . . . No, there really must be something wrong with my head.'

'Call me any name you like,' said Chapaev. 'Even Chapaev, if you like.'

'Chapaev?' I asked.

'Why not? You can even write,' he said with a chuckle, 'that I had a long moustache, and after I said that I twirled it.'

He twirled his moustache with a gentle, precise movement of his fingers.

'But I think the advice you were given applies more to reality,' he said. 'You should start writing down your dreams, and you should try to do it while you can still remember all the details.'

'They are quite impossible to forget,' I said. 'Every time I come round, I realize that it was no more than a nightmare . . . But while I am dreaming, it's impossible to understand what is real in actual fact – the carriage we are sitting in or that white-tiled hell where demons in white coats torment me at night.'

'What is real in actual fact?' Chapaev repeated after me, closing his eyes again. 'That's a question you're not likely to find an answer to. Because in actual fact there is no actual fact.'

'How do you mean?' I asked.

'Well now, Petka my lad,' said Chapaev, 'I once used to know a Chinese communist by the name of Tzu-Chuang, who often dreamed the same dream, that he was a red butterfly fluttering through the grass and the flowers. And when he woke up, he often couldn't make out whether the butterfly had dreamt it was engaged in revolutionary activity or the underground activist had had a dream about flitting through the air from flower to flower. So when this Tzu-Chuang was arrested in Mongolia for sabotage, what he said at his interrogation was that he was actually a butterfly who was dreaming about what was happening. Now since he was interrogated by Baron Jungern himself, and the Baron is a man of some considerable understanding, the next question was why this butterfly was on the communist side. He said he wasn't on the communist side at all. So then they asked him why the butterfly was engaged in sabotage, and his answer was that all the things people do are so monstrous, it doesn't make any difference whose side you're on.'

'And what happened to him?'

'Nothing. They just stood him up in front of a firing squad and woke him up.'

'And then what?'

Chapaev shrugged.

'He carried on flitting around the flowers, I suppose.'

'I understand, Vasily Ivanovich, I understand,' I said thoughtfully.

The road made another looping turn, and a dizzying view of the town opened up on our left. I spotted the yellow dot of our manor-house and the bright green patch of low trees which it had taken us so long to traverse. The shallow mountain slopes on all sides came together at their base to form a kind of chalice-shaped depression, and lying on the very bottom of the chalice was Altai-Vidnyansk.

It was not the actual view of the town that made the most powerful impression, but the panorama of the chalice formed by the mountain slopes; the town was rather unkempt and reminded me more than anything of a heap of rubbish washed down into a pit by torrential rain. The houses were still half-concealed by the final lingering wisps of morning mist. I was suddenly astonished to realize that I myself was a part of the world which lay on the bottom of this gigantic drain – where this strange, confused civil war was happening, where people were greedily dividing up the tiny, ugly houses and the crooked patches of vegetable gardens in order to gain a firmer foothold in what was literally the sink of creation. I thought about the Chinese dreamer whose story Chapaev had told me and then looked down again. In the face of the motionless world stretched out around me, beneath the calm gaze of its sky, it became inexpressibly clear that the little town at the bottom of the pit was precisely like every other town in the world. All of them, I thought, lie on the bottom of the same kind of depression, even though it may not be discernible to the eye. They are all stewing in a massive devil's cauldron on the flame that is said to rage at the centre of the Earth, and they are all simply different versions of one and the same nightmare which nothing can change for the better. The only thing that can be done with this nightmare is to awaken from it.

'If they wake you up from your nightmares the same way they did that Chinaman, Petka,' Chapaev said without opening his eyes, 'all that'll happen is that you'll drop from one dream into another. You've been flitting to and fro like that all eternity. But if you can understand that absolutely everything that happens to you is a dream, then it won't matter a damn what kind of dreams you have. And when you wake up afterwards, you'll really wake up – for ever. If you want to, that is.'

'But why is everything that is happening to me a dream?'

'Because, Petka,' Chapaev said, 'there just isn't anything else.'

The climb came to an end and we emerged on to a broad plateau. Far away on the horizon, beyond a line of shallow hills, the massive blue, lilac and purple forms of mountains thrust up high into the sky, with an immense open expanse of grass and flowers before them. Their colours were dull and faded, but there were so many of them that the overall tone of the steppe seemed not so much green as straw-coloured. It was so beautiful that for several minutes I forgot all about what Chapaev had said – and about everything else in the world.

Except, strangely enough, for that Chinese dreamer. As I looked at the faded faces of the flowers drifting past our carriage, I imagined him soaring through the space between them, pausing occasionally out of habit to paste up an anti-government broadsheet on a slim shoot of bracken, and then starting in surprise every time he recalled that it was a long time since he had had any broadsheets to paste up. And even if he had had any, who would read them?

Soon, however, I was disturbed from my meditations. Chapaev had obviously given our driver some kind of signal. We picked up speed, and everything around the carriage began to blur into stripes of colour. The Bashkir lashed the horses mercilessly, half-standing on the coach-box and shouting guttural sounds in an unfamiliar language.

The road along which we were travelling could be called that only in name. Perhaps there were fewer flowers growing on it than in the open field, and traces of some ancient rut could still be discerned at its centre, but it was far from easy to guess where it ran. Nonetheless, the surface of the steppe was so ideally even that we were hardly shaken at all. The cavalrymen in black who brought up the rear of our small detachment moved off the road, drew almost level with our carriage and formed into two groups, one on each side, so that now they were hurtling along with us over the grass in the form of an extended arc; it was as though our carriage had sprouted two narrow black wings.

The machine-gun landau in which Anna and Kotovsky were sitting also picked up speed and drew almost level with us. I noticed Kotovsky prodding his driver in the back with his cane and nodding towards our carriage. They were clearly trying to overtake us, and at one point they very nearly succeeded, hurtling along beside us at a distance of only a few yards. I noticed a design on the side of the *tachanka*, a circle divided by a wavy line into two halves, one black and one white, each of them with a small circle of the opposite colour at its centre – I thought I recognized it as an Eastern symbol of some kind. Beside it there was a large inscription, crudely daubed in white paint:

> POWER OF NIGHT AND POWER OF DAY
> SAME OLD GARBAGE ANY WAY

The Bashkir lashed our horses, and the *tachanka* fell behind again. It seemed incomprehensible to me that Anna could have agreed to travel in a carriage decorated with words of that kind. But then I suddenly had the feeling, which rapidly hardened into certainty, that she was the very one who had written the inscription on the side of the landau. How little, in actual fact, did I really know about this woman!

Our detachment hurtled on across the steppe to the accompaniment of wild whistles from the cavalrymen. We must have covered five or six miles like that – the hills on the horizon had moved so much closer that I could clearly distinguish their large rocks and the trees that grew on them. The surface of the steppe across which our carriage was racing at such speed was now less even than when we had begun our gallop; sometimes the carriage was thrown high into the air, and I began to feel afraid that the excursion would end in a broken neck for some of our company. Then Chapaev drew his Mauser from its holster and fired into the air.

'Enough!' he roared. 'Walk on!'

Our carriage slowed its pace. The horsemen, as though afraid of crossing the invisible boundary of a line projected from the rear axle of our carriage, began dropping out of view behind us one by one. The landau with Anna and Kotovsky also fell back, and within a few minutes we were again far ahead of them.

Ahead of us I noticed a vertical column of smoke rising from behind the hills. It was dense and white, like the smoke from grass and damp leaves thrown on to a fire; the strangest thing about it, however, was that it scarcely widened out at all as it rose, which made it appear like a tall white pillar propping up the sky. It was no more than a mile ahead of us, with its fire concealed by the hills. We continued our advance for a few more minutes and then halted.

The road came to an end at two low, steep-sided hillocks with a narrow path running between them. They were like gateposts to some natural gateway, and were so symmetrical that they looked like a pair of ancient towers which had sunk down into the ground many centuries ago. They seemed to mark a boundary, beyond which the landscape changed, with foothills beginning to merge into the mountains on the horizon. It seemed, too, that it was not only the landscape that was different on the far side; feeling a gust of wind on my face, I looked up in amazement at the column of smoke which rose absolutely straight from a source which must now be very close at hand.

'Why are we standing here?' I asked Chapaev.

'We're waiting,' he replied.

'For whom? The enemy?'

Chapaev did not answer. I suddenly realized that I had left my sabre behind and only had my Browning with me, so that I would find myself in a somewhat uncomfortable position if we had to deal with cavalry. But then, judging from the calm manner in which Chapaev carried on sitting in the carriage, we were not in any immediate danger. I glanced behind me and saw the landau with Kotovsky and Anna standing beside us. I noticed Kotovsky's white face; sitting there on the back seat with his arms folded across his chest, he looked rather like an opera singer poised to make his entrance. I could see Anna's back as she fiddled with the machine-guns, but she seemed to be doing it less in order to prepare the guns than to relieve her irritation at sitting beside the insufferably solemn

Kotovsky. Our mounted escort, apparently afraid of approaching the earthwork gateposts, kept a good distance, and I could make out no more of them than their dark silhouettes.

'But who are we waiting for?' I asked again.

'We have a meeting with the Black Baron,' replied Chapaev. 'I expect, Pyotr, that this will be an acquaintance you will remember.'

'What kind of terrible nickname is that? I suppose he has a name of his own?'

'Yes,' said Chapaev, 'his real surname is Jungern von Sternberg.'

'Jungern?' I repeated. 'Jung-ern . . . That sounds familiar . . . Does he have something to do with psychiatry? Has he not done some work on the interpretation of symbols?'

Chapaev looked me up and down in amazement.

'No,' he said. 'As far as I can judge, he despises all manner of symbols, no matter what they might refer to.'

'Ah, now I remember. He is the one who shot that Chinese of yours.'

'Yes,' Chapaev answered. 'He is the defender of Inner Mongolia. They say he is an incarnation of the god of war. He used to command the Asian Cavalry Division, but now he commands the Special Regiment of Tibetan Cossacks.'

'I have never heard of them,' I said. 'And why do they call him the Black Baron?'

Chapaev thought for a moment.

'A good question,' he said. 'I really don't know. Why don't you ask him yourself? He's already here.'

I started and turned my head to look.

A strange object had appeared in the narrow passage between the two hillocks. On looking closely I realized that it was a palanquin of a very ancient and strange design, consisting of a small cabin with a humped roof and four long handles on which it was carried. Both the roof and the handles appeared to be made of bronze which had turned green with age, and were covered with a multitude of minute jade plaques which glinted mysteriously, like cats' eyes in the dark. There was nobody in the vicinity who could have brought up the palanquin without being noticed, and I could only assume that the unknown bearers whose palms had polished the long handles until they gleamed had already retreated.

The palanquin stood on curved legs, giving it the appearance of something between a sacrificial vessel and a small hut supported on four short piles. Its resemblance to a hut was actually stronger, and the impression was reinforced by blinds of fine green silk netting which covered its windows. Behind them I could just discern a motionless silhouette.

Chapaev jumped out of the carriage and walked over to the palanquin.

'Hello, baron,' he said.

'Good day,' replied a low voice from behind the blind.

'I come with another request,' said Chapaev.

'I presume that once again you are not asking for yourself?'

'No,' said Chapaev. 'Do you recall Grigory Kotovsky?'

'I do,' said the voice in the palanquin. 'What has happened to him?'

'I simply can't explain to him what *mind* is. This morning he pushed me so far that I reached for my pistol. I've already told him everything that can be said, over and over again. What he needs is a demonstration, baron, something he won't be able to ignore.'

'Your problems, my dear Chapaev, grow a little monotonous. Where is your protégé?'

Chapaev turned towards the carriage where Kotovsky was sitting and waved.

The blind in the palanquin moved aside and I saw a man of about forty, with blond hair, a high forehead and cold, colourless eyes. Despite the drooping Tartar-style moustache and the cheeks covered with several days' stubble, his features were highly refined. He was dressed in a strange garment halfway between a cassock and a greatcoat, cut in the style of a Mongolian robe with a low, semicircular neck. I would never even have thought of it as a greatcoat if it had not been for the shoulder-straps bearing the zigzag lines of a general's rank. Hanging at his side was a sabre exactly like Chapaev's in every respect, except that the tassel attached to its handle was not purple, but black. And on his breast there were no less than three silver stars, hanging in a row. He climbed quickly out of the palanquin – he proved to be almost a full head taller than me – and looked me up and down inquiringly.

'Who is this?'

'This is my commissar, Pyotr Voyd,' Chapaev replied. 'He distinguished himself in the battle of Lozovaya Junction.'

'I have heard something of that,' said the baron. 'Is he here for the same reason?'

Chapaev nodded. Jungern held out his hand to me.

'Pleased to meet you, Pyotr.'

'The feeling is mutual, general,' I replied, squeezing his powerful, sinewy hand in mine.

'Just call me baron,' said Jungern, turning to face Kotovsky as the latter approached. 'Grigory, how very long . . .'

'Hello, baron,' Kotovsky replied. 'I am very glad to see you.'

'Judging from the pallor of your cheeks, you are so very glad to see me that all your blood has rushed to your heart.'

'Why, not at all, baron. That is because I think so much about Russia.'

'Ah, the same old thing. I cannot approve. However, let us not waste any time. Let us take a walk, shall we?' Jungern nodded towards the earthwork gateposts.

Kotovsky swallowed hard. 'I should be honoured,' he replied.

Jungern turned inquiringly towards Chapaev, who held out a small paper package to him.

'Are there two here?' asked the baron.

'Yes.'

Jungern put the package into the pocket of his robe, put his arm round Kotovsky's shoulders and literally dragged him in the direction of the gateway. They disappeared into the opening, and I turned to face Chapaev.

'What lies beyond that gateway?'

Chapaev smiled. 'I wouldn't like to spoil your first impression.'

The dull report of a revolver shot rang out. A second later the solitary figure of the baron appeared.

'And now you, Pyotr,' he said.

I cast a glance of inquiry at Chapaev, who screwed up his

eyes and nodded with an unusually powerful movement of his chin, as though he were forcing an invisible nail into his own chest.

I walked slowly towards the baron.

I must confess that I was afraid. It was not that I felt any real threat of danger hanging over me – or rather, it was precisely a sense of danger, but not of the kind felt before a duel or a battle, when you know that even the very worst that can happen can only happen to *you*. At that moment I had the feeling that the danger was not threatening me, but my very conception of myself. I was not expecting anything terrible to happen, but the 'I' who was not expecting anything terrible suddenly seemed to me like a man walking a tightrope across an abyss who has just sensed the first breath of a burgeoning breeze.

'I will show you my camp,' the baron said when I reached him.

'Listen, baron, if you are intending to awaken me in the same way as you did the Chinese . . .'

'Oh, come now,' he interrupted with a smile. 'Chapaev must have been telling you all sorts of horror stories. That's not what I'm really like.'

He took me by the elbow and turned me to face the earth-work gateposts.

'Let us take a stroll around the camp-fires,' he said, 'and see how our lads are getting on.'

'I do not see any camp-fires,' I replied.

'You don't?' he said. 'Try looking a bit harder.'

I looked once again into the gap between the two sunken earthen mounds, and at that very moment the baron pushed me from behind. I flew forward and fell to the ground; the sheer rapidity of his movement was such that for a second I felt as though I were a gate that he had kicked off its hinges. A moment later I felt a strange spasm run across my entire field of vision; I screwed up my eyes, and bright spots appeared in the darkness ahead of me, as though I had pressed my fingers into my eyes or made too sudden a movement with my head. However, when I opened my eyes and rose to my feet, the lights still did not disappear.

I could not understand where we were. The hills and the summer breeze had completely disappeared; we were surrounded by intense darkness, and scattered all around us in it, for as far as the eye could see, were the bright spots of camp-fires. They were arranged in an unnaturally precise pattern, as though they stood on the intersections of an invisible grid which divided the world up into an infinite number of squares. The distance between the fires was about fifty paces, so that if you stood at one it was impossible to see the people sitting at the next one; all that could be made out were vague, blurred silhouettes, but how many people there were, and whether they were people at all, was impossible to say with any degree of certainty. The strangest thing of all, however, was that the ground beneath our feet had also changed beyond recognition, and we were now standing on an ideally level plane covered with something like scrubby, shrivelled grass, but without a single projection or depression anywhere on its surface – that much was clear simply from the absolutely perfect patterning of the fires.

'What is all this?' I asked in confusion.

'Aha!' said the baron. 'Now, perhaps, I think you can see.'

'I can,' I said.

'This is one of the branches of the world beyond the grave,' said Jungern, 'the one for which I am responsible. For the most part the people who find their way here were warriors during their lifetimes. Perhaps you have heard of Valhalla?'

'Yes, I have,' I said, feeling an absurdly childish desire welling up in me to grab hold of the baron's robe.

'Well, this is it. Unfortunately, however, it's not only warriors who find their way here, but all kinds of other trash who have gone in for shooting. Bandits, murderers – the range of scum we get is amazing, which is why I have to make the rounds and check on things. Sometimes I even feel as though I were employed here in the capacity of a forest warden.'

The baron sighed.

'But then, as I recall,' he said, with a faint note of sadness in his voice, 'when I was a child I wanted to be a forester. I tell you what, Pyotr, why don't you take a good grip on my sleeve? It's not so simple to walk around here.'

'I do not quite understand,' I answered with relief, 'but by all means, if you say so.'

I took a tight hold on the cloth of his sleeve and we began moving forward. One thing immediately struck me as strange; the baron was not walking particularly fast, certainly no quicker than he was before the world had been so horrifyingly transformed, but the camp-fires past which we made our way receded behind us at a quite startling rate. It was as though he and I were walking at a leisurely pace along a platform which was being towed at incredible speed by a train, and the direction in which the train moved was determined by the direction in which the baron turned. One of the camp-fires appeared ahead, came rushing towards us and then stopped dead at our very feet when the baron stopped walking.

There were two men sitting by the fire. They were wet and half-naked, and they looked like Romans, with only short sheets wrapped around their bodies. They were both armed, one with a revolver and the other with a double-barrelled shotgun, and they were covered all over with repulsive bullet wounds. No sooner did they catch sight of the baron than they fell to the ground and literally began trembling with an overwhelming, physically palpable terror.

'Who are you?' the baron asked in a low voice.

'Hit men for Seryozha the Mongoloid,' one of them said without raising his head.

'How did you get here?' the baron asked.

'We was topped by mistake, boss.'

'I'm not your boss,' said the baron, 'and no one gets topped by mistake.'

'Honest, it was by mistake,' the second man said in a plaintive voice. 'In the sauna. They thought Mongoloid was in there signing a contract.'

'What contract?' asked Jungern, raising his eyebrows in astonishment.

'We had to pay back this loan. Slav-East Oil transferred the money on an irrevocable letter of credit, and the invoice didn't go through. So these two hulks from Ultima Thule came down . . .'

'Irrevocable letter of credit?' the baron interrupted. 'Ultima Thule? I see.'

He leant down and breathed on the flame, which immediately shrank to a fraction of its size, changing from a hot roaring torch into a pale tongue only a few inches in height. The effect this produced on the two half-naked men was astounding – they stiffened into complete immobility, and their backs were instantly covered in hoarfrost.

'Warriors, eh?' said the baron. 'How do you like that? The people who find their way into Valhalla these days. Seryozha the Mongoloid . . . It's that stupid rule about having a sword in your hand that's to blame.'

'What has happened to them?' I asked.

'Whatever was supposed to happen,' said the baron. 'I don't know. But I can take a look.'

He blew once again on the barely visible blue flame and it flared up with its old energy. The baron stared into it for several seconds with his eyes half-closed.

'It seems likely they will be bulls in a meat-production complex. That kind of indulgence is rather common nowadays, partly because of the infinite mercy of the Buddha, and partly because of the chronic shortage of meat in Russia.'

I was astounded by the camp-fire, now that I had the time to study it in detail. In fact, it could not really be called a camp-fire at all: there was no sign of firewood in the flames – instead they sprang from a fused opening in the ground shaped like a star with five narrow points.

'Tell me, baron, what is this pentagram beneath the flames?'

'A strange question,' said the baron. 'This is the eternal flame of the compassion of Buddha. And what you call a pentagram is really the emblem of the Order of the October Star. Where else should the eternal flame of mercy burn, if not above that emblem?'

'But what is the Order of the October Star?' I asked, peering at his chest. 'I have heard the phrase in the most varied of circumstances, but no one has ever explained to me what it means.'

'The October Star?' Jungern replied. 'It's really very simple. It's just like Christmas, you know – the Catholics have it in

December, the Orthodox Christians have it in January, but they're all celebrating the same birthday. This is the same sort of thing. Reforms of the calendar, mistakes made by scribes – in other words, although it's generally believed to have happened in May, in actual fact it was in October.'

'But what was?'

'You astonish me, Pyotr. It's one of the best-known stories in the world. There was once a man who could not live as others did. He tried to understand what everything meant – all the things that happened to him from day to day; and who he himself was – the person to whom all those things were happening. And then, one night in October when he was sitting under the crown of a tree, he raised his eyes to the sky and saw a bright star. At that moment he understood everything with such absolute clarity that to this day the echo of that distant second . . .'

The baron fell silent as if he were seeking for words to express himself, but was unable to find anything appropriate.

'You'd better have a talk with Chapaev,' he concluded. 'He enjoys telling people about it. The main thing though, the essential point, is that ever since that second this flame of compassion has been burning for all living beings, a flame which cannot be completely extinguished even in the line of administrative duty.'

I looked around. The panorama surrounding us was truly magnificent. I suddenly felt that I was viewing one of the most ancient pictures in the world – an immense horde which has set its camp-fires for a night halt in the open field, with warriors squatting at each of the fires, dreaming avidly into the flames, where they see the phantom forms of gold, cattle and women from the lands that lie in their path. But where was this horde moving, and what could its men be dreaming of as they sat beside these camp-fires? I turned to Jungern.

'Tell me, baron, why are they all sitting apart, without visiting each others' fires?'

'You try walking over to one of them,' said Jungern.

The distance to the nearest camp-fire, where five or six people seemed to be warming themselves, was no more than fifty paces. I looked quizzically at Jungern.

217

'Walk over,' he repeated.

I shrugged and began walking, without feeling any special or unusual sensation. Probably I had been walking for a minute or two before I realized that I had not moved any closer to the point of bright light towards which I had set off. I glanced around. Jungern was standing by the flames, three or four steps behind me, and watching me with a mocking smile.

'The fact that this place seems similar to the world which you know,' he said, 'does not at all mean that it is the same world.'

I noticed that the two frozen figures had vanished from beside the fire, and all that remained were two dark stains on the ground.

'Let's get away from here,' Jungern said. 'After all, we wanted to pay a visit to my lads, didn't we?'

I clutched at his sleeve and the camp-fires went hurtling past us once again – our speed was now so great that they extended into blurred zigzags and dotted lines. I was more than half certain that it must all be some kind of illusion, for I could not feel any wind upon my face; it was as though when the baron began to move, it was not us, but the world around us that was set into motion. I became completely disoriented and lost all concept of the direction of our movement. Sometimes we would halt for a few seconds and I could examine the individuals sitting round the nearest camp-fire – for the most part they were men with bushy beards and rifles who all looked very much like one another, and as soon as we approached they would throw themselves to the black ground beneath our feet. Once I was struck by the fact that they held spears instead of rifles, but our halt was too brief for me to be absolutely certain. After a while I realized what our manner of movement reminded me of: these crazy, unpredictable zigzags were precisely the movements of a bat flying in the darkness.

'I hope you understand, Pyotr,' the baron's voice rumbled in my ear, 'that you and I are not at present in a place where it is possible to lie? Or even not to be completely honest?'

'I understand,' I said, feeling my head beginning to spin

from the flashing yellow and white streaks and broken lines.

'Answer me one question,' said the baron. 'What do you want more than anything else in life?'

'Me?' I queried and began thinking.

This was a question which was hard to answer without telling a lie. I thought for a long moment about what I should say, but I couldn't think of anything, and then suddenly the answer came by itself.

'I want to find my *golden joy*,' I said.

The baron laughed loudly. 'Splendid,' he said. 'But what does that mean to you – your *golden joy*?'

'The *golden joy*,' I replied, 'is when *a peculiar flight of free thought* makes it possible to see *the beauty of life*. Am I making myself clear?'

'Oh, yes,' said the baron. 'If only everyone expressed themselves so clearly and so much to the point. How did you arrive at such a precise formulation?'

'It comes from my dream,' I replied, 'or rather, from my nightmare. I remembered the strange phrase by heart because it was written in a notebook from a mental home which I was leafing through in the dream – I was leafing through it because there was supposed to be something very important about me in there.'

'Yes,' said the baron, turning to the right – at which the carousel of flames around us performed a movement like a side-somersault. 'I'm very glad that you mentioned this yourself. The reason you are here is that Chapaev asked me to explain something to you. In essence, of course, he didn't ask me to explain anything special that he couldn't have told you himself. He has already told you it all before – the last time was during your journey here. But for some reason you still seem to think that the world of your dreams is less real than the space in which you get drunk with Chapaev in the bathhouse.'

'You are correct,' I said.

The baron came to a sudden halt, and immediately the camp-fires stopped dancing around us. I noticed that the flames had taken on a strangely alarming reddish tinge.

'But why do you think so?' he asked.

219

'Well, if only because eventually I return to the real world,' I said. 'To the place, as you put it, where I get drunk with Chapaev in the bathhouse. On the intellectual level, of course, I understand perfectly well what you are trying to say. More than that, I have even noticed that when I am actually dreaming the nightmare it is so real that there is absolutely no way of knowing that it is a dream. I can touch objects in the same way, I can pinch myself . . .'

'But then how do you distinguish your dream from the waking world?' the baron interrupted.

'By the fact that when I am awake I have a clear and unambiguous sense of the reality of what is happening. As I have now.'

'So you have that feeling now?' the baron asked.

'In general, yes, I do,' I said, somewhat bemused. 'Although I must confess that the situation is somewhat unusual.'

'Chapaev asked me to take me you with me so that for once at least you would find yourself in a place which has absolutely no relationship either to your nightmare about the mental home or to your nightmares about Chapaev,' said the baron. 'Take a good look around you – both of your obsessive dreams are equally illusory here. All I have to do is leave you by one of the camp-fires and you will understand what I mean.'

The baron was silent for a moment, as though allowing me time to savour the full horror of such a prospect. I looked around slowly at the blackness studded with an infinite number of unattainable points of light. He was right. Where were Chapaev and Anna? Where was that fragile night-time world with the tiled walls and the busts of Aristotle that crumbled into white dust? They were nowhere now, and furthermore I knew with absolute certainty that there was no place where they could exist, because I myself, standing here beside this strange man – if he was indeed a man – constituted the only possibility of being, the exclusive means by which all these psychiatric clinics and civil wars came into the world. And the same applied to this gloomy limbo, to its terrified inhabitants and its tall, stern sentry – all of them existed only because I existed.

'I think I understand,' I said.

Jungern looked at me doubtfully. 'What exactly do you understand?' he asked.

Suddenly there was a wild shouting from behind us:

'Me! Me! Me! Me!'

We both turned together at the sound.

Not very far away a camp-fire was burning, but it was quite unlike all the others. The colour of the flame was quite different – it was pale and gave off smoke – and something was crackling in the fire, with sparks flying off in all directions. Furthermore, this camp-fire was not aligned with the strict linear pattern of the others: it was quite obviously burning in a place where it should not be.

'Right, let's go and take a look,' Jungern muttered, tugging me sharply by the sleeve.

The men sitting by the fire were quite unlike the baron's other charges. There were four of them, of whom the most agitated was a big, burly fellow in a poison-pink jacket with a stiff crew-cut brush of chestnut hair on the top of his head that reminded me of a small cannon shell. He was sitting on the ground with his arms wrapped tightly around himself, as though his own body inspired him with an obscene passion.

'Me! Me! Me!' he kept roaring again and again.

The intonation of his shouts changed – when the baron and I first heard them, they had a certain note of feral triumph, but as we drew closer the single syllable 'me' became more like a question. Sitting beside the man who was shouting was a skinny type with a quiff, who was wearing something like a sailor's pea-jacket and staring into the flames as though paralysed. He was quite motionless, and if not for the fact that his lips occasionally moved slightly, one might have assumed that he was unconscious. It seemed as though only the third man, with a shaven head and a neat little beard, was in control of himself – he was shaking both of his companions in turn with all his might as though attempting to bring them round; he was successful to the extent that the skinny blond with the quiff began intoning something and swaying to and fro, as though he were praying. The man with the shaven head was just about to start shaking his second companion awake when he suddenly looked up and saw us. His face was instantly distorted in terror – he shouted something to his companions and leapt to his feet.

The baron swore under his breath. A hand grenade had appeared in his hand; he pulled out the ring and tossed the grenade towards the camp-fire – it fell to the ground about five yards away from our feet. In a reflex response I dropped to the ground and covered my head with my hands, but several seconds went by and still there was no explosion.

'Get up,' said the baron.

I opened my eyes to see his figure bending over me. I saw the baron now in a distorted perspective – the hand extended towards me was close beside my face and the eyes gazing attentively at me, in which the multiple reflections of camp-fires merged into a single light, seemed like the only two stars in the dark sky of that place.

'Thank you,' I said. 'What happened? Didn't it detonate?'

'On the contrary,' said the baron, 'everything worked perfectly.'

Glancing at the spot where the fire had been burning, I was astonished to see no trace of anything – neither of the fire itself, nor of those who had been sitting around it.

'What was that?' I asked.

'Oh, nothing,' said the baron, 'petty hooligans high on shamanic mushrooms. They had no idea themselves where they had ended up.'

'And you . . .'

'Certainly not,' the baron reassured me. 'Of course I didn't. I simply brought them round.'

'I am almost sure,' I said, 'that I have seen the bald one with the little beard somewhere before – in fact, I am absolutely certain.'

'Perhaps you saw him in your dream.'

'Perhaps,' I replied. The shaven-headed gentleman was quite unambiguously associated for me with the white-tiled walls and cold touch of a needle against the skin which were the standard elements of my nightmares. For several seconds I even thought I might be able to recall his name, but then my attention was distracted by other thoughts. Meanwhile Jungern stood beside me without speaking, as though he were weighing the words he was about to say.

'Tell me, Pyotr,' he said eventually, 'what are your political views? I assume you're a monarchist?'

'Naturally,' I replied. 'Why, have I given you cause for any other . . .'

'No, no,' cut in the baron. 'I simply wanted to use an example that you would easily understand. Imagine a stuffy room into which a terribly large number of people have been packed, and they are all sitting on various kinds of ugly stools, on rickety chairs, on bundles and anything else that comes to hand. The more nimble among them try to sit down on two chairs at once or to shove someone else aside in order to take his place. Such is the world in which you live. Simultaneously, every one of these individuals has an immense, shining throne of his own, a throne towering up above this world and all the other worlds that exist. This is a truly regal throne, and nothing lies beyond the power of the person who ascends it. And, most important of all, this throne is entirely legitimate. It belongs to everyone by right. But it is almost impossible to ascend it, because it stands in a place that does not exist. Do you understand? It is nowhere.'

'Yes,' I said thoughtfully, 'I was thinking about that only yesterday, baron. I know what "nowhere" means.'

'Then think about the following,' the baron went on. 'Here, as I have already said, both of your obsessive states – with Chapaev and without him – are equally illusory. In order to reach "nowhere" and ascend that throne of eternal freedom and happiness, it is enough to remove the single dimension which still remains – the one, that is, in which you see me and yourself. Which is what my own wards are attempting to do. But their chances are very slim, and after a certain period of time they are obliged to repeat the weary round of existence. Why should you, however, not find yourself in this "nowhere" while you are still alive? I swear to you that this is the very best thing you could possibly do with your life. No doubt you are fond of metaphors – you could compare this to discharging yourself from the mental home.'

'Believe me, baron . . .' I began with emotion, pressing my hand to my heart, but he did not let me finish.

'And you must do this before Chapaev puts his clay machine-gun to use. Afterwards, as you know, there will be nothing left, not even "nowhere".'

'His clay machine-gun?' I asked. 'But what is that?'

'Has Chapaev not told you?'

'No.'

Jungern frowned.

'Then we won't go into details. Just keep in mind the metaphor of leaving behind the mental home for freedom. And then perhaps in one of your nightmares you may recall our conversation. But now it is time for us to be going, the lads will be tired of waiting.'

The baron took hold of my sleeve and the chaotic streaks of light began flashing around us once again. By this stage I was accustomed to the fantastic spectacle and it no longer made me feel dizzy. The baron went on ahead, peering into the gloom; I glanced at his receding chin, his ginger moustache and the severe line at the corner of his mouth, and thought that his external appearance was the least likely thing about him to scare anybody.

'Tell me, baron, why is everyone here so afraid of you?' I asked, unable to restrain my curiosity. 'I don't wish to offend you, but I do not find anything in your appearance particularly frightening.'

'Not everyone sees what you see,' replied the baron. 'I usually appear to my friends in the guise of the St Petersburg intellectual whom I once actually was. But you should not conclude that that is what I actually look like.'

'What do all the others see?'

'I won't bore you with all the details,' said the baron. 'Let me just say that I hold a sharp sabre in each of my six hands.'

'But which of your appearances is the real one?'

'I do not have a real one, unfortunately,' he replied.

I must confess that the baron's words produced quite a profound impression on me, even though, of course, if I had bothered to think for a while, I might have guessed everything for myself.

'We're almost there now,' the baron said, in almost a casual holidaymaker's voice.

'Tell me,' I said, glancing at him sideways, 'why do they call you the Black Baron?'

'Ah,' said Jungern with a smile, 'that is probably because when I was fighting in Mongolia the living Buddha Bogdo-Gegen Tutukhtu granted me the right to use a black palanquin.'

'Then why do you ride in a green one?'

'Because in exactly the same way I was granted the right to ride in a green palanquin.'

'Very well. But then why don't they call you the Green Baron?'

Jungern frowned.

'Do you not think you are asking rather too many questions?' he said. 'You would do better to take a look around in order to fix this place in your memory – you will never see it again. That is, you could, of course, see it again, but I sincerely hope that will not happen to you.'

I followed the baron's advice.

Far ahead of us a light had appeared which seemed larger than the others. It was not hurtling towards us with the same rapidity as the other fires, but was approaching gradually, as though we really were walking towards it in the normal fashion. I guessed that this must be the final point of our walk.

'Are your friends by that big camp-fire?' I asked.

'Yes,' replied the baron. 'But I wouldn't call them friends exactly. They are my former regimental comrades: I was once their commanding officer.'

'You mean that you fought together?'

'Yes,' said the baron, 'that too. But that is not the most important thing here. We were all executed together by firing squad in Irkutsk. I wouldn't exactly say it was my fault, but even so . . . I feel a certain special responsibility for them.'

'I understand,' I said. 'If I were suddenly to find myself in such a dark and desolate place, I should probably very much want someone to come and help me.'

'You know, you should not forget that you are still alive,' said the baron. 'All this darkness and emptiness that surrounds you is actually the most brilliant light in all existence. Just stop there for a moment.'

I stopped mechanically, and without giving me a moment to grasp what he was doing, the baron gave me a sudden shove from behind.

This time, however, he did not catch me completely unawares. During the moment when my body was falling to the ground, I was somehow able to retain my awareness of that imperceptibly short instant of return to the usual world – or rather, since in reality there was absolutely nothing of which to be aware, I managed to grasp the nature of this return. I do not know how to describe it; it was as though one set of scenery was moved aside and the next was not set in its place immediately, but for an entire second I stared into the gap between them. And this second was enough to perceive the deception behind what I had always taken for reality, to perceive the simple and stupid way in which the Universe was arranged. It was an encounter which left me filled with confusion, annoyance and a certain sense of shame for myself.

The baron's movement had been so powerful that I only managed to put my hands out in front of me at the very last moment, and I struck my forehead against the ground.

When I raised my head I saw the ordinary world in front of me once again – the steppe, the early evening sky and the line of hills close by. I could see the baron's back swaying as he walked towards the only camp-fire on this steppe, from which a column of white smoke rose vertically into the sky.

I leapt to my feet and dusted down my trousers, which were soiled at the knees, but I thought better of following him. As the baron approached the camp-fire the group of bearded men in khaki uniforms and matted yellow astrakhan hats who were seated at it rose to greet him.

'Now then, my lads!' Jungern roared in a roistering commanding officer's bass. 'How's it going?'

'We do our best, your honour! We get by all right, God be praised!' came the chorus of replies. The baron was surrounded from all sides and completely hidden from view. I could see that the soldiers loved him.

I noticed a Cossack in a yellow astrakhan hat walking

towards me from the direction of the fire. His face looked so fierce that for a second I felt quite scared, but I was reassured by the sight of a bluish-green tinted tooth glass in his hand.

'Well, yer honour,' he grated as he reached me, 'you must have had a fair old scare, I reckon.'

'Yes,' I said, 'I did rather.'

'Better put yerself right then,' said the Cossack, holding out the glass.

I drank. It was vodka, and I really did begin feeling better almost immediately.

'Thank you. That was just the thing.'

'Well now,' said the Cossack, taking back the empty glass, 'you and the baron on friendly terms, are ye?'

'We are acquainted,' I said evasively.

''He's a strict one,' the Cossack commented. 'Everything by the book. We're going to chant now, and then answer questions. That is, the others is going to answer questions. I've already hit the target. I'm leaving today. For good.'

I looked at him – on closer inspection there no longer seemed to be anything fierce about his face, it was just that his features were coarse, weathered by the wind and scorched by the mountain sun. Despite this coarseness, his face bore a thoughtful, even dreamy expression.

'What's your name?' I asked the Cossack.

'Ignat,' he replied. 'And you'd be called Pyotr.'

'Yes,' I said, 'but how do you know?'

Ignat smiled ever so slightly.

'I'm from the Don,' he said. 'And you'd be from the capital, I reckon.'

'Yes,' I said, 'from Petersburg.'

'Well now, Pyotr, don't you go over to the camp-fire for the time being. His lordship the baron don't like anyone interfering with the chanting. Just let's you and me sit here and listen a while. And whatever you don't understand I can explain.'

I shrugged and sat on the ground, crossing my legs Turkish-style.

Something rather strange was taking place around the camp-fire. The Cossacks in the yellow astrakhan hats had sat down in a semicircle and the baron was standing in front of them exactly like a choirmaster, with his hands raised.

'*Oh, the nights, the weary nights,*' their powerful male voices sang out. '*And I have slept hardly at all . . .*'

'I am very fond of this song,' I said.

'How could your lordship be fond of it, if he's never heard it before?' asked Ignat, squatting down beside me.

'What do you mean, of course I have. This is an old Cossack song.'

'No,' said Ignat. 'You're mixing things up. This is a song his lordship the baron wrote specially for us so that chanting it would make us think. And so it'd be easy for us to remember, the words in it are just the same as in the song you're talking about, and the music too.'

'Then what does his contribution consist of?' I asked. 'I mean, how is it possible to distinguish the song that existed earlier from the one that the baron composed, if the words and the music are both the same?'

'Well, the song his lordship the baron wrote has a completely different meaning. Just you listen and I'll explain. Hear them singing: "*And I have slept hardly at all, but I have seen a dream.*" You know what that means? Although I couldn't sleep, I still dreamed just like as if I was sleeping, understand? That means, it makes no difference whether you sleep or you don't, it's all a dream.'

'I understand,' I answered. 'What comes next?'

Ignat waited for the couplet.

'That's it,' he said, 'listen: "*And in my dream my black steed gambolled, danced and pranced beneath me.*" There's great wisdom hidden in them words. You're an educated man, you must know that in India they have a book called the *Oopsanyshags.*'

'Yes,' I said, immediately recalling my conversation with Kotovsky.

'Well, it says in that book a man's mind is like a Cossack's horse. Always carrying you forward. Only his lordship the baron says as nowadays people is riding horses of quite a different colour . . . Nobody can manage his steed, so it's taken the bit in its teeth, like, and now it's not the rider as controls the horse, but the horse as carries him off wherever it fancies.

So the horseman's not even thinking any more about how he has to get any place in particular. He just goes along wherever the horse wanders. His lordship the baron even promised to bring us this special book – *The Headless Horseman*, it's called – seems like it was written specially all about this. But he keeps on forgetting. He's just too busy. We have to be grateful for . . .'

'And what comes next?' I interrupted.

'Next? What comes next? "*And our captain quick of wit, heard my dream then read me it . . . Oi, your wild and woolly head you are bound to lose, he said.*" The captain, like – well, that's clear enough, that's the way his lordship the baron writes about himself, he really is smart all right. And the bit about the head is clear enough, too – that's straight out of the *Oopsanyshags*. If the mind has worked itself up into such a lather that it don't know where it's going itself, it's clear enough it's done for. And there's another meaning here, too, one as his lordship only whispered in my ear not long ago. The meaning is as all this human wisdom will have to be left behind here anyway, like. But that's no cause for regretting, 'cause all that don't apply to the most important thing of all. That's why the song don't say that you're done for, only your wild and woolly head. And that's a gonner anyway.'

Ignat rested his chin thoughtfully on his hands and fell silent as he listened to the song.

> And, oh, the bitter winds did roar
> From out the East so cold and heavy,
> And the yellow hat they tore
> From off my head so wild and woolly . . .

I waited some time for his commentary, but it did not come, so I decided to break the silence myself.

'I can understand the part about the winds from the East myself,' I said, '*Ex orienta lux*, as they say. But why does the hat get blown off?'

'So as he won't have any more attachments.'

'But why is the cap yellow?'

'That's because we're Gelugpa. So we have yellow hats. If we was Karmapa, they'd be red hats. And if we was Bon-po, like down on the Don, then they'd be black. But the reality be-hind them all is the same anyhow. If the head's a gonner, then what's it care what kind of hat it used to wear? Or if you looks at it from the other side – where freedom begins, colours don't mean nothing no more.'

'Yes,' I said, 'the baron has certainly taught you well. But what exactly is that most important thing of all which starts after the wild and woolly head is gone?'

Ignat gave a deep sigh.

'Ah, that's the tricky bit,' he said. 'His lordship the baron asks that one every evening, and no one can answer him, no matter how they all try. D'you know what happens when one of the lads answers that one?'

'How should I know?'

'His lordship immediately transfers him to the Special Reg-iment of Tibetan Cossacks. That's a very special kind of force, that is. The pride and joy, so to speak, of the entire Asian Cav-alry Division, although if you think about it, a regiment like that doesn't really belong in any cavalry division, because those who serve in it ride elephants, not horses.'

It occurred to me that the man before me was probably one of those natural-born liars who can momentarily invent a story of any degree of improbability, but who always adorn it with such an abundance of detail that they make you believe it, if only for a second.

'How can you slash with your sabre from up on an ele-phant?' I asked. 'That would be most awkward.'

'Awkward all right, but that's the army for you,' Ignat said, and he looked up at me. 'Don't you believe me, your lord-ship? Well, it doesn't matter if you don't. Until I answered his lordship the baron's question, I didn't believe it either. And now I don't have to believe anything, because I know it all.'

'So you answered that question, did you?'

Ignat nodded solemnly in reply.

'That's why I can walk around the steppe like a man, and not have to stick close by the camp-fires.'

'And what did you say to the baron?'

'What I said isn't no use to you,' said Ignat. 'It's not your mouth you have to answer with. Nor your head, neither.'

We said nothing for a long time; Ignat seemed to be sunk deep in thought. Suddenly he raised his head.

'There's his lordship the baron coming over. That means it's time for us to say goodbye.'

I looked round and saw the tall thin figure of the baron approaching. Ignat rose to his feet; to be on the safe side I followed his example.

'Well, then,' the baron asked Ignat when he reached us, 'are you ready?'

'Yes, sir,' Ignat replied, 'I am.'

The baron stuck two fingers into his mouth and whistled like a street hooligan, following which something absolutely unexpected happened.

An enormous white elephant suddenly emerged from behind the low line of bushes behind us. It actually did appear to emerge from behind the bushes, even though it was ten times their height, and I was entirely unable to explain how it could have happened. It was not as though it was small when it appeared and then increased in size as it approached, nor did it emerge from behind some invisible wall that was aligned with the bushes. When it appeared the elephant was already quite incredibly huge – and yet it came from behind a tiny row of bushes behind which even a sheep would have had difficulty in concealing itself.

I experienced the same feeling I had several minutes earlier – I felt as though I were on the verge of understanding something extremely important, that any moment now the levers and cables of the mechanism that was concealed behind the veil of reality and made everything move would become visible. But this feeling passed, and the enormous white elephant was still standing there in front of us.

It had six tusks, three on each side. I decided I must be hallucinating, but then realized that if what I was seeing was an hallucination, it was not very different in nature from everything else around me.

Ignat walked over to the elephant and scrambled briskly on to its back, climbing up the tusks as though they were a ladder. He acted as though he had spent his entire previous life doing nothing but ride round plateaux created by someone's fantastic imagination on the backs of white elephants with six tusks. Turning towards the fire where the figures in khaki uniform and yellow hats were sitting, he waved, then struck the elephant's sides with his heels. The elephant began to advance, taking a few steps forward – then I saw a blinding flash of light, and he disappeared. It was so very bright that for almost a minute I could see nothing at all except its yellow and purple imprint on my retina.

'I forgot to warn you there would be a flash,' said Jungern. 'It's actually very bad for the eyesight. In the Asian Cavalry Division we used to protect our eyes with a blindfold of black material.'

'You mean such occurrences were common?'

'They used to be,' said the baron. 'There was a time when it happened several times a day. At that rate you could easily go blind. These days the lads are getting a bit thin on the ground. Well, has it passed off? Can you see?'

I could just make out the forms of objects around me again.

'Yes,' I said.

'Would you like me to show you how it was before?'

'But how do you intend to do that?'

Instead of replying the baron drew his sabre from its scabbard.

'Watch the blade,' he said.

I looked at the blade and saw a moving image on it, as though it were a cinema screen. It was a hill of sand, with a group of about ten officers standing on it; several were wearing normal military uniform, but two or three were in astrakhan hats and Cossack camouflage overalls with something that looked like cartridge-pouches instead of breast pockets. They were all wearing black blindfolds, and their heads were turned in the same direction. Suddenly I recognized Chapaev among them, despite the blindfold that concealed his eyes: he seemed a great deal younger and there were no grey hairs at his temples. With one hand he was pressing a small pair of field binoculars to the cloth over his eyes, and with the other he was slapping a riding-whip against his boot. It seemed to me that the figure in the Cossack uniform close to Chapaev was Baron Jungern, but I had no time for a good look at him because the blade turned over and the men on the hill disappeared. Now I could see the infinite and smooth surface of a desert. In the distance two silhouettes were moving against the bright sky; looking closer, I managed to discern the outlines of two elephants. They were too far away for me to be able to make out the riders, who were no more than tiny bumps on their backs. Suddenly the horizon was flooded with bright light, and when it faded, only one elephant remained. Back on the hill they applauded – and immediately I saw a second flash.

'Baron, at this rate I shall have no eyes left,' I said, averting them from the blade.

Jungern put the sabre away in its scabbard.

'What is that yellow thing over there in the grass?' I asked. 'Or do I still have spots in front of my eyes.'

'No, it's not a spot,' said the baron. 'It's Ignat's hat.'

'Ah, the raging winds have torn it off? The winds from the East?'

'It's a genuine pleasure to talk with you, Pyotr,' said the baron, 'you do understand everything so well. Would you like to keep it as a memento?'

I bent down and picked it up. The hat was exactly my size. I wondered for a while what I should do with my own – I couldn't think of anything better than simply dropping it on the ground.

'In reality I understand very far from everything,' I said. 'For instance, I simply cannot understand at all where an elephant like that could appear from in this forsaken spot.'

'My dear Pyotr,' said the baron, 'there are quite incredible numbers of invisible elephants wandering around us all the time, please take my word for it. They are more common in Russia than crows. But allow me to change the subject – it's time for you to be getting back, you see, so permit me to tell you one more thing before you go. Perhaps the most important one of all.'

'What is it?'

'It is about the place a person goes to when he manages to ascend the throne that is nowhere. We call that place "Inner Mongolia".'

'Who are "we"?'

'You can take me to mean Chapaev and myself,' the baron said with a smile. 'Although I hope that in time we will also be able to include you in our number.'

'And where is it, this place?'

'That's the point, it is nowhere. It is quite impossible to say that it is located anywhere in the geographical sense. Inner Mongolia is not called that because it is inside Mongolia. It is inside anyone who can see the void, although the word "inside" is quite inappropriate here. And it is not really any kind of Mongolia either, that's merely a way of speaking. The most stupid thing possible would be to attempt to describe to you what it is. Take my word for this, at least – it is well worth striving all your life to reach it. And nothing in life is better than being there.'

'And how does one come to see the void?'

'Look into yourself,' said the baron. 'I beg your pardon for the unintentional pun on your name.'

I pondered for several seconds.

'May I be honest with you?'

'Of course,' Jungern replied.

'The place we have just visited – I mean the black steppe with the camp-fires – seemed rather gloomy to me. If the Inner Mongolia of which you speak is anything similar, then I would hardly wish to be there.'

'You know, Pyotr,' Jungern said with a chuckle, 'when, to take an example, you unleash mayhem in a drinking-den like the "Musical Snuffbox", you may perhaps reasonably assume that what you see is approximately the same as what the people around you see – although even that is far from certain. But in the place where we have just been, everything is very individual. Nothing there exists, so to speak, in reality. Everything depends on who is looking at it. For me, for instance, everything there is flooded in blinding light. But my lads here' – Jungern nodded in the direction of the little figures in the yellow astrakhan hats who were moving around the camp-fire – 'see the same things around themselves as you do. Or rather, you see the same things as they do.'

'Why?'

'Are you familiar with the concept of visualization?' the baron asked. 'When so many believers begin to pray to some god or other that he actually comes into existence, in the precise form in which they have imagined him?'

'I am familiar with it,' I said.

'The same applies to everything else as well. The world in which we live is simply a collective visualization, which we are taught to make from our early childhood. It is, in actual fact, the only thing that one generation hands on to the next. When a sufficient number of people see this steppe, this grass and feel this summer wind, then we are able to experience it all together with them. But no matter what forms might be prescribed for us by the past, in reality what each of us sees in life is still only a reflection of his own spirit. And if you discover that you are surrounded by impenetrable darkness, it only means that your own inner space is like the night. It's a good thing you're an agnostic, or there would be all manner of gods and devils roaming about in this darkness.'

'Baron . . .' I began, but he interrupted me:

'Please do not think that there is anything in any way demeaning to you in all this. There are very few who are prepared to admit that they are exactly the same as everyone else. But is not this the usual condition of man – sitting in the darkness beside a camp-fire kindled through someone else's compassion and waiting for help to arrive?'

'Perhaps you are right,' I said. 'But what is this Inner Mongolia?'

'Inner Mongolia is precisely that place from which help arrives.'

'And so . . .' I asked, 'you have been there?'

'Yes,' replied the baron.

'Then why did you return?'

The baron nodded without speaking in the direction of the camp-fire, where the silent Cossacks were huddled.

'And then,' he said, 'I never really did come back from there. I am still there now. But it really is time for you to be getting back, Pyotr.'

I glanced around.

'But where to, precisely?'

'I'll show you,' said the baron.

I noticed that he was holding a heavy burnished-steel pistol, and I shuddered at the sight.

The baron laughed. 'Pyotr, Pyotr. What's the matter? You really should not be so very mistrustful of people.'

He thrust his other hand into his pocket and took out the package which Chapaev had given him. He unwrapped it and showed me a perfectly ordinary ink-well with a black stopper.

'Watch carefully,' he said, 'and do not look away.'

With that he tossed the ink-well into the air and when it was about two yards away from us, he fired.

The ink-well was transformed into a cloud of blue spray and minute fragments which hung in the air for a moment before scattering across the table.

I staggered backwards, and in order to avoid falling from my sudden dizziness, I braced myself against the wall with one hand. I was facing a table covered with a hopelessly stained map, beside which Kotovsky was standing, his mouth wide open. Glycerine from the shattered lamp was dripping on to the floor.

'Right then,' said Chapaev, toying with his smoking Mauser, 'now you understand what mind is, Grisha, eh?'

Kotovsky covered his face with his hands and ran out of the room. It was clear that he had suffered a powerful shock. The same, indeed, could have been said of myself.

Chapaev turned towards me and looked at me closely for a while. Suddenly he frowned. 'What's that on your breath?' Chapaev barked. 'Well, well, less than a minute goes by, and he's drunk already. And why are you wearing a yellow hat? Trying to get yourself court-martialled are you, you bastard?'

'I only had one glass . . .'

'Qui-et! Quiet, I tell you! The weavers' regiment is here, we have to settle them in, and you're wandering around drunk! Want to put me to shame in front of Furmanov, do you? Go and sleep it off! And if I catch you pulling tricks like this again, it's a court-martial, straight off! Do you want to know what my court-martials are like?'

Chapaev raised his nickel-plated Mauser.

'No, Vasily Ivanovich, I do not,' I answered.

'Sleep!' Chapaev repeated. 'And on your way to bed don't you dare breathe on anyone.'

I turned on my heels and walked to the door. When I reached it I glanced around. Chapaev was standing by the table and following my movements with an expression of menace.

'I have just one question,' I said.

'Well?'

'I just wanted to say . . . I have long known that the only real moment of time is "now". But I cannot understand how it is possible to fit such a long sequence of sensations into it. Does it mean that if one remains strictly within the bounds of this moment, without creeping over into the past or the future, it can be extended to such a degree that phenomena like those I have just witnessed will become possible?'

'And just where are you thinking of extending it to?'

'I have expressed myself incorrectly. Does it mean that this moment, this boundary between the past and the future, is itself the door to eternity?'

Chapaev jiggled the barrel of his Mauser and I fell silent. He looked at me for some time with an expression of something close to mistrust.

'This moment, Petka, is eternity, and not any kind of door,' he said. 'So how can we say that it takes place at any particular time? When will you finally come round?'

'Never,' I replied.

Chapaev gaped at me, wide-eyed.

'Well, look now, Petka,' he said in astonishment. 'Have you really understood at last?'

Finding myself back in my room, I began wondering how I could occupy myself to best calm my nerves. I recalled Chapaev's advice to write down my nightmares, and I thought about my recent dream on a Japanese theme. There was a great deal in it that was incomprehensible and confused, but even so I could recall almost every detail. It began in a strange underground train with an announcement of the name of the next station – I could remember the name and even knew where it had come from: there could be no doubt that my consciousness, following the complex rules that govern the world of dreams, had created it in the instant before I awoke from the name of the horse that some soldier was shouting under my window. Furthermore, this shout had been reflected in two mirrors simultaneously, becoming transformed, in addition to the name of the station, into the name of the football team from the conversation with which my dream had ended. That meant that a dream which had seemed to me to be very long and detailed had in reality lasted no longer than a second, but after that day's meeting with Baron Jungern and the conversation with Chapaev, nothing could amaze me any more. I sat at the desk, set several sheets of paper in front of myself, dipped my pen into the ink-well and traced the following words in large letters across the top of the first sheet: 'Next station "Dynamo"!'

I worked for a long time, but even so I managed to write down less than half of what I could remember. The details that flowed out from my pen on to the paper possessed such a glimmer of decadence that towards the end I could no longer be certain whether I was actually writing down my dream or already improvising on its contents. I wanted to smoke; I took my *papyrosas* from the desk and went out into the yard.

Downstairs everything was in a state of bustling activity, as some of the newly arrived men formed themselves into a column; there was a smell of pitch and horse sweat. I noticed a small regimental orchestra standing at the back of the column – a few battered and dented trumpets and a huge drum hung on a strap round the neck of a tall strapping lad who looked like Peter the Great without his moustache. For some reason which was incomprehensible to me, the sight of this orchestra filled me with an inexpressible, aching melancholy.

The formation was commanded by the man with the sabre scar across his cheek whom I had seen from my window. I recalled the sight of the snow-covered square in front of the station, the platform covered with red cloth, Chapaev slicing the air with his yellow-cuffed gauntlet and this man at the barrier nodding thoughtfully in response to the monstrous, meaningless phrases which Chapaev was showering on to the square formation of snow-covered soldiers. It was definitely

Furmanov. He turned in my direction, but I ducked back into the doorway of the manor-house before he could recognize me.

I went upstairs to my room, lay on the bed and stared at the ceiling. I remembered the fat man with the shaven head and the beard who had been sitting by the fire in that world beyond the grave, and I recalled his name – Volodin. From somewhere deep in the recesses of my memory a large tiled room emerged with baths secured to the floor, with this Volodin squatting naked and wet like a toad on the floor beside one of them. I felt as though I were just on the point of recalling something else, but then the trumpets sounded in the yard, the regimental drum boomed out, and the choir of weavers that I remembered so well from that night on the train roared out:

> The deadly black baron and the white hussars
> Want us to bow to the throne of the Tsars,
> But from Siberia to the North British Sea
> The strongest of all is the Red Army.

'Idiots,' I whispered, turning my face to the wall and feeling tears of helpless hatred for the world welling up in my eyes. 'My God, the idiots . . . Not even idiots – mere shadows of idiots . . . Shadows in the darkness . . .'

8

'But just why exactly did you think they were like shadows?' Timur Timurovich asked.

Volodin twitched nervously, but the tight straps securing his arms and legs to the garrotte prevented him from moving. There were large drops of sweat glistening on his forehead.

'I don't know,' he said. 'You asked me what I was thinking just at that moment. Well, I was thinking that if there was any external observer around there to watch, he'd probably have thought we weren't real, that we were nothing but flickering shadows and reflections from the flames – I told you there was a camp-fire. But then you know, Timur Timurovich, it all really depends on the observer . . .'

The camp-fire in the clearing had barely begun to blaze and was not yet giving enough light to disperse the gloom and illuminate the figures sitting around it; they appeared to be no more than blurred spectral shadows cast on an invisible screen by the branches and sods of earth lying beside the fire. Perhaps, in a certain higher sense, that is precisely what they were – but since the last of the local neo-Platonists had abandoned his shame at possessing a body shortly before the Twentieth Party Congress, there was no one to reach such a conclusion within a radius of at least one hundred miles.

It would be better, therefore, to state the facts simply – sitting in the semi-darkness around the camp-fire were three hulking brutes. Their appearance, moreover, was such that if our neo-Platonist were to have survived the Twentieth Congress and all of the insights that ensued therefrom, and to have emerged from the forest and approached the fire to discuss his topic with the new arrivals, he would very probably have suffered severe physical disfigurement as soon as the word 'neo-Platonism' disturbed the silence of the night. The signs that suggested this to be the case were numerous.

The most significant among them was the 'Toyota Harbour Pearl' amphibious Jeep standing close by; another was the immense winch on its bonnet – an item of absolutely no use whatever in normal life, but frequently to be found on the vehicles of gangsters. (Anthropologists who have devoted their efforts to studying the 'New Russians' believe that these winches are used as rams during the settling of accounts, and certain scholars even see their popularity as an indirect indication of the long-awaited resurgence of the spirit of the nation – they believe the winches fulfil the mystical role of the figureheads that once decorated the bows of ancient Slavonic barks.) In short, it was clear that the people who had arrived in this Jeep were not to be trifled with, and it would be best not to risk uttering any superfluous words in their company. They were talking quietly among themselves.

'How many bits does it take, eh, Volodin?' one of them asked.

'That depends on you,' Volodin answered as he unwrapped a paper bundle on his knees. 'For instance, I take a hundred at a time already. But I'd recommend you start with about thirty.'

'And that'll do it?'

'That'll do it, Shurik,' said Volodin, dividing up the contents of the bundle, a dark heap of something dry and brittle, into three unequal portions. 'You'll end up running all over the forest trying to find a place to hide. And you'll be running too, Kolyan.'

'Me?' the third person sitting by the fire asked in a deep bass. 'And just who am I gonna be runnin' away from?'

'From yourself, Kolyan. From your own self,' Volodin answered.

'I ain't never run away from no one,' said Kolyan, picking up his portion with a hand that looked like the body of a toy dump truck. 'You better watch your mouth. Why'd I wanna run away from meself? It don't make no sense.'

'I can only explain it by using an example,' said Volodin.

'Give us an example, then.'

Volodin thought for a moment.

'Okay, just imagine some low-life scum comes into our office, sticks all his fingers up in the air and says we should be sharing. What would you do then?'

'I'd drop him,' said Kolyan.

'You what? Right there in the office?' Shurik asked.

'That don't matter. They gotta pay for givin' us the fingers.'

Shurik slapped Kolyan on the shoulder, then turned to Volodin and said reassuringly, 'Course not in the office. We'd set up a shoot.'

'Okay,' said Volodin. 'So you set up a shoot, right? And then what happens? Let Kolyan answer.'

'Clear enough,' Kolyan responded. 'We goes round there, and when that jerk turns up I says – right mate, give us all the dirt on yerself. He starts jawin', and I waits a minute and nods my head, like, and then I blow him away . . . Yeah. And then all the rest too.'

He looked at the tiny mound of dark garbage on his palm and asked, 'Just swaller it, just like that?'

'Chew it properly first,' said Volodin.

Kolyan dispatched the contents of his palm into his mouth.

'Smells like mushroom soup,' he stated.

'Swaller it,' said Shurik. 'I've eaten mine, no problem.'

'So you blow him away,' Volodin said thoughtfully. 'So what if he gets the drop on you two first?'

Kolyan pondered for a few seconds, working his jaws, then he swallowed and said confidently, 'Nah, he won't.'

'Okay, then,' said Volodin, 'Where are you going to drop him, right there in his wheels, from a distance, or will you let him get out?'

'I'll let him gerrout,' said Kolyan. 'It's only woodentops as drops jerks in their wheels. Holes everywhere, blood too – why go spoilin' a nice set of wheels? The best kind of hit is when he comes over to our wheels.'

'Okay, so let's take the best case. Imagine he's already got out of his wheels and comes over to yours and you're just about to blow him away, when you see . . .' Volodin paused significantly, 'when you see it isn't him standing there, but you. And you've got to blow yourself away. Don't you reckon you might drop a marble or two?'

'Sure I would.'

'And when your marbles are bouncing, it's not really chicken to kick into reverse?'

'Course not.'

'So you'd cut and run, because it wouldn't be chicken?'

'If it ain't chicken, sure.'

'So it turns out you'd be running away from yourself. Get it?'

'Nah,' Kolyan said after a pause, 'I don't get it. If it ain't him, but me, then where am I?'

'You're him.'

'Then who's he?'

'He's you.'

'Nah, I just don't get it,' said Kolyan.

'Well, look,' said Volodin, 'can you imagine there's nothing at all on every side of you, nothing but you? Everywhere?'

'Yeah,' said Kolyan. 'I've been that way a coupla times from smack. Or after basing, don't remember which it was.'

'Then how are you going to blow him away, if there's nothing around you except you? No matter which way you deal it, you end up planting lead in yourself. Dropped your marbles, haven't you? Right. So instead of blasting him, you do a runner. So now try figuring that by numbers. Seems to me like you'll end up running away from yourself.'

Kolyan thought for a long time.

'Shurik'll blow him away,' he said, eventually.

'That means he'll hit you. You're all there is.'

'How come?' cut in Shurik. 'If I've still got all me marbles in place, I'll blow the right guy away.'

This time Volodin had to think longer and harder.

'No,' he said, 'I can't explain it that way. That's not a good example. Just hang about a bit till the mushrooms come on, and then we'll have another go.'

The next few minutes passed in silence. The threesome sitting by the fire opened a few cans of food, sliced some salami and drank some vodka, but it was all done without speaking, as though the words usually spoken to accompany such actions were petty and out of place against the background of something dark and unexpressed which united all present.

After the vodka the three men smoked a cigarette each, still without speaking.

'How'd the spiel get on to that track anyway?' Shurik suddenly asked. 'I mean, like, about the shoot and the marbles?'

'Volodin was sayin' as how we would end up runnin' away from ourselves through the wood when the mushrooms came on.'

'Ah. Got you. Listen, why do they say that, "come on"? Where is it they come on from?'

'You asking me?' asked Volodin.

'You'll do right enough,' answered Shurik.

'I'd say they come on from inside,' Volodin said.

'How's that then, you mean they're sitting in there waiting all the time?'

'Yeah, kind of. You could put it like that. And not just them, actually. We've got every possible high in the world inside us . . . Every time you down something or shoot up, all you do is set some part of it free. There's no high in the drug, it's nothing but powder or a few chunks of mushroom . . . It's like the key to a safe. Get it?'

'Hea-vy,' Shurik said thoughtfully, for some reason circling his head around clockwise.

'Yeah, real heavy,' Kolyan agreed, and the conversation died for a few minutes.

'Listen,' Shurik put in again, 'is there a lot of high down there inside?'

'An infinite amount,' Volodin said authoritatively. 'An inexpressibly and infinitely large amount, there's even a high you can't tune into out here.'

'Fuck me . . . You mean inside's like a safe and this high's stuck inside it?'

'Roughly speaking, yeah.'

'And can you blow the safe? Like, so as to get a lift outta the high inside it?'

'Yeah.'

'How?'

'You have to devote your entire life to it. Why do you think people go into monasteries and live all their lives there? You think they spend their time beating their heads off the walls? They're on this incredible trip, the likes of which you couldn't get out here from a fix for a grand in greens. And no stopping – get it? Morning, noon and night. Some of them even when they're asleep. On and on for ever.'

'Then what they trippin' on? What's it called?' asked Kolyan.

'It has various names. In general, I suppose you could call it grace. Or love.'

'Whose love?'

'Just love. When you feel it, you stop asking whose it is, what it's for, why it exists. You just stop thinking altogether.'

'And you've felt it?'

'Yeah,' said Volodin, 'I've been there.'

'So how's it feel? What's it like?'

'It's hard to say.'

'Give us a rough idea. Is it like smack?'

'Nowhere near it,' Volodin said with a frown. 'Compared with this smack is a heap of crap.'

'Well then, kinda like coke, is it, or speed?'

'No, Shurik. No, no, don't even try comparing it. Just imagine you've done a bundle of speed and you're tripping out – say you'll be tripping for a day. You'll want a dame and the whole works, right?'

Shurik giggled.

'And then you'll be coming down for a day. And you'll probably start thinking – what the fuck did I need all that for?'

'Yeah, it happens,' said Shurik.

'But with this gear, once it gets to you, it stays with you for ever. And you won't need any dames, and you won't get any munchies. No coming down. No cold turkey. You just keep praying for the trip to go on and on for ever. Get it?'

'Like, heavier than smack?'

'Way heavier.'

Volodin leaned over the camp-fire and stirred the branches around. It immediately flared up, as strongly as though petrol had been poured into the fire. The flames were strange – they gave off various-coloured sparks of unusual beauty, and the light that fell on the faces of the three men sitting there was also unusual, rainbow-coloured and soft, with an astonishing depth.

They could be seen very clearly now. Volodin was a plump, roundish man of about forty with a shaved head and a small, neat beard – his appearance was that of a civilized Central Asian bandit. Shurik was a skinny, fidgety little man with blond hair who made a lot of small, meaningless movements. He didn't look very strong, but his constant nervous twitching betrayed something so frightening that beside him the muscle-bound Kolyan looked like a mere wolfhound puppy. In short, if Shurik typified the élite type of St Petersburg mobster, then Kolyan was the standard Moscow hulkodrome whose appearance had been so brilliantly foretold by the futurists at the beginning of the century. He seemed to be nothing but an intersection of simple geometrical forms – spheres, cubes and pyramids – and his small streamlined head was reminiscent of that stone which according to the evangelist was discarded by the builders but nonetheless became the cornerstone in the foundation of the new Russian statehood.

'There,' said Volodin, 'now the mushrooms have come on.'

'Whoah,' Kolyan confirmed. 'And then some. I've turned blue all over.'

'Yeah,' said Shurik, 'that sure don't feel like nothing. Listen. Volodin, was all that stuff for real?'

'All what stuff?'

'All that stuff about fixing yourself up a trip that lasts all your life . . . So you just stay high all the time.'

'I didn't say all your life. The concepts in there are different.'

'You said yourself as you'd be tripping all the time.'

'I didn't say that either.'

'Kol, didn't he say it?'

'I don't remember,' mumbled Kolyan. He seemed to have dropped out of the conversation and to be occupied with something else.

'Then what did you say?' asked Shurik.

'I didn't say all the time,' said Volodin. 'I said "for ever". Keep your ears open.'

'So what's the difference?'

'The difference is where that high starts, there isn't any more time.'

'What is there then?'

'Grace.'

'And what else?'

'Nothing.'

'Can't quite get me head round that somehow,' said Shurik. 'Just hanging there in empty space, is it, this grace?'

'There's no empty space there either.'

'Then what is there?'

'I told you, grace.'

'You've lost me again.'

'Don't bother about it,' said Volodin. 'If it was that easy to get your head round, half of Moscow would be tripping for free right now. Just think about it – a gram of cocaine costs one hundred, and here this is free, for nothing.'

'Hundred and fifty,' said Shurik. 'Nah, something's not right here. Even if it was tough to bend yer head round, people'd still know about it and they'd be tripping. They figured out how to make speed out of nose drops, didn't they?'

'Use your brains, Shurik,' said Volodin. 'Just imagine you're dealing cocaine, right? One gram for one hundred and fifty bucks, and you get ten greenbacks from each gram. And in a month you sell, say, five hundred grams. How much is that?'

'Five grand,' said Shurik.

'So now imagine some scumball has cut your sales from five hundred grams to five. What have you got?'

Shurik's lips moved as he quietly mumbled some figures.

'A limp prick, that's what,' he answered.

'Exactly. You could take your whore to McDonald's one time, but as for snorting anything yourself – forget it. So what would you do with a scumball who set you up like that?'

'Blow him away,' said Shurik. 'Obvious.'

'So now do you see why nobody knows about it?'

'You reckon the dope pushers keep things tight?'

'There's far more to it than just drugs,' said Volodin. 'There's much bigger bread tied up in this. If you break through into this eternal high, then you don't need any wheels, or any petrol, or any advertisements, or any porn, or any news. And neither does anyone else. What would happen then?'

'Everything'd be fucked,' said Shurik, glancing around him. 'All of culture and civilization. Clear as day, that is.'

'So that's why nobody knows about the eternal high.'

'But who controls the whole business?' Shurik asked after a moment's thought.

'It works automatically. It's the market.'

'Don't you go giving me any spiel about the market,' Shurik

said with a frown. 'We've had it all before. Automatic. Yeah, well it's automatic when that suits, or you can make it single-shot. Or you can put the safety catch on. Someone's got all the trumps, that's all. Maybe we'll find out who later, in about forty years, not before.'

'We'll never find out,' said Kolyan, without opening his eyes. 'Come on. Just think about it. When a guy's got a million green-backs, he just sits back and takes it easy, and anyone who starts to spread the dirt about him gets dropped straight off. And the guys who're holdin' trumps or got the real power are way heav-ier than that! The most we can do is take out some hulk, or torch some office, and that's it. Nothin' but garbage men, we are, clean up the small stuff. But those guys can bring in the tanks if they can't fix anythin' by spielin'. And if that don't do it, they've got planes, an atom bomb if that's what it takes. Just look what happened when the Chechens stopped shellin' out, came down on them like a ton of bricks, didn't they? If they hadn't copped on at the last moment, they wouldn't be able to shell out for nothin' no more. And remember the White House. How could we ever come on to Slav-East like that?'

'You give over with yer White House,' said Shurik. 'Dopey bas-tard. We're not talking politics. We're talking about the eternal high . . . Listen . . . Really now . . . They said on the box that all of them in the White House were going around stoned out of their skulls. Maybe they twigged about this eternal high? And they wanted to tell everyone about it on the telly, so they went after Ostankino, only the cocaine mafia wouldn't let them through . . . Nah, now me marbles is slipping.'

Shurik put his hands around his head and fell silent.

The forest around them was filled with trembling, mysterious rainbow lights, and the sky above the clearing was covered with mosaics of incredible beauty, unlike anything a man en-counters in his gruelling, normal everyday existence. The world around them changed, becoming far more meaningful and ani-mated, as though it had finally become clear why the grass was growing in the clearing, why the wind was blowing and the stars were twinkling in the sky. But the metamorphosis af-fected more than just the world, it affected the men sitting by the fire as well.

248

Kolyan seemed to recede into himself. He closed his eyes and his small square face, which normally wore an expression of gloomy annoyance, no longer bore the imprint of any feeling at all and looked more than anything like a swollen lump of old meat. The standard-issue chestnut crew cut on top of his head also seemed to have softened, so that it looked like the fur trimming of some absurd cap. In the dancing light of the camp-fire his double-breasted pink jacket resembled some ancient Tartar war costume, with the gold buttons on it like decorative plaques from a burial mound.

Shurik had become even skinnier, more fidgety and terrifying. He was like a frame cobbled together out of rotten planks of wood, on which many years ago someone had hung out their rags to dry and then forgotten about them; in some inexplicable fashion a spark of life had been kindled in the rags, then taken such firm hold that it made life thoroughly uncomfortable for almost everyone else anywhere in the neighbourhood. He bore little resemblance to a living being, and his cashmere pea-jacket only made him look like the electrified dummy of a sailor.

No sudden changes had taken place in Volodin. Some invisible chisel seemed to have smoothed out all the sharp corners and irregularities of his material exterior, leaving nothing but soft lines that flowed smoothly into each other. His face had become a little paler, and the lenses of his spectacles reflected rather more sparks than were flying into the air from the camp-fire. His movements had also acquired smoothness and precision – in short, it was clear from many signs that he had eaten mushrooms a good many times before.

'Whoah, hea-vy,' said Shurik, breaking the silence, 'but hea-vy! Kol, how're you doing?'

'Nothin' much,' said Kolyan without opening his tightly glued eyelids. 'Some kind of lights.'

Shurik turned to Volodin and after the fluctuations produced in the ether by his sharp movement had settled down, he said:

'Listen, Volodin, d'you know how to switch on to this eternal high yourself?'

Volodin said nothing.

'Nah, I've got it now,' said Shurik. 'Seems like I've realized why no one knows and why no one's allowed to spiel about it.

But you tell me, ah? I ain't no lunk. I'll just spend my time quietly tripping out at the dacha, that's all.'

'Stop that,' said Volodin.

'Nah, you mean you don't trust me, for real? Think I'll cause trouble?'

'No,' said Volodin, 'that's not it. It's just that nothing good would come of it.'

'Aw, come on,' said Shurik, 'don't be such a tight-wad.'

Volodin took off his spectacles, wiped them carefully with the hem of his shirt and put them back on again.

'The main thing is you've got to understand,' he said, 'but I don't know how to explain . . . You remember our talk about the inner public prosecutor?'

'Yeah, I remember. The guy who can put you away if you step over the line. Like Raskolnikov when he topped that dame, and he thought his inner prosecutor'd let him go on the nod, only it didn't work out that way.'

'Exactly. And who do you think the inner prosecutor is?'

Shurik pondered the question.

'I dunno . . . probably it's me myself, some part of me. Who else?'

'And the inner brief who gets you off?'

'Probably me as well. Only it sounds a bit odd, me taking a case against myself and then getting myself off.'

'Nothing odd about it. That's the way it always is. Now try imagining this inner prosecutor of yours has arrested you, all of your inner briefs have screwed up, and you've been put away in your own inner lock-up. Then imagine that there's some other guy, a fourth one, who never gets dragged off anywhere, who you can't call a prosecutor, or the guy he's trying to get behind bars, or a brief. Who's never involved in any cases at all.'

'Okay, I've imagined it.'

'Right, then this fourth guy is the one that goes tripping on the eternal high. And there's no need to explain anything to him about this high, get me?'

'Who is this fourth guy, then?'

'No one.'

'Can I get to see him somehow?'

'No way.'

'Maybe not see him then, but feel him at least?'

'Not that either.'

'So that means he don't really exist?'

'If you really want to know,' said Volodin, 'all these prosecutors and briefs don't really exist. And you really don't exist either. If anyone really does exist, then it's him.'

'I still don't catch your drift. Why don't you just tell me what I have to do to switch on to this eternal high?'

'Nothing,' said Volodin. 'That's the whole point, you don't have to do anything. Just as soon as you start doing anything, the court's in session, right? That's so, isn't it?'

'Seems to make sense all right.'

'You see. And once the court's in session, that means prosecutors, briefs and the whole works.'

Shurik fell silent and became quite motionless. The energy that lent him life passed momentarily to Kolyan, who seemed to be suddenly roused from sleep – he opened his eyes and glared with hostility at Volodin, then he bared his teeth, revealing a gleaming palladium crown.

'You sold us a line, Volodin, with that inner prosecutor of yours,' he said.

'Why's that?' Volodin asked in amazement.

'Because. Afterwards Vovchik Maloi gave me this book with it all laid out straight down the line. Nietzsche it was wrote it. The bastard's tied it all up in knots so's no normal person can suss it, but it all adds up right enough. Vovchik hired this hungry prof. special and sat him down with a young guy as talks the spiel, and in a month the two of them sorted the whole thing so's all the brothers could read it. Translated it into normal language. Turns out all you gotta do is take out that inner pig of yours, and that's it. Then no one don't finger no one, get it?'

'Ah, come on, Kolyan,' Volodin protested gently, almost pityingly. 'Think what you're saying. D'you know what you'll get for taking out the pig?'

Kolyan laughed loudly.

'Who from? The rest of the inner pigs? That's the whole idea, you take them all out.'

'Okay, let's just suppose you've dropped all the inner pigs. That just means the inner swat team gets on your ass.'

'I can see where you're comin' from a mile away,' said Kolyan. 'Next you'll be givin' me the inner State Security, and then the "Alpha" team, and on and on. What I'm sayin' is you gotta take them all out and then make yourself internal president.'

'Okay,' said Volodin, 'let's assume you've made internal president. Then if you have any doubts, what do you do about it?'

'No problem,' said Kolyan. 'Put them down and move on down the line.'

'So you still need the internal pigs for putting down your doubts? And if the doubts are a bit bigger, will it be the internal State Security?'

'They'll be working for me now,' said Kolyan. 'I'm my own internal president. And you all ain't shit!'

'Yes, Vovchik Maloi did a good job on you. Okay, let's assume you've made internal president and you've got your own internal pigs and a huge internal security service with all those Tibetan astrologers and the works.'

'That's it,' said Kolyan. 'So's no one can even get close.'

'So then what're you going to do?'

'Whatever I wanna,' said Kolyan.

'Like for instance?'

'Like for instance I take a dame and split for the Canaries.'

'What do you do there?'

'Like I said, whatever I wanna. If I feel like swimmin' I go swimmin', if I feel like screwin' the dame I screw her, if I feel like it I smoke dope.'

'Aha,' said Volodin, and the red tongues of flame glinted in his spectacles. 'You smoke dope. Doesn't dope put ideas in your head?'

'Sure.'

'So if you're president, that means you have state ideas, right?'

'Yeah.'

'Then I'll tell you what happens next. The first dope you smoke fills your head with state ideas and your internal president ends up facing internal impeachment.'

'We'll break through,' said Kolyan, 'I'll bring in the internal tanks.'

'How are you going to bring them in? Who was it got all the

ideas? You. That means you impeach your own internal president. So then who's going to bring in the tanks?'

Kolyan thought in silence for a moment.

'Straight away you'll have a new president,' said Volodin.
'And I hate to think what the internal security service will do to
the old one so they can get in with the new one.'

Kolyan pondered.

'Well, what of it?' he said uncertainly. 'So there's a new president.'

'But you were the old one, weren't you? So now who ends up
in the inner Lubyanka for the rubber-hosepipe kidney treatment? Got no answer? You do. So now you tell me which is best
– for the inner pigs to take you in for doing the old woman, or to
wind up with the inner State Security Services as ex-president?'

Kolyan wrinkled up his brow and held his fingers up in a fan
shape as he prepared to say something, but at that point he obviously had an unpleasant idea, because he suddenly dropped
his head limply.

'Yeah, yeah . . .' he said. 'It's probably best not to stick your
head up. It's tricky all right . . .'

'Now the inner pigs have got you,' Volodin stated. 'And you
tell me, Nietzsche, Nietzsche . . . D'you know what happened to
that Nietzsche of yours?'

Kolyan cleared his throat. A gob of spittle like a tiny bull ter-
rier separated from his lips and plopped into the fire.

'You're a real bastard, Volodin,' he said. 'You've screwed my
head up again. I just saw this film on the video, *Pulp Fiction*,
about the American brothers. I felt so good after it! Like I knew
now how to carry on livin'. But talkin' with you's like getting
flushed down into some ditch full of shit . . . I'll tell you this – I
ain't never come across none of your inner pigs. If I do, then I'll
waste them, or I'll call in the shrink to get me off on an insanity
plea.'

'Why d'you want to waste the inner pigs?' Shurik put in. 'Why
bother, when you can just cut them in?'

'You mean the inner pigs are on the take too?' Kolyan asked.

"Course they're on the take,' said Shurik. 'Haven't you seen
The Godfather 3? Remember Don Corleone? To get out from
under his inner pigs, he sent the Vatican six hundred million

greenbacks. Got off with parole, even with all the guys he'd wasted.'

He turned to face Volodin.

'Maybe you're gonna tell us the inner pigs ain't on the take?'

'What difference does it make if they're on the take or not?'

'That's right,' said Shurik, 'that's not where the spiel was at. It was Kolyan started taking out the pigs. Where was we at? We was talking about the eternal high, yeah? And about some fourth guy who goes tripping on the eternal high while you're getting things together with the internal prosecutors and briefs.'

'That's right. It doesn't matter how you settle up with the inner pigs – you can take them out or cut them in or write a confession. None of the pigs or the guys who pay them off or the guys who confess actually exist. It's just you pretending to be each of them by turns. I thought you'd understood all that.'

'Not so very much.'

'Remember how you and Kolyan used to work down by Red Square before democracy? When he sold hard currency and you came over with a pig's pass and confiscated it, and took away the client? Remember how you used to say that if you didn't believe for just a moment that you were a pig, then the client wouldn't believe it either and he wouldn't walk? So you used to feel like a pig.'

'Well, yeah.'

'And maybe you actually became one?'

'Volodin,' said Shurik, 'you're a mate of mine, but I mean it, you watch your mouth.'

'This entire spiel's down to me, you just listen. D'you see what we've got here? You yourself can believe for a while that you're a pig. Now just imagine that you do the same thing all your life, only it's not the client you're fooling, it's yourself, and all the time you believe your own show. Sometimes you're a pig, and sometimes you're the guy he's fingering. Sometimes you're the prosecutor, sometimes you're the brief. Why d'you think I said they don't really exist? Because when you're the prosecutor – where's the brief? And when you're the brief – where's the prosecutor? Nowhere. So it turns out like you're dreaming them, get me?'

'Okay, okay, I get you.'

'And then apart from the pigs, you've got so many other ass-holes standing in line that life's not long enough for you to be all of them. The queue waiting for you inside is longer than any of those queues for sausage under the commies. And if you want to understand the eternal high, you have to wipe out the whole queue, get me?'

Shurik thought about it for a while.

'Ah, who needs it,' he said at last. 'I'd better do five grams of coke than go crazy. Maybe this eternal high won't give me no trip anyway – just like weed don't do nothing for me.'

'That's why no one knows about the eternal high,' said Volodin. 'That's precisely why.'

This time the silence that followed was a long one. Volodin began breaking branches and throwing them into the fire. Shurik took a flat metal flask with an embossed image of the Statue of Liberty out of his pocket, took several large gulps from it and handed it to Kolyan. Kolyan drank too, handed it back to Shurik and began spitting into the fire at regular intervals.

The branches in the flames cracked like gunfire – sometimes single shots, sometimes short bursts. The camp-fire seemed like an entire universe in which tiny beings, whose scarcely visi-ble shadows flickered between the tongues of flame, squirmed and struggled for a place beside the gobs of spittle falling on the hot embers, in order to escape for at least a few moments from the intolerable heat. The fate of these beings was a sad one – even if anyone were to guess at their spectral existence, how could he possibly explain to them that in actual fact they didn't live in a fire, but in the middle of a forest filled with the coolness of the night, and if they would only stop struggling for a place by the gobs of a mobster's spittle, then all of their sufferings would be at an end? Probably he couldn't. Perhaps the neo-Platonist who used to live in these parts could have managed it – but then the poor man had died without even living to see the Twentieth Congress.

'Verily,' Volodin said sadly, 'this world is like unto a burning house.'

'Never mind a burning house,' Shurik replied readily. 'It's a fire in a bloody brothel during a fucking flood.'

'So what d'you do? You gotta live,' said Kolyan. 'Tell me, Volodin, d'you believe in the end of the world?'

'That's a purely individual question,' said Volodin. 'If some Chechen or other blows you away, that's the end of your world.'

'We'll see who blows who away,' said Kolyan. 'What d'you reckon, is it true all the Orthodox believers are in line for pardon?'

'When?'

'At the Last Judgement,' Kolyan said quickly in a half-whisper.

'You don't mean you believe in all that garbage?' Shurik asked disbelievingly.

'Dunno if I believe it or not,' said Kolyan. 'Once I was on my way home from this kill, I felt real miserable, I had all these doubts – you know, when you feel your spirit getting weak. And there's this kiosk with these icons and these pamphlets and stuff. So I bought one of them – "Life Beyond the Grave" it was called. I read about what happens after you're dead. It was all such dead familiar stuff, honest. I recognized it all straight off. Holding cell, trial, pardon, time, article. Dying's like movin' from jail to the camps. They send the soul off to this heavenly transit jail, tribulations it's called. Everything done right, two armed escorts and all the whole works, punishment cell downstairs, upstairs – the good life. And while you're in this transit jail they slap the charges on you – your own and everybody else's too – and you gotta get yourself off on every article, one after the other. The main thing is, you gotta know the criminal code. But if the big boss feels like it, he'll stick you in solitary anyway. 'Cause under his criminal code you're fitted up under half the articles from the day you're born. For instance, there's this article says you answer for all your spiel. Not just when you mouth off out of line, but the whole thing, every single word you ever said. You get that? No matter which way you twist it, there's always somethin' they can put you away for. If you got a soul, you're in for the tribulations. But the big boss can slim your time down, especially if you call yourself a worthless heap of shit. He likes that. And he likes it when you're afraid of him. Wants everyone to be afraid of him and feel like shit. And there he is with this big-time radiance, and these big wings fanned out wide, bodyguards, angels – the whole works. He looks down at you – what you gotta say now, you lump of shit? Get the picture now? I'm readin' it and I remember – a long time ago, when I was trainin' to be a weightlifter and it was *perestroika*, they printed somethin' like it in *Ogonyok*. And when I remembered it, I broke out in a sweat. Turns out life under Stalin was like life after death is now!'

'I don't get you,' said Shurik.

'Well, look, under Stalin after death there was atheism, but now there's religion again. And accordin' to religion, after death everyone lives like they did under Stalin. Just you figure it the way it was. Everybody knows there's this window lit up in the Kremlin at night, and He's there behind it, and He loves you like a brother, and you're shit-scared of Him, but you're supposed to love Him with all your heart as well. It's just like in religion. The reason I remembered Stalin is I began wonderin' how you can be shit-scared of someone and love him with all your heart at the same time.'

'And what if you're not scared?' Shurik asked.

'That means you've no fear of God. And that means the punishment cell.'

'What punishment cell's that?'

'There wasn't much written about that. The main thing is it's dark and there's this gnashin' of teeth. After I read it I was wonderin' for half an hour what kind of teeth the soul has . . . nearly lost my marbles over it. Then I started readin' some more, and I realized that if you call yourself a pile of shit soon enough, or not just call yourself one but believe it for real, then you'll get a pardon – and then they'll let you into heaven, to see Him. The way I made it out, the main thing they have to get off on is looking at Him all the time while he's taking the parade from up on top of the tribune. And they don't need anythin' else, because for them it's either that or grindin' their teeth down in the shithole, and that's it. That's the bastard thing about it, there can't be anythin' else – it's either up on the top bunk or down in the punishment cell. I figured out the whole system, top to bottom. I just couldn't figure out who dreamed up such a heavy deal. What d'you reckon, Volodin?'

'You remember Globus?' Volodin asked.

'The one who became a banker? Sure,' Kolyan answered.

'I remember him too,' said Shurik, sipping the liberating liquid from his flask. 'Became a real big wheel before he died. Drove around in a Porsche, wore all these chains at five thousand bucks a pop. He was on television too – a sponsor, no fucking less, the whole works.'

'Yes,' said Volodin, 'and when he went to Paris for that loan, know what he did? He went to a restaurant with one of their bankers for a heart-to-heart, and he got plastered, just like he was in the Slavyansky Bazaar and started yelling – "Garçon, two pederasts and a bucket of your strongest tea!" He wasn't gay himself, but what do you do when there's no other ass in sight for twenty years?'

'No need to explain that. So what happened next?'

'Nothing. They brought the tea. And they brought the queers too. They've got the market system there.'

'And did they give him the loan?'

'It doesn't matter whether they gave him the loan or not. But just think about it. If he ended his life with ideas like that still in his head, it means he never really left the prison camps at all. He just got so big that he started driving around them in a Porsche and giving interviews. And then he even found his own Paris in the camps. So if Globus, with his jailhouse queers and his prison tea, had started thinking about life after death, what kind of thoughts do you think he would have had?'

'He never gave a thought to that stuff in his life.'

'But what if he had started thinking about it? If he doesn't know anything but the camps, but he's drawn to higher things, like any other man, then what would he have imagined?'

'I don't get you. What you drivin' at? His only high was dope.'

'I get you,' said Shurik. 'If Globus had started thinking about life after death, he'd have come up with exactly that pamphlet. And not just Globus, neither. Just think about it, Kol – the entire country was one big labour camp from the day we was born, and it'll always be a camp. That's why God's the way he is, with all them flashing lights and sirens. Who believes in any other kind round here?'

'Don't you like our country, or what?' Kolyan asked in a serious voice.

'Course I do. Parts of it.'

Kolyan turned towards Volodin.

'Listen, though. Did they give Globus the loan that time in Paris?'

'I think they did,' said Volodin. 'The banker enjoyed the show, he really liked it. Queers have never been any problem for them there, but they'd never tried tea quite like that. It became all the rage, they called it *thé à la russe nouveau.*'

'Listen,' Shurik said suddenly, 'I just had a thought . . . Agh . . . Fucking hell . . .'

'What?' asked Kolyan.

'Maybe that's not the way it really is. Maybe it's not because we live in a camp that our God is like a big boss with flashing lights, but just the opposite – we live in a camp 'cause we chose a God like a mobster with a police siren. All that garbage about the teeth and the soul, about the stove where they burn the down-and-outs, and that armed escort up in the sky – it was all dreamed up centuries ago! And here they decided to build heaven on earth. And they did build it, too! Built it for real, from all the plans! And when they built heaven it turned out it wouldn't work without hell, because what kind of heaven can there be without hell? It wouldn't be heaven at all, just boring as fuck. So . . . Nah, I'm afraid to carry on thinking like that.'

'Maybe in places where people produce less shit, God's kinder too. In the States maybe, or in Japan,' said Kolyan.

'What d'you reckon, Volodin?' Shurik asked.

'What do I reckon? As it is above, so is it below. And as it is below, so is it above. And when everything's bottom up, how can you explain that there isn't any above or below? As they say round here – at night your ass gives the orders.'

'That's some heavy trippin',' said Kolyan. 'Enough to make you jealous. How much did you eat?'

'You not tripping yourself, then?' asked Shurik. 'You just tripped all the way across the world beyond the grave, and you took us along for the ride. Turns out you got more than just a pig and a brief tucked away inside there, you got the entire Holy Synod as well.'

Kolyan held his hand out in front of him and studied it carefully. 'There,' he said. 'I've gone blue again. Why do these mushrooms keep turnin' me blue?'

'You spoil too quickly,' said Shurik and he turned to face Volodin. 'Listen, fuck you. This spiel's bouncing about like we'd lost our marbles. We started talking about the eternal high and now look where we've ended up.'

'Where have we ended up?' asked Volodin. 'Seems to me we're still sitting where we started. The fire's burning, the cocks are crowing.'

'What cocks? That's Kolyan's pager.'

'Ah . . . Never mind, they'll crow all right.'

Shurik chuckled and took a sip from his flask. 'Volodin,' he said, 'I still wanna know who that fourth guy is.'

'Who?'

'The fourth guy. Haven't forgotten, have you? What we started off talking about – that there's this inner prosecutor and this inner brief and the guy who gets off on the inner high. Only I don't get why he's the fourth. That makes him the third.'

'You've forgotten the accused, haven't you?' asked Volodin. 'The one they're all trying? You can't shift straight from being your own prosecutor to being your own brief. You have to be the accused for at least a second or two. He's the third guy. But the fourth guy isn't in on any of those deals. There's nothing he needs except this eternal high.'

'And how does he know about the eternal high?'

'Who said he knows about it?'

'You said so yourself.'

'I never said that, I said there was no need to tell him anything about the eternal high – but that doesn't mean he knows anything about it. If he knew anything' – Volodin laid a heavy stress on the word 'knew' – 'then he'd be a witness at your inner trial.'

'You mean I got witnesses inside me as well? Explain that to me.'

'Well then, imagine you've done some foul shit. The inner prosecutor says you're a scumball, the accused stares at the wall, and the inner brief mumbles something about a difficult childhood.'

'Well?'

'But for the trial to begin, you have to remember the shit you've done, don't you?'

'That's obvious enough.'

'So when you're remembering it, you become a witness.'

'From listening to you,' said Shurik, 'I must have the entire courtroom inside me.'

'Why, what else did you expect?'

Shurik said nothing for a short while, then he suddenly slapped his hands against his thighs.

'Ah!' he yelled abruptly. 'Now I've twigged it! I've twigged how to switch on to that eternal high! You've got to turn into that fourth guy, right? Like being the prosecutor or the brief.'

'That's right. Only how are you going to turn into him?'

'Dunno, I s'pose you have to want to.'

'If you want to be the fourth guy, you won't turn into him, you'll just be someone who wanted to be him. And that's a big difference. You don't turn into the prosecutor when you want to be him, but only after you really say to yourself in your heart, "Shurik, you're a real shit." And then afterwards your inner brief realizes that a moment ago he was the prosecutor.'

'Okay,' said Shurik. 'Then tell me, how can you turn into that fourth guy if you don't want to?'

'It's not a matter of whether you want to or you don't. The point is that if you want something, then for sure you're not the fourth guy, but somebody else. Because the fourth guy doesn't want anything at all. Why should he want anything when he's surrounded by the eternal high?'

'Listen, why d'you keep on being so mysterious about it? Can't you just tell me in normal words who this fourth guy is?'

'I can say anything you like, but there's no point.'

'Well, try it anyway.'

'Well, for instance, you could say he's the son of God.'

While these words still hung in the air, the three men by the fire suddenly heard the crowing of cocks on every side – which was very odd, if you think about it, because there hadn't been any chickens kept in that district since the Twentieth Party Congress. Be that as it may, the crowing came again and again, and the ancient sounds gave rise to terrible thoughts, perhaps about witchcraft and devil-worship, or perhaps about the Chechen mounted cavalry breaking through to Moscow, hurtling across the steppe with their Stingers all poised for launching, crowing like cocks to send military intelligence off on a false trail. This latter supposition seemed to be supported by the fact that the cries always came in threes, and were followed by a brief pause. It was very mysterious indeed. For a while they all listened, entranced, to this forgotten music, and then the crowing either faded away or mingled so completely with the background noise that it no longer held their interest. No doubt they simply thought to themselves that anything can happen when you're on mushrooms. The conversation picked up again.

'You just keep on trashing my brains over and over again,' said Shurik. 'Can't you just tell me straight out how I turn into him?'

'I told you, if you could just turn into him like that, then everybody would have been tripping long ago. The problem is that the only way to become the fourth guy is to stop turning into all the others.'

'You mean you have to turn into no one?'

'You have to stop being no one too. You have to not become anyone and stop being no one at the same time, get it? And the moment you're in there, you're off tripping, quicker than a flash. And it's for ever.'

Kolyan gasped quietly. Shurik gave him a sideways glance. Kolyan was sitting motionless, as though he had turned to stone. His mouth had turned into a triangular hole, and his eyes seemed to have turned inwards.

'You sure pile it on, for real,' said Shurik. 'I'll start leaking marbles any moment.'

'Let them leak,' Volodin said gently. 'What do you need those marbles for anyway?'

'Nah, that's no good,' said Shurik. 'If I drop all my marbles, then you soon won't have no marbles either.'

'How's that?' asked Volodin.

'Just you remember who your cover is. Me and Kolyan, isn't it? Isn't that right, Kol?'

Kolyan didn't answer.

'Hey, Kolyan!' Shurik shouted.

Again Kolyan didn't answer. He sat there by the fire with his back held straight up, gazing straight ahead, but not looking at Shurik sitting there in front of him, or Volodin slightly to his left. It was obvious that he wasn't looking at them at all, he was gazing

262

into nowhere. But the most remarkable thing of all was that a column of light had appeared above his head, reaching far up into the heavens.

At first glance the column looked like no more than a narrow thread, but the instant Shurik and Volodin started paying attention to it, it began expanding and growing brighter – and yet somehow it didn't illuminate the clearing or the men sitting by the fire, it only illuminated itself. Then it took in the fire and the four people sitting round it, and suddenly they were surrounded by this light, and there was nothing else around them at all.

'Fuck me!' The sound of Shurik's voice came from every side.

In reality, there weren't any sides at all, or any voices either. Instead of the voice there was a certain presence, which announced itself in a way that made it clear it was Shurik. And the meaning of the announcement was such that the best words for expressing it were clearly 'fuck me!'.

'For real. Volodin, can you hear me?'

'Yes,' Volodin answered from everywhere.

'Is this the eternal high then?'

'Why are you asking me? Look for yourself. You know everything now, you can see everything.'

'Yeah . . . What's this stuff all around us? Ah, yes, that's it . . . of course. But where's everything else gone to?'

'It hasn't gone anywhere. Everything's where it should be. Try looking a bit harder . . .'

'Oh, yeah. Kolyan, where are you? How you doing?'

'Me!' came the response from the glowing void. 'Me!'

'Hey, Kolyan! Answer me!'

'Me!!! Me!!!'

'So that's how it all really is, eh? Who'd have thought it?' Shurik went on, excited and happy. 'I'd never have guessed. Listen, Volodin, don't even bother to answer, I'll get it myself . . . Who could ever have imagined it? No way could anyone ever imagine this! No way, not ever! No way, no how!'

'Me!!!' responded Kolyan.

'Turns out there's nothing to be afraid of in the world,' Shurik went on. 'Absolutely nothing at all. I know everything, I can see everything. I can see and understand anythin' you like. Why, even . . . Well, well, well . . . Listen, Kolyan, we didn't ought to

have wasted Kosoy that time. He never took the dough. It was
. . . So it was you took it, Kolyan!'

'Me!!! Me!!! Me!!! Me!!!'

'Cut the spiel,' Volodin interrupted, 'or we'll all get thrown
out.'

'Why, the rotten bastard,' yelled Shurik, 'he threw everyone a
curve.'

'Cut it out, I said. This isn't the time. Better take a look at yourself.'

'What self?'

'So who's that talking now? Take a look at him.'

'At myself? Oh . . . Right . . . Whoah . . .'

'You see. And you said there was nothing in the world to be
afraid of.'

'Yeah . . . Right . . . Oh, fuck me! Listen, Volodin, this is real
scary. Real scary stuff. Volodin, d'you hear me? Where's the
light? Volodin? I'm scared!'

'And you said there was nothing in the world to be afraid of,'
said Volodin, raising his head and gazing wide-eyed into empty
space, as though he'd seen something there.

'Right then,' he said in a changed voice, nudging Shurik and
Kolyan, 'let's move it! Quick!'

'Volodin, I can hardly hear you!' Shurik yelled, swaying from
side to side. 'Volodin, I'm scared! Hey, Kolyan! Answer me,
Kolyan!'

'Me. Me. Me.'

'Hey, Kolyan, can you see me? Just don't go lookin' at yourself, or it'll turn dark. Can you see me, Kolyan?'

'Me? Me?'

'Move it, into the forest, quick!' Volodin repeated, and he
leapt to his feet.

'What forest? There isn't really any forest!'

'You just run, and the forest'll appear. Go on, run! You leg it
too, Kolyan. Rendezvous at the camp-fire.'

'Me?! Me?! Me?!!'

'Fucking hell! I said let's move it into the forest! Run for it!'

Even if we were to allow that the camp-fire that had been blazing in the clearing a few hours earlier really was a small universe

264

unto itself, that universe had now ceased to exist, and all the sufferings of its inhabitants had been extinguished with it. Void and darkness were upon the face of the clearing, and there was nothing but a light smoke hanging in the air above the dead embers.

The radio-telephone in the car began to ring, and suddenly some small, startled life form began rustling in the bushes. The ringing went on for a long time, and after more than a minute its persistence was rewarded. There was a crunching of twigs in the bushes, followed by rapid footsteps. A blurred shadow flitted across the clearing towards the Jeep and a voice spoke:

'Hello! Ultima Thule Limited? Of course I recognize you, of course. Yes! Yes! No! Tell Seryozha the Mongoloid not to get up my nose. No transfers. Cash ex-VAT and we tear up the contract. Tomorrow at ten in the office . . . no, not at ten, at twelve. Right.'

It was Volodin. He put down the receiver, opened up the Jeep's boot, rummaged around until he found a spray-can, the contents of which he emptied on to the remains of the fire. Nothing happened – evidently even the embers had died completely. Then Volodin struck a match and dropped it on the ground, and a bright ball of yellow-red flame rose up into the air.

He spent several minutes collecting branches and twigs in the clearing and throwing them into the flames. When Shurik and Kolyan came wandering out of the forest towards the light, the camp-fire was already blazing away.

They appeared one at a time. Kolyan appeared first; before he emerged into the clearing, for some reason he sat for a long time in the bushes at its edge, holding his hand over his eyes as he gazed into the flames. Then he finally made up his mind, went up to the fire and sat down in his old place. Shurik arrived about ten minutes later; holding his 'TT' with the long silencer in his hand, he slunk out into the clearing, looked Kolyan and Volodin over and tucked the pistol away under his cashmere pea-jacket.

'Fucked if I ever puts any of that stuff in my mouth again,' he said in a dull voice. 'Not for any money. I emptied two clips, and I don't have a blind idea who I was shooting at.'

'Didn't you like it?' asked Volodin.

'It was kinda okay at first,' Shurik replied, 'but then afterwards . . . Listen, what were we talking about just before the explosion?'

'Before what explosion?' Volodin asked in amazement.

'That, that . . . Or what could you call it . . .'

Shurik looked up at Volodin, as if hoping that he would prompt him with the words he needed, but Volodin said nothing.

'Okay then,' said Shurik, 'at the very beginning we was talking about the eternal high, I remember that. And then the spiel kinda tipped off the rails, flip-flop, and then there was this flash of fire in my eyes . . . And you was yelling yourself, telling us to leg it into the forest. As soon as I came round I thought the wheels must have exploded. Thought those jerks from Slav-East must have put a bomb in it. And then I thought that didn't make sense – there was flames all right, but there wasn't no smell of petrol. So that means it's all in the mind.'

'Yes,' said Volodin, 'that's right. All in the mind.'

'So was that your eternal high, then?' asked Shurik.

'You could call it that,' Volodin replied.

'What did you do to make us able to see it?' asked Shurik.

'I didn't do it,' replied Volodin, 'it was Kolyan. He was the one who took us in there.'

Shurik looked at Kolyan. Kolyan shrugged in puzzlement.

'Yes,' went on Volodin, gathering up the things lying by the fire and throwing them in through the Jeep's open door, 'you see the way things turn out. Take a good look at your mate, Shurik. He might never have seemed too quick on the uptake, but he was the one who pulled it off. The old spiel about blessed are the poor in spirit is sure right.'

'Are we gonna leave, or what?' Shurik asked.

'Yeah,' said Volodin. 'It's time to go. We've got a shoot with Slav-East at twelve. And by the time we get there, what with one thing and another . . .'

'I can't really remember anything straight,' Shurik summed up the conversation. 'But I feel really odd. For the first time in my life I want to do something good. Even help someone, maybe, save them from suffering. Take everyone, the whole fucking lot of them, and save them all . . .'

He turned his face up to the starry sky for a second, and it took on a dreamy and exalted expression. He sighed quietly and then, obviously taking a grip on himself, he took a step towards the camp-fire, turned his back to his two companions, fiddled with something in the region of his belt, and the tongues of flame were extinguished instantly under the heavy weight of the frothing stream.

A few minutes later they were travelling along a rough country road, more like a deep trench dug through the forest. Kolyan was snoring on the back seat. Sitting behind the wheel, Volodin was gazing hard into the darkness where the headlights sliced into it, while Shurik pondered on something and bit nervously at his lower lip.

'Listen,' he said at last. 'There's something else I don't get. You said that once the eternal high hits you it never ends.'

'It doesn't ever end,' Volodin replied, frowning as he turned the steering wheel sharply, 'not if you get in the normal way, through the front door. But you could say we climbed in through the back window. That's why the alarm went off.'

'Some heavy alarm,' said Shurik, 'real heavy stuff.'

'That's nothing,' said Volodin. 'They could easily have put us away. There are cases like that. Take that Nietzsche Kolyan was jawing about, that's exactly what happened to him.'

'But if they collar you there, where do they put you?' Shurik asked with a strange note of respect in his voice.

'On the physical plane – in the madhouse. But where they put you on the subtle plane, I don't know. That's a mystery.'

'Listen,' asked Shurik, 'can you get there as simple as that? Like, whenever you want?'

'Nah,' said Volodin. 'I . . . How can I explain it? I can't squeeze through the gap. I've picked up a lot of spiritual riches in my life. And getting rid of them afterwards is harder than cleaning the shit out of the grooves on the sole of your shoe. So I usually send one of the poor in spirit on ahead so he can squeeze through the eye of the needle and open the door from the inside. Like this time. But I didn't think that if two poor in heart got in together they would create such a rumpus.'

'What rumpus?'

Volodin was busy negotiating a complicated section of the road and didn't answer. The Jeep shuddered once, then again. For several seconds its engine roared strenuously as it clambered up a steep hillock, then it turned and drove on along an asphalt surface, quickly picking up speed. An old Zhiguli came hurtling towards them, followed by a column of several military trucks. Volodin switched on the radio, and a minute later the four people sitting in the Jeep were enveloped in the old, familiar world whose every detail was clear and familiar.

'So what rumpus was that you was talking about?' Shurik asked again.

'Okay,' said Volodin, 'we'll run through all that later. You'll have some homework to do. But for now let's think about what we've got to show Slav-East.'

'You think about it,' said Shurik. 'We're only the cover round here. You're the one pushes the wheels round.'

He was silent for a few seconds.

'All the same, I just can't get my head round it,' he said. 'Just who is that fourth guy?'

9

'Indeed, who could this fourth person have been? Who can tell? Could it perhaps have been the devil ascended from the realms of eternal darkness in order to draw a few more fallen souls down after him. Or perhaps it was God who prefers, following certain events, to make His appearance here on earth incognito, most often associating exclusively with tax-collectors and sinners. Or perhaps – and surely most likely – it was someone quite different, someone far more real than any of the men sitting by the fire, because while there is not and cannot be any guarantee that Volodin, Kolyan and Shurik, and all these cocks, gods, devils, neo-Platonists and Twentieth Congresses ever actually existed, you, who have just been sitting by the fire yourself, you really do exist, and surely this is the very first thing that exists and has ever existed?'

Chapaev put the manuscript down on the top of his bureau and looked out for a while through the semicircular window of his study.

'It seems to me, Petka, that the writer occupies too large a place in your personality,' he said eventually. 'This apostrophe to a reader who does not really exist is a rather cheap trick. Even if we assume that someone other than myself might possibly wade through this incomprehensible narrative, then I can assure you that he won't give a single moment's thought to the self-evident fact of his own existence. He is more likely to imagine you writing these lines. And I am afraid . . .'

'But I am not afraid of anything,' I interrupted nervously, lighting up a *papyrosa*. 'I simply do not give a damn, nor have I for ages. I simply wrote down my latest nightmare as best I could. And that paragraph appeared . . . How shall I put it . . .

By force of inertia. After that conversation I had with the baron.'

'Yes, by the way, what did the baron tell you?' Chapaev asked. 'Judging from the fact that you came back wearing a yellow hat, the two of you must have had quite an emotional exchange.'

'Oh, yes, indeed,' I said. 'I could sum it up by saying that he advised me to discharge myself from the hospital. He likened this world of constant alarms and passions, these thoughts about nothing and all this running nowhere, to a home for the mentally ill. And then – assuming I understood him correctly – he explained that in reality this home for the mentally ill does not exist, and neither does he, and neither do you, my dear Chapaev. There is nothing but me.'

Chapaev chuckled.

'So that's what you took him to mean. That is interesting. We shall come back to that, I promise you . . . But as for his advice to discharge yourself from the madhouse, that seems to me a suggestion which it is quite impossible to improve on. I really don't know why I didn't think of it myself. Yes, indeed, instead of being terrified by each new nightmare, these nightly creations of your inflamed consciousness . . .'

'I beg your pardon, I do not think I quite understand,' I said. 'Is it my inflamed consciousness that creates the nightmare, or is my consciousness itself a creation of the nightmare?'

'They are the same thing,' said Chapaev with a dismissive wave of his hand. 'All these constructs are only required so that you can rid yourself of them for ever. Wherever you might be, live according to the laws of the world you find yourself in, and use those very laws to liberate yourself from them. Discharge yourself from the hospital, Petka.'

'I believe that I understand the metaphor,' I said. 'But what will happen afterwards? Shall I see you again?'

Chapaev smiled and crossed his arms.

'I promise that you will,' he said.

There was a sudden crash, and fragments of the upper window-pane scattered across the floor. The stone that had crashed through it struck against the wall and fell to the floor beside the bureau. Chapaev went over to the window and glanced cautiously out into the yard.

'The weavers?' I asked.

Chapaev nodded.

'They are completely wild from drink now,' he said.

'Why do you not have a word with Furmanov?' I asked.

'I have no reason to believe he is capable of controlling them,' Chapaev replied. 'The only reason he remains their commander is because he always gives them exactly the orders that they wish to hear. He only has to make one single serious mistake, and they will find themselves another leader soon enough.'

'I must confess that I am seriously alarmed on their account,' I said. 'The situation appears to me to be completely out of control. Please do not think that I am beginning to panic, but at some fine moment we could easily all find ourselves . . . Remember what has been going on for the last few days.'

'It will all be resolved this evening,' Chapaev said, fixing me with his gaze. 'By the way, since you declare yourself to be concerned at this problem, which really is genuinely aggravating, why not make your own contribution? Help us to amuse the bored public and create the impression that we have also been drawn into their Bacchanalian revels. They must continue to believe that everyone here is of one mind.'

'A contribution to what?'

'There is going to be a concert of sorts today – you know the kind of thing, the men will show each other all kinds of ee-er . . . acts, I suppose. Everyone who has a trick will show it off. So perhaps you could perform for them as well, and recite something revolutionary? Like that piece you gave at the "Musical Snuffbox"?'

I was piqued.

'But you must understand, I really am not sure that I shall be able to fit in with the style of such a concert. I am afraid that . . .'

'But you just told me you are not afraid of anything,' Chapaev interrupted. 'And then, you should take a broader view of things. In the final analysis, you are one of my men too, and all that is required of you is to show the others what sort of tricks you can turn yourself.'

For just an instant it seemed to me that Chapaev's words

contained an excessive element of mockery; it even occurred to me that it might be his reaction to the text he had just been reading. But then I realized that there was another possible explanation. Perhaps he simply wished to show me that, when viewed from the perspective of reality, no hierarchy remains for the activities in which people engage – and no particular difference between one of the most famous poets of St Petersburg and a bunch of crude regimental talents.

'Very well then,' I said, 'I shall try.'

'Splendid,' said Chapaev. 'Until this evening, then.'

He turned back to his bureau and busied himself with studying the map laid out on it. A pile of papers was encroaching upon the territory of the map, and amongst them I could make out several telegrams and two or three packages sealed with red sealing-wax. Clicking my heels (Chapaev paid not the slightest attention to the sarcasm with which I invested this act), I left the study and ran down the stairs. In the doorway I ran into Anna as she came in from the yard. She was wearing a dress of black velvet which covered her breasts and her throat and reached down almost to the floor: none of her outfits suited her so well.

I actually ran into her in the direct sense of the word; for a brief second my arms, instinctively thrown out ahead of me, closed around her in a tight embrace, unpremeditated and clumsy, but nonetheless disturbing for that. The next instant, as through thrown off by an electric shock, I leapt backwards, stumbled over the last step of the stairway and fell flat on my back – it must all have appeared quite monstrously absurd. But Anna did not laugh – quite the opposite, her face expressed fright and concern.

'Did you hit your head?' she asked, leaning down over me solicitously and holding out her hand.

'No,' I said, taking her hand in mine and getting to my feet.

Even after I had risen she did not withdraw her hand; for a second there was an awkward pause and then I surprised even myself by saying:

'Surely you must understand that this is not the way I am in myself, that it is you, Anna, who make me the most ridiculous being in the world.'

'I? But why?'

'As if you could not see for yourself . . . You have been sent by God or the devil, I do not know which, to punish me. Before I met you, I had no idea of how hideous I was – not in myself, but in comparison with that higher, unattainable beauty which you symbolize for me. You are like a mirror in which I have suddenly glimpsed the great, unbridgeable gulf which separates me from everything that I love in this world, from everything that is dear to me, that holds any meaning or significance for me. And only you, Anna – hear me out, please – only you can bring back to my life the light and the meaning which disappeared after that first time I saw you in the train! You alone are capable of saving me.' I uttered all of this in a single breath.

Of course, I lied – no particular light and meaning had disappeared from my life with Anna's appearance, because there had not been any before – but at the moment when I pronounced these words, every single one of them seemed to me to be the most sacred truth. As Anna listened in silence, an expression of mingled mistrust and incomprehension gradually stole across her face. Apparently this was the very last thing she had expected to hear from me.

'But how can I save you?' she asked, knitting her brows in a frown. 'Believe me, I would be glad to do so, but what exactly is required of me?'

Her hand remained in mine, and I suddenly sensed a wave of insane hope surge in my breast.

'Tell me, Anna,' I said quickly, 'you love to go riding in a carriage, do you not? I have won the trotters from Kotovsky. Here in the manor-house would be awkward. This evening, as soon as it is dark, let us take a ride out into the countryside!'

'What?' she asked. 'But what for?'

'What do you mean, "what for"? I assumed . . .'

Her expression changed instantly to one of weariness and boredom.

'God, what banal vulgarity!' she said, withdrawing her hand. 'It would be better if you simply smelled of onions, like the last time.'

She walked past me, ran quickly up the stairs and entered Chapaev's study without knocking. I went on standing there for some time; as soon as I had recovered control of the muscles of my face, I went out into the yard. After a long search I managed to find Furmanov in the headquarters hut, where he seemed to have settled in and made himself thoroughly at home. Standing on the table, beside an immense ink stain, was a samovar with a vaudeville boot stuck upside down over its chimney; evidently it served them as a kind of bellows for drawing the fire. Pieces of a dismembered herring were lying on rags beside the samovar. Having told Furmanov that I would recite revolutionary verse at the concert that evening, I left him to carry on drinking his tea – I was sure that there was vodka hidden under the table – in the company of two members of the weavers' regiment. I went out through the gates of the yard and walked slowly in the direction of the forest.

It was strange, but I scarcely gave a thought to the declaration I had just made to Anna. I did not even feel particularly angry with myself. It did occur to me, it is true, that on every occasion she teased me with the possibility of a reconciliation, and then, as soon as I took the bait, made me appear quite monstrously absurd – but even this thought evaporated without the slightest effort on my part.

I walked uphill along the road, looking around me as I went. Soon the road surface came to an end; I walked a little further, then turned off the road, walked down the sloping grassy margin and sat down, leaning my back against a tree.

Holding a sheet of paper on my knees, I rapidly jotted down a text which was good enough for the weavers. As Chapaev had requested, it was in the spirit of the 'Musical Snuffbox', a sonnet with an affected rhyme scheme and a jagged rhythm that might have been ripped and torn with sabres. When it was finished, I realized that I had not included any revolutionary imagery and rewrote the final lines.

I was on the point of going back to the manor when I suddenly sensed that the insignificant effort I had made in writing these verses for the weavers had aroused my long-dormant creative powers; an invisible wing unfurled above my head, and everything else lost all importance. I remembered the death of the Emperor – this black news had been brought by Furmanov – and an almost pure anapaest threaded with interlinking rhymes flowed out as if of its own accord on to the paper. The form now seemed to me like some totally improbable echo of the past.

The poem began with a description of two sailors who seemed born from a condensation of the wind and the twilight that had settled over the world. Cleaving the foliage with the dark leather of their jackets, they were leading the bound Emperor. The Emperor was tired and resigned to his fate, but his eyes noticed many things that the sailors did not see; faces in the bushes, orderlies spitting in his beard, and the astounding beauty of this final evening. In their coarse fashion, the sailors attempted to lift the Emperor's spirits, but he remained indifferent to their words, and even to the clatter of their breech-locks. Clambering up on to a tree stump, he shouted to them:

> In the midst of this stillness and sorrow,
> In these days of distrust
> Maybe all can be changed – who can tell?
> Who can tell what will come
> To replace our visions tomorrow
> And to judge our past?

He even spoke in English, a fact, however, that did not surprise me in the slightest. Indeed, how could he, before his death (or perhaps before something else – I did not quite understand that point myself) have expressed himself in the Russian language defiled by the decrees of the Council of People's Commissars? I found the orderlies far more surprising – I simply could not make out what they meant. However, I had never understood my own poetry particularly well, and had long suspected that authorship is a dubious concept, and all that is required from a person who takes a pen in hand is to line up the various keyholes scattered about his soul so that a ray of sunlight can shine through on to the paper set out in front of him.

When I returned to the manor-house the performance was

already in full swing. In the corner of the yard stood the platform of an improvised stage, hastily cobbled together by the weavers from the planks of a dismantled fence. The men were sitting on benches and chairs which they had pilfered from wherever they could find them, attentively following the action. As I approached, a horse was being forcibly dragged away by its reins, to the loud laughter and ribald comments of the audience – the poor animal obviously possessed some talent which it had been forced to demonstrate. Then a thin man with a sabre hanging on his belt and the face of a village atheist appeared at the edge of the stage; I realized that he must be performing the function of master of ceremonies. He waited for the hubbub of voices to die away and then said solemnly:

'A horse with two pricks is nothing compared to what we have next. Your attention please for Private Straminsky, who can pronounce the words of the Russian language with his arse, and who worked in a circus prior to the liberation of the people. He talks quietly, so please keep quiet – and no laughing.'

A bald young man wearing spectacles appeared on the stage. I was surprised to note that, in contrast with the majority of Furmanov's people, his features were cultured, without a trace of bestiality. He belonged to the frequently encountered type of the eternal optimist, with a face creased by frequent grimaces of suffering. He gestured for a stool, then leaned down and supported himself on it with his hands, with his side to the audience and his face turned towards them.

'Great Nostradamus,' he said, 'tell me, do, how long will the bloody hydra of the foe continue to resist the Red Army?'

I wondered what the name Nostradamus could mean for them – perhaps some mighty hero bestriding the dark annals of proletarian mythology? The invisible Nostradamus replied:

'Not long.'

'And why does the bloody hydra continue to resist?' asked the mouth.

'The Entente,' replied its invisible interlocutor.

During the replies the lips of the man on the stage did not move at all, but he performed rapid movements with his protruding backside. The conversation was about politics and the health of the leaders – there were rumours that Lenin was in hospital again with heart problems, and only the captain of his guard was allowed to see him; the hall fell into an entranced silence.

I immediately realized how it was done. A long time before, in Florence, I had seen a street ventriloquist who had summoned up the spirit of Dante. The performance of the man on stage was something of the same kind, with the exception that the answers given by the 'spirit' obliged one to assume that Nostradamus had been the very first Marxist in Europe. It was obvious that the performer was a ventriloquist from the peculiar timbre of the replies – low, breathy and rather indistinct. The only thing that was not clear was why he needed to convince the weavers that he was uttering the sounds through his backside.

This was a genuinely interesting question. At first I thought it might be impossible to show the Red weavers a conversation with a spirit because, according to their view of the world, spirits did not exist. But then I was suddenly struck by another explanation, and I suddenly realized that the answer lay elsewhere. The performer had instinctively understood that only something thoroughly bawdy was capable of arousing lively interest from his audience. In this regard his skill in itself was entirely neutral – as far as I understood it, ventriloquists do not even speak with their bellies, they simply pronounce the sounds of speech without opening their lips – and therefore he had to present his act as something repulsively indecent.

Oh, how I regretted at that moment that I did not have one of the St Petersburg symbolists there with me. Could one ever possibly find a symbol deeper than this – or, perhaps I should say, wider? Such will be the fate, I thought with bitterness, of all the arts in this dead-end tunnel into which we are being dragged by the locomotive of history. If even a fairground ventriloquist has to resort to such cheap tricks to maintain his audience's interest, then what can possibly lie ahead for the art of poetry? There will be no place at all left for it in the new world – or rather, there will, but poems will only be considered interesting if it is known on the basis of sound documentary evidence that their author has two pricks, or at the very least, that he is capable of reciting them through his arse. Why, I asked myself, why does any social cataclysm in this world always result in the most ignorant scum rising to the top and forcing everyone else to live in accordance with its own base and conspiratorially defined laws?

In the meanwhile, the ventriloquist forecast the imminent demise of the kingdom of capital, then recited a weary, worn-out joke which no one in the audience understood, before issuing in farewell several protracted sounds of a vulgar physiological nature, which were greeted by the audience with enthusiastic laughter.

The master of ceremonies appeared again and announced my entrance. I ascended the sagging wooden steps, assumed my stance at the edge of the stage and gazed out without speaking at the assembled public. It was a far from pretty sight. It sometimes happens that the glass eyes of a stuffed wild boar project the semblance of some expression, some feeling which might have been expressed if the animal had been alive; the impression is in turn fleshed out by the mind of the observer. Some similar effect seemed to be in evidence here, except in reverse; although the multitude of eyes staring at me were actually alive and I seemed to understand the feeling reflected in them, I knew that they did not express to even the very slightest degree what I was imagining. In reality I would never be able to decode the meaning that glittered in them; indeed, it was probably not worth the effort.

Not everyone was looking at me. Furmanov was engaged in conversation about something with his two aides-de-camp – in their case the etymology of the term 'aides' could be traced back, beyond the slightest possible doubt, to the word 'hades'. I noticed Anna sitting in one of the most distant rows. She was chewing on a straw with a smile of contempt on her face. I do not think the smile was intended for me, she was not even looking at the stage; she was wearing the same black velvet dress she had worn a couple of hours before.

I set one foot in front of the other and folded my arms on my chest, but carried on standing there in silence, gazing at some point in the gangway. Soon the audience began murmuring restlessly, and in a few seconds the murmur had swollen to a rather loud rumble, providing a muted background for the more distinct sounds of whistles and hoots. Then, in a deliberately quiet voice, I began to speak:

'Gentlemen, I feel I must beg your forgiveness for making use of my mouth in order to address you, but I have had neither the time nor the opportunity to master the accepted modes of intercourse here . . .'

Nobody heard the first words I spoke, but by the end of this phrase the noise had dropped so noticeably that I could distinguish the buzzing of the multitudinous flies circling above my audience.

'Comrade Furmanov has asked me to recite some poetry for you, something revolutionary,' I continued. 'As a commissar, there is one comment I would like to make in this regard. Comrade Lenin has warned us against excessive enthusiasm for experimentation in the field of form. I trust that the artist who preceded me will not take offence – yes, yes, you, comrade, the one who spoke through your arse. Lenin has taught us that art is made revolutionary, not by its unusual external appearance, but by the profound inner inspiration of the proletarian idea. And by way of an example I shall recite for you a poem which speaks of the life of various princes and counts, but which is, nonetheless, a very clear example of proletarian poetry.'

Silence had established its total and undisputed reign over the seated rows of the public. As though saluting some invisible Caesar, I raised my hand above my head, and in my usual manner, using no intonation whatsoever but merely punctuating the quatrains with short pauses, I recited:

Princess Mescherskaya possessed a classy number, a fine little
Tight-fitting velvet dress, black as the Spanish night.
She wore it to receive a friend newly back from the capital,
Who shook and trembled and fled from the sight.

How very wearisome, the princess thought, oh what a painful bore,
I'll go and play some Brahms now, why should I care less?
Meanwhile her visitor concealed his naked self behind the *portière*,
A bagel painted black a-trembling in his passionate caress.

This story will seem no more than a joke
To little children who will never guess
How bloodsuckers exploited common folk,
Oppressed the peasants and the working class.
But now each working man can wear a bagel
As bold as any count was ever able.

For several seconds the silence hung in the air above the
seats, and then they suddenly erupted into louder applause
than I had ever managed to elicit even in 'The Stray Dog' in St
Petersburg. I noticed out of the corner of my eye that Anna had
risen and was walking away along the aisle, but just at that moment it did not bother me in the least. If I am honest, I must confess that I felt genuinely flattered, even to the extent that I forgot
all the bitter thoughts I had been thinking about my audience. I
brandished my fist at some invisible foe, then thrust my hand
into my pocket, pulled out my Browning and fired twice into
the air. The response was a rumbling cannonade from the
bristling forest of gun-barrels that had sprouted above the audience, followed by a roar of sheer delight. I gave a brief bow
and left the stage, then skirted round a group of weavers who
were still clapping, before heading for the manor-house.

My success had somewhat intoxicated me. I was thinking
that genuine art is distinguished from its false counterpart by
its ability to beat a path to even the most coarse and brutal-
ized of hearts, and its ability to exalt to the heavens, to a
world of total and unfettered freedom, even the most hope-
less victim of the infernal global trance. However, I came to
my senses soon enough as I was stung by the realization,
painful though it was for my own vanity, that they had applauded me simply because my poem had seemed to them to
be something in the nature of a warrant which widened by a
few extra degrees the scope of their unlimited and unpun-
ished licence: to Lenin's maxim that we should 'plunder what
has been plundered' had been added permission to don a

bagel, however unclear the repercussions of that might yet be.

I went back to my room, stretched out on the divan and stared at the ceiling with my hands clasped behind my back. I thought of how everything that had happened to me during the past two or three hours was a magnificent illustration of the eternal, unchanging fate of the Russian intellectual. Writing odes about Red banners in secret, but earning his keep with verses in honour of the name-day of the Head of Police – or the opposite, perceiving with his inner eye the final appearance of the Emperor, while mouthing off about the hanging of a count's bagels on the horny genitals of the proletariat.

Thus it will be always, I thought. Even if we were to allow that power in this terrifying country might not be won by one of the cliques warring for it, but could simply fall into the hands of villains and thieves of the kind to be found in all the various different 'Musical Snuffboxes', the Russian intelligentsia would still go running to them for business like a dog's barber.

While thinking all of this, I had already fallen half-asleep, but I was summoned back to reality by an unexpected knock at my door.

'Yes, yes,' I shouted, without even bothering to get up from the bed, 'come in!'

The door opened, but no one came in. I waited for several seconds until my patience was exhausted and I raised my head to look. Anna was standing in the doorway, wearing that same black velvet dress.

'May I come in?' she asked.

'Yes, of course,' I said, rising hurriedly, 'please. Have a seat.'

Anna sat down in the armchair – the second when her back was turned was just long enough for me to sweep a tattered puttee lying on the floor under the bed with a movement of my foot.

Once in the armchair, Anna folded her hands on her knees and contemplated me thoughtfully for several seconds with a gaze that seemed clouded by some thought that was not yet entirely clear even to her.

'Would you like to smoke?' I asked.

She nodded. I took out my *papyrosas* and placed them in front of her on the table, then set beside them the saucer which served for an ashtray and struck a match.

'Thank you,' she said, releasing a thin stream of smoke in the direction of the ceiling. There seemed to be some kind of struggle taking place within her. I was about to make some banal remark in order to start the conversation, but I stopped myself just in time when I remembered how that usually ended. Then suddenly Anna herself spoke.

'I cannot say that I really liked your poem about that princess,' she said, 'but in comparison with the other participants in the concert you cut rather an impressive figure.'

'Thank you,' I said.

'And by the way, I spent all last night reading your poems. The garrison library turned out to have a book . . .'

'Which one?'

'That I do not know. The first few pages were missing, someone must have torn them out for rolling cigarettes.'

'Then how could you tell that the poems were mine?'

'I asked the librarian. Anyway, there was one poem, a reworking of Pushkin, about opening one's eyes and seeing nothing but snow, empty space and mist, and then on further and further . . . It was very good. How did it go now? No, I can't remember. Ah, yes:

> But desire burns within you still,
> The trains depart for it,
> And the butterfly of consciousness
> Flits from nowhere into nowhere.

'Yes, I recall it now,' I said. 'The book is called *Songs of the Kingdom of I.*'

'What a strange title. It does sound rather smug.'

'Not really,' I said. 'That is not the point. It is simply that in China there once used to be a kingdom whose name consisted of a single letter – "A". I was always amazed by that. You know, we talk about "a" forest or "a" house, but here all we have is "a". Like an indication of something that lies beyond a point at which words come to an end, and all we can say is "a", but "a" *what* exactly is impossible to say.'

'Chapaev would immediately ask you whether you can say what you mean when you say "I".'

'He has already asked. But in relation to the book – it really is one of my weakest, by the way, I must give you the others some time – I can explain. I used to do a lot of travelling, and then at some moment I suddenly realized that no matter where I might go, in reality I can do no more than move within a single space, and that space is myself. At the time I called it "I", but now I would probably call it "A".'

'But what about other people?' Anna asked.

'Other people?' I queried.

'Yes. You write a lot about other people. For instance,' she knitted her brows slightly, evidently in the effort of remembering, 'take this:

> They gathered in the old bathhouse,
> Put on their cufflinks and their spats,
> Then banged their heads against the wall,
> Counting out the days and the miles . . .
> I hated the sight of their faces so badly
> That I could not live without their company –
> The sudden stench of the morgue
> Refines the language of recall, and I . . .

'Enough,' I interrupted her, 'I remember. I would not say that is really my best poem.'

'I like it. And in general, Pyotr, I liked your book terribly. But you have not answered my question: what about other people?'

'I am not sure I quite understand what you mean.'

'If everything that you can see, feel and understand is within you, in that kingdom of "I", does that mean that other people are quite simply not real? Me, for instance?'

'Believe me, Anna,' I said passionately, 'if there is one thing in the world that is real to me, then it is you. I have suffered so much from our . . . What can I call it – our falling-out – that . . .'

'That is my fault,' said Anna. 'I do have such a bad character.'

'What nonsense, Anna, I have nobody to blame but myself.

You have shown such patience in bearing all the clumsy, absurd . . .'

'Don't let us try to outdo each other in politeness. Tell me simply – do I really mean as much to you as it might appear from the phrases you have uttered at certain times?'

'You mean everything to me,' I said with complete sincerity.

'Very well then,' said Anna. 'I believe you suggested that we should go for a ride in the carriage? Into the country? Let us go.'

'This very moment?'

'Why not?'

I moved closer to her.

'Anna, you can never . . .'

'I beg you,' she said, 'not here.'

Driving out of the gates, I turned the carriage to the right. Anna was sitting beside me, the colour had risen in her cheeks, and she was avoiding looking at me. It began to seem to me that she already regretted what was happening. We drove to the woods in silence; as soon as the vault of green branches had closed over our heads I stopped the horses.

'Listen, Anna,' I said, turning towards her. 'Believe me, I appreciate your impulse immensely, but if you have begun to regret it, then . . .'

She did not allow me to finish. She put her arms around my neck and set her lips against my mouth. It happened so quickly that I was still speaking at the moment when she began kissing me. Naturally, I did not value the phrase I was pronouncing so much as to try to stop her.

I have always found kissing to be an extremely strange form of contact between human beings. As far as I am aware, it is one of the innovations introduced by civilization; it is well known that the savages who inhabit the southern isles and the peoples of Africa who have not yet crossed that boundary beyond which the paradise originally intended for man is lost for ever, never kiss at all. Their lovemaking is simple and uncomplicated; possibly the very word 'love' is inappropriate for what takes place between them. In essence, love arises in solitude, when its object is absent, and it is directed less at the person whom one loves than at an image constructed by the mind which has only a weak connection with that original. The appearance of true love requires the ability to create chimeras; in kissing me Anna was really kissing the man behind the poems which had affected her so strongly, a man who had never existed. How was she to know that when I wrote the book I was also engaged in a tormented search for him, growing more convinced with each new poem that he could never be found, because he existed nowhere? The words left by him were simply an imposture, like the footsteps carved in the rock by slaves, which the Babylonians used to prove the reality of the descent to earth of some ancient deity.

This last thought was already about Anna. I felt the tender touch of her trembling tongue; between their half-closed lids, her eyes were so close that I felt I could have dived into their moist gleam and dissolved in them for ever. At last we grew short of breath and our first kiss came to an end. Her face turned to the side so that now I saw it in profile; she closed her eyes and ran her tongue across her lips, as though they were dry – all of these small mimetic gestures, which in other circumstances would not have meant a thing, now moved me with a quite unbelievable power. I realized that there was no longer anything keeping us apart, that everything was possible; my hand, from lying on her shoulder, which only a minute ago it would have seemed like sacrilege merely to touch, moved down simply and naturally to her breast. She leaned away from me slightly, but only, as I realized immediately, in order that my hand should not encounter any obstacles in its way.

'What are you thinking of now?' she asked. 'Only honestly.'

'What am I thinking of?' I said, moving my hands together behind her neck. 'Of the fact that progress towards the zenith of happiness is in the literal sense like the ascent of a mountain . . .'

'Not like that. Unfasten the hook. No, no. Leave it, let me do it. Forgive me, I interrupted you.'

'Yes, it is like a difficult and dangerous ascent. As long as the object of desire lies ahead, all of one's feelings are absorbed in the process of climbing. The next stone on which to set one's foot, a tuft of grass which one can grab hold of for support. How beautiful you are, Anna . . . What was it I was saying . . . Yes, the goal gives all of this meaning, but it is completely absent at any single point in the movement; in essence, the approach to the goal is superior to the goal itself. I believe there was a certain opportunist by the name of Bernsteen who said that movement is all and the goal is nothing . . .'

'Not Bernsteen, but Bernstein. How does this thing undo . . . Where on earth did you find such a belt?'

'My God, Anna, do you want me to go insane . . .'

'Carry on talking,' she said, looking up for just a second, 'but don't be offended if I am unable to maintain the conversation for a while.'

'Yes,' I continued, leaning my head back and closing my eyes, 'but the most important thing here is that as soon as one has ascended the summit, as soon as the goal has been attained, at that very moment it disappears. In its essence, like all objects created by the mind, it is ultimately elusive. Imagine it yourself, Anna, when one dreams of the most beautiful of women, she is present in one's imagination in all the perfection of her beauty, but when she is actually there in one's arms, all of that disappears. What one is dealing with then is reduced to a set of the most simple and often rather crude sensations, which, moreover, one normally experiences in the dark . . . O-o-oh . . . But no matter how they may rouse the blood, the beauty which was calling to you only a minute before disappears, to be replaced by something, to strive for which was ridiculous. It means that beauty is unattainable. Or rather, it is attainable, but only in itself, while that goal which reason intoxicated by passion seeks behind it, simply does not exist. From the very beginning beauty is actually . . . No, I cannot go on. Come here . . . yes, like that. Yes. Yes. Is that comfortable? Oh, my God . . . What did you say was the name of the man who said that about the movement and the goal?'

'Bernstein,' Anna whispered in my ear.

'Does it not seem to you that his words apply very well to love?'

'Yes,' she whispered, gently biting the lobe of my ear. 'The goal is nothing, but the movement is everything.'

'Then move, move, I implore you.'

'And you talk, talk . . .'

'Of what exactly?'

'Of anything at all, just talk. I want to hear your voice when it happens.'

'By all means. To continue that idea . . . Imagine that everything which a beautiful woman can give one adds up to one hundred per cent.'

'You bookkeeper . . .'

'Yes, one hundred. In that case, she gives ninety per cent of that when one simply sees her, and everything else, the object of a thousand years of haggling, is no more than an insignificant remainder. Nor can that first ninety per cent be subdivided into any component fractions, because beauty is indefinable and indivisible, no matter what lies Schopenhauer may try to tell us. As for the other ten per cent, it is no more than an aggregate sum of nerve signals which would be totally without value if they were not lent support by imagination and memory. Anna, I beg you, open your eyes for a second . . . Yes, like that . . . yes, precisely imagination and memory. You know, if I had to write a genuinely powerful erotic scene, I would merely provide a few hints and fill in the rest with an incomprehensible conversation like the . . . Oh, my God, Anna . . . Like the one which you and I are having now. Because there is nothing to depict, everything has to be filled in by the mind. The deception, and perhaps the very greatest of a woman's secrets . . . Oh, my little girl from the old estate . . . consists in the fact that beauty seems to be a label, behind which there lies concealed something immeasurably greater, something inexpressibly more desired than itself, to which it merely points the way, whereas in actual fact, there is nothing in particular standing behind it . . . A golden label on an empty bottle . . . A shop where everything is displayed in a magnificently arranged window-setting, but that tiny, tender, narrow little room behind it . . . Please, please, my darling, not so fast . . . Yes, that room is empty. Remember the poem I recited to those unfortunates. About the princess and the bagel . . . A-a-ah, Anna . . . No matter how temptingly it might lure one, the moment comes when one realizes that at the centre of that black bage . . . bagel . . . bagel . . . there is nothing but a void, voi-oid, voi-oi-oooid!'

'Voyd!' someone yelled once again behind the door. 'Are you in there?'

'*Merde*,' I muttered, getting up from the bed and casting a crazed glance around my room. Outside the window the twilight was thickening. 'Damn you to hell! What do you want?'

'Can I come in?'

'Come in.'

The door swung open, revealing a blond-haired, bow-legged hulk of an individual standing in the doorway. In theory he was my orderly, but after several weeks of the demoralizing influence of the Reds, it was no longer quite clear just exactly what he had on his mind, and so now every evening, just to be on the safe side, I pulled off my own boots.

'What, sleeping, was you?' he asked, looking round the room. 'Woke you up, did I? Sorry. You give us a real surprise today. Here's a present as the men wants you to have.'

Some object wrapped in newspaper flopped down on to the bed in front of me; it had a strangely familiar smell. I unwrapped the bundle. Inside there was a bagel, one of those that were sold in the bakery on the main square, except that it was black, and it smelt of the coal-tar dubbin which the soldiers used for blacking their boots.

'Don't you like it, then?' he asked.

I looked up at him, and he immediately took a step backwards; before I could find the butt of my Browning in my pocket, he had disappeared from the doorway, and the three bullets which I fired into the empty rectangle ricocheted off the stone wall of the corridor like the song of angels.

'All. Women. Suck.' I said in a loud voice, and collapsed back on to the bed.

For a long time no one disturbed me. Outside the window I could hear constant drunken laughter; several shots were fired and then apparently a long, feebly fought fight broke out. To judge from the sounds that reached my ears,

288

the concert had developed into an evening of total outrage, and it was very doubtful whether anybody at all was capable of controlling this tempest of the people's rage, as the St Petersburg liberals had liked to call it. Then I heard quiet steps in the corridor. I felt a brief, fleeting hope – after all, I thought, there are such things as prophetic dreams – but it was so weak, that when I saw the broad-shouldered figure of Kotovsky in the doorway, I was not really disappointed. It even seemed rather funny to me that he should have come back to continue haggling over the trotters and the cocaine.

Kotovsky was wearing a brown two-piece suit; perched on his head was a dandified hat with a wide brim, and he had a leather portmanteau in each hand. He set them down on the floor and raised two fingers to his forehead.

'Good evening, Pyotr,' he said. 'I just wanted to say goodbye.'

'Are you leaving?' I asked.

'Yes. And I have no idea why you are staying,' said Kotovsky. 'Tomorrow or the next day these weavers will torch the entire place. I simply cannot understand what Chapaev is hoping for.'

'He was intending to resolve that problem today.'

Kotovsky shrugged.

'You know,' he said, 'problems can be resolved in various ways: you can simply drink yourself into a fog, and then for a while they will disappear. But I prefer to deal with them, to sort them out – at least until they begin to sort me out. The train leaves at eight o'clock this evening. It is still not too late. Five days, and we are in Paris.'

'I am staying.'

Kotovsky looked at me carefully.

'You do realize that you are mad?' he asked.

'Of course.'

'It will all end with the three of you being arrested and that Furmanov in supreme command.'

'That does not frighten me,' I said.

'You mean you are not afraid of arrest? Of course, all of us in the Russian intelligentsia do retain a certain secret freedom *à la Pushkine*, even in the madhouse, and it is possible . . .'

I laughed. 'Kotovsky, you have a quite remarkable talent for detecting the rhythm of my own thought. I was actually pondering on that very theme only today, and I can tell you what the secret freedom of the Russian intellectual really consists of.'

'If it will not take too long, I should be most obliged to you,' he replied.

'A year ago, I think it was, there was a most interesting event in St Petersburg. Several social democrats arrived from England – of course, they were appalled by what they found – and we had a meeting with them on Basseinaya Street, organized through the Union of Poets. Blok was there, and he spent the whole evening telling them about this secret freedom which, as he said, we all laud, following Pushkin. That was the last time I saw him, he was dressed all in black and quite inexpressibly morose. Then he left and the Englishmen, who naturally had not understood a thing, began asking us exactly what this secret freedom was; nobody could give them a proper answer, until a Romanian who happened for some reason to be travelling with the Englishmen said that he understood what was meant.'

'I see,' said Kotovsky, and he glanced at his watch.

'No need for concern, this will not take long. He said that the Romanian language has a similar idiom – *haz baragaz*, or something of the kind – I forget the exact pronunciation, but the words literally mean "underground laughter". Apparently, during the Middle Ages Romania was frequently invaded by all sorts of nomadic tribes, and so the peasants constructed immense dugouts, entire underground houses, into which they drove their livestock the moment a cloud of dust appeared on the horizon. They themselves hid in these places as well, and since the dugouts were quite excellently camouflaged, the nomads could never find a thing. Naturally, when they were underground the peasants were very quiet, but just occasionally, when they were quite overcome by joy at their own cunning in deceiving everyone, they would cover their mouths with their hands and laugh very, very quietly. There is your secret freedom, the Romanian said, it is when you are sitting wedged in among a herd of

foul-smelling goats and sheep and you point up at the roof
with your finger and giggle very, very quietly. You know,
Kotovsky, it was such a very apt description of the situation,
that from that evening onwards I ceased being a member of
the Russian intelligentsia. Underground giggling is not for
me. Freedom cannot be secret.'

'Interesting,' said Kotovsky. 'Interesting. But I am afraid it
is time for me to be going.'

'Let me see you to the gate,' I said, rising to my feet. 'There
is the very devil of a commotion out there in the yard.'

'As I was saying.'

I put the Browning into my pocket, picked up one of Kotovsky's portmanteaus and was on the point of following him
along the corridor when I was suddenly struck by a strange
presentiment that I was seeing my room for the very last time.
I halted in the doorway and looked around it carefully; two
light armchairs, a bed, a small table with copies of *Isis* for
1915. My God, I thought, if things really are that bad, what
does it matter that I shall never come back here? What does it
matter that I do not know where I am going? How many
places have I already left behind for ever?

'Have you forgotten something?' asked Kotovsky.

'No, it's nothing,' I replied.

The sight that greeted us when we emerged on to the porch
of the manor-house reminded me in some indefinable manner of Briullov's painting *The Last Day of Pompeii*. There were
not actually any collapsing columns or clouds of smoke
against a black sky, just two large bonfires burning in the
darkness and blind-drunk weavers wandering everywhere.
But the way in which they slapped one another on the shoulder, the way they stopped to relieve themselves in public or
to raise a bottle to their lips, the way some half-naked,
drunken women were laughing as they staggered around the
yard, together with the menacing red glow of the fires that illuminated the entire Bacchanalian scene – all served to in-
duce a sense of impending menace, final and implacable.

We walked quickly to the gate without speaking; some
men with rifles sitting by one of the bonfires waved for us to
join them and yelled something indistinct, and Kotovsky

nervously stuck his hand in his pocket. Nobody fell in behind us, thank God, but the last few yards to the gate, when our defenceless backs were exposed to this entire drunken rabble, seemed extremely long. We went out of the gate and walked on another twenty steps or so, and then I halted. The street winding spiral-fashion down the hill was deserted: a few street lamps were burning, and the damp cobblestones gleamed dully under their calm light.

'I will not go any further,' I said. 'I wish you luck.'

'And I you. Who knows, perhaps we shall meet again some time,' he said with a strange smile. 'Or hear news of each other.'

We shook hands. He raised two fingers to the brim of his hat once again, and without turning to look back, he set off down the street. I watched his broad figure until it disappeared round a bend, and then began slowly walking back. I stopped at the gates and glanced in through them cautiously. The window of Chapaev's study was in darkness. I suddenly realized why I had felt such horror at the sight I had seen in the yard – there was something about it which reminded me of the world of Baron Jungern. I did not feel the slightest desire to walk back past the bonfires and the drunken weavers.

I realized where Chapaev might be. I walked along the fence for another forty yards, then glanced around. There was no one in sight. Jumping up, I grabbed hold of the top plank, managed somehow to haul myself up and over it and jumped down.

It was dark here; the flames of the bonfires were hidden behind the dark silhouette of the silent manor-house. Feeling my way by touch between the trees still wet from the recent rain, I scrambled down the slope into the gully, then slipped and slid into it on my back. The invisible brook was babbling somewhere off to my right; I walked towards it with my hands extended in front of me and after a few steps I glimpsed the brightly lit window of the bathhouse between the trunks of the trees.

'Come in, Petka,' Chapaev shouted in response to my knock.

He was sitting at the familiar rough wooden table, which once again bore a huge bottle of moonshine, several glasses and plates, a kerosene lamp and a plump file full of papers; he was wearing a long white Russian shirt outside his trousers, unbuttoned to the navel, and he was already extremely drunk.

'How's things?' he asked

'I thought you were intending to resolve the problem of the weavers,' I said.

'I am resolving it,' said Chapaev, filling two glasses with moonshine.

'I can see that Kotovsky knows you very well,' I said.

'That's right,' said Chapaev, 'and I know him very well, too.'

'He has just left for Paris on the evening train. It occurs to me that we have made a serious mistake in not following his example.'

Chapaev frowned.

'But desire still burns within us,' he chanted, 'the trains depart for it and the butterfly of consciousness flits from nowhere to nowhere . . .'

'So you have read it too? I am very flattered,' I said and was immediately struck by the dreary thought that the word 'too' was somewhat misplaced. 'Listen, if we leave straight away, we could still catch the train.'

'So what's new for me to see in this Paris of yours?' Chapaev asked.

'I suppose just what we'll be seeing here soon,' I answered.

Chapaev chuckled. 'Right you are, Petka.'

'By the way,' I said with concern, 'where is Anna at the moment? It's not safe in the house.'

'I gave her a task to do,' said Chapaev, 'she'll be here soon. You just take a seat. I've been sitting here all this time waiting for you – already drunk half the bottle.'

I sat down facing him.

'Your health!'

I shrugged. There was nothing to be done. 'Your health, Vasily Ivanovich.'

We drank. Chapaev gazed moodily into the dim flame of the kerosene lamp.

'I've been thinking about these nightmares of yours,' he

said, laying his hand on the file. 'I've reread all these stories you wrote. About Serdyuk, and about that fellow Maria, and about the doctors and the gangsters. Did you ever pay any attention to the way you wake up from all of them?'

'No,' I said.

'Well, just try to remember, will you?'

'At a certain moment it simply becomes clear that it is all a dream. That's all there is to it,' I said uncertainly. 'When I really begin to feel too bad, I suddenly realize that in fact there is nothing to be afraid of, because . . .'

'Because what?'

'I am struggling to find the words. I would put it like this – because there is a place to which I can wake up.'

Chapaev slapped the table with his open hand.

'Where exactly can you wake up to?'

I had no answer to that question.

'I do not know,' I said.

Chapaev raised his eyes to look into mine and smiled. He suddenly no longer seemed drunk.

'Good lad,' he said. 'That's the very place. As soon as you are swept up in the flow of your dreams, you yourself become part of it all – because in that flow everything is relative, everything is in motion, and there is nothing for you to grab hold of and cling to. You don't realize when you are drawn into the whirlpool, because you are moving along together with the water, and it appears to be motionless. That's how a dream comes to feel like reality. But there is a point which is not merely motionless relative to everything else, but absolutely motionless, and it's called "I don't know". When you hit it in a dream you wake up. Or rather, the waking up pushes you into it. And then after that,' – he gestured around the room – 'you come here.'

I heard a staccato burst of machine-gun fire beyond the wall, followed by the sound of an explosion, and the panes of glass rattled in the window.

'There's this point,' Chapaev continued, 'that is absolutely motionless, relative to which this life is as much of a dream as all your stories. Everything in the world is just a whirlpool of thoughts, and the world around us only becomes real when

294

you yourself become that whirlpool. Only because you *know*.'

He laid heavy emphasis on the word 'know'.

I stood up and went over to the window. 'Listen, Chapaev, I think they have set fire to the manor-house.'

'What's to be done, Petka?' Chapaev answered. 'The way this world is arranged, you always end up answering questions in the middle of a burning house.'

'I agree,' I said, sitting back down facing him, 'this is all quite remarkable, this whirlpool of thoughts and so forth. The world becomes real and unreal, I understand all that quite well. But any moment now some rather unpleasant individuals are going to arrive here – you understand, I am not trying to say that they are real, but they will certainly make us feel the force of their reality in full measure.'

'Make me?' asked Chapaev. 'Never. Just watch.'

He took hold of the big bottle, pulled a small blue saucer over to him and filled it to the brim. Then he performed the same operation with a glass.

'Look at that, Petka. In itself the moonshine doesn't have any form. There's a glass, and there's a saucer. Which of the forms is real?'

'Both,' I said. 'Both of them are real.'

Chapaev carefully drank the moonshine from the saucer, then from the glass, and threw each of them in turn hard against the wall. The saucer and the glass both shattered into tiny fragments.

'Petka, watch and remember,' he said. 'If you are real, then death really will come. Even I won't be able to help you. I'll ask you one more time. There are the glasses, there's the bottle. Which of these forms is real?'

'I do not understand what you mean.'

'Shall I show you?' asked Chapaev.

'Yes, do.'

He swayed to one side, thrust his hand under the table and pulled out his nickel-plated Mauser. I barely managed to grab hold of his wrist in time.

'All right, all right. Just don't shoot the bottle.'

'Right you are, Petka. Let's have a drink instead.'

Chapaev filled the glasses and then became thoughtful. It

was as though he was searching for the words he needed.

'In actual fact,' he said eventually, 'for the moonshine there is no saucer, and no glass, and no bottle – there's nothing but itself. That's why everything that can appear or disappear is an assemblage of empty forms which do not exist until they are assumed by the moonshine. Pour it into a saucer and that's hell, pour it into a cup and you've got heaven. But you and me are drinking out of glasses, and that makes us people, Petka. D'you follow me?'

There was another loud bang outside. I no longer had to go over to the window to see the reflected crimson glow flickering in the glass.

'By the way, about hell,' I said, 'I cannot remember whether I told you or not. Do you know why these weavers have left us alone for so long?'

'Why?'

'Because they believe quite sincerely that you have sold your soul to the devil.'

'Do they now?' Chapaev asked in amazement. 'That's fascinating. But who sells the soul?'

'How do you mean?'

'Well, they say – he's sold his soul to the devil, or, he's sold his soul to God. But who is the person who sells it? He must be different from the thing he sells in order to be able to sell it, mustn't he?'

'You know, Chapaev,' I said, 'my Catholic upbringing will not allow me to joke about such things.'

'I understand,' said Chapaev. 'I know where these rumours come from. There was one person who came here to see me in order to ask how he could sell his soul to the devil. A certain Staff Captain Lambovsky. Are you acquainted?'

'We met in the restaurant.'

'I explained to him how it can be done, and he performed the entire ritual most punctiliously.'

'And what happened?'

'Nothing much. He didn't suddenly acquire riches, or eternal youth either. The only thing that did happen was that in all the regimental documents the name "Lambovsky" was replaced by "Serpentovich".'

'Why was that?'

'It's not good to go deceiving others. How can you sell what you haven't got?'

'Do you mean to tell me,' I asked, 'that Lambovsky has no soul?'

'Of course not,' said Chapaev.

'And you?'

For a second or so Chapaev seemed to be gazing deep inside himself, and then he shook his head.

'Do I have one?' I asked.

'No,' said Chapaev.

My face must have betrayed my confusion, because Chapaev chuckled and shook me by the elbow.

'Petka, neither I, nor you, nor Staff Captain Lambovsky have any sort of soul. It's the soul that has Lambovsky, Chapaev and Petka. You can't say that everyone has a different soul and you can't say everyone has the same soul. If there is anything we can say about it, it's that it doesn't exist either.'

'I really do not understand a single word in all of that.'

'That's the problem, Petka . . . That's where Kotovsky made his mistake. Remember that business with the lamp and the wax?'

'Yes.'

'Kotovsky understood that there is no form, what he didn't understand is that there is no wax either.'

'Why is there not?'

'Because, Petka – listen to me carefully now – because the wax and the moonshine can take on any form, but they themselves are nothing but forms too.'

'Forms of what?'

'That's the trick, you see. They are forms about which all we can say is that there is nothing that assumes them. D'you follow? Therefore in reality there is no wax and there is no moonshine.'

For a second I seemed to be balancing on some kind of threshold, and then a heavy drunken dullness descended on me. It suddenly became very difficult to think.

'There may not be any wax,' I said, 'but there is still half a bottle of moonshine.'

Chapaev stared at the bottle with murky eyes.

'That's true,' he said. 'But if you can only understand that it doesn't exist either, I'll give you the order from my own chest. And until I do give it to you, we won't be leaving this place.'

We drank another glass and I listened for a while to the sounds of shooting outside; Chapaev paid absolutely no attention to it all.

'Are you really not afraid?' I asked.

'Why, Petka, are you afraid of something?'

'A little,' I said.

'What of?'

'Death,' I answered, before pausing. 'Or rather, not death itself, but . . . I do not know. I want to save my consciousness.'

Chapaev laughed and shook his head.

'Have I said something funny?'

'That's a good one, Petka. I didn't expect that of you. You mean you went into battle with thoughts like that in your head every time? It's the same as a scrap of newspaper lying under a street lamp and thinking that it wants to save the light it's lying in. What d'you want to save your consciousness from?'

I shrugged. 'From non-existence.'

'But isn't non-existence itself an object of consciousness?'

'Now we're back to sophistry again,' I said. 'Even if I am a scrap of newspaper that thinks that it wants to save the light in which it is lying, what difference does it all make if I really do think that, and it all causes me pain?'

'The scrap of newspaper can't think. It's just got the words written across it in bold italics: "*I want to save the light of the street lamp.*" And written beside that is: "*Oh what pain, what terrible suffering . . .*" Come on, Petka, how can I explain it to you? This entire world is a joke that God has told to himself. And God himself is the same joke too.'

There was an explosion outside, so close this time that the panes of glass in the window rattled audibly. I distinctly heard the rustling sound of shrapnel ripping through the leaves outside.

'I tell you what, Vasily Ivanovich,' I said, 'why don't we

finish up with the theory and try to think of something practical.'

'To be practical, Petka, I can tell you that if you're afraid, then both of us are for the high jump. Because fear always attracts exactly what it's afraid of. But if you're not afraid, then you become invisible. The best possible camouflage is indifference. If you're genuinely indifferent, none of those who can cause you harm will even remember you exist – they just won't think about you. But if you go squirming about on your chair the way you are now, in five minutes' time we'll have a roomful of those weavers in here.'

I suddenly realized that he was right, and I felt ashamed of my nervousness, which appeared particularly pitiful against the foil of his magnificent indifference. Had not I myself only recently refused to leave with Kotovsky? I was here because I had chosen to be, and it was simply foolish to waste what might be the final minutes of my life on anxiety and fear. I looked at Chapaev and thought that in essence I had never discovered anything at all about this man.

'Tell me, Chapaev, who are you in reality?'

'Better tell yourself, Petka, who you are in reality. Then you'll understand all about me. But you just keep on repeating "me, me, me", like that gangster in your nightmare. What does that mean – "me"? What is it? Try taking a look for yourself.'

'I want to look, but . . .'

'If you want to look, why do you keep on looking at that "me" and that "want" and that "look", instead of at yourself?'

'Very well,' I countered, 'then answer my question. Can you give me a simple answer to it?'

'I can,' he said, 'try it again.'

'Who are you, Chapaev?'

'I do not know,' he replied.

Two or three bullets clattered against the planks of the walls, splinters flew up into the air, and I instinctively ducked my head. I heard quiet voices outside the door, apparently discussing something. Chapaev poured two glasses and we drank without clinking them together. After hesitating for a moment, I picked up an onion from the table.

'I understand what you are trying to say,' I said, biting into it, 'but perhaps you could answer me in some other way?'

'I could,' said Chapaev.

'Then who are you, Vasily Ivanovich?'

'Who am I?' he echoed, and raised his eyes to my face. 'I am a reflection of the lamplight on this bottle.'

I felt as though the light reflected in his eyes had lashed me across the face; suddenly I was overwhelmed by total understanding and recall.

The blow was so powerful that for a moment I thought a shell must have exploded right there in the room, but I recovered almost immediately. I felt no need to say anything out loud, but the inertia of speech had already translated my thought into words.

'How fascinating,' I whispered quietly, 'so am I.'

'Then who is this?' he asked, pointing at me.

'Voyd,' I replied.

'And this?' he pointed to himself.

'Chapaev.'

'Splendid! And this?' he gestured around the room.

'I don't know,' I said.

At that very moment the window was shattered by a bullet and the bottle standing between us exploded, showering both of us with the last of the moonshine. For several seconds we gazed at each other in silence, then Chapaev rose, went over to the bench on which his tunic lay, unpinned the silver star from it and threw it across the room to me.

His movements had suddenly become swift and precise; it was hard to believe that this was the same man who had just been swaying drunkenly on his stool and gazing senselessly at the bottle. He snatched up the lamp from the table, unscrewed it rapidly, splashed the kerosene out on to the floor and tossed the burning wick into it. The kerosene flared up, followed by the spilt moonshine, and the room was illuminated by the dim glow of a fire just beginning to take hold. Deep shadows were cast across Chapaev's face by the flames from beneath, and it suddenly seemed very ancient and strangely familiar. He overturned the table in a single gesture, then bent down and pulled open a narrow trapdoor by a metal ring.

'Let's get going,' he said. 'There's nothing left for us to do here.'

I felt my way down a ladder into cold damp darkness. The bottom of the shaft proved to be about two yards below the level of the floor; at first I could not understand what we were going to do in this pit, and then the foot with which I was feeling for the wall suddenly swung through into emptiness. Coming down behind me, Chapaev struck my head with his boot.

'Forward!' he commanded. 'At the double!'

Leading away from the staircase was a low, narrow tunnel supported by wooden props. I crawled forward, struggling to distinguish anything ahead of me in the darkness. To judge from the draught I could feel, the exit could not be very far away.

'Stop,' Chapaev said in a whisper. 'We have to wait for a minute.'

He was about two yards behind me. I sat down on the ground and leaned my back against one of the props. I could hear indistinct voices and other noises; at one point I clearly heard Furmanov's voice yelling: 'Get back out of there, fuck you! You'll burn to death! I tell you they're not in there, they've gone! Did you catch the bald one?' I thought of them up above, rushing about in thick clouds of smoke among the repulsive chimeras created by their collective clouded reason, and it all seemed incredibly funny.

'Hey, Vasily Ivanovich!' I called quietly.

'What?' responded Chapaev.

'I just understood something,' I said. 'There is only one kind of freedom – when you are free of everything that is constructed by the mind. And this freedom is called "I do not know". You were absolutely right. You know, there is an expression, "a thought expressed is a lie", but I tell you, Chapaev, that a thought unexpressed is also a lie, because every thought already contains the element of expression.'

'You expressed that very well, Petka,' responded Chapaev.

'As soon as I know,' I continued, 'I am no longer free. But I am absolutely free when I do not know. Freedom is the biggest mystery of all. They simply do not know how free they are. They do not know who they are in reality. They . . .'

– I jabbed my finger upwards and was suddenly contorted by a spasm of irrepressible laughter – 'they think that they are weavers . . .'

'Quiet,' said Chapaev. 'Stop neighing like a mad horse. They'll hear you.'

'No, that's not it,' I gasped, choking on the words, 'they don't even think that they are weavers . . . They *know* it . . .'

'Forward,' he said, prodding me with his boot.

I took several deep breaths to recover my senses and began edging my way ahead again. We covered the rest of the distance without speaking. No doubt it was because the tunnel was so narrow and cramped that it seemed to be incredibly long. Underground there was a smell of dampness, and also, for some reason, of hay, which grew stronger the further we went. At last the hand I was holding out in front of me came up against a wall of earth. I rose to my feet and straightened up, banging my head against something made of iron. Feeling around in the darkness that surrounded me, I came to the conclusion that I was standing in a shallow pit underneath some kind of flat metal surface. There was a gap of two feet or so between the metal and the ground; I squeezed into it and crawled for a yard or two, pushing aside the hay that filled it, and then I bumped against a broad wheel of moulded rubber. I immediately remembered the huge haystack beside which the taciturn Bashkir had mounted his permanent guard, and I realized where Chapaev's armoured car had gone to. A second later I was already standing beside it – the hay had been pulled away to one side to expose a riveted metal door, which stood slightly ajar.

The manor-house was enveloped in flames. The spectacle was magnificent and enchanting, much the same, in fact, as any large fire. About fifty yards away from us, among the trees, there was another, smaller fire – the blazing bathhouse where only recently Chapaev and I had been sitting. I thought that I could see figures moving around it, but they could easily have been the dappled shadows of the trees shifting every time the fire swayed in a gust of wind. But whether I could see them or not, there were undoubtedly people there: I could hear shouting and shooting from the direction of both conflagrations. If I had not known what was actually happening there, I might have thought it was two detachments waging a night battle.

I heard a rustling close beside me, and I pulled out my pistol.

'Who goes there?' I whispered nervously.

'It's me,' said Anna.

She was wearing her tunic, riding breeches and boots, and in her hand she had a bent metal lever similar to the crankhandles used for starting automobile engines.

'Thank God,' I said, 'You have no idea how worried I was about you. The mere thought that this drunken rabble . . .'

'Please don't breathe onion on me,' she interrupted. 'Where's Chapaev?'

'I'm here,' he answered, crawling out from underneath the armoured car.

'Why did you take so long?' she asked. 'I was beginning to get worried.'

'Pyotr just would not understand,' he replied. 'It even reached the point where I had resigned myself to staying there.'

'But has he understood now?'

Chapaev looked at me.

'He didn't understand a thing,' he said. 'It was just that the shooting started up back there . . .'

'Now, listen here, Chapaev,' I began, but he stopped me with an imperious gesture.

'Is everything all right?' he asked Anna.

'Yes,' she said, handing him the crank-handle.

I suddenly realized that Chapaev was right, as always; there had not been anything that I could be said to have understood.

Chapaev rapidly swept aside the hay covering the armoured car's inclined bonnet, inserted the crank-handle in the opening in the radiator and turned the magneto several times. The engine began to purr quietly and powerfully.

Anna opened the door and got in, and Chapaev and I followed her. Chapaev slammed the door and clicked a switch, and the light, quite blindingly brilliant after the underground darkness, revealed a familiar interior: the narrow leather-upholstered divans, the landscape bolted to the wall, and the table, on which lay a volume of Montesquieu with a bookmark and a packet of 'Ira' *papyrosas*. Anna quickly clambered up the spiral staircase and sat on the machine-gunner's revolving chair, the upper half of her body concealed in the turret.

'I'm ready,' she said. 'Only I can't see anything because of the hay.'

Chapaev caught hold of the speaking-tube that communicated with the driver's compartment – I guessed that the Bashkir was there – and spoke into it.

'Scatter the haystack. And don't get a wheel stuck in any hole.'

The armoured car's motor began to roar, the heavy vehicle shuddered into motion and moved forward several yards. There was some kind of mechanical noise above us – I looked up and saw that Anna was turning something like the handle of a coffee-mill, and the turret and seat were turning together around their axis.

'That's better now,' she said.

'Switch on the floodlights,' Chapaev said into the tube.

I put my eye to the spy-hole in the door. The floodlights turned out to be installed around the entire perimeter of the armoured car, and when they came on, it was as though someone had switched on the street lights in some shadowy park.

It was a strange vista indeed. The white electric light falling on the trees was a great deal brighter than the glow from the fire; the dancing shadows which had looked like people darting through the darkness disappeared, and I could see that there was no one near us.

But our solitude did not remain inviolate for long. Weavers with rifles in their hands began appearing at the edge of the pool of light. They stared at us in silence, shielding their eyes from the blinding glare of the searchlights. Soon the armoured car was trapped in a living circle bristling with rifle barrels. I could even hear snatches of shouting: 'So that's where they are . . . nah, they won't get away . . . they've already run away once . . . put that grenade away, you fool, it'll blast our own lads to bits . . .'

They fired several shots at the armoured car and the bullets bounced off the armour-plating with a dull clanging sound. One of the searchlights burst, however, and a roar of delight ran through the crowd around us.

'Well, then,' said Chapaev, 'everything comes to an end some time. Make ready, Anna . . .'

Anna carefully removed the cover from the machine-gun. A bullet struck the door close beside the spy-hole, and just to be on the safe side I moved away from it. Leaning over the machine-gun, Anna put her eye to the sights, and her face distorted itself in a grimace of cold fury.

'Fire! Water! Earth! Space! Air!' Chapaev shouted.

Anna rapidly twirled the rotational handle, and the turret began revolving around its axis with a quiet squeaking. The machine-gun was silent, and I looked at Chapaev in amazement. He gestured reassuringly. The turret made a single complete revolution and came to a halt.

'Has it jammed?' I asked.

'No,' said Chapaev. 'It's all over already.'

I suddenly realized that I could no longer hear any shots or voices. All the sounds had disappeared, and only the quiet purring of the motor remained.

Anna climbed down out of the turret, sat herself on the divan beside me and lit a *papyrosa*. I noticed that her fingers were trembling.

'That was the clay machine-gun,' said Chapaev. 'Now I can tell you what it is. It isn't really a machine-gun at all. It's simply that many millennia ago, long before the Buddha Dipankara and the Buddha Shakyamuni came into the world, there lived the Buddha Anagama. He didn't waste any time on explanations, he simply pointed at things with the little finger of his left hand, and their true nature was instantly revealed. When he pointed to a mountain, it disappeared, when he pointed to a river, that disappeared too. It's a long story, but in short it all ended with him pointing to himself with his little finger and then disappearing. All that was left of him was that finger from his left hand, which his disciples hid in a lump of clay. The clay machine-gun is that lump of clay with the Buddha's finger concealed within it. A very long time ago in India there lived a man who tried to turn that piece of clay into the most terrible

305

weapon on earth, but no sooner had he drilled a hole in it than the finger pointed at him and he himself disappeared. After that it was kept in a locked trunk and moved from place to place until it was lost to the world in one of the monasteries of Mongolia. But now, for a whole series of reasons, it has found its way to me. I have attached a butt-stock to it and I call it the clay machine-gun. And we have just made use of it.'

Chapaev stood up, opened the door and jumped out. I heard his boots striking the earth. Anna climbed out after him, but I went on sitting there on the divan, gazing at the English landscape on the wall. A river, a bridge, a sky covered in clouds and some indistinct ruins; could it possibly be, I wondered, could it?

'Petka,' Chapaev called, 'what are you doing still sitting in there?'

I got up and stepped out.

We were standing on a perfectly level circular surface covered with hay, about seven yards in diameter. Beyond the bounds of the circle there was nothing at all – nothing was visible except an indistinct, even light, which it would be hard to describe in any way. At the very edge of the circle lay half a rifle with a bayonet attached. I suddenly recalled the moment in Blok's 'Circus Booth' when Harlequin jumps through the window and breaks the paper with the view of the horizon drawn on it and a grey void appears in the tear. I looked round. The engine of the armoured car was still working.

'But why is this island left?' I asked.

'A blind spot,' said Chapaev. 'The finger pointed at everything there was in the world beyond the bounds of this area. It's like the shadow from the base of a lamp.'

I took a step to one side, and Chapaev grabbed me by the shoulders.

'Where do you think you're going . . . Don't get in front of the machine-gun! All right, Anna, put it out of harm's way.'

Anna nodded and carefully made her way to stand under the short protruding barrel.

'Watch carefully, Petka,' said Chapaev.

Anna squeezed her *papyrosa* tight in her teeth, and a small round mirror appeared in her hand. She raised it to the level of the barrel, and before I could understand what was going on, the armoured car had vanished. It happened instantaneously and with unbelievable ease, as though someone had switched off a magic lantern, and the picture on the linen sheet had simply disappeared. All that was left were four shallow hollows from the wheels. And now there was nothing to disturb the silence.

'That's it,' said Chapaev. 'That world no longer exists.'

'Damn,' I said, 'the *papyrosas* were still in there . . . And listen – what about the driver?'

Chapaev started and looked in fright first at me, and then at Anna.

'Damn and blast,' he said, 'I forgot all about him . . . And you, Anna, why didn't you say anything?'

Anna spread her arms wide. There was not a trace of genuine feeling in the gesture and I thought that despite her beauty, she was unlikely ever to become an actress.

'No,' I said, 'there's something wrong here. Where's the driver?'

'Chapaev,' said Anna, 'I can't take any more. Sort this out between the two of you.'

Chapaev sighed and twirled his moustache.

'Calm down, Petka. There wasn't really any driver. You know there are these bits of paper with special seals on them, you can stick them on a log, and . . .'

'Ah,' I said, 'so it was a golem. I see. Only please don't treat me like a total idiot, all right? I noticed a long time ago that he was rather strange. You know, Chapaev, with talents like that you could have made quite a career in St Petersburg.'

'What is there new for me to see in this St Petersburg of yours?' Chapaev asked.

'But wait, what about Kotovsky?' I asked excitedly. 'Has he disappeared too, then?'

'Inasmuch as he never existed,' said Chapaev, 'it is rather difficult to answer that question. But if you are concerned for his fate out of human sympathy, don't worry. I assure you that Kotovsky, just like you or I, is quite capable of creating his own universe.'

'And will we exist in it?'

Chapaev pondered my words.

'An interesting question,' he said. 'I should never have thought of that. Perhaps we shall, but in precisely what capacity I really can't say. How should I know what kind of world Kotovsky will create in that Paris of his? Or perhaps I should say – what Paris he will create in that world of his?'

'There you go again,' I said, 'more of your sophistry.'

I turned and walked towards the edge of the circle, but I was unable to reach the very edge; when there were still about two yards left to its edge I suddenly felt dizzy and I slumped heavily to the ground.

'Do you feel unwell?' Anna asked.

'I feel quite wonderful,' I replied, 'but what are we going to do here? Conduct a *ménage à trois*?'

'Ah, Petka, Petka,' said Chapaev, 'I keep on trying to explain to you. Any form is just emptiness. But what does that mean?'

'Well, what?'

'It means that emptiness is any form. Close your eyes. And now open them.'

I do not know how to describe that moment in words.

What I saw was something similar to a flowing stream which glowed with all the colours of the rainbow, a river broad beyond all measure that flowed from somewhere lost in infinity towards that same infinity. It extended around our island on all sides as far as the eye could see, and yet it was not an ocean, but precisely a river, a stream, because it had a clearly visible current. The light it cast on the three of us was extremely bright, but there was nothing blinding or frightening about it, because it was also at the same time grace, happiness and infinitely powerful love. However, those three words, so crudely devalued by literature and art, were quite incapable of conveying any real impression of it. Simply watching the constant emergence of new multicoloured sparks and glimmers of light in it was already enough, because everything that I could possibly think of or dream of was a part of that rainbow-hued stream. Or to be more precise, the rainbow-hued stream was everything that I could possibly think of or experience, everything that I could possibly be or not be, and I knew quite certainly that it was not something separate from myself. It was me, and I was it. I had always been it, and nothing else.

'What is it?' I asked.

'Nothing,' replied Chapaev.

'No, not in that sense,' I said. 'What is it called?'

'It has various names,' Chapaev replied. 'I call it the Undefinable River of Absolute Love. Ural for short. Sometimes we become it, and sometimes we assume forms, but in actual fact neither the forms nor we ourselves, nor even the Ural exists.'

'But why do we do it?'

Chapaev shrugged. 'I don't know.'

'But what if you try to explain?' I asked.

'One has to do something to occupy oneself in all this eternal infinity,' he said. 'So we're going to try swimming across the river Ural, which doesn't really exist. Don't be afraid, Petka, dive in!'

'But will I be able to dive out again?'

Chapaev looked me over from head to toe.

'Well, you obviously could before,' he said. 'Since you're standing here.'

'But will I be myself again?'

'Now, Petka,' Chapaev asked, 'how can you not be yourself when you are absolutely everything that possibly can be?'

He was about to say something else, but at this point Anna, having finished her *papyrosa*, carefully ground it out under her foot, and without even bothering to look our way, threw herself into the flowing stream.

'That's it,' said Chapaev. 'That's the way. What's the point of all this shilly-shallying?'

Fixing me with a treacherous smile, he began backing towards the edge of the patch of earth.

'Chapaev,' I said, frightened, 'wait. You can't just leave me like this. You must at least explain . . .'

But it was too late. The earth crumbled away under his feet, he lost his balance and flung out his arms as he tumbled backwards into the rainbow-hued radiance. It parted for a moment exactly like water and then closed over him, and I was left alone.

For a few minutes I stared, stunned, at the spot where Chapaev had been. Then I realized that I was terribly tired. I scraped together the straw scattered around the circle of earth and gathered it into a single heap, lay down on it and fixed my gaze on the inexpressibly distant grey vault of the sky.

Suddenly the thought struck me that since the very beginning of time I had been doing nothing but lie on the bank of the Ural, dreaming one dream after another, and waking up again and again in the same place. But if that were really the case, I thought, then what had I wasted my life on? Literature and art were no more than tiny midges hovering over the final pile of hay in the Universe. Who, I wondered, who would read the descriptions of my dreams? I looked at the smooth surface of the Ural, stretching out into infinity in all directions. The pen, the notepad and everyone who could read those marks made on its paper were now simply rainbow-coloured sparks and lights which appeared and disappeared and then appeared again. Will I really simply fall asleep again on this river bank, I wondered.

Without giving myself even a moment's pause for thought, I leapt to my feet, ran forwards and threw myself headlong into the Ural.

I hardly felt anything at all; the stream was simply on every side of me now, and so there were no more sides. I saw the spot from which this stream originated – and immediately recognized it as my true home. Like a snowflake caught up by the wind, I was born along towards that spot. At first my movement was easy and weightless, and then something strange happened; I began to feel some incomprehensible friction tugging at my calves and my elbows, and my movement slowed. And no sooner did it begin to slow than the radiance surrounding me began to fade, and at the very moment when I came to a complete standstill, the light changed to a murky gloom, which I realized came from an electric bulb burning just under the ceiling.

My arms and legs were belted tight to the chair, and my head was resting on a pillow covered in oilcloth.

Timur Timurovich's thick lips materialized out of the dim half-light, approached my forehead and planted a long, wet kiss on it.

'Total catharsis,' he said. 'Congratulations.'

10

'*Eight thousand two hundred miles of emptiness,*' sang a male voice trembling with feeling from the radio, '*and still no place to spend the night . . . How happy I should be if not for you, Mother Russia, if not for you, my homeland . . .*'

Volodin stood up and turned the switch. The music stopped.

'Why'd you turn it off?' asked Serdyuk, looking up.

'I can't bear listening to Grebenschikov,' replied Volodin. 'He's talented, of course, but he's far too fond of over-complicated phrases. His songs are all just full of Buddhism – he doesn't know how to use words in a straightforward way. You heard that song he was singing just now about the homeland – d'you know where it comes from? The Chinese White Lotus Sect had this mantra: "Absolute emptiness is the homeland, the mother is the unborn." But he's wrapped it all up in code so you could burst your brains trying to understand what he's talking about.'

Serdyuk shrugged and went back to his work. As I kneaded my Plasticine, I looked over every now and then at his quick fingers folding paper cranes out of pages from an exercise book. He performed his task with quite incredible dexterity, without even bothering to look at what he was doing. There were paper cranes scattered all around the aesthetics therapy room; many of them were just lying on the floor, although only that morning Zherbunov and Barbolin had swept a huge pile out into the corridor. Serdyuk took no interest whatsoever in the fate of his creations; once he had pencilled a number on each crane's wing, he just tossed it into the corner and immediately set about ripping the next page out of the exercise book.

'How many still to go?' asked Volodin.

'I've got to get them all done by spring,' said Serdyuk, then transferred his gaze to me. 'Listen, I've just remembered another one.'

'Go on then,' I answered.

'Okay, it goes like this. Petka and Vasily Ivanovich are sitting boozing, when suddenly this soldier comes dashing in and says: "The Whites are coming!" Petka says: "Vasily Ivanovich, let's leg it quick." But Chapaev just pours another two glasses of hooch and says: "Drink up, Petka." So they drink up. Then the soldier comes dashing in again. "The Whites are coming!" Chapaev pours another two glasses and says: "Drink up, Petka!" The next time the soldier comes running in and says the Whites are almost at the house now. So then Chapaev says: "Petka, can you see me?" And Petka says: "No." And Chapaev says: "I can't see you either. We're well camouflaged."'

I sighed derisively and picked up a new piece of Plasticine from the table.

'I know that one too, but with a different ending,' said Volodin. 'The Whites come bursting in, look round the room, and say: "Damn, they got away again."'

'That one is a little closer to the truth,' I responded, 'but it is still very wide of the mark. All these Whites . . . I simply cannot understand how everything could have been distorted so grossly. Well, does anybody have another one?'

'I remember one,' Serdyuk answered. 'Petka and Vasily Ivanovich are swimming across the Ural, and Chapaev's clutching this attaché case in his teeth . . .'

'O-oh,' I groaned. 'Who on earth could possibly invent such nonsense?'

'Anyway, he's almost on the point of drowning, but he won't dump the case. Petka shouts to him: "Vasily Ivanovich, drop the case, or you'll drown!" But Chapaev says: "No way, Petka! I can't. It's got the staff maps in it." Anyway, they barely make it to the other bank, and when they get there, Petka says: "Right then, Vasily Ivanovich, show me these maps we almost drowned for." Chapaev opens up the case, Petka looks inside and sees it's full of potatoes. "Vasily Ivanovich," he says, "what kind of maps do you call these?" So Chapaev takes out two potatoes and says: "Look here, Petka. This is us – and this is the Whites."'

Volodin laughed.

'That one lacks even the slightest glimmer of sense,' I said. 'In the first place, if, after another ten thousand lives you, Serdyuk, should have the chance to drown in the Ural, you may regard yourself as extremely fortunate. In the second place, I simply cannot understand where all these Whites keep appearing from. I suspect that the Cheka crew must have been at work there. In the third place, it was a metaphorical map of consciousness, not a plan of military positions at all. And they were not potatoes, but onions.'

'Onions?'

'Yes, onions. Although for a number of highly personal reasons I would have given a great deal for them to have been potatoes instead.'

Volodin and Serdyuk exchanged a protracted glance.

'And this is the man who wants to discharge himself,' said Volodin. 'Ah, I've remembered one now. Chapaev is writing in his diary: *"Sixth of June; we have driven the Whites back . . ."*'

'He did not keep any diary,' I interjected.

'*"Seventh of June; the Whites have driven us back. Eighth of June; the forest warden came and drove everybody out."*'

'I see,' I said, 'no doubt that one was about Baron Jungern. Only he didn't come, unfortunately. And then, he was not actually a forest warden, he simply said that he had always wanted to be a forester. I find this all very strange, gentlemen. In some ways you are really quite well informed, and yet I keep on getting the feeling that someone who does indeed know how everything really happened has attempted to distort the truth in the most monstrous fashion possible. And I simply cannot understand the reason for it.'

Nobody broke the silence again for a while. I became absorbed in my work and started thinking through my forthcoming conversation with Timur Timurovich. The logic of his actions still remained entirely opaque to me. Maria had been discharged a week after he broke the bust of Aristotle over my head, but Volodin, who was as normal a man as any I had ever seen in my life, had recently been prescribed a new course of drug therapy. On no account, I reasoned with myself, must I think up answers in advance, because he might not ask a single one of the questions for which I might have prepared myself, and then I would be bound to throw out one of my ready-made answers at entirely the wrong moment. All that I could do was trust to chance and luck.

'All right, then,' Volodin eventually said. 'Why don't you give us an example of something that has actually been distorted? Tell us how it really happened.'

'What exactly are you interested in?' I asked. 'Which of the episodes that you have mentioned?'

'Any of them. Or we can take something else. Like this, for instance, I can't imagine what could possibly have been distorted in this one. Kotovsky sends Chapaev some red caviar and cognac from Paris, and Chapaev writes back: "Thank you, Petka and I drank the moonshine, although it smelled of bedbugs, but we didn't eat the cranberries – they stank of fish."'

I laughed despite myself.

'Kotovsky never sent anything from Paris. But there was indeed a rather similar incident. We were sitting in a restaurant and actually drinking cognac with red caviar – I know how bad that sounds, but they had no black caviar in the place. Our conversation concerned the Christian paradigm, and therefore we began discussing its terminology. Chapaev commented on a passage from Swedenborg in which a ray of heavenly light shines down to the bottom of hell and the spirits who live there take it for a dirty, stinking puddle. I had understood this in the sense that the light itself had been transformed, but Chapaev said that the nature of light does not change, and everything depends on the subject of perception. He said that there is no power that would prevent a sinful soul from entering heaven – but it happens that it simply does not want to go there. I could not understand how this could be the case, and then he explained that one of Furmanov's weavers, for instance, would have taken the caviar we were eating for cranberries that smelled of fish.'

'I see,' said Volodin, who for some reason had turned rather pale.

I was struck by an unexpected idea.

'Just a moment now,' I said, 'where did you say the cognac came from?'

Volodin did not answer.

'What difference does it make?' asked Serdyuk.

'Never mind,' I said thoughtfully, 'but now at last I seem to have some idea of who could be responsible for all this. It is rather strange, of course, and it does seem quite unlike him, but all the other explanations are so completely absurd . . .'

'Listen, I've remembered another one,' said Serdyuk. 'Chapaev comes to see Anka, and she's sitting there naked . . .'

'My dear sirs,' I interrupted, 'are you not taking things just a little too far?'

'It wasn't me that made it up,' Serdyuk replied insolently, tossing another paper crane into the corner of the room. 'So anyway, he asks her: "Why haven't you got any clothes on, Anka?" And she says to him: "I haven't got any dresses to wear." So he opens the wardrobe, looks inside and says: "What's all this then? One dress. Two dresses. Hi there, Petka. Three dresses. Four dresses."'

'Really,' I said, 'I ought to just punch you in the face for saying such things – but somehow instead it brings back a deep feeling of melancholy. In actual fact it was all quite different. It was Anna's birthday, and we had gone out for a picnic. Kotovsky immediately got drunk and fell asleep, and Chapaev began explaining to Anna that a human personality is like a wardrobe filled with sets of clothes which are taken out by turns, and the less real the person actually is, the more sets there are in the wardrobe. That was his present to Anna on her birthday – not a set of dresses, but his explanation. Anna was stubborn and she refused to agree with him. She attempted to prove that what he said was all very well in theory, but it did not apply to her, because she always remained herself and never wore any masks. But Chapaev simply answered everything she said by saying: "One dress . . . Two dresses . . ." and so on. Do you understand? Then Anna asked, if that was the case, who was it that put on the dresses, and Chapaev replied that there was nobody to put them on. That was when Anna understood. She said nothing for a few seconds, then she nodded and looked up at him, and Chapaev smiled and said, "Hello there, Anna!" That is one of my most precious memories . . . But why am I telling you all this?'

I had suddenly been overwhelmed by a veritable whirlwind of thoughts and ideas. I remembered Kotovsky's strange smile at our parting. I do not understand, I thought, he could have heard about the map of consciousness, but how would he know about the camouflage? He had left just before that . . . Then I suddenly remembered what Chapaev had said about Kotovsky's fate.

In an instant everything became absolutely clear. Kotovsky, however, had failed to take one important factor into account, I thought, feeling the malice seething within me, he had forgotten that I could do exactly the same thing that he had done. And if that cocaine-riddled lover of trotters and secret freedom had condemned me to the madhouse, then . . .

'Now I would like to tell a joke,' I said.

The feelings that had taken possession of me must have been visible in the expression on my face, because Serdyuk and Volodin glanced at me in genuine alarm; Volodin even shifted his chair a little further away from me.

Serdyuk said, 'Just don't get yourself upset, all right?'

'Are you going to listen or not?' I asked. 'Right, then. Now . . . Aha, I have it. Some savages have captured Kotovsky and they say to him: "We are going to eat you, and then make a drum out of your bald scalp. But now you can have one last wish." Kotovsky thought for a moment and said: "Bring me an awl." They gave him an awl, and he took it and jabbed it into the top of his head over and over again. Then he yelled: "So much for your drum, you bastards!"'

I laughed ferociously, and at that very moment the door opened and the moustachioed face of Zherbunov appeared. He glanced warily round the room until his gaze came to rest on me. I cleared my throat and straightened the collar of my dressing-gown.

'Timur Timurovich wants to see you.'

'Straight away,' I replied, getting up from my chair and carefully placing the unfinished bagel of black Plasticine on the table that was cluttered with Serdyuk's toy cranes.

Timur Timurovich was in an excellent mood.

'I hope, Pyotr, that you understood why I called what

happened to you at the last session total catharsis?'

I shrugged non-committally.

'Well then, consider this,' he said. 'I explained to you once that misdirected psychic energy may take on the form of any kind of mania or phobia. To put it in rather crude terms, my method consists in approaching such a mania or phobia in terms of its own inner logic. For instance, you say you are Napoleon.'

'I do not say anything of the sort.'

'Let us assume that you do. Well then, instead of trying to prove to you that you are mistaken, or administering an insulin shock, my answer is: "Very well, you are Napoleon. But what are you going to do now? Land in Egypt? Declare a continental blockade? Or perhaps you will abdicate the throne and simply go back home to your Corsican Lane?" And then, depending on how you reply to my question, all the rest will follow. Consider your colleague Serdyuk, for instance. That Japanese who supposedly forced him to slit open his belly is quite the most vital element in his psychological world. Nothing ever happens to him, not even when Serdyuk himself suffers symbolic death, in fact in his imagination he even remains alive after Serdyuk is dead. And when he comes round again, he can think of nothing better to do than make all those little aeroplanes. I am sure they advised him to do it in some new hallucination. In other words, the illness has affected such extensive areas of his psyche that sometimes I even contemplate the possibility of surgical intervention.'

'What do you have in mind?'

'It doesn't matter. I only mention Serdyuk for purposes of comparison. But now consider what has happened to you. I regard it as a genuine triumph for my method. The entire morbidly detailed world that your clouded consciousness had constructed has simply disappeared, dissolved into itself, and not under any pressure from a doctor, but apparently by following its inner own laws. Your psychosis has exhausted itself. The stray psychic energy has been integrated with the remaining part of the psyche. If my theory is correct – and I would like to believe that it is – you are now perfectly well.'

'I am sure that it is correct,' I said. 'Of course, I do not understand it in all of its profundity . . .'

'There is no need for you to understand it,' Timur Timurovich answered. 'It is quite sufficient that today you yourself represent its very clearest confirmation. Thank you very much, Pyotr, for describing your hallucinations in such detail, not many patients are capable of doing that. I hope you will not object if I make use of excerpts from your notes in my monograph?'

'I should regard it as a signal honour.'

Timur Timurovich patted me on the shoulder affectionately.

'Come now, no need to be so formal. I'm your friend.'

He picked up a rather thick file of papers from his desk.

'I just want to ask you to fill in this questionnaire, and to take the job seriously.'

'A questionnaire?'

'A pure formality,' said Timur Timurovich. 'They're always thinking up something or other in the Ministry of Health – they have so many people there with nothing to do all day long. This is what they call a test for the assessment of social adequacy. There are all sorts of questions in it, with different possible answers provided for each. One of the answers is correct, the others are absurd. Any normal person will catch on immediately.'

He leafed through the questionnaire. There must have been twenty or thirty pages of it.

'Sheer bureaucracy, of course, but we get the official circulars here the same as everywhere else. This is required for discharge. And since I can't see any reason for keeping you here any longer, here's a pen, and off you go.'

I took the questionnaire from him and sat down at the desk. Timur Timurovich tactfully turned away to face the bookshelves and took down a thick, heavy volume.

There were a number of sections in the questionnaire: 'Culture', 'History', 'Politics' and a few others. I opened the section on 'Culture' at random and read:

32. At the end of which of the following films does the hero drive out the villains, waving a heavy cross above his head?
a) Alexander Nevsky

b) Jesus of Nazareth
c) The Death of the Gods

33. Which of the names below symbolizes the all-conquering power of good?
a) Arnold Schwarzenegger
b) Sylvester Stallone
c) Jean-Claude Van Damm

Struggling not to betray my confusion, I turned over several pages at once to a point somewhere in the centre of the history section:

74. What was the target at which the cruiser *Aurora* fired?
a) the Reichstag
b) the battleship Potemkin
c) the White House
d) the firing started from the White House

I suddenly recalled that terrible black night in October 1917 when the *Aurora* sailed into the estuary of the Neva. I had raised my collar as I stood on the bridge, smoking nervously, staring at the distant black silhouette of the cruiser. There was not a single light to be seen on it, but a vague electrical radiance trembled at the ends of its slim masts. Two people out for a late stroll halted beside me, an astonishingly beautiful young schoolgirl and a fat governess chaperoning her, who looked like one of those stout columns intended for displaying posters in the street.

'Look at it, Miss Brown!' the young girl exclaimed in English, pointing towards the black ship. 'This is St Elmo's fires!'

'You are mistaken, Katya,' the governess replied quietly. 'There is nothing saintly about this ship.'

She peered sideways at me.

'Let's go,' she said. 'Standing here could be dangerous.'

I shook my head to drive away the memory and turned over a few more pages:

102. Who created the Universe?
a) God
b) the Committee of Soldiers' Mothers
c) I did
d) Kotovsky

I carefully closed the questionnaire and looked out of the window. I could see the snow-covered crown of a poplar, with a crow perched on it. It was hopping from one foot to the other, and snow was sprinkling down through the air from the branch on which it was sitting. Down below an engine of some kind roared into life and startled the bird. Flapping its wings ponderously, it took off from the branch and flew away from the hospital – I watched it go until it was reduced to an almost invisible black speck. Then I slowly raised my eyes to Timur Timurovich, meeting his own attentive gaze.

'Tell me, what is this questionnaire needed for? Why did they invent it?'

'I don't know that myself,' he replied. 'Although, of course, there is a certain logic to it. Some patients are so cunning that they can wind even the most experienced doctor round their little finger. So this is just in case Napoleon decides for the time being to admit that he is mad, in order to obtain permission to leave the hospital and inaugurate the One Hundred Days . . .'

A sudden startled thought glinted momentarily in his eyes, but he extinguished it immediately with a flick of his eyelids.

'But then,' he said, walking over quickly to me, 'you're perfectly right. I've only just realized I've been treating you as though you're still a patient. As though I didn't trust you myself. It's terribly silly, but it's just my professional reflex response.'

He pulled the questionnaire from my grasp, tore it in half and threw it into the waste-paper basket.

'Go and get ready,' he said, turning towards the window. 'Your documents have already been prepared. Zherbunov will show you to the station. And here is my telephone number, just in case you need it.'

The blue cotton trousers and the black sweater that Zherbunov issued to me smelled of dusty broom cupboards. I was extremely displeased that the trousers were crumpled and stained, but as Zherbunov explained, the domestic services unit had no iron.

'This isn't a laundry, you know,' he said caustically, 'nor the bleeding Ministry of Culture neither.'

t on the high boots with the patterned soles, the round
p and the grey woollen coat, which would actually have
rather elegant if not for a hole with scorched edges in the

;ot plastered, probably, and one of your mates burnt
with his fag,' Zherbunov commented as he donned a
.sonous-green jacket with a hood.

It was interesting to note that I did not feel in the least bit offended by these boorish outbursts, which he had never per-
mitted himself in the ward. Quite the contrary, they were like
music to my ears, because they were a sign of my freedom. In
actual fact he was not even being rude, this was merely his
usual manner of speaking to people. Since I had ceased to be a
patient, and he had ceased to be an orderly, the rules of professional ethics no longer applied to me; everything that had
bound us together had been left hanging on that nail
crookedly beaten into the wall, together with his white hospital coat.

'And the travelling bag?' I asked.

His eyes opened wide in feigned astonishment.

'There wasn't any travelling bag,' he said. 'You can take
that up with Timur Timurovich if you like. Here's your purse,
there were twenty roubles in it, and that's what's in it now.'

'I see,' I said. 'So there is no way to get at the truth?'

'Well, what did you expect?'

I made no attempt to argue any more. It was stupid of me
even to have mentioned it. I limited my response to the
stealthy extraction of the fountain pen from the side pocket of
his jacket.

The doors of freedom swung open in such a banal, everyday fashion that I actually felt slightly disappointed. Beyond
them was an empty, snow-covered yard surrounded by a
concrete wall; a pair of large green gates, oddly decorated
with red stars, stood directly opposite us, and beside them a
small lodge with pale smoke rising from its chimney. In any
case, I had already seen all of this many times from the window. I went down the steps from the porch and glanced back
at the faceless white building of the hospital.

'Tell me, Zherbunov, where is the window of our ward?'

'Third floor, second from the end,' answered Zherbu. 'There, you see, they're waving to you.'

I caught a glimpse of two dark silhouettes in the window One of them raised his open hand and pressed the palm against the glass. I waved to them in reply and Zherbunov tugged rather rudely at my sleeve.

'Let's get going. You'll miss the train.'

I turned and followed him towards the gates.

It was cramped and hot in the lodge. An attendant in a green peaked cap with two crossed rifles on the cockade was sitting behind a small window; in front of it the passage was blocked by a boom made of painted iron piping. He took a long time to study the documents which Zherbunov passed over to him, several times looking up from the photograph at my face and then down again, and exchanging a few quiet comments with Zherbunov. Finally the boom was raised.

'See what a serious guy he is,' said Zherbunov, when we emerged. 'He used to work in a Top-Secret Facility.'

'I see,' I answered. 'Interesting. And did Timur Timurovich cure him as well?'

Zherbunov gave me a sideways glance, but he said nothing.

A narrow snow-covered path led away from the gates of the hospital. At first it wound its way through a sparse birch wood, and then for ten minutes it led along the edge of the wood before plunging back into the trees. There were no traces of civilization to be seen anywhere, apart from the thick cables sagging down between identical metal masts that looked like the skeletons of immense Red Army men in their helmets. Suddenly the forest came to an end, and we found ourselves beside a set of wooden steps leading up to a railway platform.

The only structure on the platform was a brick shed with a feebly smoking chimney that bore a remarkable similarity to the gate-lodge at the hospital. The thought even occurred to me that this might be the dominant form of architecture in this unfamiliar world – but of course, I still had too little experience to make such broad generalizations. Zherbunov went over to a little window in the hut and bought me a ticket.

ay then,' he said, 'here's your train coming. Fifteen min-
Yaroslavl Station.'

lendid,' I replied.

oking forward to the ladies, then?' he sneered.

as only a little shocked by the directness of the question.
my long experience of associating with soldiers, I knew
among the lower classes the shameless discussion of the
mate side of life fulfils approximately the same function as
conversation about the weather for the upper classes.

I shrugged. 'I cannot say that I have pined too badly for
what you call ladies, Zherbunov.'

'Why's that?' Zherbunov asked.

'Because,' I replied, 'all women suck.'

'That's true enough,' he said with a sigh. 'But all the same,
what are you going to do? You've got to work somewhere,
haven't you?'

'I do not know,' I replied. 'I can write poetry, I can command a cavalry squadron. Something will turn up.'

The electric train came to a halt, and its doors opened with
a hiss.

'That's it, then,' said Zherbunov, proffering me a crablike
hand. 'Be seeing you.'

'Goodbye,' I said. 'And please give my very best wishes to
my wardmates.'

As I shook his hand, I suddenly noticed a tattoo which I
had not seen before on his wrist. It was a blurred blue anchor,
and above it I could just make out the letters 'BALTFLOT' –
they were very pale and indistinct, as though someone had
tried to erase them.

Entering the carriage, I sat down on a hard wooden bench.
The train set off and Zherbunov's stocky figure drifted past
the window and disappeared for ever into non-existence. At
the very end of the platform, protruding above the barrier on
two metal poles I saw a board bearing the inscription: 'LOZO-
VAYA JUNCTION'.

Tverskoi Boulevard appeared exactly as it had been when I last
saw it – once again it was February, with snowdrifts everywhere and that peculiar gloom which somehow manages to

infiltrate the very daylight. The same old women perched motionless on the benches, watching over brigh dressed children engaged in protracted warfare among t snowdrifts; above them, beyond the black latticework of the wires, the sky hung down close to the earth as though it were trying to touch it. Some things, however, were different, as I noticed when I reached the end of the boulevard. The bronze Pushkin had disappeared, but the gaping void that had appeared where he used to stand somehow seemed like the best of all possible monuments. Where the Strastnoi Monastery had been, there was now an empty space, with a sparse scattering of consumptive trees and tasteless street lamps.

I sat on a bench opposite the invisible statue and lit a cigarette with a short yellow tip which had been kindly given to me by an officer wearing a uniform that looked as though it belonged in some operetta. The cigarette burnt away as quickly as a Bickford fuse, leaving me with a vague taste of saltpetre in my mouth.

There were several crumpled bills in my pocket – in appearance they differed little from the rainbow-coloured hundred-rouble Duma notes which I remembered so well, although they were rather smaller in size. Zherbunov had told me at the station that this would be enough for a single lunch at an inexpensive restaurant. I sat there on the bench for quite a long time, pondering what I should do. It was already beginning to get dark, and on the roofs of the familiar buildings huge electrified signs lit up with messages in some barbarous artificial language – 'SAMSUNG', 'OCA-CO A', 'OLBI'. In this entire city I had absolutely nowhere to go: I felt like a Persian who for some inexplicable reason has run the distance from Marathon to Athens.

'And have you any idea what it is like, my dear sir, when you have nowhere left to go?' I murmured to myself, gazing at the words burning in the sky, and I laughed as I remembered the Marmeladov-woman from the 'Musical Snuffbox'.

Suddenly I understood exactly what I had to do next. Getting up from the bench, I walked across the road and held out one hand in order to hail an automobile. Almost immediately a rattling old vehicle shaped like a drop of water and splattered

r with dirty slush pulled up alongside me. Sitting at the
ℓ was a bearded gentleman who reminded me vaguely
unt Tolstoy, except that his beard was rather shorter and
ᴇr.

ᐧhere to?' he asked.

ᐧou know,' I said, 'I am afraid I cannot remember the pre-
ᐧ address, but I need a place called "The Musical Snuff-
ᐧx". A café. Somewhere not far from here – down along the
boulevard and to the left. Quite close to Nikitsky Square.'

'You mean on Herzen Street?'

I shrugged.

'I've never heard of such a café,' said the bearded gentleman. 'I suppose it only opened recently.'

'No,' I said, 'quite a while ago, actually.'

'Ten roubles. Money up front.'

I opened the door and sat beside him. The automobile set
off and I stole a glance at his face: he was wearing a strange-
looking jacket cut in a manner reminiscent of the military tu-
nics so beloved by the Bolshevik leadership, but made of
material patterned in a liberal check design.

'You have a fine automobile,' I said.

He was obviously flattered by my remark.

'It's old now,' he replied, 'but after the war, there was no
finer car in the world than the "Pobeda".'

'After the war?' I asked.

'Well, of course, just after the war. But for five years at
least. But now they've completely screwed everything up.
You just wait and see, and the communists will come to
power.'

'Please do not talk about politics,' I said, 'I understand absolutely nothing about it and I always get confused.'

He gave me a quick look.

'That, young man, is precisely the reason why everything
has fallen apart the way it has, because you and people like
you understand absolutely nothing about it. What's politics
about anyway? It's about how we can carry on with our lives.
If everyone thought about how we could sort things out in
Russia, then they wouldn't need any sorting out. And that, if
you'll pardon the expression, is the dialectic.'

'And just where do you intend to hang this dialecti
asked.

'Excuse me?'

'Nothing,' I said, 'it doesn't matter.'

We stopped at the beginning of the boulevard. There was a
long queue of vehicles ahead of us – there were horns sounding and orange and red lights flashing. The bearded gentleman said nothing, and I thought he might have found my
words a little unfriendly. I felt I wanted to smooth over the
awkwardness.

'You know,' I said, 'if history teaches us anything, then it is
that everybody who has tried to sort things out in Russia has
ended up being sorted out by Russia instead.'

'That's right,' said the gentleman. 'That's precisely why we
have to think about how to sort things out here – so that it
won't happen again.'

'As far as I am concerned, I have no need to think about it,'
I replied. 'I know perfectly well how to sort things out in
Russia.'

'Oh yes? And how's that?'

'It is all quite simple. Every time the concept and the image
of Russia appears in your conscious mind, you have to let it
dissolve away in its own inner nature. And since the concept
and the image of Russia has no inner nature of its own, the result is that everything is sorted out most satisfactorily.'

He looked at me carefully.

'I see,' he said. 'That's just what the American Zionists
want to hear. That's exactly how they poisoned the minds of
your entire generation.'

The automobile began to move again and turned on to
Nikitskaya Street.

'I do not entirely understand what you are talking about,' I
said, 'but in that case all that has to be done is to take all the
American Zionists and sort them out as well.'

'And just how would you go about sorting them out, I
wonder?'

'In precisely the same way,' I replied. 'And America
should be sorted out as well. But then, why bother going into
every particular case? If one is going to sort things out, one

might as well sort out the entire world at once.'

'Then why don't you go ahead and do so?'

'That is exactly what I intend to do today,' I said.

The gentleman wagged his beard up and down condescendingly.

'Of course, it's stupid of me to try to talk to you seriously, but I should point out that you are not the first person ever to talk such drivel. Pretending that you doubt the reality of the world is the most cowardly form of escape from that very reality. Squalid intellectual poverty, if you want my opinion. Despite all its seeming absurdity, cruelty and senselessness this world nonetheless exists, doesn't it? And all the problems in it exist as well, don't they?'

I said nothing.

'Therefore talk of the non-reality of the world does not signify a highly developed spirituality, but quite the opposite. In not accepting the creation, you also fail to accept the Creator.'

'I do not entirely understand what "spirituality" is,' I said. 'But as for the creator of this world, I am rather briefly acquainted with him.'

'And how's that?'

'Oh, yes. His name is Grigory Kotovsky and he lives in Paris, and judging from everything that we can see through the windows of your remarkable automobile, he is still using cocaine.'

'And is that all you have to say about him?'

'I think I can also tell you that his head is presently covered with sticking-plaster.'

'I see. And would you mind me asking exactly which psychiatric hospital you escaped from?'

I thought for a moment.

'I think it was number seventeen. Yes, there was a big blue board hanging by the door, with the number seventeen on it. And it also said that it was a model hospital.'

The automobile came to a halt.

I looked out of the window and saw the building of the Conservatory. We were somewhere close to the 'Snuffbox' already.

'Listen, we should try asking someone the way.'

'I won't take you any further,' the gentleman said. 'Get out of the car and go to the devil.'

I shrugged, opened the door and got out, while the automobile shot off in the direction of the Kremlin. It was rather upsetting that my attempts to speak honestly and sincerely had met with such a reception. But then, by the time I reached the corner of the Conservatory, I had already completely sorted out the bearded gentleman and his devil as well.

I glanced around me on all sides – the street was definitely familiar. I walked along it for about fifty yards and saw a turn to the right and, almost immediately, the familiar gateway in the wall where Vorblei's automobile had stopped on that memorable winter's night. It was exactly the same as it had been, except that I think the colour of the house had changed, and standing on the road in front of the gateway were a great many automobiles of various different shapes and styles.

Quickly crossing the inexpressibly depressing courtyard, I found myself facing a door surmounted by a futuristic-looking canopy of glass and steel. A small signboard in English had been hung on the canopy:

JOHN BULL: Pubis International

Light was showing through the pink blinds drawn halfway down several windows beside the door. From behind them I could hear the mechanically plaintive note of some obscure musical instrument.

I tugged the door open, revealing behind it a short corridor hung with heavy fur coats and men's overcoats, ending in an unexpectedly crude metal partition. A man in a canary-yellow jacket with gold buttons who looked like a convict rose from a stool to meet me; in one hand he had a strange-looking telephone receiver with the wire broken off to leave a stump no more than an inch long. I could have sworn that only a second before he got up he had been talking into it – moreover, he had been holding it incorrectly, with the broken-off wire sticking upwards. This touchingly childlike ability to become totally immersed in a fantasy world, so unusual in such a thug, inspired me with a feeling close to sympathy for him.

'Entry is for club members only,' he said.

'Listen,' I said, 'I was here quite recently with two friends,

ber? One of them hit you in the groin with the butt of
n.'

canary-yellow gentleman's hostile face suddenly ex-
weariness and revulsion.

remember?'

he said. 'But we've already paid.'

ot here for money,' I replied. 'I would just like to sit
a while. Believe me, I shall not be here for long.'

ave a forced smile, then opened the metal partition to
veal a velvet curtain, which he pulled aside, and I entered a
dimly lit hall.

The place had not changed very much – it still looked like a
run-of-the-mill restaurant with some pretensions to chic. The
public seated among the dense clouds of smoke at the small
square tables was quite varied and I think someone was
smoking hashish. It was all illuminated by a strange spherical
chandelier which rotated slowly around its axis, and the
spots of dim light it cast drifted around the hall like glimmers
of moonlight. Nobody took any notice of me, and I sat at a
small table not far from the entrance.

The hall was bounded on one side by a brightly lit stage on
which a middle-aged man with a black, feral beard was
standing behind the keyboard of a small organ and singing in
a repulsive voice:

Kill no one – I have never killed.
Be faithful – I have never failed.
Thou shalt not pity – I would give the shirt from off my back.
Thou shalt not steal – That's where I really cut myself some slack.

It was the chorus. The song appeared to be about the Christian commandments, but the treatment was rather original.
The manner of singing, quite unfamiliar to me, was obviously
popular among the audience – every repetition of the mysterious phrase 'that's where I really cut myself some slack' was
greeted with audible ripples of applause and the singer
bowed slightly, without ceasing to caress his instrument with
his immense hands.

I began to feel a little sad. I had always prided myself on
my ability to understand the latest developments in art and

recognize the eternal and unchanging elements concea̶
hind the unpredictable complexities of form, but in thi̶
the rift between my customary experience and what I
was simply too wide to be bridged. There could have bee̶
simple explanation, of course; someone had told me that b̶
fore he made Chapaev's acquaintance, Kotovsky had been little more than a common criminal – this could well have been
the reason for my inability to decipher the strange culture
which had produced the manifestations that had baffled me
so completely in the madhouse.

The curtain at the entrance quivered, and the man in the canary-yellow jacket stuck his head and shoulders out from behind it, still clutching the telephone receiver in one hand. He
clicked his fingers and nodded towards my table. Immediately a waiter appeared in front of me, wearing a black jacket
and a bow-tie, holding a leather folder with the menu.

'What would we like to eat?' he asked.

'I do not wish to eat,' I replied, 'but I would happily drink
some vodka. I am chilled.'

'Smirnoff? Stolichnaya? Absolut?'

'Absolute,' I replied. 'And I would also like – how shall I
put it? – something to help me relax.'

The waiter gave me a dubious look, then he turned to the
canary-yellow gentleman and made some kind of card-
sharper's gesture. The latter nodded. The waiter leaned down
to my ear and whispered:

'Amphetamines? Barbiturates? Ecstasy?'

I pondered the indecipherable hieroglyphics of these
names for a moment or two.

'I tell you what. Take ecstasy and dissolve it in Absolute.
That will be just right.'

The waiter turned to the canary-yellow gentleman once
again, gave a barely perceptible shrug of his shoulders and
twirled one finger in the air beside his temple. The other man
frowned angrily and nodded again.

An ashtray and a vase holding paper napkins appeared on
my table. The napkins were most à propos. I took the fountain
pen that I had stolen from Zherbunov out of my pocket,
picked up a napkin and was just about to start writing, when

suddenly I noticed that the pen did not end in a nib, but in a hole that looked like the mouth of a gun barrel. I unscrewed the barrel, and a small cartridge with a black lead bullet without any casing tumbled out on to the table; it was like those they sold for Montecristo guns. This clever little invention was even more welcome – without my Browning in my trouser pocket I felt something of a charlatan. I carefully replaced the cartridge, then screwed the pen back together and gestured to the pale gentleman in the canary-yellow jacket to bring me something with which I could write.

The waiter arrived with a glass on a tray.

'Your order,' he said.

I drank the vodka in a single gulp, took the pen from the fingers of the canary-yellow gentleman and immediately absorbed myself in my work. At first the words simply did not come, but then the mournful sounds of the organ bore me up aloft and an appropriate text was ready in literally ten minutes.

By this time the bearded singer had disappeared. I had not noticed the moment of his departure from the stage, because the music continued to play. It was very strange – there was an entire invisible orchestra playing, ten instruments at the very least, but I could see no musicians. Moreover, it was quite clearly not the radio, to which I had grown accustomed in the clinic, nor was it a gramophone recording; the sound was very clear, and quite certainly a live performance. My confusion evaporated, however, when I guessed that it was the effect the waiter's concoction was having on me. I began listening to the music and suddenly made out a very clear phrase in English, sung by a hoarse voice very close to my ear:

> You had to stand beneath my window
> With your bagel and your drum
> While I was waiting for the miracle –
> For the miracle to come . . .

I shuddered.

This was the sign I had been waiting for – it was quite clear from the words 'miracle', 'drum' (which undoubtedly referred to Kotovsky) and 'bagel' (no commentary was required here). It was true that the singer did not seem to know English

331

too well – he pronounced 'bagel' like 'bugle' – but that was not so important. I stood up and drifted towards the stage through the pulsating aquarium of the hall, swaying as I went.

The music had stopped most opportunely. Clambering up on to the stage, I leaned against the small organ, which replied with a long extended note of an unpleasant timbre, and then looked around at the tense, silent hall. The customers were a very mixed bunch, but as has always been the case throughout the history of humanity, it was pig-faced speculators and expensively dressed whores who predominated. All the faces I saw seemed to merge into a single face, at once fawning and impudent, frozen in a grimace of smug servility – and beyond the slightest doubt this was the face of that old moneylender, the old woman, disincarnate but as alive as ever. Several young fellows looking like overdressed sailors with cheeks rosy pink from the frost appeared by the curtain that covered the entrance. The canary-yellow gentleman rattled off something to them, nodding in my direction as he did so.

Removing my elbow from the rumbling organ, I raised the napkin covered in writing to my eyes, cleared my throat and in my usual manner, using no intonation whatsoever but simply making brief pauses between the quatrains, I read:

Eternal Non-Return

Hundreds of years spent filing at the bars set in the frame
And shifting form and face through flux and dissolution,
A madman bearing Emptiness for his name
Flees from the clutches of a model institution.

He knows quite well there is no time to flee,
Nowhere to go, no path on which to go there,
But more than that, this self-same escapee
Himself cannot be found, for he is nowhere.

To say the process of the filing does exist
Or that there are no file or bars is all the same.
The madman Voyd clutches his rosary in his fist –
All answers to all questions he disclaims.
For since the world keeps moving but we know not whither,
Better say at once both 'No' and 'Yes', but swear to neither.

At these words I raised Zherbunov's pen and fired at the chandelier. It shattered like a toy on a Christmas tree, and a blinding electric light flashed across the ceiling. The hall was plunged into darkness, and immediately I saw the flashes of gunshots from over by the door where the canary-yellow gentleman and the ruddy-faced young fellows had been standing. I went down on all fours and slowly crawled along the edge of the stage, wincing at the intolerable racket. Someone began firing back from the opposite end of the hall, from several barrels at once, and the ricochets struck sparks into the air from the steel door. I realized that I should not be crawling along the edge of the stage, but back into the wings, and I made a turn of ninety degrees.

I heard a groan like the howl of a wounded wolf over by the steel door. A bullet knocked the small organ off its stand and it tumbled on to the floor right beside me. At last, I thought as I crawled towards the wings, at last I had managed to hit the chandelier! But – my God! – was that not always the only thing of which I had been capable, shooting at the mirror-surfaced sphere of this false world from a fountain pen? What a profound symbol, I thought, what a pity that no one sitting in the hall was capable of appreciating what they had just seen. But then, I thought, who knows?

In the wings it was just as dark as in the hall – it seemed that the electricity had failed throughout the building. At my appearance someone dashed away down the corridor, stumbling and falling. They did not get up again, but simply remained concealed in the darkness. Rising to my feet, I set off along the invisible corridor holding my hands out in front of me. It turned out that I remembered the way to the stage door very well. It was locked, but after fiddling with the lock for a minute or so, I opened it and found myself on the street.

A few gulps of frosty air restored me to my senses, but I still had to lean against the wall – the walk along the corridor had been incredibly tiring.

The main door, from which I was separated by about five yards of snow-covered asphalt, swung open and two men came dashing out, ran over to a long black automobile and

333

opened the lid of its baggage compartment. Terrifying-looking weapons suddenly appeared in their hands, and they ran back inside without even bothering to close the lid again, as if the one thing they were most afraid of in all the world was that they might be too late to join in what was happening. They did not even spare me a glance.

New holes appeared, one by one, in the dark windows of the restaurant; the impression I had was that several machine-guns must be working in there simultaneously. I thought that in my time people were hardly any kinder, perhaps, but the times themselves were certainly less cruel. However, it was time for me to be going.

I staggered across the courtyard and out into the street.

Chapaev's armoured car was standing exactly where I had expected to see it, and the cap of snow on its turret was just as it should have been. The motor was working, and there was a grey-blue cloud of smoke swirling in the air behind the back of the vehicle. I walked up to the door and knocked. It opened, and I climbed inside.

Chapaev had not changed in the slightest, except that his left arm was now supported by a strip of black linen. The hand was bandaged, and I could easily guess that there was empty space under the gauze where the little finger should have been.

I was quite unable to say a single word – it took all the strength I could muster to drag myself on to the divan. Chapaev immediately understood what was wrong with me. He slammed the door shut, murmured a few quiet words into the speaking-tube, and the armoured car moved off.

'How are things?' he asked.

'I don't know,' I said, 'it is hard to make sense of the whirlwind of scales and colours of the contradictory inner life.'

'I see,' said Chapaev. 'Anna sends her greetings. She asked me to give you this.'

He stooped down, reached under the seat with his sound hand and took out an empty bottle with a gold label made out of a square of metal foil. Protruding from the bottle was a yellow rose.

'She said you would understand,' said Chapaev. 'And it

seems that you promised her some books or other.'

I nodded, turned towards the door and set my eye against the spy-hole. At first all I could see through it were the blue spots of the street lamps slicing through the frosty air, but we kept moving faster and faster, and soon, very soon we were surrounded by the whispering sands and roaring waterfalls of my dear and so beloved Inner Mongolia.

Kafka-Yurt
1923–1925